WASHOE COUNTY LIBRARY
3 1235 03400 5954

D0828378

Halldór Laxness

The Great Weaver from Kashmir

Translated from the Icelandic by Philip Roughton

archipelago books

First published as *Vefarinn mikli frá Kasmír* by Forlagið, Reykjavík, 1927

First Archipelago Books Edition

Published by agreement with Licht and Burr Literary Agency, Denmark.

Archipelago Books
232 Third Street #A111
Brooklyn, NY 11215
www.archipelagobooks.org

Printed in Canada

Library of Congress Cataloging-in-Publication Data
Halldór Laxness, 1902–1998.
[Vefarinn mikli frá Kasmír. English]
The great weaver from Kashmir / by Halldór Laxness ;
translated from the Icelandic by Philip Roughton.
p. cm.
ISBN 978-0-9793330-8-8
I. Roughton, Philip. II. Title.
PT7511.L3V3713 2007
839'.6934–dc22
2008015345

Distributed by Consortium Book Sales and Distribution
www.cbsd.com

Cover art: *Svanasöngur* (*Swansong*), 1966, Jóhannes S. Kjarral (1885–1972)

This publication was made possible with support from Lannan Foundation, Bókmenntasjóður/the Icelandic Literary Fund, the National Endowment for the Arts, and the New York State Council on the Arts, a state agency.

Ma nondimen, rimossa ogne menzogna,
tutta tua visïon fa manifesta;
e lascia pur grattar dov' è la rogna.

Ché se la voce tua sarà molesta
nel primo gusto, vital nodrimento
lascerà poi, quando sarà digesta.

DANTE ALIGHIERI
(*Par.* XVII. 127–132)[1]

Book One

1.

Once two swans flew overhead, eastward.

The world is like a stage where everything has been set up for an extravagant musical: the fragrance of birchwood in the lava fields at Þingvellir,[2] cold gusts of wind from Súlur, violet light in the Esja sky, the azure deep and cold over Skjaldbreiður, but darkness no longer descends. Nightlessness and insomnia in all directions.

The basalt Ylfingabúð[3] stands on a grassy strip of land between crevices in the surrounding lava rocks. The wild birch is shaken by the gusts and scrawls invisible signs on the evening sky, and a young girl comes out from the house onto the veranda on the south side. She looks westward beyond the path leading through the copse and leans out upon the railing. She stretches her neck like a mountain grouse, tilts her ear to the west and listens, innocent and bright like a mythic character who has grown up alongside white, wild lambs. The clock inside the house strikes ten.

An old woman wearing a long, dark dress, her hair beginning to gray and her appearance imposing and distinguished, steps out onto the veranda.

"Diljá," she says, "I simply can't understand why they haven't arrived yet. I mean, it was nearly eight when Örnólfur called to say that they were leaving. God help Jófríður, to have to board ship tomorrow – didn't you just hear a clatter?"

"No, Grandma, not a single clank," answered the young girl ruefully.

"Who knows? Maybe something went wrong. Haven't I always said that those automobiles aren't very reliable? They'll probably end up watching the ship sail away from shore from somewhere up on Mosfellsheiði! Run inside, Diljá dear, and fetch my knitting and bring me my shawl. I'm going to sit out here on the veranda for a bit, since the weather's decent."

The girl came back out onto the veranda after a few moments, chewing. She had put on a white flannel jacket, and was holding a half-eaten cookie.

Although her eyes were young and clear, they were not devoid of a kind of heavy miragelike grayness that is often a sign of hysteria, her lips damp with youth and purity, spongy and red, with lines slightly drawn around her mouth, as if a sculptor used his scraper to shape her head in outline only. The rest of her body was much the same: a seedling, fresh and tender, like an ear of grain in the spring, when the new moon watches over the fields, burnished white and slender. Her hair was the only part of her young body that had volume: it was thick, glossy, and bright, twisted into one braid, with crisp curls hanging down around her cheeks.

"Imagine it, Grandma," said the girl, after she'd handed the old woman her things and munched down the rest of the cookie. "It wasn't until I read about it in *Morgunblaðið*[4] yesterday that I found out the Grímúlfur family was planning to sail away! And Steinn Elliði, who tells me everything, didn't say a single word about it a week ago when we were together in Reykjavík. We walked out to Laugarnes. Why are they leaving so suddenly like that?"

"They'd been planning it for a long time," answered the old woman, as she made the first of her stitches. "But folk hardly know about the brothers' plans until they're well under way. The last time Örnólfur was abroad he opened a new market, as they're called. He was in Portugal and southern Italy. One of them's got to stay down there in the south pretty much all of the time in order to manage the market. One can't trust foreign office workers to keep things running when so much is at stake. But they kept it fairly quiet that it was Grímúlfur who was going to be moving, until the last minute."

"As if Jófríður wouldn't die of anxiety down there in the south just like anywhere else!" said the girl. "She can't put up with much for long, what with her consumption and her nerves – I predict that she won't be able to stick it out very long down there! And what business does Steinn Elliði have down there, when he's all wrapped up in his art and literature?! And hardly anyone down south can read! As if Steinn wouldn't miss home, as if he wouldn't turn right around and come back to see Iceland, that Steinn of ours! Our Steinn, who worships the mountains! I couldn't see myself going to Italy even if someone invited me. What's so great about Italy anyway?"

"The Ylfingur Company doesn't really concern itself with whatever's great about Italy, Diljá my dear," said the foster mother. "Ylfingur isn't interested in anything but the market. And you should know that the pope can read. But as far as Jófí is concerned, she's never more contented then when she's out and about, and I couldn't wish anything better for little Steinn than for him to leave Reykjavík, so that he can get away for a while from that gang of boys that's always hanging around him because of his father's money, not to mention those damned dreams of his of being a poet, which are sure to end up ruining him."

Although it was evening, the breeze could not be called cold; in fact it was wholesome and peaceful, and the girl regarded her foster mother, Valgerður Ylfingamóðir.[5] This woman was a superior power: she respected neither youth nor talent, misunderstood Steinn Elliði, and put no stock in poets. She was from an old plutocratic family and thought about things as if she were a bailiff from the days when regents governed Iceland. But tonight the girl was in no mood for submission, and she shook her index finger haughtily at her foster mother as she spoke.

"No, Grandma, I really must inform you that Steinn Elliði doesn't have friends just because of Grímúlfur's money. Steinn has friends for completely different reasons than the fact that Ylfingur sells salt-fish. Because Steinn Elliði is far richer than his father, Grímúlfur, let me tell you, yes, even richer than the Ylfingur Company itself. You'll see later, when Steinn becomes famous. Yes, just wait a few years, although you might smirk at the thought now. What did his lyceum teachers say? Didn't they say something along these lines: that Steinn was the most incredibly gifted boy who'd graduated from there in years? Didn't he graduate with honors in philosophy in the spring, eighteen years old? And what did the German professor say, the one Steinn traveled with up north last year? Weren't these his exact words: that he'd never encountered such fiery talent in all of Germany? 'Eine feurige Begabung,'[6] that's what he said to Örnólfur,

Grandma! And what do his friends say, many of whom are both famous and cultured? They adore him and worship him, because he's such a great poet, so inspired, so innovative, so astute–"

The girl was so ardent that from her lips flew words one never sees except in *Eimreiðin* and *Skírnir*.[7] She was clearly determined to convince her grandmother.

But Valgerður Ylfingamóðir's only reply was "Well now." She glanced sharply at her foster daughter and smiled faintly at her simplistic enthusiasm for the words "innovative" and "astute," but could not be bothered to make any further reply.

As she peered down at her knitting her mind was drawn away from her grandson to her sons, those steady, tight-lipped men who had known better how to follow their own lead than even those Icelanders most renowned for innovation and astuteness. The control that they had over the management of the national household determined to a significant extent what might be called the order, the security, or the welfare of Icelandic national prosperity. She was the mother of kings.

2.

One of the Ylfingurs' personal cars, a bulky brownish yellow vehicle, came driving quietly up to the veranda two minutes later, and the fragrance of the copse was blended with the stench of grease and gasoline.

The director of the fishing company, Örnólfur, sat behind the wheel. He tipped his thin felt hat courteously toward Diljá and his mother, who had come down the veranda steps to smile at the new arrivals. Steinn Elliði was sitting next to Örnólfur and didn't wait for the vehicle to stop, but instead threw open the car door and leaped out in order to be the first one to greet the women, extending one hand to his grandmother and one to Diljá. Grímúlfur pulled down the handle of the rear door with thin bluish fingers and helped his wife step out. They all kissed each other, except for Örnólfur, who circled the house in order to turn the car around, and then began checking it over like a true chauffeur before going inside.

Steinn Elliði acted as spokesman for the new arrivals. "Well, old toughie!" he said to his grandmother. "It's an old custom that those who go to sea receive the blessing of their matron, and you've hopefully remembered to cook some pancakes for us. Twenty-four hours from now we'll have lost sight of land, heading south, Grandma, south, toward warmer regions. Imagine Leith, that great city on the other side of the sea, where the cargo cranes howl like the elements and giant Belgian hacks thrust out their tongues and snort in the coal dust!"

And without giving a second thought as to whether his grandmother had heard him or not, he turned to Diljá and continued to speak in the same tone of cavalierish nonchalance:

"Now then, Diljá! It hasn't been more than, say, three or four days since I learned what the fates had up their sleeves. Father told us about it at the breakfast table two days before yesterday, almost as an afterthought, just as if it had nothing to do with anything. He said that I could actually decide for myself whether I stayed or went, and I thought about it for two days. Finally I came to the conclusion that I must go. Who else was going to read out loud for Mother from nonsensical theosophical essays and English half-crown novels written for 'benevolent readers' with crazy hair and bad teeth, wearing boots with lopsided heels and artsy bow ties? And who was going to lead the missus through the museums in Firenze and show her the masterpieces by Cranach and Michelangelo in the Galeria Pitti? Who, if not me? Isn't the son born into this world to support and pamper his mother? Diljá, damn it, you should have said you'd come with us! And just look at you! Are you angry?"

He grabbed her quickly by the shoulder and spun her around like a top; suddenly they were staring straight at each other. Usually they laughed at everything whenever they met, but this time no joy shone in her eyes. And this caught him off guard. Neither of them could manage a laugh. He took his cigarette case out of his trouser pocket and fingered it nimbly for a moment, then stuck it back in again.

"I need to talk to you," he said, and they went into the house.

3.

He was about eighteen years old, but full grown, big and strong, his body agile and svelte. His disposition revealed itself passionate at times, bearing witness to the intractable power of his soul. He was a stately man no matter how one looked at him: neither timidity nor bashfulness obscured his splendid deportment. His bearing, freewheeling and blustery, had effects similar to sunshine hues: the dashing youngster's look captivated others like an apparition in the sweltering banality of everyday life. His forehead was particularly high, although not quite as wide, and oddly rounded on top. His hair was reddish blond, dense and firm. It was combed back and swept in long locks down the back of his head: this splendid mane lent his face a magnificent and imposing quality. Nothing in his person was, however, as charming as his eyes; they had a deviant gleam; they were jewels; it was tempting to stare into their radiant azure; they were deep-set, and their beauty revealed itself best when he glanced upward; they were protected by long eyelashes. His eyebrows were thick and strong; sometimes he knitted them tightly into a ball and looked quickly upward, reminding one of the commander of an army. These eyes either radiated the wild joy of his multifaceted genius' soul or reflected tranquil refulgence, as if his consciousness were raised in an instant over all visible things and shed light on a hidden world; he had been granted an extra personality that had its home on the other side of everyday life. If one looked, however, from his eyes to his mouth, one noticed something imbalanced in his features. The irregular shape of his mouth drew attention; his upper gums jutted out a little, and his two front teeth were always visible, except when he closed his lips; his mouth seemed fixed in a sneer. At a glance this sneer seemed only to lend a manly look of discontentedness to his face, bearing witness to the easily forgiven complacency of a youth who has the whole world at his feet. On closer inspection, one could read in this look a cold refusal to acquiesce: impudence, even shamelessness. And finally, this sneer could be taken as an outspoken witness to the fact that this man was forever prepared to oppose, to respond mercilessly, savagely. It was just as detrimental to stare too long at his smile as it was comforting to gaze at the psychic beauty of his eyes.

His hands were small, with thick palms, his fingers short and slender at the tips, the backs of his hands and wrists covered with blond hair all the way up under the cuffs of his sleeves. He appeared to have come directly from a social gathering, clad in a dinner jacket, potato yellow socks and broad-heeled but slender-cut patent-leather shoes, a long muddy-gray overcoat covering the rest of his clothing, a bright hat upon his head. He held snow-white gloves in one hand.

4.

The old woman took one of her daughter-in-law's hands in both of hers and listened compassionately to her despondent complaints about the pressing concerns of the last few days and various other afflictions. She had been struggling to decide on what she did not want to bring with her, to put things in order in trunks and cabinets, and finally to sort out her luggage: pack, pack. No one but God could imagine what a bother all of this had been. Three of the maids had been up to their ears in the work for four days. Finally, however, an end to it had come into sight, thank goodness. But who knows, maybe the girls had skimped on the packing material, and everything would be smashed and shattered to smithereens if the trunks were overturned!

Madam Jófríður sighed. But she comforted herself with the

thought of being able to get some rest tonight, here in the peace and quiet of Þingvellir – if, that is, she could catch a wink of sleep with all of this nonsense going on – it was as if she had just arrived from a flight over the North Pole! She had decided to come here tonight to get away from the ruckus in Reykjavík – as usual, whenever someone decides to go somewhere, everyone else suddenly shows up, wanting to do this and that; it's only then that people realize how much they'll miss someone. "Oh, Madam Valgerður, how poorly I've felt since the blood appeared in my saliva last spring; my only hope is a prolonged stay in the warm air down south."

Although Madam Jófríður was the mother of an eighteen-year-old son, she bore none of the marks of a middle-aged woman. On the contrary, her skin was smooth and youthful, her body chubby, swollen with full-flower femininity, her face milky pale, her lips kelp-red, and her hair auburn, but her dark eyes burned with dangerous embers, bearing witness to a number of different things at once: passion, consumption, hysteria; her eyebrows were two dark arches high above her eyes. In her facial expression, however, there was something that recalled a mask, the stylized face of an automaton or a wax image, but which had one thing beyond those, in that it was made of flesh and blood. But despite the ever-vigilant womanhood that shone from her with each word, every glance of her eye, every movement, there still appeared from time to time in her bearing something that reminded one of a tired child. She was not just formed of astoundingly delicate, perishable material, but she also seemed to know precisely how precious, fragile, and costly she was. She was like a vase made of Oriental glass. Every slight occurrence in her vicinity distressed her; she was perpetually afraid, perpetually annoyed, perpetually confused; it seemed as if she would die, were she to dip her hand in cold water. There was a depressed comeliness in her fumbling hand movements.

"Alright, Jófí dear! And what are you planning to do with your house in Rauðarárvík?" replied the mother-in-law. "Have you decided to leave it empty?"

"Yes, and I was the one who got to decide," she answered with childish pride. "Grímúlfur wanted either to sell the house or to rent it, because he says that it's foolish not to earn interest on one's possessions. But I don't find it foolish; I absolutely refuse to listen when Grímúlfur starts talking about interest or compound interest. Don't you think I'm right, Mama? Haven't I always said that Grímúlfur is and always will be a child in everything that touches on our family's welfare? Because when our house is sold we'll be left without a home in the world. Who knows, maybe one day I'll find out that it's better to own an empty house up near the North Pole than nothing in the lands to the south. And then there's Steinn, who so dearly loves the beautiful view from the west windows, who has sat there so often in the spring, writing beautiful things at sunset."

Grímúlfur sat down discreetly in one of the wicker chairs on the veranda; his mood was pensive. He cared as little about the beauty of Þingvellir as he did the smoke coming from his cigar. He was still a man in his prime, yet somewhat short – he scarcely reached all the way up to his son's shoulders, but he was burly, with prominent shoulders and an evenly shaped head. His face was marked with deeply drawn lines, and he had large, bushy eyebrows. His eyes were gray and keen, shielded with gold-rimmed glasses. His upper lip was carefully shaven, while his hair was dark and grizzled, parted meticulously in the middle of his forehead. His face retained an aura of dry business concerns. It was obvious that this man's work was the only reality that concerned him.

Suddenly from inside the house came the sounds of singing and the grand piano being played, just as Örnólfur came up the veranda steps after having finished tinkering with the car. He kissed his mother on the forehead and asked what was new at Þingvellir, and when he was told that everyone at the Ylfingabúð was doing fine he said:

"Since tomorrow is Sunday I'm going to do nothing but enjoy the peace and quiet of Þingvellir until tomorrow night. Father and son can hopefully handle driving south tomorrow morning."

He glanced at his hands – his fingers were dirty from touching the grimy engine parts. "I'm going in to wash up," he said, and he smiled and went into the house.

He could still be called a young man, not yet thirty-five years old, his hair longish and thin, he himself well-built and dashing, with manly shoulders. His manner was calm and determined, almost crafty. His face bore the same qualities of thoughtfulness and acuity as his elder brother's, was marked with similar lines from the nose to the corners of the mouth, but on his forehead, over the bridge of his nose, were runelike marks that would deepen with age. His eyes were quicker and livelier than Grímúlfur's, his eyebrows at least as bushy, his hair dark. Something in this man's face would have reminded one of an eagle or a hawk lying in wait to snatch its prey, had not another quality come into play that spoiled his raptor's likeness: namely, his gentle, modest smile, and the beauty that it lent to his face. The smile played about his lips every time he spoke. It also appeared every time he listened to others speaking. In fact, every time he looked into someone's face, even if he were just passing through a room where others were gathered, this smile appeared on his face and warmed everything around him. No one was more skillful at sealing business deals than this great industrialist with his gentle smile. His personality contained an energy that found its outlet in pliancy.

After Örnólfur went inside, Madam Jófríður shook her head and looked plaintively at her mother-in-law.

"What really gets to me," she said, "is when I hear this man complain about laziness, because if any man is going to die from ungodly overstress it'll be Örnólfur. That Kristján, one of their managers, was even talking about it with me yesterday at breakfast. It's been nearly a week now since Örnólfur came back from his little trip to Akureyri, on some kind of wretched fishing tub, and Kristján said that he would venture to swear an oath that this entire week he hasn't slept more than three hours out of twenty-four, if in fact he even tried to sleep at night at all! 'It's no mortal man who works like the director of this fishing company'; those were his exact words. He, who's in charge of so many offices. He confided to me that Örnólfur didn't just think for and control the company, but literally knew every single thing that concerned the company inside and out, both at sea and on land, by night or day. He knows where every ship is stationed at all times; he knows about every worker in the company, man and woman, what each one is supposed to be doing at all times; he knows about every truck, yes, every wheelbarrow! It's as if he knows every item by rote, every number in the accounts, both small and large, and I'm sometimes close to believing that he flies off on his broomstick to the company's offices in Genoa and Barcelona so that he can get their numbers as soon as they're written down. He's the kind of man I would dare to trust with a kingdom."

After concluding this description Madam Jófríður added: "I've never heard anyone talk about a mortal man the way the workers talk about Örnólfur."

"That's right," answered Madam Valgerður, without taking her eyes off the door, which had closed behind her son. "How often haven't I said to the boy: 'You must have built such an expensive summerhouse here for something if it's not just for your foreign guests, like the ones who were here last year and the year before, or for me, the old lady, and those impetuous girls, Diljá and her girlfriends.' Last week there were sometimes seven of them here, surrounding me with their constant music and racket. He himself has never enjoyed a single week's rest here in this blessed beauty–"

"No, it's not a week's rest that Örnólfur needs," interrupted Jófríður, "and the last time I told him that was yesterday, when I stopped him in the foyer of the National Bank and ordered him under threat to invite me to midafternoon coffee at Hotel Iceland. It's something else he needs to be getting. He needs a wife. And I said to him: 'I would have been willing to be your wife if your brother hadn't already spoken for me twenty years ago. You should get yourself a darling young wife and a comfortable home; you obviously have your choice of women both here and abroad,' said I; '. . . a beautiful and loving wife, yes, a devoted wife, dear Örnólfur, who waits impatiently for you to come home from your office at three and serves you your afternoon coffee; receives you with both hands whenever you return from a trip abroad, throws her arms around your neck, kisses your eyes and mouth, and runs her hands through your hair. Just like that,' said I, 'that's what you need, my boy.' There's nothing like a wife. Nothing can keep a man in line but a wife. A wife's the best elixir of life there is if you pick the right one."

"And what was his reply?" asked Madam Valgerður in a low voice.

"Oh, it was completely useless! He smiled and said, 'Mmhmm; first we'll wait and see how the new markets are doing in Portugal and Sicily.'"

"Oh, yes, I've heard such answers before; Lord knows how I've been put to the test by Örnólfur's eccentricities!" said Madam Valgerður.

Both of them shook their heads and looked sadly into the distance. Grímúlfur was still sitting pensively, waiting for both his cigar to burn out and the moment when it would suit the women to get up and his mother to invite him to coffee. No more music came from the parlor. The clock in the house struck eleven.

5.

He had greeted her as cheerfully as ever. But, truth to tell, there had been no joy in their parting. It was night; he had come to say goodbye; in the morning he was gone.

He said he had come to speak to her, but he ended up saying nothing. All he did was ask her to play the grand piano; he would accompany her. But it hadn't worked – neither of them was in any mood to play or sing. They couldn't even laugh at their own awkwardness.

She stood up and walked across the room, although on no particular errand, and he went to the piano and closed it; the curtains in the parlor were thick and shadows filled the room. She leaned up against the windowsill and watched him attend to the piano; night closed over her face.

"Are you leaving tomorrow morning?" she asked, abruptly and dully.

"The ship leaves just before noon," he said. "It's been nothing but parties since the voyage was announced. Tonight we were supposed to have gone to yet another party, but Mother chose to come out to Þingvellir and visit Grandmother, instead of sitting up until midnight in the company of potbellied misers. I myself went to a party that started at five today – there were young poets and artists, schoolmates and a few girls, toasts and good-byes, a bit of dancing. At eight-thirty the car honked outside; there was silence in the hall, a moment's sadness, then the shouting of good-byes: 'Farewell, Steinn Elliði!' said my friends. 'Hail, ye who put to sea in your golden magical swift-sailing vessels, to search for new lands, explore new worlds, new philosophies, new mythic worlds of the living arts! And sail home again hale, arrow of southern fire, laden with holy power, the bearer of the new arts to your people in the north, Icelandic ambassador to the new dawn in the culture of a youthful Europe!'"

She didn't care a whit for the clever words of his friends' farewells, and instead asked in a faraway voice:

"Why do you have to go, Steinn? You're not going to sell fish?!"

"I go because I want to go! Of course I will go, go, go! What further business do I have among these rustics, surrounded by barbaric boors and avaricious fisherfolk in this land of plebeian wisdom, where the vanguard of culture is composed of beggars, grannies, fortune-tellers, and retired bailiffs? I'll never be the main character in a romance with a setting and characters such as these! God bless the mountains of Iceland!

"I want to go out into the world, dear Diljá, to where the world wars were fought, in countries where cathedrals were shot at just for the fun of it and widows' hearths were leveled due to unscrupulous mistakes. You must have heard of such things. I want to see the day dawn over broken roods and carven images of Christ cut in half, over grapevines torn asunder and grapes trampled underfoot, forests uprooted; see the blessed human being who lies exhausted in the grass and either praises the Lord for the victory or curses the Devil for the defeat as he licks at his swollen wounds. I want to greet the day that dawns over the nurslings from the summer of 1914, who lost their fathers as offerings to the hands of the Kaiser, the fatherland, and the lie, freedom, slogans, and the Devil. I want to go, Diljá; Diljá, I want to see. I'm born to see; born for the wide world, the great huge world with its countless kingdoms and cities, a world full of monuments, crumbling or intact, from untold ages of culture, from ages of ascendancy and periods of decline, a world that hopes to see seven suns of new culture rise over the crumbling walls of palaces and tumbled-down towers."

She was silent for several moments, half-hypnotized by his passionate outburst, but when she regained her senses, she said:

"I thought perhaps, Steinn, that you would have found it difficult to leave Iceland, the mountains, and your friends, but now I can hear that you're in seventh heaven. Don't you know that Italy is teeming and swarming with crooks, thieves, and murderers, and that it's totally corrupt? Folk there are like savages, and they worship idols that they call saints."

He walked over to the window where she was sitting and, with the intention of ridiculing her, laughed out loud.

"Where in the hell did you acquire all of this wisdom about Italy?" he asked.

But she only looked down at her toes, avoiding his glance, and without looking up fled over to the piano once again. She recalled having read it somewhere: in her history book, or in Karl Finnbogason's *Geography.*[8] But maybe she hadn't read it anywhere; she just knew it offhand; in fact she'd never given a thought to Italy before yesterday.

A maid knocked at the door, then stuck her head in and announced that the coffee was ready in the dining room. Neither Steinn nor Diljá moved. Steinn Elliði fiddled with his cigarette case and lit a cigarette; neither of them said anything. But the air around them quivered with future tidings, burned with secrets. The clinking of tableware was heard from within the room at the other side of the hallway, where everyone else had gone for coffee. The grandmother called out:

"Children! Come while the coffee is warm!"

Diljá came to her senses and said:

"Yes, what are we doing here alone like asses?"

He cleared his throat and replied, in an annoyed, impatient tone:

"There's never any peace with these old grannies about! They grumble and rumble like spinning wheels, three or four at a time. Do they think we're all better off just because we've poured lukewarm coffee down our throats? Didn't I just tell you, Diljá, that I need to discuss an important matter with you?"

In the next instant his tone changed; he held out his hands like a rhetorician and said abstractedly:

"I ought to tell you something, Diljá. I was up all night thinking about the heavenly divinity that radiates from the face of this earthly world; I was thinking of what things I should say to you before I left. What is disturbing me, Diljá, is of no small consequence. All spring long I sat by my window in the brilliant sunshine and composed a princely hymn to the sun, in between skewering fish flies with my fountain pen. No one in the world has ever conceived such magnificent thoughts as I did this spring."

"Don't you think then that you ought to lie down and get some sleep before morning, Steinn?" she asked.

"Me?" he asked warily. "Do you think that I'm the kind of creature who could sleep here tonight? No, tonight I'm planning to stay awake, to gaze at the mountains and talk. And if no one wants to listen, then I'll talk to the mountains.

"Diljá," he added quickly, imploringly, "I have to speak to you tonight after everyone goes to bed! Stay awake!"

But she still lacked any coquettish promptitude in her responses.

"Stay up, me?" she replied hesitatingly. "I don't know about that. The idea never really crossed my mind. But what is this, boy, you're going to miss the coffee!"

Then she added, in a lower voice: "At least Grandma mustn't know about it if I do stay up."

6.

The clock in the house strikes one, just one tiny stroke.

It is noiseless and still; he starts up at the dulcet metal sound and looks around the loft where his bed had been prepared. Had he drifted off? Was he the kind of creature who would let himself fall asleep? Hadn't he been dreaming of a girl with golden arms and red lips? Damn. Or had he dreamt that the night before? Or was it a memory of an even older dream? Damn.

The day would soon dawn behind Ármannsfell – it was much brighter now than it had been at midnight. Everyone was surely asleep, guests and residents; nothing stirred except for a window hasp that dangled from the frame of an open window somewhere on the back side of the house, and the flag rope that smacked at the gable at long intervals. They hadn't set a time for their meeting, but he snuck downstairs in complete certainty that she was waiting for him, and found the veranda door open. Only those doors through which someone is expected to come stand open like this at night, he thought, and he stepped out onto the veranda. He peered about; the maid had stacked the chairs before she went to sleep, to speed up her morning cleaning duties. He peeked through the windowpanes: the parlor window to the right of the door, the dining room window to the left, but no one was there.

A high-pitched screech sounded from the lava to the west: someone was whistling through bentgrass. He turned on his heels and saw her. She was sitting out by the road, just on the other side of the bridge over the cleft closest to the house, on the rim of a notch in the lava rocks, with her feet down in the grass-grown crack. Her face was turned away from the Ylfingabúð, as if she had neither looked in that direction nor seen Steinn. She held her hands to her mouth, engrossed in signaling. Had he not been slightly nearsighted, he would have seen her immediately from the open veranda door. He walked straight over to her.

She had buttoned her coat up around her neck, but sat in a rather careless posture, as adolescent girls do. The hem of her coat reached to just above her knees, her strong calves stuck obtusely out, and she was not in the least bit conscientious about revealing her extraordinarily stout knee joints. This unhindered, imprudent pose was a reliable witness to a maidenhood too cloudless and untouched to know anything about protecting itself from danger. And yet there was a hot gleam in her steel gray, unswerving eyes.

He swelled with joy and jumped into the air:

"Tonight I'm as happy as an American boxer," he said. "Or as Douglas Fairbanks, who leaps over fences from happiness and grins like a horse."

But she had waited for him for an entire hour out in the night breeze, and when she heard how happy he was she was annoyed. She did not look up even though he was standing right in front of her; she looked at her open palm, which was green and wet from squeezing the grass between her hands.

Why couldn't she look up and smile? Hadn't it been her nature, since the time she had entered this world, to look up and smile? And hadn't he composed a poem about the girl who looks up and smiles? Had she changed and become someone else?

He waited. From the beginning he had always been accustomed

to her sitting and standing whenever he wanted. Wasn't she going to behave normally? He glowered at her silently.

But the longer this went on, the more difficult it became for her to look up. What did he think he could get from her when all he did was carry on with his ridiculous gladness? Why hadn't he gone to sleep? She had nothing left to say to him! Those who looked forward to leaving should leave quietly! He shouldn't expect that she would ever look at him again! She should get a lump in her throat; she should start crying, yes, start wailing and sit here all night and get a sore throat and a cold; but look at him, no, that she should never do.

Finally she jumped up and walked curtly over to the road and stopped there. She looked westward toward Þingvellir, then started walking again after a moment's thought, weaving her way along the path like a drunkard, slow, downcast, kicking with her toes at the gravel. All of her behavior came as a complete surprise to him. Finally he couldn't contain his resentment. He walked over to the road and called out after her, sharply and gruffly:

"Diljá!"

The voice that now tore through the still of the night and startled the girl was the old domineering, unreasonable one that had struck fear into the hearts of the other children with whom Steinn had once played. He jogged after her and caught up with her in the blink of an eye; she took one last wavering step, and then dared no more. He came up close to her, grabbed her by one arm, and tried to look into her eyes, but she bowed her head lower and lower.

"Diljá, what has become of you? You didn't act like this when we walked to Laugarnes last Sunday night! Have I offended you? Or have you heard something about me? How am I to interpret this behavior?"

He was no longer her childhood friend and playmate; that was the one thing she noticed. He was something different and something more; she could feel so clearly that he was a man, a young man. And he was the only man she knew, the only one she wanted to know, the only one she had ever planned to get to know. And he was leaving and might never come back. She had grown up since yesterday, grown and become a woman at the thought that she might never see him again; she was a daisy sprung up overnight. It terrified her to feel his strong hand upon her arm; her whole body trembled. And she hid her face with her free hand, bowed her head and cried; the tears fell down her hand as if from the sepals when a stem bends under the weight of the dew on a flower.

"I'm so sad that you're leaving!" she moaned in desperation.

He let go of her arm and looked at her indecisively, as if he didn't believe her. Finally he pronounced her name in a voice that blended pity and reproach.

"Diljá!"

But she continued to sob into the hollows of her hands, and the tears continued to trickle down them and fall onto the road.

"I'm in anguish," she sobbed again. "I know that it's terribly ugly of me to cry, I'm sorry that I should have started to cry, but I get so sad when someone leaves; I'm just seventeen."

He put his arm loosely around her waist and directed her with manly confidence off the road, since otherwise she would have stood there and cried until morning. She had no further will; she just let herself be directed, crying, wherever it might be. They wound up in a brake alongside the road; he pulled the scrubby birch branches apart, but still they hooked onto her dress; he let her walk ahead. They came to a flat mossy area. He pushed more than led her, sorrowful and stooping with her scarf covering her nose and mouth, until they came to a hollow growing with buttercups, wood crane's bill, green grass and many other types of vegetation, and there they sat down.

Her tears were somewhat stilled; all the same she was still reluctant to look at him. She was weak and frightened and only seventeen. He watched as she wiped her nose and mouth and cleared her throat; she ran tear-moistened fingers through her hair; her face was swollen and red from weeping, and he noticed how, while all of this had been going on, her face had taken on the look of a full-grown woman. Finally he said:

"Diljá. I don't understand why you're taking this so hard. I haven't seen you cry in many years. Imagine how painful it is for me to see you crying, when I've always turned to you for happiness. You who fill everything around you with lighthearted sunshine laughter! When I see you crying, it reminds me of the winter of plague, the day that I walked behind you in your father's funeral train. You were only fourteen then and you cried all the way to the churchyard, and I thought about how I was always going to be so good to you after that. I haven't seen you cry since then."

Finally she looked up with tear-filled eyes. She recalled that raw, cold November day in 1918, when she was left with nothing else in the Lord's entire wide world to love. The sob in her breast had been stifled.

"Diljá, to see you saunter off like that made me angry. I'm sorry

I shouted your name so harshly. Yet I couldn't help but think: has Diljá become like all the others? Whom else could I then trust with my divine revelations? If you were to change then I wouldn't know anyone any longer. All of the people that I know are slaves to licentiousness, and it gets on their nerves like a silly prank if someone says anything about his soul. My dear Diljá, tonight I want to talk to you about God and about me. I want to confess to you now, in this, the temple of my mountains, on my last night here. Be as you were!"

"Steinn, I'm sorry!" she said in a suppliant voice. "I was so tired of waiting for you; I'd grown so cold," she lied quickly, in order to excuse her capriciousness.

He gave her his hand and they walked up to the road again, and from there followed it side by side westward through the lava field.

7.

He reached into his case, took out a cigarette and stuck it quickly between his lips, then immediately took it back between his fingers and gesticulated as he started talking.

"What I wish to confide in you, Diljá, is neither more nor less than the fact that I've been reborn."

Here he paused for a moment as if he wanted to cover the silver of his words with the gold of his silence. She waited for more and avoided looking up, because she feared that he would grow angry again over the lack of understanding that her face would surely reveal. Then he continued, slowly and deliberately at first, but with ever-increasing passion the more he spoke.

"I don't know if you understand the word 'rebirth.' I don't understand it very well myself. I've discovered that writers of dictionaries don't understand it either. I don't know if anyone has ever understood it. But we live and move in God, so it is quite to be expected that we understand nothing. We only know that various things happen to us, and we give those things various names. It's only obsolete know-it-alls who have pretended to understand things.

"As far as I'm concerned, I don't understand what has happened. I'm entirely the same as I was before, but God has spoken to my soul. That's what has happened. It happened up on Öskjuhlíð on the fourth of May. I've kept quiet about it until now because it's so peculiar."

When he reached this point his inspiration flared up and a hot draft swelled his voice. He tossed his unsmoked cigarette out into the lava and continued:

"What I mean is, God has given me new perspective. I know that he will also lead me to new and more beautiful lands. The great and powerful God has lifted me, a blind wretch, up from his road; he has invited me to his home and created in me new eyes with new pupils; he has taken me up in his hands like a hatchling that has landed on a barbed-wire fence and broken its wing. And behold, I have flown like a newly created Brazilian butterfly from the talons of the Almighty! I am new and everything around me is new, my being most like a refulgent pattern woven yesterday on the loom, and I myself helped to draw the thread through the heddles, a work of creation piping hot and fragrant like warm loaves of bread from the baker's oven. I was remade so that I might be suited for composing perfect poems on the beauty of God. To be reborn – it is to learn to turn one's back on old masters and ancient loves and compose like God's firstborn. I've made a pact with the Lord about becoming the most perfect man on Earth."

She looked up quickly and asked:

"Why do you want to become so perfect?"

But he would not grant an answer to such an ignorant question.

"I have vowed to leave no further room in my soul for anything other than the celebration of the spiritual beauty of creation. No soulless wish or physical longing, no fleshly desire or pleasure. I am betrothed to the beauty on the visage of things. I intend to travel back and forth through existence like a jubilant monk of the world who beholds the smile of the Holy Mother in everything that exists. My bread and wine will be the glory of God on the face of creation, the image of the Lord on the Lord's coins. I am a son of the Way in China, the perfected Yogi of India, the Great Weaver from Kashmir, the snake charmer in the Himalayan valleys, the saint of Christ in Rome."

"I think that you might have lost your marbles!" said the girl, and she stopped to look in his face, because she understood nothing. They stood silently upon the road.

"It's as true as day, just as the sun will come up over there by Ármannsfell in a little while!" he averred.

She riveted her eyes on him until she herself was swept away by his devotion and felt that all of the holy foolishness shining from his face was the truth and reality, and that everything would happen just as he said: within a short time he would be gone, swept away and lost somewhere out in the realm of incomprehensibility, gone east to Kashmir to weave silk and satin.

All she could do was lower her head and sigh; his name died out half-spoken on her lips. And they hurried off spontaneously, side by side, two creatures from an Oriental romance.

8.

The first whimbrel cried out to the southwest like a young, sleepless drunkard. Otherwise the birds were not yet stirring. Two sheep, staid and respectable like old housewives, stepped leisurely along a narrow path a short distance away, their gait gentle and notable; they were thinking. The gentle breeze had given way to a dead calm; everything begins to glisten with dew. The birch-grown leading edge of the lava field smells sweet.

And finally, she absolutely could not help but ask: "Then you're not planning to get married?"

"I've vowed never to touch a woman again," he answered curtly, pithily.

"Again?" she asked, without fully realizing what she was asking.

"It is imperfect to betroth oneself to any human creature," he said. "A perfect man marries only his ideals. Had matrimony been the way to raise mankind from its sins, Jesus Christ would have redeemed the world by marrying and setting up a carpenter's shop in Jerusalem, with a sign over the door. The apostle Paul would have bought dining room furniture and a piano and settled down with his wife, like an English missionary. If a man's soul became powerful and strong by sacrificing burnt offerings upon the altar of lust within the so-called temples of matrimony, the masters in Tibet would fall to their knees before red-cheeked chastity imps, and the saints and martyrs would fawn like buffoons on lewd doxies in décolleté negligé. It is horrendous to be betrothed to a woman: one can't go for a refreshing walk in the cool of evening, like the Lord, without having a whole side of female meat hanging on to one. And what's more, a man has to endure this infectious carcass in his bed at night, lying over him, smacking her lips and groaning in her sleep, puffing and snuffling. Marriage is an ignominious capitulation."[9]

"Steinn, shame on you! I suppose you think that a woman doesn't have a soul like a man, you cad?"

He answered without hesitating:

"Oh, it could very well be that a woman has a soul; when did I say that a woman doesn't have a soul? It just doesn't matter at all whether she has a soul, and anyway no one has ever cared a whit about that up until now. It would be worse if a man had to marry a soul. As if any man has ever at any time since the days of Adam looked at a woman because she had a soul – what nonsense! If anyone brought me a woman's soul in a glass jug, I would immediately have the jug taken down to the cellar and put into the little closet where my father keeps the empty bottles."

The girl tried to run out into the lava, but he grabbed her, held her by the arm, made her follow him whether she wanted to or not, and poured from the cornucopia of his eloquence out over her wordlessness.

"Diljá, don't you have the nerve to watch as my heart is opened and the naked truth steps forth? Or do you think that I'm standing here in front of you, trying to talk sense, for the fun of it? No, Diljá, no one does such a thing for fun. Diljá, stand still here for just a moment and look at me as one human being to another, and not like a Spiritualist looking at an ectoplasm. Consider once who I am without wrapping my image in a foolish shroud of sanctity. You mustn't believe that I speak like a master because I have sipped from nirvana! No, I speak like a bombastic poetaster from the days of Klopstock, because doggerel has been my life."

He made her stop on the road to look at him and he pointed again at his chest:

"I forbid you once and for all to look at me like a photographer who fixes and refixes his overhead lights, his ground lights, and his prop lights on his test subject. Look here!" – and he again pointed at his chest:

"Here is where sin dwells! Here dwells the chief foe, the arch-enemy, that untiring torturer of the soul, who eternally seeks to cajole my spirit out into damnation: *cupiditas carnis.* Since I was a child at least half of all my spiritual strength has been pushed this way and that by passion and lust, has revolved around debauchery and pornography, the female body and copulation. There aren't any sexual misdeeds that I haven't become more cordially acquainted with than I have ever prayed the Lord's Prayer. Now it's been six years since I lost my virginity in the arms of a disgusting, stinking slut in the laundry room in the basement at home. That same summer and the following winter I joined in, as a rule, with several older chums in the drinking binges we held whenever we had the chance. We sat around with girls far into the night and acted as if we were possessed by devils. If I didn't come home until the next day, I pretended to have been with the Væringjar boys [10] in Hafnarfjörður, or out at Rauðavatn, or here at Þingvellir. If it seemed better to tell a different lie, I told a different lie.

"At home I've always been worshipped like an idol, since I never lied to any other individual so openly or so unscrupulously as my mother. She is the one person to whom I have never spoken truthfully from the first time that I can recall anything about myself. My mother is egotistical, passionate, and ingenuous, and because she never thinks about anything but herself, she can never have any suspicion of what might be hidden beneath someone else's cagey cant. It proved to me to be an easy game to clothe myself in the fraudulent cloak of the delightfully smiling, darling dear child in her presence. I have generally kept the whole truth of my demeanor locked up, except when I was with my comrades, who have seen the most splendid manhood revealed in the most depraved debauchery. When, for instance, did you ever hear that I was out carousing around?"

He waited a moment for an answer, and when she finally looked up she smiled at him, as if she thought that all of the sins of the world could be wiped away with one smile, and asked:

"Why are you telling me such ugly things, Steinn, on your last night here? Do you really think that I believe half of what you say?"

"Of course not!" he said. "That's obvious! All that you know is this: Steinn Elliði is brilliant, poetic, beautiful. As if I didn't know what you all say! From my childhood it has been my pleasure to pursue the arts; that's true. I'm not going to start musing on the reasons for it, but artistic ability has had a special place in my life. I have never had, nor do I have, any other dream for my future more beautiful than to be an artist. If half of my life is sin, then the other half is poetry, and maybe more.

"I am convinced that in this century no other young person here in this country has thought more than I have. I have conceived a heavenly verse, Diljá, such a one as cannot be put into words. I have had thoughts as strange as the Seven Sisters or the Mother of God who stands on the moon, or as the three-headed angel or the creatures in the Book of Revelation; no, it's not possible to put such thoughts into words. I have sat or stood in Rauðarárvík entire spring nights, my being reeling with the Almighty like a pagan idol in a thick cloud of incense, and I didn't come to my senses until dawn, when I found that I'd been composing hymns of praise all night and skipping stones and scratching comets on the wall of the solar system–"

He stopped and looked around: the dusky blue peaks peered out over the lumpy, copse-grown lava, through which the crevices branched out like ripples on the sea, shadowy, quiescent, and cool, silver at the bottom, Skjaldbreiður to the east, gentle, cold, and pure.

"God bless the mountains," he said suddenly. "What a pleasure it is to be able to spend this night at the heart of one's country. In this church I would wish to die if all else were to fail!"

Next he touched her arm to bring her even with him, and they continued on their way. He started right in again where he had left off.

"Diljá. A man has two natures; there's nothing one can do about it. One ascends to Heaven, if you can understand that, up into the rarefied space beyond the atmosphere, all the way to God. The other pursues a downward course, down into the Earth, a thousand shovel's lengths below all diggable ground, all the way down into the fiery and icy depths of Hell. Man has a soul, and man has a body, and what the soul demands is at odds with what the body desires, and the body desires whatever it is that kills the soul. In Latin this is called *spiritus adversus carnem.* The world contains both good and evil and man is free to choose between them. Man has two choices, perfection or perdition. You might find this to be too commonplace, but it's not as worthless as the Psalter or *Faust.* For a little less than two years I thought that everything Christianity had to say about Heaven and Hell, God and the Devil, was a bunch of lying rubbish, and that the Christian religion could be boiled down to the political dodges of old bishops. The threat of damnation seemed to me to be nothing other than an invention used to make the guileless rabble bend beneath the pope. Now it's my opinion that Christianity is the absolute flat-out truth from start to finish. This suddenly occurred to me one night in the spring. I was taken by the scruff of the neck. I was ripped into. Some higher being spoke to me through the mouth of God. And this happened up on Öskjuhlíð, in that scraggly scrap of a wood where no one has ever had a revelation before. Yes, Diljá, now that I've started to speak, it would be best if I were to tell you everything and leave no stone unturned."

He spoke with feverish passion, in short sentences broken by quick silences.

"You must remember the spring when Mother and Father went north for ten days. Gone was the taciturn, destitute rigidity that reigns in the house when Father is at home. You yourself know our house and know how high the ceiling in the foyer is. You remember how murky the foyer is: it's like a countryside church in Spain, where carnal vices have been satiated with pharisaic blessings, clouds of incense, and Latin chant for many hundreds of years. A gleam of light comes down from somewhere above, and the lacquered craftwork, the burnished chairs and the table, are there for nothing: no one ever sits there, much less eats or drinks; and the creepers stretch up over all the walls, blackish green and ugly. There is no human abode as monstrous as the foyer at home.

"And for ten days there was no one at home except for myself and Helga, the parlor maid – no one besides the servants in the basement. I was sitting up in my room reading; I hadn't felt like getting dressed that day, but instead sat in front of the fireplace in my nightclothes and robe. I'd recently bought some voguish novels; I still remember their titles, but we won't go into that.

"Novels can make one giddy, because they open one to the expansiveness of human life. I didn't know what I was doing, Diljá. I went and got the keys, snuck down, and opened the wine cellar. And I took a whole armful of bottles up to my room and started drinking. No, Diljá, I didn't know what I was doing. I felt so fiendishly great. This blissful devilish determination to sin burned in every last little part of my body. The greatest bliss in the world is to sin. The next greatest is to determine to sin. The saints covet sin. I rang the bell. A few moments passed.

"Then the door opened.

"Helga stood in the doorway and waited to hear what it was I wanted, quiet and modest as usual. And when she saw the wine on the table before me she became even shier than usual. That was the first time I looked on her in a different way than as a master on his servant.

"'Helga,' said I, 'I would like to offer you a glass of champagne, because I have no one to drink with.'

"But she didn't want to take it, said that she never drank, had only tasted alcohol twice or thrice in her life and then only a few drops, didn't dare it, thought she would get drunk. She looked me straight in the eye and said no. But I kept on nagging her until she gave in and promised to drink half a glass, but absolutely no more. It was out of the question that she would take a seat; no, she would just sip from the glass standing, since I of course needed to drink with someone.

"But before she knew it she was sitting. Yes, she didn't realize it until she'd drunk an entire glass filled to the brim. She said she'd never tasted wine so good, in general had never thought that wine could be so good–

"Under my parents' roof I beguiled this poor girl disgracefully, deprived her of her virginity, in lustful euphoria made her swear that she wouldn't betray me, and treated her like a harlot for three whole days and nights."

He lit a cigarette absentmindedly and peered into the darkness along the road as he exhaled several thick streams of smoke. He let his story be for the time being. They walked on silently, he out upon the farthest edge of the road to one side, and the smoke from his cigarette drifted to her senses in the calm air.

9.

"On the morning of the fourth day a message came from my parents. They were setting out from Akureyri.

"I kissed my mistress's feverish lips with a last exhausted kiss, threw off the stained and sweat-dampened bedsheets, got up, and opened the windows to let the cold north wind coming over the strait blow through the house. I was jaded and befuddled from the drunkenness of the last several days, but I put on my clothes and staggered out.

"I stood before the door like a brown beggar dog that has swallowed some filthy thing down on the beach. I pondered whether I in fact could find refuge anywhere on all of God's green Earth, and whether there was in fact anyone whom I could now allow to look me in the face. And not a single living soul came to mind, not one single creature. Imagine it, Diljá! There come those times when a man actually has no friend at all! This anguish can cut one so quickly to the heart that no comfort can assuage it, no friendly handshake can shake it off, no smile can soothe it, no mother's tears can wipe it clean, no lover's heart can conquer it with forgiveness and affection. Who could possibly grant resurrection to a man who has enlisted as a soldier for the enemy of his soul? Only time can wash one's wounds in the waters of Lethe. Eternity confirms whether the wounds are healed.

"I sauntered from Reykjavík up and over the fields; the last thing I could think of doing was to head downtown where every other jackass would doff his hat to me, smiling deferentially, as when drunken men say hello to telephone poles and Good Templars, because I felt sure that I wanted nothing to do with looking into the faces of those so-called friends of mine. I rambled a bit southward, over walls and fences, ditches, fens, hills, heaths, and mires, and avoided all human paths. I sat on stones on the hills and in my distress scratched sorcerers' crosses, concentric circles, and cuneiform runes with the heels of my boots or rolled around in the white withered grass on the slopes and crests of hills.

"Yes, Diljá, my chest rose and fell like a broken accordion; I rolled and rolled in the gray turf and asked the Lord God to allow me to crumble back into the dust that I once was, never to have to rise up again, not even on Doomsday. My head was like a universal madhouse where the Devil and all the idiots of the solar system press against the windows and stare at God and twist their faces into grimaces because of the glare.

"I sat in a pub in Hafnarfjörður for the rest of the day without looking up. I sat in a nook behind a door that was constantly being opened and shut, but I didn't pay attention; I drank coffee as strong as lye from a thick clay cup. And there, around midafternoon, I ate fish and potatoes and rice pudding.

"I walked back home in the evening, just as aimless as in the morning, except for when I skirted the margin of the sea and wasted time taking detours out onto all the spits and tongues as if to discover whether my own corpse had washed up anywhere in the kelp. I took off my clothes and tried to scrub away my wantonness in the cold sea. And when I walked up Öskjuhlíð that evening, it was around nine and the sun shone over Faxaflói.

"The breeze still blew from the north, clean and fresh, and I left my shirt unbuttoned to air out my heart. And as I stood there that evening and gazed out into blue space, I was spoken to through the mouth of the Lord; truth was poured into my soul. In a single moment I understood the nature of everything, like a character in a psychological work by William James.

"'Behold,' said Almighty God, 'how this night is sinless and beautiful. Look at the visage of things. Feel how pure the breeze is! Why will you not worship the world that I your God have given you, sink your thoughts into the glory of God, which the world reflects, and forget yourself in the presence of the Almighty like the saints? Do you think that you must sell your soul to the passions of the flesh and the demands of the beast within you? For what reason do you think that I have entrapped you in human form? No, my friend, you should let your spirit rejoice in me! The grass is coming up in the Fossvogur homefield! And aren't the mountains that I have given you splendid and soft? Here is Esja, and there Helgafell and Mosfell, bare like the mountains of the moon. Now the farmers in the Eyrar district and the Mosfell dale are discussing whether it might not soon be possible to start letting the cows out to graze. Behold the cars on the Hafnarfjörður road, glistening in the nightshine; all day they bring folk back and forth between Hafnarfjörður and Reykjavík for one króna fifty. And there stand the radio towers on Melar; behold how they stretch their slender fingers out into endless space and the eternal blue! They are like supernatural trees of the forest, hiding their crowns in the cabalistic ether and drinking in political news from the east, from Shanghai and Bombay.'"

10.

They had come as far west as the plain, and they stopped; she would not challenge him further on anything. He stood on the edge of the road on one side, she on the other. She looked at him.

Yes, yes, she should always look at him; look at him with tears in her eyes and a sob in her throat; whatever wickedness he wished to tell her, he should always be able to count on the fact that she was prepared to stop on the road and look him in the eye. He could wind his way through every misfortune, every one; she was supposed to smile at him and the smile was supposed to rise from the depths of her soul; she should take him by the hand if that would be of any relief to him. Yes, even if his hands were spattered with blood, she should always be prepared to wash them with her warm tears. They stood on opposite edges of the road and looked at each other. And she whispered his name so quietly that it could scarcely be heard: "Steinn Elliði"; these two difficult words emerged onto her lips involuntarily, a noiseless groan.

It might never have been clearer to her than tonight that Steinn Elliði was more gifted than others and more of a man than any other. And if he ran into any trouble, it was not because he was wicked, because no one was better than him. It was because he was more gifted than others and more of a man than any other. Woe to whomever might try to convince her that someone had been found in the world more illustrious or better than him! Steinn, Steinn, she thought. Even if you were to reject your God, you would never reject me.

They had watched each other grow. Once she had been six years old and he eight. What had changed? They hadn't been aware of any changes, but even so, they stood here tonight on opposite sides of the road, full-grown.

And when he beheld her smile, unsteady and weak, he understood that he had not confessed gratuitously; she was raised above all sin and forgave everything. She was too pure to comprehend that there was anything foul in sin. She loved those who were in trouble, that was all. And at that moment the sun rose over Ármannsfell.

In fact it was unlike any other sun; it was truly more like blood gilded with fire, gushing from a fissure on the mountain. It erupted in all directions. A tall man could easily have stuck his hands into it and let it foam like soap through his fingers. It must have been healthy for a sinful man to wash himself in this blood.

He quickly took her by both hands, like a man in a poultry shop grabbing two chickens that he wants to buy. They walked down to the grassy plain through Fagrabrekka in order to watch the fire, and sat down entirely unconcerned that the dew would wet their clothing. The air was cold and clear. The morning stepped ever higher; the chaos over the mountain soon changed into sunshine. The dew began to glisten. In an hour a snow-white fog would extend itself over the entire copse. Everything was still drowned in shadow although the sky was radiant. "Chastity is the highest of all blessings," he said.

"A chaste man is a holy man; whatever he does is holy. Chastity is the fount and foundation of what old chronicles call virtue. Chaste men, and no others, are possessed of a strong will, unfailing powers of accomplishment, an all-seeing intellect, an affectionate heart, an alien beauty, and a magnetic personality. A chaste man puts a yoke on his flesh for the freedom of his soul. Freedom is formed beneath the yoke and nowhere else but there. No one is free but a chaste man. The most powerful establishment in the world, the Roman Catholic Church, is founded upon chastity. It is thanks to chastity that it has not collapsed. When its monks swerved from its ideal of chastity its success diminished. When the ideal of chastity came once again to the fore it experienced a renaissance. If I believed in even half of all the truth found in the Bible, I would become a Catholic monk and dedicate my soul to God and Joseph, the Virgin Mary, the holy Anna, and that entire household. But no matter what, my life must become a hymn of praise to chastity. Poetry is my lover, the new poem. God himself has told me that if I am pure enough, I can inspire a new era in world literature, like Dante Alighieri.

"Diljá, this is no phantasm!" he reiterated, and he gave himself over to the power of his inspiration. "Diljá, I am gifted and strong! Powerful! I believe that I can rule a huge kingdom! My childhood dream was to subdue all of Asia to the east of a line from Kamchatka to Persia, and I still feel that I was born to be king over the largest country in the world. Diljá, I love the world and all that is in the world!

"I could die for the world if I wanted to, let myself be crucified for all that is in the world. I love all men, love them all, love them like infants in white gowns, like French girls on parade, innocent, bright, and helpless. I long to take them all into my arms and stroke their cheeks with my hand, erase struggles, trials, and sins. Come all ye to my breast, my friends! I love the most vicious criminal among you just as passionately as the holiest saint! My Holy God, no one understands better than I why you should have wished to become a man and live among us."

He buried his face in his hands for a few moments, and when he looked again toward Heaven his eyes were drenched with tears.

"I love all of it," he continued in a passionate, quivering voice, "all that exists, all that there is! The glorious radiance of the universe overwhelms me. I am prepared to kneel before everything, everywhere. God, take me unto you!"

His rapture was like a flood bursting all riverbanks; he was forced to fall silent. Finally he spoke again, more calmly than before.

"I love the asphalt street in the evening after rain, the life of the street, the whirling jungle of the pavement, and the lampposts with their shining electric fruits, the streets of the city with all their thousand-and-one-wheeled reality. The huge advertisements that the merchants paste up on the walls along the streets inspire me no less than the oil paintings from Pompeii do the English tourists, who examine them with the aid of three guidebooks. I read the classified advertisements in the newspaper with just as much inspiration as old women do the Bible or the bourgeoisie the masterworks of poetry. And whereas it took no less than a symphony orchestra in the Queen's Hall in London to inspire the old poets, I am filled with blissful admiration for the rhythmless caterwauling of a harmonica down in Melar, and it is an aesthetic pleasure for me to listen to the false notes played on the flutes of beggars on the squares down south in Barcelona. And I am seized with no less mystical joy when paying attention to the hens, which peck dainty, glittering grains from the rubbish on the side streets of Þingholt, than when watching the golden plover or ptarmigan on the mountains, about which the great poets sang glorious odes. Nothing touches me more deeply than the simple and plain, things whose power resides in being whatever they are. My most precious gift is that I have been given an aesthetic soul, the ability to worship the glory on the visage of things."

After several silent minutes he pulled the end of one sleeve back from his watchband and looked at his watch.

"Diljá," he continued. "I'm leaving and have come to say good-bye. I am for the moment standing at the heart of my country, but within a few hours I will have embarked upon the sea, with foreign shores before the ship's prow. I feel as if I'm setting out into pitch-black eternity, alone, on foot, over countless seas. I have of course been abroad every second or third summer since I was a child, but this is the first time that I've felt as if I were leaving. Now I'm leaving. Who knows, perhaps I shall never return, Diljá. Father and friend of all that is, tend to this green plot!"

And after a short silence:

"What else might lie before me than to become lost? A man who has spoken to God must become lost. And I yearn to be sucked into the whirlpool of life until I have become a tiny pupil that peeks out along the streets of some huge city, a tiny songbird's tongue so that I can sing about what I am. When I finally leave this place, I wish that these might be my parting words: 'What I saw was beyond compare.'

"Have you heard the story that most suits the calling of the poet? It is the story of Vyasa. Vyasa composed a poem that is seven times more sapient than all the Holy Scriptures. The poem is called the Bhagavad Gita. And it starts out by saying that Vyasa sang this poem, '. . . but concerning Vyasa nothing is known, neither when he lived nor where.' God grant that I might become forgotten and lost like Vyasa, but that my verse might live; that I might be forgotten like the king Shah Jahan, who built for his deceased queen the Taj Mahal palace, the most glorious building in the world. Peace be to Vyasa, peace be to Shah Jahan and his wife. I pray for the same peace. God grant that those of other faiths exalt my verse in the temple while they kowtow in praise of the One who gave me my harp! God grant that the children in the side streets sing my verse in the evenings while they dance beneath the street lamps, Hesperus gleaming beyond the wall. Diljá, we may never see each other again."

His last words slipped into her heart like an arrow; she gasped quickly for breath and slowly shut her eyes. Then she moved just a touch nearer to him as if cuddling up to him were foremost on her mind. All that he did was give her a stern, investigative look.

"Yes, Diljá, I'm leaving," he repeated, with unswerving emphasis on every syllable, perhaps from premeditated cruelty. And she looked at him in a way that showed her ignorance of the art of language, although the pious sorrow and the anguished affection on her face were mightier than words. And he was suddenly stymied.

"Diljá," he said suddenly, "I shall never, ever forget you."

His voice burned with passion for a single moment, and it was clear that he had to constrain himself into silence. He looked down at the grass. They sat a little distance apart from each other and did not touch. She also looked down at the grass and said:

"I'm never going to get married either."

It was as if she knew how peculiar and clumsy these words sounded coming from her mouth, because she added, with eager conviction:

"I made that vow a long time ago."

She looked him straight in the eye, and it was apparent that she herself did not know whether she was telling the truth or a lie. She wasn't about to start carrying on about asceticism in grandiose poetic prattle or mystical exhortation, but the determination and passion in her voice were not affected. In the next instant she cast herself facedown onto the field.

And she lay there before him young and fair, pressed herself down into the luxuriantly thick spring grass, herself nothing but a personification of the fertile earth. When she drew in her feet her clothing tightened over her hips, revealing their agreeable roundness; this slender, resilient body rested here in the spring grass, and the male partner in the tango could sway like a reed in the dance. She was a woman, fit to become the mother of generations, like Egill Skallagrímsson's queen at Borg. But the ascetic would not take the opportunity to lift her into his arms in order to kiss her on the eyelids.

"Arise, Diljá! Take my hand! This hour is holy. I am bidding farewell to my childhood and leaving. And the sun has risen."

And he added, as if performing an old ritual bungled together by prelates:

"Let us pledge to each other to offer our souls and bodies to the truth that is concealed behind creation and that radiates from the visage of things."

A moment passed and she did not move. She seemed not to have heard his words. She could just as well have been sleeping or dead. When she finally stood up it was as instantaneously as when she had thrown herself down. Her face was wet. She had been crying, silently, without a sob. She came so near to him at that moment that her face was no farther away than a few inches from his chest. It was as if she were dead drunk. With closed eyes and an exhausted sigh she reached out to him with her warm, damp hands, which she could just as well have folded onto her own naked bosom.

"Diljá, we call God as witness to this vow of chastity," said he, in a deep, solemn voice, as he looked at her eyelids. And she let the words echo in her mouth: "We call God as witness."

Then she looked up. The eyes of this living soul were aglow with suffering. She looked into his face and sighed once more. She tilted her head back, as if she thought that a cup would be raised to her lips.

"Yes," she whispered with a shudder, and swallowed the sob that arose in her throat when she started to speak. "We call God as witness. We call Almighty God as witness."

They squeezed each other's hands as hard as they could and gazed with drowning eyes at each other's lips.

Book Two

11.

Steinn!

Now winter has come and it's been almost seven months since you left. You left in July; now it's Christmas. It was bright then; now it's dark. But more than likely winter only visits me, not you. You must be so happy there in the south.

No snow falls to the earth in the south and you never experience a sunless day or a night of storm. Every day there is like a fairy tale, and at night everyone can sleep. The people there think only about God and the solar system and the glory on the visage of things. But at home boats are always sinking and men are always falling off of trawlers. And collections are taken for widows at every church door, burlesque shows are put on, dances and evenings of comic songs are held for the benefit of orphans. And here no one ever talks about the glory on the visage of things; they just insult each other in the newspapers.

How could anyone possibly believe that you have a thought remaining for the ones you left behind in the cold and polar darkness;

how could I be so foolish as to think that? The longer you're gone the better I see how foolish I am.. Forgive me for being such a child! Forgive me for being so paltry compared to you.

I waited here impatiently for every ship that came, all the summer and all the fall, as if I expected that they would bring me greetings from Steinn. But those huge strong ships that come all the way from the continent never bother to bring me greetings. They rush into the bay like mighty whales and blow their horns in the harbor so loudly that the mountains shake. But I sit fearfully by my window.

Couldn't I just as well have assumed that Steinn would forget, forget, and never again remember what once was? Shouldn't I have known you well enough to know that every past event in your life is like a hundred-year-old old wives' tale to you? No one was more eager to forget! Your life happens in leaps and bounds. And you never stop anywhere except on mountaintops where the winds of the sky come to meet you. On every peak four winds blow around you. How could you possibly recall what once was?

12.

Steinn!

Have no fear that I'll ever send you this letter. Never. Just forget, forget, forget! Blessed are those who forget! Never shall a letter from an idiotic girl near the North Pole disturb your peace there in the south. Think in peace about everything great and holy! Think in peace about God, the great God! I congratulate you on your great God who shines like phosphorescence from the visage of things. I hope that you write a beautiful poem about him, much more beautiful than the one you wrote about me. He rewards you much better than I do. Of course he promises you that you'll reach Heaven. And all that I am is one of his creatures, just a little girl. Forgive me for that.

No, Steinn, I'm not writing because I think that you or anyone else should read this. In any case you wouldn't grant my letters such respect as to read them. God wouldn't allow you to read them. He would call down fire and brimstone over them. There's no glory shining from them. They're nothing but the sleepless blabber of a young girl. I write because I feel so bad. I'm so bored. I'm young, weak, scared, and alone. No one understands me. I feel like a little human child raised by trolls, and one of these days the trolls will come and eat me. At night before I go to bed I look at myself in the mirror. And then I pray to God to help me, because I'm afraid. What am I? At night I don't sleep. I cry.

Everything is dark and meaningless around me. Tell me, Steinn: is anything worthy of a single daydream? Will you never return?

It isn't any fun anymore for me to meet my girlfriends. It's like they've taken sides with the trolls. No one understands me or knows me but you. You made me what I am. I was the clay between your hands. I wanted to be everything and do everything that you wanted. If I never see you again, I'll never get over having sat with you by the sea. And when I think about all of this I find it simply disgusting to be a girl. Steinn, forgive me. Should I become a nun? Or should

I become an actress? Or should I become a dancer? Steinn, I'm nimble and quick. Last evening after my bath I would have dared to let you see me dance.

Sometimes I feel like it's nothing but an illusion that I exist. When have I ever had any inkling of whatever it is that's called reality? Remember when you taught me the poem about "the painted veil, that those who live call life"?[11] What is reality? Sometimes I feel like death is the only reality, and the rest an illusion! My mother died giving birth to me. Isn't it horrible that I should have been born to kill my mother? Why wasn't I allowed to die, and my mother to live? I never asked to be born, and my mother was happy. I'm always full of fear and despair, but there's nothing wrong! I woke up one Sunday last summer at Þingvellir and saw that my life, sixteen-and-a-half years, had been nothing but a dream. I feel that whatever time I have left to live will be uninterrupted sleeplessness. Then death will come.

Sometimes I look forward to dying because then the illusion will come to an end. Sometimes I shudder at the thought of being buried. Imagine it, Steinn, letting your body be buried in the earth! Often when the terror overcomes me I get up out of bed at night, and I take out my picture of Mother. I kiss it and cry. And then I hate my own body, Steinn, because it cost my mother her life. God grant that I never have a child! I'm afraid of my body, afraid of my soul, afraid of myself, afraid of everything. And you're gone.

13.

Steinn!

Since you'll never see this letter then I might as well write everything. Everything? No, so little can be put in words. Words can never reveal the heart. Words are wise, precise, and strict like teachers, and I'm afraid of them, but the heart is none of these things. I usually stayed quiet when you were around because I felt that words couldn't say what was in my heart. I want to speak a completely different language than the one contained in words. As if I could put into plain words how I felt in my heart that day in the summer when you left!

I went to bed and fell asleep after you drove away. When I woke up it was pouring rain. I got up out of bed and went to the window. And Ármannsfell, where the sun had come up in the morning, was covered with clouds. And huge drops fell outside my window. And oh, how everything was dreary! I woke up alone in the wilderness, and your ship had put out to sea seven hours before. And I listened to the rain fall, and memories rained down in my mind. I recalled your words and everything that had happened. Your words are beautiful and terrible. I tremble when you start to speak. Everything that you say and do is beautiful and terrible. Maybe you'll get up without any warning, come straight over to me, plunge your hand into my breast, and take away my heart.

I felt that the farther away you went, the more beautiful and terrible everything that you had said would become, the more beautiful and terrible everything that had happened. Tell me why we swore oaths! Were we serious? Steinn, is it true that you're going to try to become so perfect? Isn't that just poetic fancy like so much else? How can anyone become so perfect? I'm positive that I can never become perfect. I'm so frightened. Steinn, don't ask me to become perfect, because I don't want to, but tell me that I can believe in you, because that's the only thing that I want to be allowed to do.

Your name was in the paper the next day:

"*Gullfoss* sails today for Leith and Copenhagen. Among the passengers: Director and Mrs. Grímúlfur Elliðason, Steinn Elliði Grímúlfsson, cand. Phil. . . ."

Every time I see your name in print, Steinn, it's as if something seizes my heart. Strangers had printed your name there in black, lifeless letters, people who couldn't care less about you, people who had no clue as to what you'd said before you left, where you'd been your last night here, how you were completely smitten with grandiose plans, how your voice was passionate and inspired, your eyes bright. And you had held the hands of your little tearful girl and made her swear an oath. Steinn, what did we mean? I don't dare to think about you becoming so perfect!

I look out over the lava, gray in the rain, toward the wilderness, and think about you who are gone. And it's like I'm reading a big book. I don't recall anything before you. Once you had a straw hat with a wide brim and a red walking stick with a crook. I remember it like it was yesterday. I was sitting on someone's lap, and you walked with your stick straight through and into the next room. That's my first precise memory of you, because I thought it extraordinary how big you were, with your hat and stick. You're the big boy and I'm the little girl, just a little speck next to you. I've always looked up to you with awe and admiration, and the same went for the last time, when you drove away from the Ylfingabúð, you sitting behind the steering wheel with your parents in back. A cloud of blue smoke trailed behind the car as it rushed west over the ridge; in the next moment it had vanished into Almannagjá. The last thing I saw was when you grabbed your hat with one hand and pushed it down over your forehead so that it wouldn't fly off in the wind. Now I've been dreaming of you for seven months. I can meet your eyes in the stars, because they're all that we can both see at the same time. But that only awakens an even deeper longing to see you. The language that you speak today is completely different from mine. And your thoughts are like earthquakes.

14.

Do you remember when we went up to Mosfellssveit with your mother and grandmother? Our maid was with us, and a boy from the company drove. It was on a warm, sunny day in the middle of the week, the channel as blue as Esja, the hayworkers with their long wagons on the road. Everything was calm, pure, and blue. Don't you remember how our summer joy was deep and sweet when we were little? We didn't stop until we were a long way out in the countryside; we parked the car on a gravel bed just off the road and hiked up to the foot of a mountain. The boy brought our lunches. We chose a grassy spot by a little stream. The maid heated cocoa; we ate eggs and bread, crackers and fruit. Oh, how hungry we were! Don't you remember how exciting that was?

But suddenly you were lost. You had hiked up along the stream and disappeared behind a hill. A long time passed, and you were lost. Then I hear a shout, and I look up. And you're standing up on the hill, making a trumpet with your hands around your mouth and calling to me. I ran to you as I always did whenever you called. And you took me by the hand and led me to a little field between two stony hills. You could be so serious and solemn when you were a boy, and I was always scared. "Diljá," you said, "come here and listen to something!"

And there was a tiny hole in that hard field. It was so narrow that you couldn't stick your foot in it. And grass grew over the opening, making it almost unbelievable that anyone should have been able to find it. And it was so deep that I thought it went all the way through the Earth. And then you said: "There's a dwelling down there, and folk talking."

We threw ourselves down flat and put our ears close to the hole. And it was true! We could hear people's voices far, far down in the Earth. I still remember how serious you were, but I was scared. "Almighty!" I said. "What if it's spirits? We should get out of here! Come on!"

But you weren't scared; you just wanted to listen longer. And I was tempted to listen again. At first we heard the same murmur of calm, strange speech, as if someone were speaking in the other world, or in his sleep. But the longer we listened, the more eerie the things we heard became. Finally we heard an instrument being played.

Someone had brought out a guitar and was plucking the strings gently, as if playing for a small child. And far, far away it was answered with the deep, deep tones of an organ. We stood up and looked at each other: they played instruments in the other world!

15.

In the summer of 1914 you were twelve, and I was ten. You had gone abroad with your mother, and you didn't plan to be back until the fall. And then the war started. And the sea was filled with mines, and ships were blown up. Good gracious me, I was scared! No, you could certainly never suspect just how scared a little girl can be!

Every night I prayed to God to keep your ship from being blown up. And I said that he could let all the other ships be blown up if he would just protect your ship. And I said to him that even if he had never heard my prayers before, it didn't matter: I could forgive him everything if he would hear my prayer just this once. "Keep watch over them, my dear God," said I. "Don't let them perish!"

Every morning I asked: "Did a ship come from abroad today?" But my blessed father was serious and strict, much like your father, and he had a lot to think about. That summer Örnólfur was home on his last summer holiday from the university. And Örnólfur was always so kind, the only one at home who had a soul. No better man exists than Örnólfur. He was always willing to talk to me. I often felt like Örnólfur was a little boy, he was so sincere and humble. He always went and got a copy of *Morgunblaðið* when I asked, and checked on the ships. And ship after ship came, but some were blown up. And finally I started thinking that your ship had sunk.

The atmosphere at home was like this when Örnólfur was gone, that a little girl never dared to say anything about what was on her mind. But I got my chance one morning when Örnólfur was alone in the dining room after breakfast, and I asked: "Örnólfur, do you think that their ship will sink?" He was reading foreign newspapers, but he looked up, stroked my cheek, and said: "No, no, Diljá dear, they don't cross a danger zone. Steinn Elliði will make it home just fine."

And he stroked my cheek again and looked at me for a long time.

One morning early in September, Örnólfur came to Grandmother and me and said: "The *Bothnia* has reached Grótta. Grímúlfur and his wife sent a telegram from the ship yesterday, but it wasn't delivered until this morning. They'll be in the harbor in half an hour."

I was overcome by such joy when I heard this wonderful news that I forgot to thank God for hearing my prayer until half a month later. And when we reached the pier the ship was just anchoring. The passengers leaned over the railing, smiling and greeting their friends on the pier. Your father was standing there in his plain black overcoat with its silk collar, serious as usual. Next to him stood your mother in a new fur coat, and you slipped your hand under her arm. I can still see you there, in a blue sailor suit, your trousers reaching down to your heels, with new patent-leather shoes, in a gray, unbuttoned overcoat, not wearing a hat, your hair parted to one side like a grown-up man. I wouldn't let you out of my sight. You disembarked before your parents and said hello to us. I gave you my hand without a word. I was only ten and you were twelve. And I felt like you'd come home from war. I thought that during the last few months you'd heard nothing but the roar of cannons and seen nothing but fire.

But all I could think was "Jeremiah!" because when it came down to it you were so incredibly full of yourself. You bowed to us as if you were greeting strangers overseas, and when you bumped into someone you said, *"Um verzeihung,"* because you'd been with your mother at a German spa during the summer, while your father was down south in Spain. You were so arrogant that whole day that I didn't dare to look at you, except in secret. I didn't dare to come into the dining room while you ate breakfast with us. I stayed in the kitchen with the maids. Oh, how terribly disappointed I was!

But on the next day you came to us alone. Grandmother gave us chocolate and fruit. You were completely different than the day before: you'd put on shorts, a sweater, and waterproof shoes like every other Reykjavík boy, and you were starting lyceum in the fall. You spoke more naturally and told us about everything you'd seen. You'd seen everything. You'd seen ropedancers, and black men swallow fire, and bears ride bicycles, and horses dance polkas. And you'd seen all the soldiers parading through the streets in Germany. And when you looked down on the soldiers from the balcony of your hotel, it was as if you were looking out over meadows of incredibly tall grass, and wind was blowing through the grass. But that was the bayonets on the soldiers' shoulders, all tilted in the same direction. You said you hoped that the Kaiser in Germany would conquer the whole world. And when Grandmother got tired of listening, you told just me about everything you'd seen. And I said nothing; I just gazed at you and sighed. No one can believe how happy a little girl can be when she reclaims her playmate from death.

16.

After you moved to your new home in Rauðarárvík we saw each other less often than when you lived in town. During the winters you were completely busy studying, during the summers either abroad with your mother or on some trip with the Væringjar boys. One summer you were up north in Akureyri. Often weeks went by when I didn't see you, sometimes months. And every time I did see you I felt that you'd become a greater man than when I saw you last. I continued being a little girl and had no clue as to what was happening in the world, didn't understand what people were talking about, but you lived and moved in reality. My thoughts were like fog in the spring.

And there were all kinds of stories being told about you. Your schemes were supposedly endless. One person said that you were a brawler, another that you were a boor. My girlfriends talked about you: some were with you in lyceum, had crushes on you, and were never more attracted to you than when they told ugly stories about you. I often wanted to ask you when I met you next whether this or that story was true. But when we finally met you were so gloomy that I completely forgot what I'd wanted to ask you. Is it true that you once climbed from the street up onto the balcony of the parliament building and had the boys yell, "Down with the king!" and that you were admonished by the rector for it? Is it true that you once got some of the boys to help you light a shed on fire up in Mosfellssveit, and that your father had to pay for it? Is it true that you once knocked out one of your classmates with a billiards cue?

Steinn, to this day I still shudder at one particular story, so you can imagine how I felt when I first heard it. Sigga P. told me. I cried most of the night. I've never blamed you, Steinn, not once then, no, not even once then. But that night I wasn't a child; I don't know what I was! I would gladly have come to you on my knees and begged you to be good to me. I felt like a foal caught in an earthquake or a dog in a thunderstorm. If I'd ever before thought that I had you measured, whatever I'd used to measure you was turned into a child's toy. I realized that you were beyond all measure, like a force of nature.

You once had four cats; do you remember? You kept them in a little room in the basement, never let them out, and fed them yourself. Everyone knew that sometimes you spent hours at a time alone with the cats, and that you'd come back scratched and bloodied. And when we came to visit you always took me down to the basement to show me the cat-folk. Rúrik and Hansína are a couple, and Hans and Rúsína too, you said, since you'd given the cats those silly names. And they all meowed around you before you'd even gotten through the door, jumped up to your shoulders or hung on to your clothes. I couldn't help but feel disgusted by it.

But once during the summer you invited me home to see something new. And I came over. You took me back down into the basement and opened the little room with a key. And how it surprised me to see a bunch of birds there, and the cats' den empty! "Look!" you said, and you started making chirping noises, and some of them came and sat on your hand and others on your shoulders. And you fed them from the palms of your hands.

"Those damned cats were nothing but trouble," you said. "They've been set free. I had a fellow from the countryside get me these finches. There're seven of them. They're picky about their food and impatient, just like me. They long to be out in the open air just like me. But they're not any worse for wear by being exposed to human life."

Steinn, where were your little birds the next time I came to visit you? Why didn't you invite me to come and have a look in the basement? Why did you ignore it when I asked about your pets? You'd decided to become a musical virtuoso. Up until then you'd been too lazy to practice. Now you practiced from morning till night, said your mother, and took a lesson every day. No one said anything about your birds.

It wasn't until the fall that I found out everything. Sigga P. and I were out taking a walk at the southern end of Tjörnin[12] in the moonlight. We walked back and forth over the bridge ten times or more. She heard the story from her mother's maid, who had heard it from your maid:

"He said that he was completely bored with pampering the creatures. The cats continued to roam around the house, skinny and starving and an embarrassment to the household. And sometimes three or four days in a row would pass when he wouldn't bother to feed the birds, but instead wandered around God knows where with the key to the room in his pocket. And those poor little things cheeped all day from hunger and thirst, and no one could get in to give them something to eat. And one night when he came home the housekeeper started scolding him for how he treated the poor creatures. And what did Steinn Elliði do? He went and rounded up all of his cats and took them to the basement. He didn't come up to go to bed until after midnight. Next morning the bird room was open, and there were bird feathers scattered all over the floor, along with half-eaten bones. He'd been amusing himself the night before by letting the cats hunt, thought the housekeeper. But what had become of the cats? That wasn't discovered until a week later when they went to do the laundry. In the laundry room was a tub full of water, and down in the water was a sack full of something, with the head of a sledgehammer tied to it. After he had finished amusing himself watching the cats hunt he stuck them all in the same bag and sank it. Then he went to bed. And after that he decided to become a musical virtuoso."

You probably think that because of this I started thinking: Steinn Elliði is a scoundrel whom I don't want to know anymore! No, Steinn, nothing is further from the truth. In my heart I pitied those blessed birds and those poor cats, but nothing was further from my mind than to blame you. I just saw you in a new light, mightier than before, savage, horrible, and at the same time raised above everything that has the name of good and right, the laws that others obey. I saw you as mysterious, incomprehensible, and limitless. No one but Grettir Ásmundarson[13] or Steinn Elliði could have come up with that. I thought the same thing on our last night at Þingvellir when you told me everything . . .

When I see you walking down the street, it's like seeing a phantom;

when you recite your poems, your voice gushing with passion, or even if you do nothing but lift your head and look at me, it's like lightning – I get frightened and know only this: you're from a world that nobodies like me can't measure.

When I do something bad it's because I'm imperfect and lack the strength to do what's good. And when I do something good it's because I lack the nerve to do something bad. But even your sins are enchanting, like in a myth. Even over your sins there burns an awful beauty, like cairn-fire.

17.

Just this, Steinn; I always find this same thing to be your chief characteristic the longer and the more that I think about you: you have grown beyond your work. Just as soon as you've composed something, whether it's "beautiful" or "ugly," you walk away from it, like a shepherd from the embers of his fire. I've never known anything to capture your heart as much as something you haven't yet done. You would disappear for a few days, sometimes whole weeks; you'd lock yourself in your room and forget everything except for your new project. And when you finished your project you'd never mention it again. You only talked about what you planned to do next. All that mattered was what you planned to do next. What you'd done no longer existed.

You practiced the piano for half a year. Then you got sick of the sound and never mentioned music again. Once you wrote a play. You came to me with the script in a beat-up old briefcase and started reading it. But you didn't read to me for more than an hour. Then you left. I didn't see you again until a week later, and then I asked you when you were going to read to me next. But you just shrugged your shoulders and didn't answer. You'd lost the manuscript. "Where?" I asked. Either down in Hafnarfjörður or up at Rauðavatn. Once you sat for a whole day in the office at our house, and no one was allowed to come visit you. You were writing poetry. In the evening a boy came to take you to the cinema. And you were gone. On the desk lay a half-written drápa[14] on a pile of scribbled-up sheets of paper. When I reminded you a few days later that you'd left a half-written poem at our house, you'd already forgotten it.

You never took anything so insignificant into your hands that it didn't become a living world while you held it. And you never laid aside any precious thing that didn't afterward become worthless, dead, and forgotten to you.

Your schoolbooks became books of revelation to you while you were reading them. Sometimes you spoke with burning inspiration about the miracles in chemistry, the logic in a Latin text; next you were in seventh heaven over the Pythagorean theorem or some amazing thing from world history. Everything that appeared before your eyes was precious and beyond compare, everything new. And just as soon as you finished your exams in the spring you didn't give a second thought to what you'd learned. Once you said that the goal of an educated man was to forget everything he'd learned.

18.

You often told me, Steinn, that I was the only soul in the world who understood you. That was incredible exaggeration; I often understood you only halfway, sometimes not at all. You never suspected how hard I tried to become your spiritual companion, ever since I was twelve or thirteen until the time you left. I hid all my efforts from you. Actually everything I busied myself with, either consciously or unconsciously, was aimed at trying to make myself fit to understand you, but in the end my thoughts were nothing but a weak echo of you. I drank up poem after poem, read author after author, everything that I thought would make me more worthy to follow you, which is also why I started taking French and German classes on my own initiative when I was just thirteen. For an awful long time I felt that I'd never be able to learn those complicated, peculiar languages; I was so slow; no one knew how much energy I put into them or how often I despaired. But I was driven by the conviction that the one thing that could make me worthy of your friendship was knowledge and understanding, and I vowed never to give up. But it was like you knew everything and understood everything automatically; it was easy for you to learn a whole language in a few days; while I was trying to break through the German verb declensions you amused yourself by reading Unamuno in Spanish and Pirandello in Italian.

The summer that I was fifteen years old you were overseas again with your parents, but I'd been sick that winter and had gone up to Borgarfjörður for the better part of the summer to recuperate. I stayed at a nice farm and the children there were wonderful; there were four, all under ten years old. And what do you think I started doing there in the blessed countryside? I started writing stories for the children. They were incredibly simple and foolish, but I was proud of them, and I looked forward to showing them to you in the fall. I rewrote them again and again, wanting to make them as beautiful as possible, and finally I copied six of them in a little book, not larger than half the size of my palm, with pink pages gilded on the edges, bound in blue velvet. I wanted to give you this book when you came. One longs so much to be like those whom one believes in. I both looked forward to it and shuddered at the thought that you might read my little stories. When I came to Reykjavík in the fall you'd already arrived, two days ahead of me. You came to visit us as soon as you heard that I was home.

Imagine that fall evening when I saw you again! You came suddenly into the room where we were sitting. I said hello to you and blushed. I'd been in the countryside during the summer and was tan and fat, my hands red and ugly. And there you came into the room, like a phantom, and walked straight toward me like lightning. You'd grown taller, I hardly recognized you. And you were wearing summer clothes with a tiny checkered pattern, a green necktie and green silk socks, and your collar was in a style I'd never seen before. The curls in your hair were like a work of art, your hands snow-white, and your nails shone as if you'd made a habit of going to a manicurist; you smoked perfumed cigarettes. While I'd been strolling alone in the Icelandic mountains, up ravines and slopes covered with heather, up along streams or in birchwood copses, you'd been in Madrid and Barcelona, Paris and London, writing voguish poetry in hotel parlors in the mornings, dancing at five o'clock teas in the afternoons, listening to concerts in the evenings, and driving home in an automobile at midnight.

You brought back with you a fresh breath of air from out in the world. You'd devoured the latest works of the modernist masters, and now no poetic style was worth anything to you except for Dadaism and Expressionism, which you called "Essentialism." You reeled off to me from memory whole pages of word games by Max Jacob and Mayakovsky, talked about André Breton, Soupault, and Ehrenburg as if you were talking about divine revelations, and professed your faith in the redemptive spirit that the Russian Revolution had for the arts as well as for everything else. And I listened to you like a dimwit, having never heard these writers' names before, let alone comprehended anything concerning the redemptive spirit of the Russian Revolution.

You were beside yourself with joy and inspiration and spoke to me in newly composed sorcerers' chants and witches' spells, and when you saw how dim-witted and unlearned I was you stroked my face:

Hush, I know you,
    How little you are,
        Little and strange!

For I am a Safir,
    From Sahara in Aharabia,
        Saba in Abaria

And I know all;
Abari from Sabari
Saraba in Arabia
And I know allallallallallallall.
All.

Táta,
Come Táta,
Come little Nótintáta
To kiss Pótintáta
Out in the woods.
For my name is Máni from Skáni,
Come from Spáni
To see you
Spámáni from Skáni,
Skámáni from Spáni,
From Skámánaspáni,
And I'm coming to get you, get you–

You didn't speak like a man, but instead like a caricature of a man or, more correctly, like a caricature of life itself; everything you said was hallucinatory and made me more and more frightened:

Eia, I am the forest,
The forest itself,
The morning forest driven with dew,
The diamond land,
No, I am the afternoon forest,

The throstleharp,
The chirruping evening forest,
The crepuscule wood
Swathed in white fog
Greenclad cuckoomonth
Of the godless earthdream,
Heavenly prurience
Of the heathen earth.
And all creation drinks itself drunk beneath
my leaves.
I am the hundredcolored fallforestsymphony;
Behold my leaves fall;
They fall to the earth
And die,
Trampled by the birder's boots,
While the hawks perch in white branches.
And the sorcerer's hounds prowl in my pale
leafhair.

I was a little girl, ignorant and primitive, and I could do nothing but blush. And after you left I hid my blue silk book in a place where no one could find it, and looked at my hands and started to cry.

19.

The King's Three Sons

A Legendary History by Little Bjössi

Once there was a great king in the Southlands called Hexameter, and he had three sons with belts and swords and three golden crowns upon their heads. And so he sent them to war to fight with a terribly cruel king up north in Finnmark. And they made their way through a thick forest and were so tired and hungry in the evening that they wanted to die. And then the moon came up, and they saw a little house nearby, and in front of it was a little silver blue lake. And they went into the house, and there they found a table with a tablecloth and three fried trout and cream in three jugs. Goodness me, how the king's sons were delighted!

Snati

From the Memoirs of Little Sigga

Poor old Snati, who rests his head on his paws outside the storehouse door, what might he be thinking now? Remember, my dear Snati, when we were little, when we both went sledding? All of a sudden there blew such a gust that I thought trolls were coming to take me. Do you remember once when we were down by the sea gathering shells, and you hopped around me? That was such fun, dear Snati! But now you are old and I am grown up, and you lie outside the storehouse door, but I am home helping Mama in the pantry. Good-bye, dear Snati; I'm going in to kiss Mama.

In the Homefield

A Fairy Tale by Little Gauja

Look at the little blue cuckooflower in the homefield. It's teasing the buttercup, saying: "The calf doesn't want to eat you, you're so tart!" Then the dandelion comes and says, "Hush! There's no milk in you like there is in me!"

And because of all this the buttercup started to cry; and the cuckooflower also started to cry. But the milk in the dandelion has a terribly bitter taste. And just then the calf came up and ate the cuckooflower. And sister Sigga swished up the sunflower and stuck it in her hair. And little brother grabbed up the dandelion and drank all of its milk and got such a terrible stomachache that Mama and Kitty both had to come looking for him out in the homefield. And Kitty went hunting sparrows all over the homefield.

The Crow in the Tower

A Fairy Tale for Children

In a church tower in Spain is a terribly ugly crow. Once an evil robber with a black beard came and tried to do something that he wasn't supposed to do. Then the crow came, sat down on his hat, and said:

"Fie, fie, evil robber, I'll peck out your eyes if you don't beat it back up the mountain where you live with all the other evil men."

The robber was frightened, because even though he was bad he didn't want to be blind. And he went back to all the bad men on the mountain and said:

"There's a terribly ugly crow in the tower."

And the poor ugly crow sang through its rusty windpipe all day, because it was so happy. And the poor ugly crow shall always have its home in the tower.

La pomme qui dort

A Foreign Story for Children

On a tree between green leaves hangs a little apple. Its little cheeks are so red that it's easy to see that it's sleeping. Under the tree stands a little child, who calls out:

"Apple, apple, wake up! You've slept enough!"

Thus begs the little child, but do you suppose the apple woke up? No, the apple didn't even stir in its air nest between the green leaves.

Just then the dear, blessed Sun was taking a walk in Heaven.

"Oh, listen to me, my dear Sun!" said the child. "Wake up the apple for me; it's slept enough!"

"Why not?" answered the Sun, and he shed his rays on the face of the apple and embraced it kindly.

We Send Our Best Wishes

It is incredibly beautiful up by the stream. And the little trout play in the sunshine, and they are colored so beautifully. And there's a completely different sound in the brook up on the hill than down in the field. And should I tell you what the brook is saying in the sunshine as it runs down the hill? It's saying:

"I'm on my way down into the district to have a talk with the bailiff's children. I'm going to talk to Steini and Little Tobba and Little

Imba and tell them the news from the mountains. The elves wear blue jerkins and dance in the dells, and I think that an outlaw lives in the canyon."

My dear brook, give our best to Steini and Little Tobba and Little Imba!

20.

Hotel Britannique, Naples. January 1922. I address these pages to you, dear Diljá, and send them to you. I'm writing to relieve some tension; time is going by too slowly. And I know that you understand me because you've turned eighteen years old, as I was when I married, and besides that you are an intelligent girl and keep yourself away from all the disgusting *pruderie* of a small town; oh, Heaven knows that I have suffered like a fish on dry land in that priggish atmosphere at home, where every woman drapes herself in *poésie,* lies, and sanctimony, and no one can speak except under the rose for fear that the scandalous stories might lose their sweet savor. Yes, I know that you, a woman who cannot be scandalized by anything between Heaven and Earth, can imagine what I had to put up with, living all those years in the sanctimonious and poetic joylessness of the world of the nineteenth-century woman.

That does not mean that I am overjoyed to have traveled here to the south; no, nothing could be further from the truth. Because even though all the Pharisaism was crushing me and suffocating me at home, solitude is even worse, when all the things that one knows are thousands of miles away and those whom one loves are gone. No, I've been dreadfully lonesome, and my health isn't getting any better, always a cough, often blood, my heart either weak or crazed. And always this fear, just as before, and long sleepless nights. The noise here is absolutely dreadful: all the livelong night a clattering of carriages and cracking of whips, and all during the later part of the day the city hums with the endless shouts and calls of the street vendors, packs of gypsies, and madmen. If a man braves the traffic he is surrounded by those *lazzaroni*[15] who bully foreigners with all kinds of *gotaterri*.[16] It must have been a wretched idiot who invented this idiom: "*Vedi Napoli e poi muori*."[17]

Oh, I saw everything there was to see of this life in huge hotels a long, long time ago: servants practically kowtowing from courtesy and pretense; orchestras as cold and spiritless as barrel organs; Americans with diamond rings mollycoddling European mistresses without having the slightest clue concerning civilized customs; English mummies with bulldog snouts, their hands stuck in their pants pockets, brooding over their wives or escorts while Italians wait on them with precisely the same vain gusto that was in fashion five hundred years ago; oh, those Italians live in an entirely different century than other races!

And when I come home in the evening with my English maid, having been disappointed at the San Carlo Opera or the Teatro Bellini, or having watched some cinematic rigmarole until I was half dead, there is no one that I can talk to, because I'm bored with this poor English maid, and then maybe I sit alone long into the night, and my thoughts revolve only around me, my whole life, about all the wild vitality of youth and all my hunger for the fulfillment of life, which was assuaged by nothing but banality and apathy, discouragement, boredom, fear, nervousness, ruefulness, and sickness. The pantomime of my memories passes through my conscience: I yearn for one thing and one thing only, and what I yearn for is the one thing that I've never gotten, but everything else I have gotten, both what I didn't desire and also what I feared. I never found my own life.

My final disappointment occurred when my boy turned his back on me and forsook me. I had decided not to go with Grímúlfur in the hope that Steinn and I could be together, since as long as we, mother and son, were together, it was possible for us to have something resembling a home even if Grímúlfur was always fluttering about. But even the sturdiest knot can come undone. Steinn commended me to the dreariness of exile one October night last fall. I was left standing alone in the railway station, and his train vanished into the darkness.

As you know, we, mother and son, as well as my English maid, stayed during the two hottest summer months in Brighton, since I was reluctant to come here to the south in the worst of the heat. Grímúlfur continued on without stopping in England; he doesn't notice the difference between warm and cold.

During our first days in Brighton, Steinn was like a considerate and good son: in the mornings he went with me on walks by the sea, along King's Road and Marine Parade, and we often went together to the Regent Palais de Dance in the afternoons, and he was still a good boy, courteous and delightful, and often danced with me a bit. But what do you think it is that took him away from me? What do you think captivated my boy so in the most splendid city in England, and made him turn his back on his mother? What but a decrepit old fellow in a white linen suit, rust brown in the face. It's incredible but true: several days after Steinn met this detestable ghost at the Hotel Metropole, where we were staying, he became an entirely different child. Imagine it, when I went out alone with my maid in the mornings I could expect to meet them on the coast road where they rambled along absorbed in palaver and walking arm in arm! It was simply grotesque!

"Steinn," I said, "show me a little more consideration, at least while the guests in the hotel are watching, and don't sit down to chat with this Carrington while everyone can see that I am sitting alone at my table!"

And what do you imagine he answered? "I am forced to inform you, dear woman, that the time is past when sons are to be daughters to their mothers!" Imagine it – he said "dear woman"! And when my maid, Miss Bradford, found out that I'd been crying all day because of this rude reply, she couldn't keep from bringing it up with him that evening. And what do you imagine he answered the poor girl? "I don't want you to speak to me!" – that's what she got.

Nevertheless, I convinced Steinn to come south with me in September; first we stayed several days in Rome, and then here, but his mind had turned away from his mother. He was cold toward me and silent, but I found out that he kept up a steady correspondence with this Carrington fellow. One morning here at the Hotel Britannique he tells me, completely out of the blue: "I'm going to England tonight."

My tears and prayers were of no avail. He left that night without giving me an address or any idea at all of what he was planning. Since then I've gotten two postcards from him, but he didn't write his address on either of them. His father, who had been staying in Palermo since last summer but has recently gone to Genoa, hasn't had a single word from him.

Imagine, Diljá dear, how lonely I am, left behind in this lunatic town like in a lion's den, consumption and memories of an aimless life my company. No one loves me but Death, who prowls around me day and night like an abominable adulterer.

21.

I would have found it plausible if you had asked me why I married a man like Grímúlfur, as young as I was. Many people have asked me the same thing, few have understood it, most have reproached me; everyone knows that we are no more alike than two creatures from different planets.

But in fact there is nothing more comprehensible than that I should have taken this destiny-laden step in the heedlessness of my youth. I was raised in complete affluence, yes, in far greater freehanded indulgence than you could ever suspect, and had never been acquainted with anything but luxury from my earliest childhood. And precisely when everyone thought that our power was at its peak my father went bankrupt, and died shortly afterward. We siblings were left orphans, and wound up with our father's friends, except for the two oldest, who went abroad and made their own livings. I was sixteen years old at the time and ended up with Madam

Valgerður, your foster mother. And about a year later I became her daughter-in-law, tacitly and calmly. I would gladly have become the daughter-in-law of any other woman in the country, had it not now pleased chance to hang me around the neck of her son. And I was ready to throw my arms round the neck of any man whatsoever; I was wild about men.

This was a few years after Grímúlfur and your father, Þorsteinn, started in on their business enterprise; business boomed, and out of it grew Ylfingur. Grímúlfur was more like Örnólfur in those days than now. Of course he was never so charming nor as beautifully built as his younger brother, nor as talented, but a lot of girls desired him, because he was a renowned financier and had everything it took to become fabulously wealthy. One winter he asked me to a dance; I'll tell you about it in as few words as possible, because the story of our coming together is in fact so unremarkable. I was in fairly poor condition: I looked horrible, and I knew it. Even if I was fully mature by my eighteenth year and had long been used to being looked upon as a grown-up girl, on that particular night the gentlemen wouldn't give me a second glance. I suppose that even then I was already considered Grímúlfur's betrothed. Long before the dance was over I went to him and asked him to take me home. My throat was tight from holding back sobs, and I couldn't say anything. He wanted to take my arm, but I wouldn't let him. I wanted to make him follow me, but this didn't work and I felt even more resentful. By the time we reached the foyer back home, I was completely deranged and no longer knew what I was doing. Just as soon as he had taken my cloak, I threw my arms with no warning around his neck and cried loudly at his breast in some sort of lunatic ecstasy, begged him to help me, said that I loved him, and so on. Thus was the groundwork laid for my marriage to Grímúlfur, Diljá dear.

When we married I celebrated having been consecrated into the same sort of life of luxury in which I was raised, and I looked forward to the joys of wedlock, because in my childishness I had often thought that marriage meant the fulfillment of all hopes. This is what all of us women think before we wake up to reality; and our bosoms bubble and boil like mud springs from this incomprehensible yearning to encompass all the happiness of Heaven and Earth.

But nothing is further than marriage from being able to satisfy the desires of a true woman – I don't mean those soulless female things that let themselves be used like dull screws in the machine of society. The true woman soon discovers that the happiness of marriage is not the fulfillment of all hopes, but rather the relinquishment of all hopes: "resignation"; and that without this relinquishment there is no happiness. Marriage is a shipwreck in which the cruise ship is tossed against a cliff, a bankruptcy in which youth has nothing left over but debt. Nothing is more empty and sad than the long insomniac days of the first year of marriage, unless, perhaps, the grave itself. Imagine the young wife as she sits at home sleepy and alone and breathes in the revolting stenches of the new home, or else invites her girlfriends over, reluctant, cold, and matured after the fresh experience of her honeymoon. But the man doesn't come home until evening, because he promised himself to another bride before his wife: his business, and its demands come before all others. And when a newly wedded woman finds herself at home surrounded by the brand-new furniture in her living room, she discovers that she herself is actually nothing but a piece of furniture, purchased to complete the ridiculous unit that the man calls his home. And when she takes her girlfriends from room to room to show them the wedding gifts, oh, all that disgusting cursed rubbish made of gold and silver and who knows what! – living room furniture, dining room furniture, the salon, the boudoir, the bathroom, the bedrooms – oh the smell, the smell! – then in her heart she feels almost the same as if she were showing them the crypt where her corpse is to wait for Doomsday.

The man she marries is never the same whom she saw in her dreams, never the one she expected. The man she marries is never anyone but the one she let take her, the one into whose arms she threw herself in a kind of bewilderment, because she couldn't find the one about whom she dreamt. The man she married was the one who offered her gold and green forests. She uses all of her powers of self-deception to settle for whatever he lacks of the outstanding qualities of her dream man, and even succeeds from time to time in convincing herself that her husband is a perfect image of the one she longed for, and determines to do everything she can to enjoy with him what she had imagined enjoying with her dream man. But all the time she knows this one thing, despite all the deception: that he is still not the same man she had desired. She might live with him her whole life and raise children for him, but nothing else is guaranteed except that deep, deep within her is hidden the hope that in spite of her fate and her ruined palaces, the moment might come when her sweetheart will suddenly sweep into her dull, everyday life: she quickens when he grasps her hand, trembles at his glance, her heartbeat is irregular, and all of the pillars of her past tumble down like a house of cards. And then she knows that nothing can hinder her any further, and she seizes the first opportunity to cheat on her husband and drown herself in the embrace of the man who gives her everything, and she is lost. In sin alone is the fulfillment of all her hopes.

"Who gives her everything" – how misguided it is to say such a thing! Because her lover gives her nothing but one gift: he takes everything from her. From her husband she makes demands without giving; to her lover she gives without making demands. She is ungrateful to her husband because he gave her a different kind of car than the one she had dreamt of. She makes little show though he brings her costly gifts every month. But she is ready to kiss the earth if her lover cuts a lock of his hair for her. Love: it is not a bounteous home filled with merriment and dinner parties, or big families and blue-eyed children. And there are no calm winter evenings, full of *tendresse sans passion,*[18] when husband and wife sit at home and discuss the day's events or the newest books or whatever has appeared most recently in the daily papers, or make their plans for the future, go over the details for their next trip abroad or what dishes they should serve at the next party. No, this is not love, dear Diljá. All of this is vanity.

Love, dear Diljá, is a great sacred thing, behind all the farce we women make, the core of the unspeakable, the mystery of the most blessed misfortune, the marvel that hushes all other voices, *la meta profetata fuori del mondo*.[19]

The desire to destroy all honor and happiness, body and soul, all at one moment, that's what it is to be in love. To sit on the steps before her lover's door and not to get in, to ramble throughout the city in darkness like a drunken harlot in her despair, that's what it is to be in love. To bathe her lover's hands in her tears and look with a shudder into his eyes, as into the depths of her own destiny, that's what it is to be in love. When a woman is no longer anything but a wretched sacrificial lamb under the cumbersome hands of the tormenter, naked, with no will, powerless, dead to herself, quaking, weeping, dizzy, burning, then she loves; and the dogs wait at the door ready to tear her to pieces when she slinks out into the silence of the night.

22.

My husband gave me everything: gold, green forests – everything but what I longed for and was born to enjoy. He was not a man who could take anything from me. He was a businessman, not a lover. He was distracted when he came home at night, and was gone in the mornings. His caresses were businesslike, his embraces mild and prudent as if he were reckoning his accounts. He never broke the seal placed over my heart.

Seasons passed, and what do you think happened? I became pregnant! I had never actually thought that a person could become pregnant. I scarcely believed it when my maid told me. It started with nausea and dizziness, and one day I vomited and passed out. "Madam is surely pregnant," said the girl. "What damned nonsense is in you?" said I. "Shame on you!"

And when my husband came home that night he had hardly sat down to eat before he took out his pocketbook and started to jot down some numbers. I observed him in secret and realized that I despised the man. For a week I didn't allow him to come to bed with me at night. I had determined to drag it out as long as possible before telling him that I was with child. But I was so helpless and grief-stricken, because there was no way of escape, and finally I felt that there was nothing else to do but try to love him. And one evening I sat down at his knees and whispered this impudent news to him: I was with child.

"Is that so, my dear?" he asked.

Could you imagine a more revolting reply?

But at the birth of Steinn a new sun arose in my life. Feelings wakened that I could never have possibly suspected were hidden in my breast; I lost myself in motherly joy, was reborn.

I loved my child wildly at first, and then I worshipped him. I determined to live for the boy. And I lived for him. I could scarcely tolerate anyone coming near him but me. I stayed awake for him at night, bathed him myself in the morning, looked after all his needs alone, thought of nothing but him all day. My delight was to gaze at him and serve him! I looked upon him as divinity. My beloved little boy – no one has seen a more beautiful boy; his blue eyes were deep and clear, and from his skin and golden locks beamed a dazzling light. He could speak perfectly by the age of two, and he understood everything. Nothing got past him; he asked me about everything, was amazed at everything, admired everything, and all things took on a new shape in my own eyes because I became used to looking at everything from the perspective of the boy.

I felt as if I owned him exclusively, and that everything existed because of him. I felt as if no other child had ever been born in the world except for him, and that no child like him would ever be born again. Grímúlfur wanted us to have a girl, but I flatly refused, protected myself against becoming pregnant again and was cold and capricious toward the boy's father. I felt as if he no longer mattered to me now that I had the boy.

Three years passed.

Grímúlfur set sail and planned on staying abroad for half a year. He asked me to come with him, said that we would take the boy with us, but I chose to stay at home. What did I care about wandering off to another country when I could have this little god to myself at home? Grímúlfur left; the child and I stayed.

That was in the winter. Several months passed. I was scarcely ever up and about, hardly ever went visiting, because the boy put a spell on me. If I stayed more than two hours away from him, I was no longer myself.

One winter night I came home from a party; there I'd been quite warm, but when I came home the house was so cold. I caught cold in the evening, and in the morning I was dangerously ill. It was pneumonia.

I lay for weeks between life and death, because the pneumonia was followed by pleurisy, which caused chronic bronchitis. The doctors urged me to take extreme care.

Finally spring arrived. Grímúlfur came home and had a specialist investigate me carefully, and then it came to light that I had tuberculosis.

That day was one of the most terrifying I have ever lived. Since childhood my lungs had been weak, and I had always feared tuberculosis like a death sentence. Now I was told that I had become the prey of what I had feared most: the doctor's diagnosis spelled out my doom!

My first thoughts were of Steinn. I broke into convulsive sobs in the doctor's sight, and asked through my tears if God could truly be so unmerciful as to tear me away from my child and topple me into the grave so young, leaving my angel behind, an orphan. I cursed my existence in my derangement and wished that I had never given birth, but instead had been able to enjoy life in ecstasy this fleeting moment, enjoy it like a harlot or a barren woman without having to behold the fruit of my sins, and be allowed afterward to die blissfully. Finally I rose to my feet and shouted: "No, I don't want to die; I can't die and leave my boy! God can demand anything else from me!"

The doctor tried to explain to me that there was no reason for fear. He advised me to move to a more wholesome climate in the fall, said that he could assure me of an improvement by the following spring. And in the hope of my returning home in a year, fully recovered and able to serve my son, it was decided that I should set sail that summer with a Danish girl for a companion. And little Steinn wept in his father's arms and stretched out his hands in the direction of the ship when it left shore with his mother.

But all our hopes come to naught. My stay in Nice, the city of the sun, was a sad exile; my life of recovery was truly a prison sojourn. I was sick almost all winter, sick in body and soul, inert from homesickness. Twice in the winter I coughed up blood, the second time very badly. At that time I was convinced that I would die soon, that now my time was up, and I had no other wish than to be able to return home to see my child once more before I died. The doctors did all they could to dissuade me from such a dangerous expedition, but I refused to listen, said that I knew I was going to die and wanted to die at home. And I recovered strength at the hope of going north. I left in the middle of the summer. After an eleven-month stay abroad I finally embraced my boy again.

23.

Those who never fasten their hopes to one thing over another are blessed; they are deceived less than I. My boy had grown big. He was four years old, and the memory of his mother had faded from his mind. He wasn't a whit fonder of his mother than of the housekeeper or the maid. It was no longer his delight to sit at his mother's knees and tell her about all the wonders of the world. Now it was most fun to gather whole crowds of boys, drag them into the house, and romp around with them from room to room, or to go visit his playmates in other homes; he was away half the time. And I was sick, had to live according to strict rules, couldn't be on my feet more than a short period of time each day, couldn't go out except at certain times, and then had to walk slowly and calmly without thinking of anything but getting well. My boy didn't want to go with me because I was sick: it was much more fun to harass the maids than to accompany Mother. I was no longer the only one who loved him; everyone loved him.

Everyone wanted to have him near because he was so beautiful and bright. I was left in the cold because I was sick.

You ask how Grímúlfur and I got along? Yes, he met me at the harbor and helped me climb into the car. But I found only that this arid businessman was a total stranger to me, and that I actually did not understand how he could have wanted me. The last year and a half I had scarcely ever given him a thought. I neither loved nor hated him; I was sincerely indifferent about him. I even paid little heed to wifely modesty although he saw me at those times when women would rather be unseen by their husbands. When he spoke to me I answered him as I would a man in a railway car or a toilette attendant.

And so went that year – I scraped by. Yes, although it might seem incredible, I did not become any sicker, but stayed fairly the same. I even ventured several times to attend some social affairs, which did not cause any harm.

But in my interior being something started to stir – something that had lain dormant for months and even years; hidden fires began to blaze anew. One bright day I suddenly saw myself as I was, like a man who had forgotten who he was and what he was named. For several years I had forgotten who I was and what I was named! I discovered that in fact I was still just a little girl, even if life had bestowed on me the experience of a full-grown woman, the tribulations of a shipwrecked man. My body was delicate, my soul perhaps even more delicate, but in among the infirmities was hidden an untiring power. My desires had been pricked by a sleep-thorn,[20] but now they were awake, passionate and wild, and they begged to be allowed to sing out with all the magic of life in one mighty song.

Oh, with what sick, entrenched passion didn't I desire at that time to meet the man who was fit to love me, to take me as I was, bound to another, hysterical, emaciated. I was eager to sacrifice my honor if I could only find someone who would be man enough to love a woman as she desires most of all: illicitly. And to be loved illicitly in return. I lived for that man, for the hope of meeting him. I dreamt about him day and night. I dressed up for him in the morning, changed clothes every three hours, preened myself for him. And I undressed for him at night, and thought thoughts that he wanted me to think, sleepless night after sleepless night. Perhaps it was this, my thirst for love, that saved me from the grave.

Twice I thought I had found him; but both times I was deceived. Always my hopes were deceived. I trusted both of these men with my misfortune, affliction, and desire. They saw my soul in all its nakedness. But I was a child: a woman should never show a man her soul in all its nakedness. When a man has seen to the bottom of a woman's soul he looks at her body as if it were an empty vase, and it is as if he thinks that the vase would break if he were to touch it: he pities her and leaves.

One was a foreign consul who left the country. I haven't seen him since, and have never wanted to. I still blush when I think of what I said to him. The other was an artist whom I met several months later. He came daily, sat alone with me and played the grand piano. Everything he said was nonsense, but there was something refreshing in his bearing that touched me the first time I saw him. I realized little by little just how deprived he was of everything that a woman actually desires to find in a man. We kissed. But one day I saw him crying. It was repulsive: he felt sorry for me or for himself or for both of us. He wasn't man enough to bear his own passions. Nothing is more repugnant than a man who cries.

24.

When Steinn was seven years old I went abroad with Grímúlfur and took the boy with me. It was on that trip that we quarreled, the only quarrel we've had in our marriage all these years. It happened in a hotel in London one night. I still forbade him to touch me as his wife and pleaded my sickness as an excuse.

"You're not sick anymore," he said. "It's all hysteria, if not complete pretense."

"Of course I'm sick," I said. "Leave me alone! I forbid you to touch me!"

"Then you can sail your own sea," he said. "Keeping you going doesn't expand my bank account!"

"You make the same demands of me as a harlot!" I said.

"Parasite!" he answered.

"Rapscallion, liar, villain!" I said.

"Just fine!" he said. "I'll remember this. And I can get five hundred harlots for a far lower price than what you alone have cost me."

"What are you going to do with the boy if you get rid of me?"

"That's none of your business!"

"The boy is mine!"

But after several silent minutes I calmed down a bit and said:

"Grímúlfur, you can take as many harlots as you want, whenever you want, instead of me. I understand that and would never resent you for it. But I can't, I can't."

In the morning he gave me a hundred pounds and left, left me behind with the boy. Several days later a letter came from him, from Bilbao; he asked for my forgiveness. He met me again in Folkestone in the fall, and our life together continued as before, as if nothing had happened.

My health always wavered, like a flickering candle flame. I participated in the vanity of everyday life like everyone else, but depression and apathy weighed on me every moment that I was alone. My only joy was that the boy's consideration toward me grew stronger the more he learned. My stay in England alone with him linked him to me. Now Grímúlfur had to spend another half year in Bilbao. I asked if the boy and I could come with him, and that's what we did.

Grímúlfur had quite a few friends down south in Spain, and I suddenly found myself part of a joyful social life. I've actually never been happier than I was that winter, caught up in the enchanting elegance and the refinement that characterizes the social habits of those who live in the south, in which the pulse of passion throbs through everything in the form of lyric poetry and every emotion is spoken in magic spells.

25.

Then I met José, who pressed his lips hardest of all against mine. And it is about the memory of this alien young man that my dreams have most often played since my feelings for him first awakened. And yet I sent José away with death in his heart.

Why did I start loving José, by all means? I have often thought about this, but it is one of the mysteries of love that anyone should love one person more than another. Because one man is in fact never more remarkable than a thousand others. Or does a woman perhaps love this one particular man because there is no way that she can ever love all the others? José certainly wasn't any more handsome or charming than the others.

Maybe I loved him, like the woman in *L'invitation au voyage,* because he was even more alien than the others, born in South America? Or did I love him because he had a broader and more pliant baritone than the others? His voice was like velvet, deep and warm, and I drowned my senses in it when he sang. Or perhaps because the fire in his flint black eyes burned even more passionately than the fire in the eyes of others? Or because he was eight years younger than I was, and seemed as if he was created to dance on embers? José, José, your name reminds me of the name of Jesus in an Irish saint's life that I read in my childhood!

His speciousness gave him an air of fairy-tale elfishness, something distant and dangerous, which made him exotic even among his countrymen, a foreigner when he spoke his own language. And he had a kind of wondrous way of speaking English without understanding it. Nothing was more delightful than to hear him speak so fluently a language that he couldn't make heads or tails of.

José's character was from the other side of the Earth, where the sun rises in the evening and sets in the morning. Sometimes I could see him with strange mountains in the background, sometimes alone on a never-ending prairie. Thus burn the coals in the eyes of those who are raised in a land where a veiled power dwells in the mountains and bloodthirsty beasts roam the jungles. The dreaminess and depression that sometimes made his face and bearing so gloomy, like fog over the land, are seen only in a man who has looked out over endless prairie in his youth and never beheld its limit. José was neither more handsome nor more gallant than a thousand other men, but he was the man about whom I had dreamt throughout my youth, created for this alone: to love a woman who trembles before the charming power of her own dreams. And yet I sent José away with death in his heart.

I had lived unforgettable days with José, evenings drunk with happiness. We danced in tea salons in the afternoons, visited the most jocund cabarets in the evenings. We drank wine; we drove up into the mountains. For a long time not a single thing happened between us, because José was a noble-minded man and respected my marriage. But the walls crumbled one by one, until finally our lips met over wine in a drawn-out kiss.

Grímúlfur was far away. He was in the south, and several days passed. José came with his car in the morning, and we drove to a small village several kilometers away. This was on a mild Spanish winter day. We ate breakfast at a café out in the countryside; we laughed like children in love and reclined over wine that glowed in the sun. José sat by my side. The smoke from his cigarette took on marvelous shapes in the rays of the sun. We sat close to each other; I felt his arm around me and leaned up against him, and we watched the sunbeams play in the wine and the cigarette smoke in the sunbeams. Finally my name was whispered in my ear:

"Jófí!" was whispered, and his breath played over my cheeks, filled my senses, fragrant with wine.

"Jófí!" he whispered again. "*Cuándo?*"

At first I said nothing, but red-hot currents flowed through me. Finally I straightened myself in my seat and turned toward him to look into his eyes. And we gazed for a long time into each other's eyes in silent comprehension of everything. We knew that all of the walls had fallen down; all formalities were now in vain. The kiss broke every seal. I leaned back again in my seat and my whole being trembled. I closed my eyes; my breath fluttered. And the answer came involuntarily to my lips, from my innermost depths, like bubbles that ascend to the surface of a spring from far down below.

"José, come to me, tonight, late."

We got to our feet and drove to town without saying another word, then parted with a silent handshake. I knew that his eyes were burning when we parted, but I did not look up. I showed him only my eyelids and fled in the next instant into the hotel.

26.

I had done everything to gratify the whims of my soul; perfumed the cushions on the sofa; burned incense in a little brazier on the mantelpiece. Wine stood on the table in cold, clammy bottles with faded labels and dusty necks: this wine had waited for eager lips for a hundred years, and in a hundred years its spirit, its magic, and its fire had intensified in the dark cellar. Tonight the consecration was imminent.

I had finished my perfumed bath and dressed myself in my softest silk, both outerwear and undergarments. I had put the boy to bed an hour earlier and instructed the maid to leave me alone. The clock struck ten; I threw myself down onto the soft sofa and waited. I listened motionless and silent to every sound that could be heard out in the hall, my senses as delicate and keen as an animal's. Sometimes I tiptoed to the door and listened. But there was still no José.

Was everything still safe?

I peeked out into the hotel hallway, but no one was about. My maid was sleeping somewhere on the top floor. My guests usually rang at my apartment's front door without the intercession of the staff, so everything should have been safe.

But then I started thinking about the boy. Would he sleep through it? I thought. My goodness, what if the boy should wake up! This thought struck me immediately with terrible fear. The boy slept in my room, farther down the hall, and when I considered how sensitive he was to everything that happened around him I thought that there was nothing more likely than that he would wake when

I least expected it. Our whispering would wake him; the slightest tinkling of a glass or creaking of a chair would be enough to startle him awake. Maybe he would suddenly be standing between the portieres to check on his mother out in the parlor, standing there in his white nightgown, his eyes deep and blue, wide and inquisitive, like the sky itself, his golden locks a mess. He runs his eyes around the room and spies his mother; yes, spies his mother. No, my dear God, that must never happen! Never, never could the boy know that his mother was – that she was – no, never!

I've got to double-lock the bedroom door, I thought, and stole into the bedroom to make sure that he was asleep. At his bedside burned a dull night-light, which cast a faint gleam on his innocent and beautiful face as he slept there with one palm under his cheek. My beloved little boy! His locks fell over his little hand; his sleep was deep and tranquil. I stood for several moments over his bed and lost myself in gazing at this angel face-to-face, this holy untouched being who was flesh of my flesh and blood of my blood, this, my little god, with which my womb had been graced. And when I forced myself to look back into the parlor where everything was prepared, like a chapel where I had planned to offer my body as a sacrament, I was suddenly seized by ice-cold terror. It was as if my heart frosted over in my breast; I thought that I would faint. My dear God, what had I been planning to do?

How could I have ever thought to commit this crime against my child? What sort of excuse could I ever make to this unsuspecting, unstained, innocent child after such defilement? Because what I planned to do was the same as dishonoring the child itself, my own flesh and blood! How could an adulterous female ever be so audacious as to lay a fingertip on her child's body, embrace such a holy angel, even if he had once been the flesh of her flesh? In the morning I would be neither a mother nor a woman anymore; I would be an abominable beast, smitten with filth, a soulless animal, a sow that has rolled itself over in the chaff!

And with what feelings would I look into my husband's eyes when he came home next? What a crime against him! All these years he has surrounded me with luxury, me, more ungrateful, more selfish than any harlot, and I have actually intentionally refused to fulfill the most basic obligations of the wife despite all of his benefactions. I've been demanding and wasteful all these years without once extending him a hand, or anything else for that matter, for his gifts. Whenever he wanted he could have shown me out the door of his house like a parasite that had no rights at all! But his patience and benevolence have been untiring. And in these rooms, which he paid for with his money, where every single thing around me was a gift from him, yes, every thread in my clothing, where his child slept safe and sound in his innocence, I did not hesitate to use the first chance that presented itself to drink from the cup of the whore. No, God Almighty, save me from this sin!

Wake up, dear Steinn; wake up! My dear, wake up and sit with Mama a little while. Mama wants to give you pieces of chocolate with rum inside, as many as you want! Listen to me, my dear Steinn, stay awake with Mama for a bit! Mama feels so bad.

A few minutes later a confidential knock came on the door, so quiet that it could barely be heard. And the door opened. There stood José. He was clearly startled when he saw the boy by my side on one of the sofas. His glance was like red-hot iron.

"Pardon me!" he said. "I thought that you were alone!"

"Please, señor," said the boy at my side. "Have some rum chocolate!"

"No, José, forgive me!" said I, and I stood up with my breath caught in my throat and walked to the door. "Forgive me, but I must ask you to leave! I dare not, José; I cannot; will not! I wasn't in my right mind this morning. It didn't mean anything. I didn't know what I was saying."

First he looked at me, then at the boy, and because the boy was watching us he was hesitant to touch me.

"Make the boy go!" he whispered commandingly. "I'll take you! A man cannot be ridiculed in such a way!"

"No, the boy will remain here. If you don't go, the boy will defend me. Go!"

Then he addressed the boy and said: "Why don't you go to your room to sleep, dear boy? I have to speak to your mother a little about something that wouldn't interest you."

But I knew that the moment I was out of the boy's sight, José would take me in his arms and I would in the same instant lose all my will and all my self-control. My determination would immediately burn to ashes before his eyes. By receiving a cruel kiss from his lips my soul and my body would be in his power.

"No, Steinn, stay here!" I said.

José waited for a moment at the door and looked at me; that was the first and perhaps the last time that I have stood face-to-face with the background of my being, *la meta profetata fuori del mondo.* His glance contained the universe of my dreams: another hemisphere, an unknown power, mountains on the other side of the Earth, the silence of the rain forests, the prairie, the whole prairie in its insatiable endlessness, death, the fulfillment of all. And I lacked the courage this first, perhaps last time.

"So you are sending me away?" he said, and added, when I nodded my head in agreement: "With death in my heart."

He put on his hat in the doorway and turned to go. For a moment I stood as if deranged; I know only this one thing for certain, that in that second I forgot my child – yes, I believe that I would have lost myself in the sight of the child had not José's magnanimity determined the outcome: he had turned from me.

"No, José," I said, and touched his arm with my fingertips.

"No, José," I pleaded. "Not with death in your heart!"

But he had reached the foyer and did not turn to look. I took two steps after him and pleaded:

"Forgive me, José!"

But he was gone.

27.

Early the next morning I sent my husband a telegram: "Come immediately; I must speak to you."

He telephoned immediately and came that night. I met him at the train station and kissed him. I said that I loved him and was his wife, but that José had tried to steal my love. I said that I hated José.

That night I begged him to forgive me for everything that I had done against him. And he forgave me. “From now on I am entirely yours, as I was before Steinn was born,” I said. All the same his caresses were a torture, a mortification, a physical and spiritual injury. And in just a short time he was asleep. I woke just before dawn and looked at him in the gleam from the night-light, at how he slept. I hated him; I wanted to cut his throat. I loved José. I regretted having missed my chance: I had lacked the courage to be craven. One is never gripped with such aching regret as when one has lost the opportunity to sin. The world’s misfortune springs from people’s lack of courage to sin.

I had cast away the cup of bliss that sin alone is able to offer. Maybe I would have been allowed to die in José’s arms that night. The highest bliss is to die in sin. But José had gone to South America. Perhaps he is dead. And my husband brought me to Iceland a little later, home to the tepid banality, home to the poesy, the lie, and the dissimulation.

Love is the only true life. Only love is life. Only love is reality. Everything but love is a lie. Without love everything is worthless and there is no comfort but death. And death, perhaps, is the lover par excellence. A true woman would much rather sacrifice her tears and blood to the murderer of her soul than allow her hunger and thirst for the mystery of the most blissful misfortune be disgraced in the tepid banality of marriage. A woman can never have a higher goal in life than to seize her opportunities to steal from the tree of knowledge.

28.

Diljá threw down the pale, irregularly written pages; no, she had no desire to read any more, had skipped whole sections and still had more than half left to read. She felt as if her hands were filthy, as if a raw egg had been cracked open over them. She hurried over to the windows to look into the face of reality. Spring had arrived in all its glory, the sky over the fresh and green Landakot meadow blue and deep. It was hardly possible, when one looked into this sky, to believe anything other than that life was beautiful, and as eternal as it was beautiful.

Love, love: the most divine thing in life, she thought.

No, dear God, it cannot be that life is sinful. This blue sky would not vault the Earth if it were as abominable as what was contained in these pages. Sacrilege had been committed against her most cabalistic dreams: in place of visions that are dreamt of in maidenhood's unperturbed mind, her soul had been violated and horrid pornographic pictures smeared onto the wall. From now on this repugnance would form the backdrop to her dreams and would bully her night and day. "My dear God, obliterate these awful visions!" she cried out loud, as she clutched her head like a man losing his mind, rocked backward and forward in her seat. My God, allow me to behold love in its proper light! Love that is holy, inexpressible, how could the most blissful dream of the human heart be a crime against – the holiest thing that anyone can know! Allow me to disappear into the spring sky, out into the purity of Heaven, the eternal blue farthest, farthest out, because I am so frightened!

She looked with the eyes of her friend into the vast, immeasurable blue, because only Steinn Elliði knew what was right and what wrong.

Love; love, chastity, God, Heaven – he understood everything. She cannot think, knows nothing; she hears only several nonsensical words trickle down like rain, or better put, tumble down like hail:

"Steinn Elliði; Steinn Elliði; Steinn Elliði."

At that moment her desire was so overwhelming that she felt as if her heart would soon be unable to stand it any longer.

29.

She walks up Laugavegur one day at the start of June, alone, having set herself the task of pilfering books from Steinn Elliði. His books had always been available to her, and they were more interesting than most other books. It was a dry, bright day; a fresh breeze from the north, fish trucks on perpetual journeys back and forth as one enters the city, the sides of the trucks painted with black tasteless letters: h/f Ylfingur,[21] and she shrinks back now and again from these gorgons; they raise a cloud of dust, bellow and screech. The girl is relieved to turn at last onto the private drive to Grímúlfur's house down by the sea. His lawn is soft and green like lustrous webwork, and the cuckooflower with the desolate pallor of its chaste eye stares like a young girl out into the verdure and the blue. On the edge of the ditch alongside the road the buttercups tilt their heads, their faces mini-reflections of the sun, fat and blissful. From the lawn ascends an intoxicating and pleasant scent that mingles with the gentle breeze to pervade the girl's senses, blended with the smell of kelp and sea salt from the straits.

Goodness gracious, how blue the straits are today, thinks the girl, so deep blue and dark blue under the sun, just barely white-misted where the water pulls away from the land, where the waves break; and on the opposite side of the straits stand the peaks, Skarðsheiði like a half-chiseled masterpiece by Einar Jónsson,[22] Esja bowed like a sorceress in prayer, and over all this artwork towers the sky, blue as God, eternity, and death.

The girl steps in pretty shoes along the dazzling road, and who should come to meet her but the breeze, which thrusts itself up against her as if it owns her, making her dress flutter, and then does various other things that it is not permitted to do.

The house at Rauðarárvík was more opulent than it was beautiful, built of white-painted concrete, with a red roof, low balconies on the south side, broad steps leading up to an expressionless main door, its style cold, lacking nuance, devoid of all artistry, displaying only the appearance of mechanical calculations.

An elderly woman shows her in to the custodian in the basement: a comely sitting room, portraits of Jón Sigurðsson[23] and Jesus Christ, and sitting in a modest easy chair, Guðmundur in his shirtsleeves, wearing glasses with rusty frames and smoking a pipe, reading from yellowed issues of *Politiken* that lie in great stacks on the floor. He is a bald man with a gray smiling mustache, one of those kinds of men who start their existence on the parish, slave away afterward like hacks for sixty years without keeping the pot boiling, finally hit the jackpot in their sixties by pure luck, and are now beside themselves with joy from gratitude toward God and men.

"Bless you, Diljá my dear," he says with long, drawn-out emphasis on every syllable. "Blessed little lady, my how she has grown big. Gunna, Gunna! Come here, my dear, and look at this! What do you think the boys are saying?! How many years has it been since she had two braids behind her head and wanted to play ball games out here in the yard? Gunna, do you hear that? How are you now, my blessed darling? How is all that blessed family doing down south? You don't suppose they'll make an appearance here in our blessed cold country this summer? No? Here everything's always the same, as the girl can see, absolute affluence, God be praised, and I tending our saplings here in the yard now and then, and damn it if the grass hasn't become absolutely gorgeous seven weeks in, since we didn't spare the manure on it in the winter, let me tell you! I mowed three times last year though it was hardly worth it the last time, and now it's almost a month since I took the shutters off the windows, and I open all the windows from time to time to let in the blessed breeze, and in between all that I sit here comfortably like the Count of Monte Cristo and fumble my way through the Danish newspapers that I found in a trunk in the storeroom. And the older they are the more amusing's the stuff that's in them, such as, for instance, the Alberti scandal and the Dreyfus affair; how I remember all those grand events now.

"I was at sea in Reyðarfjörður the year that Alberti got in his mess, but these days nothing remarkable happens anymore; all it is now is endless whining about politics–"

After obtaining the keys from the custodian she opened the foyer door and went into the house. Of course Steinn Elliði's library was on the second floor, but she automatically found herself walking straight into the living room as she was accustomed to doing when the family was home. It was here that boring guests usually sat over their coffee in deep chairs and soft sofas, rattling off vanities for Jófí's amusement; here there was usually wine on the tables and blue cigarette smoke hovering over the dark furniture, but now it was bleak looking, all the comforts of home piled one on top of the other like wares in a storage room, the window curtains pulled down and the parquet floor bare.

Only the grand piano, that old friend of the family, had not been moved: it and the girl shared common memories; she longed to thank it for everything old and good by stroking its toothed mouth! There was once a time when Steinn had sat upon its stool and decided to become a musical virtuoso on a par with Franz Liszt. She had sat there in the corner and patiently listened to him play after all the others had fled. Several months later it was she who had sat at the instrument, while he stood behind her and sang like Enrico Caruso. There had often been singing here, but now all those notes were lost out in the immeasurable.

At one time there had been no other composer in the world but Edvard Grieg. And Steinn had been uncommonly quick to learn his works, even his most chameleonic song:

Jeg kaldte dig mit lykkebud,
Jeg kaldte dig min stjerne[24]

He had sung this song after only a half-hour's practice, whereas Diljá had finally lost heart and given up before its peculiar military cadence, after she'd practiced it a hundred times a day for half a month. Its progressions deceived her.

A little later no other composer in the world but Schubert captured Steinn's soul. Nothing expressed the human heart with more melancholy magic than the serenade *Leise flehen;* it held him spellbound night after night; finally he got up one morning around daybreak and slunk down to the parlor, sat down at the piano and began to play the prelude, cautiously, cryptically. He sang:

Leise flehen meine Lieder
durch die Nacht zu dir;[25]

The window stood open; his voice was carried out; it chimed over the straits in the still of the night, chimed out into the blue, cloudless, serene spring night, out into eternity; he must have been in love! The people in the house started up from their sleep.

A week later he had forgotten this song, and instead sang the *Doppelgänger.*[24] She thought that if he'd been in love when he was most fond of the serenade, he had probably killed his love by the time he took a fancy to the *Doppelgänger,* because he sang his translation of this song of Heine's in a dirgelike voice that was as acrimonious as his enthusiasm had been passionate and rich when he had started in on the first notes of *Leise flehen:*

Silent the night, the city lies sleeping,
Days past and gone my lover dwelt here;

Lost dreams of union once our keeping,
Forlorn the moonbeams on rooftops appear.

So outcast he stares in stolid conviction,
His sorrow stinging with deathly pale shine;
Wounded and bleeding sore affliction,
There smiles the moon on this semblance of mine.

And wakened within me a passionate trembling,
A soul in peril clouds my sight
Aping a lucid face resembling
Pallidly lumined shade of night.

On the grand piano lay a thin red volume, *Élégie* by Massenet, the song that had always reminded her of fiddles and prairies. She wished that she could play this song on the piano's strings once more, in memory of bygone days. But the grand piano was shut.

Ô, doux printemps d'autrefois
vertes saisons
vous avez fui pour toujours.[27]

It was like a miracle or an oracle: *Pour toujours, pour toujours,* she told herself.

These songs will never be sung again.

Book Three

30.

Autumn in Europe, 1921.

The Italian peasant no longer smokes his pipe on his doorstep after completing his day's work. The evening no longer brings a fresh breeze after a hot day. He pulls his chair back in over the threshold. In the summer Hesperus ascends into the blue twilight sky and gleams like steel over the peasant's roof. Now at night the air is raw and bleak, and black storm clouds cross the sky, following peculiar paths. Huge cold raindrops fall onto the layer of white dust on the street, noiseless like heavenly tears or eerie expectorations. Before one knows it, a heavy downpour commences and the street turns into a muddy river. The winter raillery of the elements is close at hand; hailstorms and tempests dance on the peaks of the Alps.

Steinn Elliði sits one evening in a second-class compartment on the Rome-Paris express, which has reached Modane, the French border town. He sits by the window, enwrapped in a thick coat, staring out and waiting for the train to continue on its way to Paris. He shares the compartment with an elderly British couple, sleeping like marmots, the wife covered by a huge blanket, the husband hidden behind the continental edition of the *Daily Mail.* The stop at the border station is long and tiring. Outside the window stands a man with a wagonload of pillows, which he advertises for rent for two lira. "My ladies and gentlemen," repeats the man over and over, "soft pillows, two lira!" Refreshment vendors and newspaper sellers wind their way around each other, red and blue from shouting, their voices either distressed or threatening. Porters, railway workers, customs officers, and policemen bump into each other as they work to save the nation, and no one quite understands this bustle, since the passengers have long since been dealt with and most boarded the train. Soldiers with long sabers and cigarettes in their mouths strut back and forth along the platform and make crude remarks about the girls in town. An addled traveler who has made some mistake as well as lost his hat stands remiss in front of three officers of the state and is written up. Several experienced travelers pace around the station platform, knowing that it is useless to make a fuss, and instead use the delay to stretch out after spending the whole day sitting in their seats.

Steinn leans into the corner by the compartment window and waits passively, except for now and then when he reaches into his coat pocket for a nut; he crushes the shell on the ashtray fastened to the wall, then shoves the kernel into his mouth.

Finally!

The train jerks into motion, first backward as if it is planning to jump, then slightly forward; next it makes a decisive leap and sets off. At the last moment a new passenger carrying a little handbag steps in; he walks down the passageway, searching for seats, until he sets his eyes on the empty ones in Steinn's compartment. He bids good evening in French, puts his bag up on the net, and sits down at the window opposite Steinn. He takes off his hat, black, low-crowned, quite nappy; the crown of his head is bald, but a thin, soft stripe of black hair covers the front, the sides, and the back. He is wearing a shoe-length overcoat, which he unbuttons because he is hot from running. Beneath it is a black shoe-length habit, and a scapular the same color can be seen beneath the edge of the habit. Protruding from his sleeves are white hands, small and handsome.

Steinn recognizes immediately from the man's clothing that this new arrival to the compartment is a monk. They glance quickly at each other's eyes. Then the monk takes his Psalter from his pocket, leafs through it for a moment until he has found the reading for the day, makes the sign of the cross, adjusts himself in his seat, and in the next breath is deep in his prayer readings, oblivious to his surroundings.

For the first time in his life Steinn sits opposite a man who has been shaped by Christian asceticism; he is therefore more than a little curious about trying to determine the psychological value of the lines in the face of such a person, and finds his opportunity to do so while the monk is reading.

The investigation resulted in the greatest promotion of Christianity's honor. Steinn came to the conclusion that if the Church counted in its flock of canons many sheep of this variety, it could easily call together a ministerial cabinet that many a state would envy. The stature of this man, the shape of his head and his physiognomy bore clear signs of an exceptionally virtuous personality. In civilian dress such a heroic figure would have immediately drawn the attention of the man on the street. The crown of his head was big and powerful, his nose large and hooked; his chin and the lines beneath his small delicate mouth witnessed his strong will. His eyes were exceptionally clear. Yet his expression had an aura that Steinn could not help but connect with either a musical virtuoso or a mathematician, something that avouched a strong, resolute interest in phenomena beyond the realm of the visible, something that ran the risk of being considered arrogance. Almost everything in this man's countenance would have found its home in a portrait of a genius, and Steinn could not help but think, despite the nobility of his asceticism, that in the end it would be a pitiful mistake of providence to shut this man behind an unclimbable wall, behind an iron door, which screeches the few times it is opened. He would undeniably have been better suited as an orator standing in the sunshine on a green hill, with thousands of people below shouting hurrah.

31.

The train rolls westward into France like a tremendously large, oblong insect from Earth's primeval times, howling and rattling, but the man with the shaven crown is engrossed in heavenly adventures; he is standing in the city of Zion, gazing at the Lord with the cherubim, seraphim, and blessed saints. At least an hour passes by, and Steinn is slightly annoyed that the man should not care about what is happening on Earth. But finally he finishes his prayers, takes his leave of Almighty God by crossing himself, puts the *Breviarium Monasticum* back into his pocket, and looks up. Once again they exchange quick glances, Steinn and the monk; next the latter leans back in his seat and closes his eyes. He had apparently traveled a long way, just like Steinn, and was tired. The train rushes noisily on.

But Steinn Elliði burned with the desire to talk. He had scarcely said a word since he parted from his mother at the station in Naples, and the three-day journey had awakened in him a great many thoughts. Besides that, it was foolish to let the opportunity to compare books with a Catholic ascetic slip by once it had presented itself. And he heard himself start to speak before he had any clear idea as to what he wanted to say:

"Excuse me, dear sir," he said, "but this is the first time that I have been granted the pleasure of sitting face-to-face with a true Christian son of the Catholic Apostolic Church, so I hope that you do not take it amiss if I address you. I should mention that you do not need to fear that I am as ignorant concerning Catholicism as any ordinary heretic; no, far from it, sir: I've read Cardinal Newman and have no qualms about placing him on the same pedestal as the gods of the nineteenth century. I've read three volumes of the apologetics of Weiss, who is sufficiently middle-of-the-road to merit being called both logical and extravagant. I've read old Bossuet, who I must admit is nothing other than a clever fool, unfortunately; I would have denied it on oath that it would be possible to write as dishonest a world history with as good a conscience as he has succeeded in doing. Concerning Pascal, I must truly say that I abhor him. Of the more recent Catholic writers I dare say that I have read the ones that are most well-known on the continent; thus I can name names such as Huysmans and Bordeaux, Paul Bourget, René Bazin, all petty bourgeois except for Huysmans; Léon Bloy, Marsis, Robert Hugh Benson, Hilaire Belloc, Chesterton, Johannes Jørgensen; and just recently I finished the new book by Papini, *Storia di Cristo,* which of course is nothing more than flowery, prideful, chattery prattle and a regression in style from when he published *Un uomo finito,* 1912. What do you think?"

"It is a genuine pleasure to speak with such a well-read man," said the monk, and Steinn saw immediately that his smile concealed French charm, but his voice was exceedingly bright, almost lyrical, yet entirely masculine. "I will take the liberty to deduce that the gentleman is a British or Scandinavian artist, and likely a poet, on his way home from sunny Italy, blessed with beautiful memories and lofty dreams."

Steinn acknowledged this: he was a Scandinavian, descended from Viking ancestors on his father's side. He was a worshipper of beauty. His soul was replete with sublime dreams. The monk had also come from Italy: from Monte Cassino, the great Benedictine abbey, where he had stayed for two months, lecturing to the novices. His home monastery was actually in Belgium. They exchanged cards, Steinn and the monk.

"It is truly instructive to meet an ascetic of the order of Benedict of Nursia in the year 1921," said Steinn. "It only goes to show that asceticism is neither one of the fads of the Middle Ages nor a worthless inheritance from Eastern heathendom, but rather one of the passions of human nature. I must inform you that I admire asceticism and would likely have entered a monastery had I not been raised in heretical doctrine. As you know, the spiritual life in the Nordic countries has for centuries lacked the treasures contained in the mystical nature of Christianity. The Christianity of the Nordic countries is as far removed from the ancient Catholic teachings as Theosophy is from Lamaism. The Catholic faith and Protestantism are two distinct religions, writes Cardinal Newman in *Loss and Gain,* and I would say that they are more than distinct religions: they are two opposing views of life that will never be reconciled. Catholicism is something that a man cannot help but call true; Protestantism is independent thinking gone awry. A man does not need to be more than middling keen to perceive the curse of excommunication that drifts like the stench of rotting flesh from every Protestant church door. The Apostolic Church has slung over the Lutherans an irrevocable ban, which presses down on us like a yoke and fills us with hatred and bigotry toward the truth; we would feel the same in a Catholic church as Swedenborg's demons straying onto the stage of the angels by mistake. Whenever I had the chance to stick my nose into a Catholic church I trembled in my soul like a man who fears being roasted on a spit. Yet I can assure you, sir, that in Scandinavia many hearts beat strongly and passionately with reverence for the Catholic Church and yearn for it. For my part, I thirst for its beauty, its authority and power, and for its ideals, especially its ideals of asceticism, which cannot be separated from unconditional belief in this so-called Lord of ours, Jesus Christ. And I despise with all my heart this latter-day Christianity, which some Saxon boors and wretches put together here recently just to tickle the ears of simpletons and strengthen the power of petty German kings. I was even convinced for three consecutive weeks this past spring that all of this deathly rubbish about atonement, the saints, and the infallibility of the pope was the highest truth that could possibly be achieved on our level of being. And I am, as I mentioned, still not entirely averse to the idea that Christianity, as the Catholic Church teaches it, is the truth. I am not more eager to believe in anything between Heaven and Earth than this: that Jesus Christ is the son of God, the incarnation of the Almighty, and has not only established a supernatural church, but was also begotten in a supernatural way, died in a supernatural way, and rose from the dead in a supernatural way. *The New Testament* is still the most remarkable book that I know, and *La Vie de Jésus* by Monsieur Ernest Renan is and always has been the most inconsequential book that I know. And just as the New Testament becomes more remarkable in my eyes the more that I study it, so too does *La Vie de Jésus* become more banal and insignificant.

"But *allegro ma non troppo,* sir, and so I turn to the truth, for that is the one thing about which I still long to ask: namely, what in the name of the Devil himself do we have, generally speaking, to do with truth?

"It has been asserted that the truth sets men free. It has likewise been proven that a piece of chalk the size of your fingertip contains enough power to propel a huge ship across the Atlantic Ocean. Still, in the real world people use coal and oil; and thus the difference between the validity of the truth and a lie vanishes, sir. A lie makes you scarcely less free than the truth. A lie is at least as secure a path to one's goal as the truth: that is to say, a poorly preached lie will naturally turn out to be a fool's mate before a well-preached truth, but the truth can't even begin to resemble smoke from burning hay leavings before a well-preached lie. And a lie is scarcely less suited to making a man happy than the truth. It has, for example, been shown that the truth about Jesus Christ and Almighty God has never been enough to free Christians from such a ridiculous thing as war. After Christians had prided themselves on this truth for two thousand years, boasted of it in front of extraordinarily learned mandarins in China, foolish Moors in Africa, and apish aborigines in Australia, they made a complete mockery of it and went to war. And they would go to war again tomorrow if they had the money for it. The entire Christian world rewrote the Lord's Prayer as the Devil's with their deeds, sir. The Catholic Church admits the legality of a defensive war, but since this is so, it admits the legality of all wars, in defiance of the commandment about the right and left cheeks, because war is best waged when one defends oneself against the encroachment of another; all wars are defensive wars. Yes, it is common knowledge that Catholic priests sprinkled holy water on cannons and made the sign of the cross over them in the last war, which is no less incredible than the pope in the old days making the sign of the cross over the swords that he gave to his minions. In general I don't understand how God could have come up with the idea of entrusting his Church to such ragamuffins as Europeans, when in the Orient there exist races of people of much nobler descent, with culture so incredibly old that European culture can't even begin to compare with it.

"The only ones who fought against this universal disgrace of the Christians, the world war, were several contemptible proletarians of the likes of Jaurès and Liebknecht, men who floundered in heresy and confusion and, while the continent was consumed by fire and sword over property, preached the barefaced lie that proprietary rights were not rights at all and that individuals should not be allowed to own anything. Of course patriotism and Machiavellianism shouted all such voices into silence, because if their lies and heresies had been heeded, we would of course have avoided a whole deluge of blood and tears and half of God's Ten Commandments would have been invalidated; and what would those of us here west of the Suez Canal preach if God's Ten Commandments were gone?

"Is it any wonder that I am of the opinion that a truth which after two thousand years of tautology is no more fit than this to better mankind is extraordinarily inconsequential? It may well be that Jesus Christ is the true God, and everything true that is taught about him, whether in the Church or in the Bible, but when the nations set out to destroy each other in the name of Jesus Christ, and when year after year they continue to slaughter the fathers of innocent children in the name of Jesus Christ and wreck the world from pole to pole with crime and sabotage, all in the same name, one begins to feel somewhat indifferent as to whether Christianity is true or a lie. I must admit that since people feel no shame about holding another such feast for the Devil as the world war was, after two thousand years of Christianity, and since they become worse children of Hell the more boisterously they profess their faith in the one true God before the mandarins and aborigines, then I find that the question becomes quite moot. Wouldn't you also agree that it might be advisable to bring something more wholesome to mankind's table, some sort of healthier chicken?"

There was a hint of something in the smile on the canon's face that made it resemble that of an uneducated girl who is prohibited from understanding what is being discussed around her and therefore decides that it is best to smile rather than appear dumbfounded. And this exceptionally pleasant, problematic smile tempted Steinn to pitch even more of the dialectic of truth out over the soul of the saint.

"Since I have made bold to mention politics, sir," he continued, "then I cannot refrain from dredging the truth up before you as it must appear to any man who has eyes in his head: it is a blind man who does not see that communism is the social polity of the future. These are mournful tidings, sir, in the first place because of how many prophets will surely be stoned before it is accomplished, and in the second place because of how many stupid old wives' tales will be spread in order to put it to shame. The Church in its role as a worldly institution most resembles a monarchy, and holds that monarchy has its foundation in the will of God, among other things because Christ considered it just to pay taxes to Caesar. The Church has been an untiring advocate of knightly riffraff and tribes of berserks, the so-called noble classes that in the old days sprang up like mushrooms on manure heaps after every war, convinced themselves that they owned the Earth and looked upon themselves as some sort of supermen whom the masses ought to bear upon golden chairs. It certainly was deft of the Church to take sides with the nobility in order to secure itself souls. But now it has had to watch as the will of God concerning monarchy and the nobility has gone the same way as the twenty-four royal dynasties of Egypt. First the bourgeoisie devoured the will of God, and then the plutocracy devoured the bourgeoisie. Society in our time is subservient to the despotism of adventurists! Society in our time is camouflaged anarchy: every hand is raised against the next; everyone fights and hates everyone else, and it's sheer coincidence that grants the victory! Coincidence creates kings like Rothschild and Stinnes, Vanderbilt, Rockefeller and Morgan, Field and Astor; but human reason and human virtue are trampled down beneath the feet of dogs and men.

"Reality is what has happened and we must look it straight in the eye. No matter what the will of God might be according to the theological sciences, God has let everything happen as it has. It is too late to speak for kings nowadays, when the noblemen have become dancers in coffeehouses, streetcar attendants, and shoeshine boys. Anarchy joins in a game of blindman's bluff with a gullible public under the mask of parliamentary democracy, which is an illusion, freedom of speech, which is cant, and philanthropy, which is venality. In other words, the time has come for human reason to stand up on its own two feet and change the course of the game.

"Human reason, sir, is the most vicious power under the sun. When human reason takes to its feet, it shovels the masses like cast-iron rods into enormous crucibles and lights an engulfing fire beneath; then it forges from them a sharp-edged weapon, which it whets quite diligently, sir, because it will not cease from killing until the blood drips from the bleeding trunks of the last enemies of mankind. This is what has been done in Russia, and is what will be done throughout the world. In each and every country wise men are sharpening their weapons for the decisive battle, and the weapons are the masses; the battle is the revolution.

"When I read in the world newspapers about the fear of communism as a reactionary response propagated by members of the Catholic Church, it seems to me that between the lines one can read the pope's fear concerning whether the Church will stand or fall because of the backwardness or imperfection of the social order; in other words, the fear that Christ will break his promise, which the Church is constantly shouting, that he will keep watch over it until the end of the world. Am I in the wrong, sir? Or does the Church fear that its teachings concerning charity will become invalid in communist society? If so, why did your father, Benedict of Nursia, found a communist society? When Christian monks founded a society in Paraguay it was communist, not unlike what is happening in Russia now. In your rule the greatest care is taken to ensure that the individual is not a passive witness to an imperfect social order; each individual stands in a legally binding position to the whole; everyone is given work according to his own abilities; every single individual is a limb on the societal body, he exists for the sake of the community, the community for his sake; if anyone becomes sick he is nursed without a word; those whom old age bends are allowed to live their days without care or worry; no one is allowed to suffer need; all receive their daily bread, but nothing beyond that. The abbot is not superior to the brothers except in his gift for organization and his abilities as a leader, which he has received from God, in addition to the cross upon his chest, as a sign of the one in whose name he governs. Very fine, sir: in this collective state of yours, Christian love of one's neighbor and God's Ten Commandments are put into practice in a simple manner, not with lotteries, collections, and vaudeville shows, nor with cobbled rags to be distributed to the poor at Christmas, but rather with simple government, organization founded on human reason. And it is the same kind of government, the same kind of system, founded on the same kind of human reason, that is described in Marxist doctrine: cooperation in place of endless war, collective ownership of the Earth's endowments in place of matches of tug-of-war over them, the legally binding position of the individual in relation to the whole, in place of armed despotism in which the most brazen adventurist tyrannizes the masses; in other words, Benedict of Nursia in place of Alexander Borgia.

"Doesn't the Church have two thousand years of experience of this: that in a social order in which people are denied everything except for the fight for the necessities of life, the doctrine of love for mankind is nothing other than seed strewn about for the birds of the air? Will it not learn any lessons from current events? Does it turn a deaf ear to the Great World War, which speaks the clearest language about the sterility of the doctrine of confraternity in a society founded on conflict between men? Does it not see that it has been playing the fiddle for two thousand years while Rome has been burning? Or does it intend to wait for the Christian world to rewrite the Lord's Prayer for the Devil with an even more appalling war than the Great World War?"

32.

At home Steinn was accustomed to needing only five minutes to win over those who listened to him, and he would have found nothing more natural here than for the monk to rise to his feet, throw off his cowl, renounce the one true faith, and shout: *"Eviva la bandiera rossa!"*[28] But this did not happen. This man must have been living in a hideout of firmly rational thought. He smiled the entire time that Steinn rambled on.

"I find it a true pleasure to listen to you speak," he replied finally. "I admire your elocution. And I sincerely rejoice to meet a strong young soul who not only finds himself compelled to take a stand and reproach men for their errors, but also to carry a clean slate."

And although the monk did not take any steps to expound the excellence of the true faith or make excuses for Christian culture to this elated Scandinavian, it was far from it that he considered him worthless: instead he looked him over long and carefully, while Steinn let his blazing eyes rest on the man who slept under the continental edition of the *Daily Mail*.

Why didn't the monk answer? Why didn't he try to defend Christianity? Does he think that it's sufficient proof of the pope's infallibility to let all of the criticism rush past his ears like wind and pay me some empty compliments? Steinn thought it reasonable that a Benedictine monk should be ready and willing to haggle about his faith no less than someone sitting in a café in Reykjavík.

But the monk seemed not to give any thought to approaching the field where Steinn had wanted to force their conversation into pitched battle, and instead finally asked, courteously, and yet perhaps not entirely unsarcastically:

"Would it be too importunate if your fellow traveler, whom you might never see again, were to be so bold as to reveal that he is slightly curious to know what such a brilliant thinker has in mind to do?"

Steinn looked straight at the man and answered without hesitation:

"I am in search of perfection, like you. And I will not stop until I find it. I have no waking interest in anything but perfection. This is why my face is savage when I turn it toward others. You think that I am a communist? No, sir, I am a much greater revolutionary than that. The communist movement is worthless, per se. The communist movement is only an inside-out capitalist movement, per se. I despise those who think that mankind would be happy if the masses were to take over the Kremlin, Buckingham Palace, or the Vatican, or were to get honey to eat instead of horse fat. On the other hand, it is a person with cataracts who does not see that the communist system is the social order of the future.

"But in my eyes everything is worthless but God. I find him so remarkable that I have decided to write fifty poems about him in English. It is another matter whether he exists. My soul is like Kashmir, the valley of roses; I have been given glorious talents, and what's more, the calling to put them to use. I have a friend in England, a professor at an Indian university, a man who is able to appreciate my talent, and I am now on my way to him to learn the English language thoroughly. He will be staying at home in England for three years. I intend to use the British Empire as a receiving set. Would you like to hear the headings? I have them all written here in my notebook. The world has never suspected that such poems could be slumbering in the harp of any poet. I plan to spend the next three years in seclusion."

The monk finally smiled in such a way that Steinn thought he understood everything.

"And you have no hesitations about subjecting yourself to such a long period of self-denial for fifty poems?" he asked.

"It's not for the fifty poems, but for the sake of perfection, for the sake of God," corrected Steinn.

"Eh bien," said the monk.

"No, sir. I have no hesitations. My powers know no bounds. 'The weakest power of my soul is more far-reaching than Heaven and earth,' says Master Eckehart. I don't feel that any ordeal is beyond my strength. My will is strong. Nothing between Heaven and Earth can ever subdue it. What I have firmly resolved shall be accomplished. Three years from now you will see the world shouting from the rooftops the things that I whisper in your ears tonight."

Now, finally, after Steinn had brought his political chatter to a close and had started to speak of his soul, the face of the canon gleamed with understanding. And the more unexpectedly that his prevarication had struck Steinn before, the more unprepared Steinn was now for the monk's lack of perplexity, as he made his first affirmative remarks: "You intend," he said, "to compose fifty perfect poems for God. *Très bien.* But has it never occurred to you, who have such a strong brain, that in fact it might not be your poems that God asks of you? Has it never occurred to you that perhaps God is served as little whether you give him either perfect poems or nothing at all? Has it never occurred to you that in fact it might not be your gifts that God demands, no matter how precious they might be?"

This time it was Steinn Elliði who was tongue-tied, and he looked at the monk for a moment with questioning eyes. Is he trying to confuse me? he thought, and felt it worst that he did not know how to score a point against the monk; he was, however, on his guard not to endanger his own perspective under the weight of dialectic, preferring to allow the monk to explain his own view before they went any further. It was as if he suspected the cloaked man of having the ability to best his opponents with their own tricks.

"If God is not served with perfect works, then I admit that I would be curious to hear you clarify the idea of God. What does this God of yours demand?"

"With our external works, *opera externa,*" said the monk, "it is quite easy for us to become famous on rooftops, even overthrow entire states and subdue kingdoms. But of what avail is that? We will never subdue God's kingdom with external works. One Lord's Prayer, prayed at night while everyone is asleep, is a greater event than the revolution in Russia, even if no one will hear about it until Doomsday. If you had any notion as to what one sigh means for those who seek God in the night, the most famous, magnificent deed would become as worthless chaff in your eyes. The truth is not the external, but rather the internal. If you do not trust God to watch over the welfare of the world without you, then it would be healthy for you to remember that he created the world with all of its solar systems without you. Your poems and achievements may be incredible. 'Your gifts are worth nothing to me,' says the Lord. 'I only ask for you yourself.' It must be wonderful to hear one's name praised from the rooftops, but *'Quantum unusquisque est in oculis tuis, domine, tantum est et non amplius,'* says Bonaventura, which he learned from the humble man from Assisi: 'What you are in the eyes of God, that you are and no more.'"

Whether Jesuit disputational tricks or appeals to mysticism were being employed here, this unmilitant man knew the art of fixing his argument precisely, in sentences that were difficult to work one's way around, and he also knew the power of letting his glance, mild, calm, and steady, accompany his words unyieldingly. And Steinn was becoming more and more convinced that the man was not a lamb, but an eagle; again he found himself at a loss for words.

"I have never thought such a merciless thought as the one that you have planted in my mind, sir," he said, "that perhaps art itself is one of the devil's traps. Or what else could you possibly mean? Art, however, demands a sacrifice, sir! It demands self-denial no less than monasticism, and perhaps even more toil, more sleepless nights, more constant moments of despair. A true artist sacrifices everything for his gifts of grace; he renounces life's fortune, even peace of mind; he renounces all human joy and celebrates only the fact that he is able to take on his shoulders all of the burdens that are bound to mankind, and he lies down like a camel to let himself be loaded with them."

It was almost as if Steinn's voice contained a hint of a plea for mercy. But the monk was still too secure to dispute with him. And Steinn felt more and more that everything he had said, and even what he still had to say, would only come across as vain prattle in the ears of the stranger.

"Once I knew a young man who had planned to follow the same path as you," began the monk again. "He was also seeking the true reality. And he would not let anyone dissuade him. A young man demands the right to secure for himself, at a high price, the experience of life that he is in fact offered for free in the admonitions of his elders. The Way is all there is for a man, and those who are not on The Way are seeking The Way. Everyone chases his own dream: one to Brazil to play the violin, another to London to compose beautiful poems. No one can escape his fate. And yet The Way leads neither through Brazil nor through the British Empire. But do not forsake this one thing, and think about it when the time comes when you feel that the solar system will burst asunder and the Earth shatter under your feet: one thing has higher value than anything else, and that is *la vie spirituelle,* the working of grace on a man's inner being."

Steinn looked silently at the monk's smile and listened to his bright, pure voice, without being able to determine from his words whether he was a lunatic or a sage.

"It would be my true pleasure to be able to meet you sometime later in life," said the monk finally. "And should the time come when you find yourself compelled to discuss essential matters with a humble servant of the most holy Church of our Lord Jesus Christ, then you know where such an insignificant person can be found."

Steinn thanked his fellow traveler for his amity, found of course no impulse within him to consider such a visit as things stood now, but asked if he might send the canon a letter at his later convenience; in fact there were still quite a few things left that he wished to say to the Church.

They said nothing more to each other; only the night spoke; the stars flew like sparks outside the window. But the monk's words continued to echo in Steinn's ears, although sleep fettered his tongue: God does not ask for your gifts, but rather for you. They were as indelible as unintelligible runes carved on a young tree. More than anything else, Steinn was overcome by a feeling approximating shame. He felt as if he had gotten more than he bargained for. He had behaved like an actor in a burlesque show before this unassuming man of the cloth. The monk was like a powerful oak tree, planted a thousand years ago, its roots deep in the Earth – but I am like a rootless, gripless walking stick that some vagrant stuck in the grass yesterday to the disgrace of God, he thought. He felt that he was becoming smaller and smaller in the silence; he knew nothing, was nothing. In the same way, the monk grew larger; his silence was more powerful than his words, deeper. Perhaps he was inspired by the deepest verity of being, was perhaps more than a man, his humanity a revelation of a nobler world. He was perhaps a two-thousand-year-old master and the mouthpiece of the highest spirit, perhaps Krishna. Steinn Elliði was King Arjuna. And the train sped westward through France, like an immense insect from Earth's primeval days.

When Steinn woke in the morning in the Gare de Lyon in Paris he was alone in the cabin; the English couple had risen from death and the monk had vanished completely. But in his breast pocket he found a name-card with these words: *Fr. Alban, moine bénédictin.*[29] *Sept Fontaines. Belgique.*

33.

Sussex, summer 1924. Highly esteemed sir. My deepest thanks for the edifying discussion we had in the train that autumn night in 1921. I make no secret of the fact that your personality has made a deep impression on me. I have not been able to forget you. Of course, I did not understand you completely and have long since forgotten what you said, but the more that time passes the stronger suspicion I have that there was wisdom in it. I have often thought about writing to you, sometimes even to come visit you. When we spoke together, I thought that I was on the right path. It is characteristic of those who are completely lost, that though they go in empty circles and arrive ten times at the same place, it is almost impossible to convince them that all they've done is go in circles. They even think that rivers run uphill. After I had composed twenty-eight poems I was finally able to see that I had gone in twenty-eight circles. I discovered that I was not on any path at all. I had sailed a fresh fair wind out into the blue. I have a great number of opinions as to what is right and what wrong, but unfortunately I must admit that I do not know what is right and what is wrong. The main point, says Maurice Barrès, is to be convinced that there exist only points of view, *manières de voir,* that they all contradict each other, but that we can with a little effort acquire them all regarding the same thing. But in spite of everything, I lack nothing so much as the dexterity to have all of the world's opinions concerning the same thing at once. All of my *manières de voir* continuously miss the point, and all of my misfortune arises from this. There is not a shred of tranquility within me. I am a roaring lion in the desert. I am the Flying Dutchman, the Wandering Jew:

Johohoe! Johohoe! Hojohe!
Traft ihr das Schiff im Meere an,
blutrot die Segel, schwarz der Mast?
Auf hohem Bord der bleiche Mann,
des Schiffes Herr, wacht ohne Rast!

Hui! – Wie saust der Wind! Johohe!
Hui! – Wie pfeift's im Tau! Johohe!
Hui! – Wie ein Pfeil fliegt er hin,
ohne Ziel, ohne Rast, ohne Ruh![30]

Sometimes I ponder the welfare of mankind and hate those who take an interest in anything else. Sometimes I ponder myself and the immeasurable inside myself, but despise mankind. Sometimes I thirst for nothing but the one true Almighty God and despise myself, but give not a single thought to mankind. When we spoke I mentioned a British friend and said that he was able to appreciate my gifts. But in the end I could no longer bear his presence. I suffer in the company of men who do not suffer. Now he is gone, this British bull, this colonial jackal, gone to Hell to preach to the souls in prison: the Indians in the rat trap of the British Empire; and he has entrusted to me the keeping of his residence in Hounslow near London. Now I am on a two-month gad around southern England in search of myself. I am going to try to collect myself. I am like jetsam scattered along a long beach.

Forgive me for writing to you. But I have no friends whom I trust. At home in the town where I was born I had several companions, but they are simpletons. They comb their hair. Everything is "cosmic" to them. The world is, in their eyes, a foreign magazine. I have not combed my hair once in two years. I have swallowed the entire world. I do not speak; I scream. I do not debate; I give orders. I am a wolf in the fold. I should be imprisoned like a dictator. I should be quartered. The scraps of my body should be scattered about to nourish the birds of the air. All of this I trust you will do.

34.

After I composed the twenty-eighth poem, I said *"Basta!"* I threw that rubbish out like a man on the street who eats nuts and spits the shells here and there; like the Lord of the universe, who shakes suns like ten-aurar coins out of his heavenly jester's sleeves, absentmindedly and nonchalantly, not even to amuse himself, let alone others; or like a wagon driver who used to be the servant of his donkey and cart, but who now, after both donkey and cart have tumbled off a cliff, stands behind on the ledge, empty-handed, and celebrates his victory. But what do you think this Carrington did?

He stole the poems and took them to a printer without my knowledge, and has newspapers and magazines harp on them as masterpieces.

Of course they are masterpieces, but God does not lack masterpieces. God needs souls. Mankind does not need masterpieces. Mankind needs *panem et circenses*.[31] Neither I nor others compose masterpieces for God or mankind. Delusion! Poets have never carried the people's burdens. They are the enemies of the people. They are the harlots of the people. They howl at the people. They spit at the people. They cajole the people. They lie. They dress themselves up in sacred linen before the people like hellish sorcerers. They shriek like a woman in the pangs of childbirth. They swallow fire, turn somersaults and contort themselves before the people, all in the hope of subduing them, elbow their way onto the highest seats so that queens can anoint their feet with balsam and dry them with their hair. Their goal is like that of the Roman emperors, to be deified and worshipped in life. They are lovelorn men. The artist's essential being is nothing but *obsession du sexe*. They're oversexed. They think that they have special permission to break all the commandments of God and man at once. "The simplest form of art is love," says André Breton. The one who understands this understands the entire hoax. In the future, artistic madness will be cured by a simple operation. The artist has no moral interests, says the preface to *Dorian Gray*. The artist is an immoral intellectual. Art is one of the indulgences of the intellectual. Art refuses to be one of the weapons that are used in the war over the values of life. Art for art's sake is a settled question – and last but not least in favor of the artist. Art is the kingly dream of the peasant, the cocaine craze of the psychopath who lacks the fortitude to work, the tool of the man who sees in it his life's goal of being published in the culture section of newspapers, like the weather forecasts.

Dear sir, I understand all of this now.

35.

The sage has three choices. He can choose whether he will live for himself, for God, or for men. I mull over these three choices. I examine them minutely under a microscope and take a determined stand toward each of them: which is to say, I take a stand toward none of them. I am the ass that dies between rows of drying hay.

I lack the coarseness of the old noblemen; no, I lack sufficient faith in myself to count myself a god and make people my slaves, like the superman. And I lack sufficient faith in God to be able to throw myself down in the mud beneath the cross. But I pity the people, not because they are created in God's image, but because they are created in my image. It is of course a weakness to pity people, but it is also a weakness to implore the God of the weak. But the greatest weakness is to believe in oneself. That is a resort that either ends in madness or suicide. After Nietzsche lost his faith in the theory of evolution, and at the same time in the superman as a higher form of man, he counted himself a god and went mad. For what is man? *Homo vanitati similis factus est: dies ejus sicut umbra prætereunt:* man is like vanity; his days flit by as a shadow.[32] Even a superman is a vain superstition. If a superman were conceivable, he would also be a prisoner of nature, a prisoner of his existence like a man, and his only reason for being born would be to die, like a man. All flesh is hay. A superman is situated just as far from the eternal absolute spirit as a man. The deeper that I delve into Nietzsche, the more dismal a mirage the superman becomes to me.

A similar case applies to the ordinary Lord. He has in fact never been real to me. He has at most been an ornament in my poems. If I were to repeat the story of my childhood thoughts, I could say that he appeared to me most often as a morbid phantasm. I also doubt that he had been anything but a morbid phantasm in the minds of the martyrs. They would never have endured martyrdom for their convictions, as they were called, if those convictions had been to them as unequivocal as the Earth upon which they stood or the air that they breathed. It would never cross anyone's mind to let oneself be put to death for the conviction that one stands upon the Earth.

Men let themselves be put to death for sick imaginations and lapses of reason, not for their convictions.

From my childhood my conception of God was nothing but a touch of mild hysteria that reappeared again and again in various forms, but might just as well have appeared as chronic gastritis or an inflammation of the gallbladder. My rebirths and reconversions were never anything other than lyrical disturbances of my mind.

If I presume, on the other hand, that God exists, then I can't see that he and man could have anything to do with each other. It is nothing but bombast to say that men must struggle to become perfect because God is perfect. Spiritual superiority revealed in moral perfection never touches the plane of the notion of God. The ideal of perfection has its end and origin in the idea of man. If God were a perfect spirit, his control over the world would be the pinnacle of moral perfection. But if any God rules the world, he rules it with nothing but foolish caprice and infringement upon the underdog.

Powerful spirits come into the world to fight for human welfare, and they sacrifice everything. They love mankind; its prosperity is their wine and bread. But while these pioneers of perfection fight for the success of mankind, the Lord commands the seas to swallow the supporters of poor families and lets the wind blow the roofs off of orphans' huts. He shakes Messina with earthquakes and in one night slaughters fourteen thousand innocent men who had no suspicion of danger. And he lets a million children die of starvation in Russia, Austria, and Germany during our own era. Why does he let a million children suffer starvation in Russia, Austria, and Germany? Why doesn't he help those wailing wretches? What have they done to deserve it?

God is not a moral being. God is far beyond any such thing. God is not moved. Man can become morally perfect. Man can sacrifice everything for the happiness of his brothers. God does not care about men's happiness. I am what I am, says the Lord. When Christ asks God to be merciful, he chooses men as his model. He does not say let us forgive one another as God forgives us, but rather the opposite: forgive as we forgive.

How in the world can Christianity, a nineteen-hundred-year-old ghost story from Asia, be expected to have any influence on contemporary Europeans? The time has long since passed when men yearned to reach the Kingdom of Heaven. Men no longer sin; they make blunders. They conduct themselves foolishly and inadvisably because they make false calculations and are uneducated. They play blindly. They curse each other because they live in a society in which one man's death is another man's bread. They comport themselves ridiculously, lamentably, grotesquely, and piteously. But they do not sin.

Men live in reality, and there they are condemned to help themselves. God has sentenced man to help himself. God does not help him; that is evidenced everywhere. It is also evidenced everywhere that the more faith men put in God, the more liable they are to wallow in idiocy and penury, the less liable to rise up against their enemies, against lies and tyranny. In just a short time the holiest names of Christianity will not be seen upon anything other than fatted calves, lapdogs, soft drinks, and laundries.

36.

"Greif hinein ins volle Menschenleben!"[33]

A perfect man fights against the enemies of mankind. Perfect labor is a karmayogic philosophy. The philosophy of work for the sake of work is an opiate. It is suited to ascetics who lack the energy to fight in the war for the values of life. Perfect work is vanity, per se. The history of mankind is the history of war over the price of life, the value of life. On the one side are perfect men, on the other side the enemies of mankind. A man is worth precisely as much as the ideal that he proclaims to be the goal of his battle. That labor is most valuable which brings the greatest happiness to the greatest number of people, says Bentham. Labor that does not aim at achieving a valuable ideal is weed, no matter how beautiful it is.

The vintners of the generations are coming. Thousands wait only for the coming of the spiritual princes, who will eclipse the sun and the moon. And they are coming. They shout the slogan, and all throng to their weapons. Woe to those who try to rise up against the vintners of the generations and their troops! Woe to those who do not apprehend the time of their arrival, when the reappraisal of all value is at the door! "Brothers!" cries the apostle Paul. "You are limbs on the body of Christ!" And before one knows it every rascal has become a limb on the body of Christ and a powerful empire is founded on the back of one carpenter. Rousseau gives the order: "Return to nature!" And the people reply: "We shall return to nature!" and they start a revolution. Marx: "Workers of the world, unite!" And grimy coal men and exhausted dockworkers tear down emperors and gods, raise the land up and dump it over the sea.

The vintners of the generations are merciless tyrants who will not spare kings. They have only one goal, to lead thousands to a new settlement where all things look completely different, where man's gifts can be nurtured under better conditions, and where the powers are exalted in concord. They all invite mankind to a greater and more beautiful feast. They hold bridal feasts and betroth mankind to its ideals. The enemies of mankind will be cast out into utter darkness.

Heaven help those who rule states and kingdoms! Heaven help those who dictated what war cries would be used during the years 1914–1918! Heaven help those condemned souls who turned the continent into a field of blood in the name of the king, the fatherland, and freedom. It is high time that the people came to understand thoroughly each and every slogan that was trumpeted in their ears during the World War. The people will learn that the king is a combination of a decoy and a sacrament, dangled by parliamentary democracy before them, a walking old wives' tale, a historical addition to the menu at feasts, and that parliamentary democracy is a mask covering the despotism of a small group of adventurists who usurp the dividend of the fruits of the Earth. And it will come to know that the fatherland consists in reality of nothing other than these adventurists, groups of golden-toothed, balding potbellies who set up their industrial conglomerates and trading companies throughout the world and compete to dominate the global market. Freedom is the mud on the field of battle; it is mutilation; it is a shameful death on the *champ d'honneur,* the profligate arena of sabotage; it is unemployment when the soldiers come home maimed and insane; it is the hunger that sucks the marrow from their children's bones; and finally it is a tiny buttonhole badge worth five aurar, distributed for free to those who make the greatest strides in killing the people from the other fatherland, raping the women, and burning the churches.

37.

I am one of those big strong men needed by the world to fight in the merciless battle against the enemies of mankind. And this is what tips the scales: I fully comprehend the manners of the age and know precisely what demands must be made of philanthropists who are ill-equipped to fight against a better-armed tyrannical power than any other that one could cite from the past, a power that fights with carefully cultivated hereditary lies or hereditary truths, a power that has usurped all the tools of information, schools, newspapers, and publishers, and places bribed orators in its advance guard, to distribute lies and deceptions in a hundred million different places every day, a power that has not only conquered the legislature, the police, and the courts, but also religion and the arts and sciences, and has a million soldiers like pathogenic bacteria stored in its back pocket to spread out over the masses if all else fails.

To me ideas mean action. I concern myself only with the conclusion of the contest, and not with the passage of arms. As a soldier I do not expect to wage honorable or valiant war, and I would certainly break any pact made with my enemies over the correct conduct of battle. I am a savage of the twentieth century: I have no other choice but to fight as a criminal for my freedom against those in whose hands every single branch of civilization becomes a deadly mistletoe.[34] There are no means conceivable that I would fail to utilize if they would allow me to reach my goal. The ends justify the means, no matter what they are. Honorable war is a sport, a game, a swindle, a bluff. He who fights for life or death has the right to utilize all of his tricks: he is higher than all rights. Ruthlessness, effrontery, and impudence are the most unfailing weapons that an idealist of our time can use to gain and maintain control, and I have been endowed with these gifts in full measure.

In ages past men suffered martyrdom for their convictions. The martyrdom craze raged again and again like the plague. Men sprawled themselves out on the torture racks in lecherous joy. I despise those masochistic inclinations of the men of old; they are perverse, unnatural. I assure you, I will not let myself be butchered for my convictions. I would sooner tell five hundred lies and live than let a hysterical longing to prate about my convictions before some abject court, or on the streets and crossroads, be the cause of my death. He who is not as cunning as a serpent does not deserve to possess an ideal. Just as soon as some despot demands it of me, I shall take back everything today that I said yesterday; I would even have no scruples about asking for forgiveness. But I would start anew in all earnestness tomorrow, and begin where I had to stop before, only at a more suitable place, so that I could rest safely assured that my enemies were not able to profane my person. Woe to the man who claims to be fighting for an ideal in our time and does not know how to give a false impression of himself! He is defeated even before the duel begins.

I sail into the faces of my enemies under a false banner and lay my mines furtively under their fleet. I greet my enemies under an assumed name, grasp their hands sincerely, hold councils with them and look into their eyes frankly and boldly like a polite boy, accept their invitations for visits and discuss matters of the heart with their wives, innocent and holy like Rasputin or Cagliostro, while I work the whole time on gathering fiery embers over their heads. I come to them like a man of God with my dagger concealed in my crucifix.

I am ready to have every tenth man in the world beheaded if need be. If ten men stand against an ideal that otherwise would benefit ninety men, I would not hesitate to give my servants the order to take those ten men out and execute them. If the ideal is of more worth than those who oppose it, then it is plain that those who resist must die.

The personality, the magnetism of the iron will, this blessing that even sages were denied, this is my most precious cradle gift. The duty to mankind that was placed on my shoulders is to preserve my self-made mettle. I must not bend. I must never swear allegiance to anyone. Men like me commit deadly sins against mankind if they allow their mettle to be fouled by impurities. They are born to be pure and alone.

Of all the disciplines, chastity is the most powerful guardian spirit of the personality. To chastity I sing a hymn of praise. Nothing better fortifies a man's spirit nor amplifies his psychological greatness, nothing hardens him better against pliancy nor softens him better against rigidity, nothing makes him more warlike nor more immune to hurt, nothing else endows him with a more irreconcilable power to face peril nor a more unfailing endurance in the prolonged battles, and no more intense savagery in exterminating dragons. Chastity is a guarantee that the intentions of great minds are pure, and stains fall neither onto the shield nor the ideals of the chaste man; he never fights for himself. When I hear about a man's heroic deeds, the first thing I ask is: was he chaste? I have no confidence in the leadership of a man who is an intellectual being by day and a sexual being by night. Such a vacillatory spirit never runs the greatest risks. I do not trust leaders who wake at dawn to the sound of the war bugle with pins and needles in their limbs after a lukewarm night. Call me a dog if the woman, the butcher's bills, and the family portraits do not make the threshold of his door into a nearly unscalable cliff. A married man is not just bound to his wife, since society is never so bad that he is not wed to it as well. "A wife is like thirty tyrants," says the Tobacco Company of Iceland, Ltd.

The chaste man is married to his ideals. He is married to the battle for the welfare of mankind. He eats dry bread and has no roof over his head except when the state throws him into prison. Everything that makes war against the freedom of his soul is his enemy; the upkeep of his body is only cruel necessity. He is a manifestation of a higher manhood, of the free and perfect reality, an independent intellectual being, higher than good and evil, a mystic phenomenon, a Buddha with ten thousand women in his belly, a god with the trembling prayers of entire nations in the grip of his omnipotent hands. He is solitary and alone, but solitude is the mother of power. He has no friends, no one that he loves, except for mankind.

38.

I discovered early that woman appealed only to what was evil in my being. Everything that I could conceive of was evil insofar as my mind was directed toward her. Every one of my thoughts about woman is a stain on my soul. To the angel in my being nothing exists that is called "woman." The man in my being is repelled by woman as by a disgusting beggar. The beast in my being sees its most desired soul mate in her. My Satan nature relishes woman with eager joy.

It beseems no thinker to avoid such a serious concept, like an unsolved puzzle.

It is true: woman is a strange sphinx of the desert. And it is also true that the face of the lion-maiden is concealed by a veil that few succeed in lifting, and none is better for doing so. It is not too far from the truth to say that most men die who dare to lift the veil from the face of Isis, just as those who behold the face of Yahweh. At least no one who has lifted the veil from the face of Isis remains unchanged.

I have seen through the web of deception. Woman in all of her glory no longer has any effect on me. When I was a child she was a mirror and a puzzle to me. Her glance flashed over my body like lightning over a lightning rod. The gleam from her flesh slew my soul with magic spells. I looked at woman with similar eyes as I did the Bible or fairy tales and I quivered before this mystery: woman, so entirely cabalistic in her manner of being, was my dreamland. But the deeper that I dug into the hiding places of mortal nature, the more barren became the mysterious land of my dreams; finally nothing else appeared to me but the bare mountains of the moon, which glow like red-hot showers of iron smelting in the fires of the sun. Whereas woman had at first appeared to me as the Bible, I discovered now that she was nothing but a textbook on homeopathy. A woman's beauty was no longer a supernatural fairy gleam, but the external skin of the life of her passions: her attractiveness stands in direct proportion to her nymphomania. The puzzle had become a petty card trick, the mystery a ballad whistled in public squares.

Women have appeared to me in visions as I sat there by The Way, meditating. They came in huge groups and long caravans, came laughing, came singing, and took their places on the road before the eyes of the sage. There they spun on their heels and stopped in the midst of the dance, with one foot on the ground and the other in the air *in pose orridamente oscene.* I have seen them all and know them all. I have seen the first Eve and the last, the women who lived before the Flood and after the Flood, women from the east, women from the west, women in Paris, women in Rome, thousands of women, tens of thousands of women, all the women in the world. Women are the same everywhere. I have seen young women who were so succulent from love and fertility that one's hands became damp by touching them; they were wondrous like the fog in Laugardalsskógur on a warm spring morning. I have seen other women who were as elegant as amber, woven of moonlight and algal gloss, who understood before any words were spoken and saw before anything was shown; women who were attuned to my most hidden thoughts like magnetic currents and quivered before my glance like young deer shying at a whistling in the forest. I have seen women who were sinewy, strong, and nimble, like wild beasts from primeval jungles, their hands like tongues of fire, long, slender, and poisonous, as if they were made to claw deeply into the flesh of martyrs and saints. I have seen women with gentle smiles, calm and dreamy like summer-green valleys in the mountains, replete with luxurious growth like sedge-grown meadows in midsummer; their fire burned mildly and tranquilly, like light over a baby's cradle on the feast of Saint Þorlákur, the day before Christmas. I have seen women who raged like prairie fires, supple women and women deranged, fleet like gazelles, dressed to kill, hot and fuming like mares pulling the Pharaoh's wagon, their Venus breasts laden with lustful terrestrial power. I have seen women who were plump like loaded trawl nets; their bodies glossy like soft-paste porcelain, the folds of their skin hiding layers of fat five fingers thick, like porkers; in their drowsy glance there appeared abominable, slothful aphrodisiac dreams; they could have been roasted and eaten. And I have seen a four-thousand-year-old maiden from Egypt; she is housed in the British Museum, sits there unmoving, completely naked, on display for one and all to see. Her breasts are like moldy raisins, her hair most like the hurds on a twenty-five-aurar doll, her mouth a black rift like a crack in tree bark; her nose has fallen off, her eyes are two black hollows, her skin resembles a strung-up, soot-strewn liverwurst wrapping.

39.

What especially captured my attention when I walked for the first time into the chief cathedral of the Christians, Saint Peter's Basilica in Rome, was when I read those ludicrous warnings on the doors, written in four languages: *"Vietato l'ingresso alle signore indecentemente vestite,"* "Immodestly dressed women refused entrance."

The inscription "Jesus Nazarenus Rex Judæorum" was only written in three languages, I thought.

Posted on the cathedral door in Florence is a detailed set of regulations concerning how female visitors there are obliged to conceal their flesh. They may not be bareheaded. Bareheaded women, *garçonnes,*[35] customarily borrow the hats of the men accompanying them before they enter the church. Women's dresses must reach some distance below the knees – anything higher than that comes from the Devil. They may not be cut lower than two inches below the neck, so as to remind no one of the Rococo period. The sleeves must reach at least midway between the wrists and the elbows. Finally a woman must not be clothed in anything transparent – otherwise the regulations would be worth little!

But when I started to think about it more carefully, I realized that it is not a question of vanity that a woman is obliged to conceal her flesh as carefully as possible if she would dare to enter the temple of God. A woman is, namely, neither more nor less than the most dangerous rival of God and competitor in the contest for a man's soul. There are two divine powers in our earthly existence, and both are engaged in a tug-of-war over a man's soul. On the one hand is God, as he is called, the limit of man's spiritual desire; on the other hand is a woman's flesh. Both love man in their own way; neither wants to be a spare horseshoe; both demand to possess him entirely, possess him in body and soul. More correctly put, man has only two choices when the time comes for him to choose: God or woman. There are no other roads than the broad one that leads to Hell, as Jesus Christ worded it so delectably and so ruthlessly, and the narrow one that leads to perfection.

If he makes woman his reality, God will become to him an unreal poetic fancy, at the most a Bible bound in sharkskin, something showy that he moves along with his clock into the temple that he has built for his woman and that he names his home. If he chooses God, woman becomes for him an image of the perishable world; he views her as an emissary of vanity, a personification of the illusion.

Most of the songs in the world have been sung to these two lords of Heaven and Earth. There are various opinions concerning which were more beautiful, but certainly those that were sung to God are fadingly few in comparison to the enormous quantities that have been sung to woman. Every seventh day men go before the Lord, worship him like a magnificent but unreal poetic vision; for the other six days they lay their offerings at the altar of woman. Very few men sacrifice one night of their lives to keep vigil in the sight of the Lord; most offer woman all the nights of their human existence.

In my childhood I roamed throughout my father's house, full of mystic inspirations and love poems. Here and there throughout my native city I had my own sanctuaries, at least twelve as sacred as the Stations of the Cross are to the faithful, on streets where my beloved darlings had their homes. I composed verses about the chimneys on their houses, and the poor people in the cellars of those houses became more remarkable than other folk for living under the same roof as my Hallas, Huldas, and Svafas. Man is a polygamous animal. The love poem that I composed for one was intended for all.

I gave devout consideration to the type of reverence accorded to women. Men kissed her hand when they greeted her. In her ears they whispered the best things they could think of, the most beautiful things they knew. Men took care not to contradict her and paid more attention to what she said than to their own male kindred, even if what she said was pure nonsense. The more beautiful she was the more greedily men accepted every scatterbrained remark that blew from her lips. Men took her by the hand and helped her out of the car, led her up the steps and opened the door for her, sought to become her servants – even the wisest men. Men presented her with the most precious gifts, diamonds, ivory, feathers and furs, gold, incense, and myrrh. Men built houses and palaces for her and planted fruit trees in her gardens; men swamped her with beautifully veneered furniture, costly instruments, artists' masterpieces, tableware of porcelain and precious metals, Oriental rugs, antique silver, terra-cotta pitchers. And the poets sang for her their fairest odes; they adored her far beyond the Lord, yes, beyond Dionysus himself, raised her above the clouds, beat their breasts before her, paraded in front of her in sackcloth and ashes, tore out their hair, turned somersaults to her glory, and contorted themselves like the burlesque clown before the Virgin Mary in Anatole France.

It is a pitiable man who cannot content himself with any illusion, because he is much too strong to live among men. I am one of those strong, pitiable men: the hymns that have been sung to love are nothing but lies, hypocrisy, cant, baby talk, dupery, swindle, and bluff. Poetry, courtesy, all of this adoration, all of this creeping before a woman's feet: flowery obscenity, *obsession du sexe*. The poems and blandishments, kisses on the hand and bowing before her, all of this is for only one goal.

Love is so bound to a man's genitalia that a castrated man cannot feel it, a phenomenon so dependent on nutrition that a man who fasts is independent of its movements. It has been scientifically proven that a man and a woman who pledged each other their love for life will hate each other like devils after being starved in the same little room for half a month. It is the same story that Jóhann Sigurjónsson tells in the play about Fjalla-Eyvindur and his wife, the most profound drama written in a Nordic language.[36]

For some time I tried to imagine that there did in fact exist the thing that lyrical souls name Platonic love. But I have also seen to the bottom of the clamor about that.

It is true: easily awoken in men is admiration and enthusiasm for things that reveal to him spiritual beauty and higher dignity; noble love exists, love for God and men, ideals, and a better world. And spiritual sympathy exists between two souls who share the same God. But love is limited by sex. It is impossible to raise love above nature. On the other hand it might be said, concerning Platonic love, that it certainly exists – except between a man and woman. It is possible to love the Virgin Mary or Mona Lisa in a platonic way, like the thief who stole the latter from the Louvre one year, because Lisa is a picture and Mary a fairy tale. Those men are conceivable who fall in love with the "the idea of girlishness," which is a phrase that has been applied to one of Marcel Proust's characters,[37] who worship female portraits in fashion papers, even love flies, in one type of scarcely definable zoophytical eroticism, like the man in the story by Hamsun. It must be possible to love a telephone pole in a Platonic way – a woman never. A man loves and will love a woman because of her physical form, as Dr. Weininger puts it in one place in a more candid and coarse way than I care to repeat.

40.

In the kingdom of the lie and hypocrisy there is certainly no more heinous crime than to speak of love and woman without beating around the bush. Whoever has the nerve to speak of love and woman in any other language than lyrical gibberish "spoils youth," "sets fire to the foundation of society," is a "wolf in the fold, an obscene rogue, a misanthrope," and is either accused of indecency or declared insane, because one of the chief pillars of this kingdom is formed of the lies inherited from savagedom concerning the relationship between the sexes. If someone accuses society of having, as far as laws against exposure of children are concerned, no other goal than to produce cannon fodder for the enemies of mankind, encourages women to sublimate their femininity, and considers childbearing justifiable when the child is deposited like living payment in a welfare fund of the aggregate, then all of the world's hereditary lies go into a kind of bovine rut and savagedom devours that person with its fiery red jaws. The man who demands that women be something other than and more than sexual beings and childbearing machines is a pervert and a lunatic!

Ownership of women is the basis of all ownership.

Society is founded upon relics of tribal organization: the home, the family, and, as the cornerstone, man's ownership of women. And it is for this petty kingdom of his, built around his idol, woman, that a man fights. During times of peace one competes against all and all against one, and society is a bubbling witches' brew of "free-market competition," but during times of war those who profit from the ordering of society, the power-holders, trumpet the call of the fatherland, and the citizen sets out for the field of battle, filled with false hopes of conquest, fame, spoils, and every other conceivable emolument that he can lay on the altar of his wife.

But the World War was a great blessing, although a costly one. Nothing has focused man's critical faculties so much upon the millenial lies and deceptions of white society. The war taught men, among other things, how to live without women for four years, and to stare death in the face. Men took deep, long looks at themselves during those years.

It is proven better with each passing day that the school of the war was not worthless. Contemporary man no longer worships woman in the same blasphemous way as before; the basis of bourgeois society, ownership of women and the home, has lost validity in his eyes. His understanding of society has matured more in four years than it ever did in four centuries – in the direction of a socialist ideal. He has come to understand little by little that the health of the multitude is of far more value than the middle-class hearth, the value of culture higher than the value of women. And women will be forced to make one choice: to wake from their sexual giddiness, to rise against the spirit of the past that has pricked them with sleep-thorns, to dedicate their lives to the cultural values of the new world. Children are no longer raised under sooty rafters as soldiers of a petty kingdom; the children of modern man are raised by the great aggregate household; on the ruins of family life the communist state builds its magnificent nurturing sanctuary, where the child's soul gains the chance to connect itself to the collective soul of mankind, the brotherhood.

We squatted in the trenches for four years, say veterans of the

Great War. The mud reached up to our knees, rockets whined relentlessly over our heads, we suffered more torments than the condemned in Hell, and we thought of our women back home. We blessed those women who guarded our hearths, commending us to God in their prayers. We fight for you who endure at home, we thought. For your sake we long to become heroes; for your sake we undertake the most terrifying mortal trials.

We consoled ourselves by thinking that they were taking part in our lot in their thoughts; that they waited expectantly for all the news of the war, were sincerely grateful to us for our willingness to sacrifice. We were eager for the reunions, for the moments when they would lay their heads under our cheeks and would listen in blessed love-filled devotion to our stories of feats of prowess, as faithful as Odysseus' wife.

But what really happened?

We came home exhausted like old jades, with slackened vitality, shattered nerves, distraught dispositions. And do you think then that the women cared to sit at our knees to hear about the war? No, good fellows, they didn't care a bit about our recent sorrows; they yawned sullenly as soon as we recounted our adventures at Marne or Verdun; they wanted for Heaven's sake not to hear about our victories or defeats, let alone the terrors that we had faced day and night for four years while they sat idle by the fireside at home. Is anyone such a child as to believe what the great poets of the fatherland have written in books, that they blanketed us with tender passion and comforting affection? No, good gentlemen, they wanted to drink and dance. They asked us for new dresses and made us take them to glitzy nightclubs where existence was crystallized in the shimmy and the fox-trot. And there they introduced us to young gallants with monocles, waxed hair, and manicured nails. These were the lovers whom they had taken while we were abroad, while we danced with the Devil in the mud on the *champ d'honneur.* Before we left we forgot to girdle their thighs with chastity belts, as men did during the Crusades.

41.

Wife and harlot are two ghastly relics of the past, two waymarks on the same path pointing in the same direction, two congruent concepts. Both are products of a society that stands and falls with barbarian ideas of social order, condemned to have their loves turned into marketable commodities, of a society that has turned everything between Heaven and Earth into commercial wares, even the mercy of God and the boons of the virtuosos.

The harlot is the wife; the wife is the harlot. The one I buy for lifelong intercourse. All her life she receives beautiful clothing and food and drink at my table for being my whore. The other I buy for intercourse for one night, and on the next morning I give her one pound sterling so that she can get something to eat in an inexpensive teahouse and buy herself new shoes so that her feet won't get wet; for her feet are sensitive. What is the difference? One is hired by contract; the other sails in the wind; both give me the same thing. I am tied to one, and independent of the other. One is pretentious, the other content with little. One is fat, conceited, and stupid, like a general or an archbishop, because she knows that she is in a secure position. The other is poor, penniless, and experienced in life, like an Icelandic poet. One is impudent, more hypocritical, and more vacillating; the other is meek, guileless, and unostentatious. One is highly esteemed in silly charitable clubs, and there does what she can in order to keep her little light burning in a society that turns half of mankind into slaves and paupers. The other is the image of self-denial, ever-sacrificing; she sacrifices her honor and happiness, body and soul, sacrifices her entire self to everyone, everywhere. One raises children that are later used as cannon fodder for the king, freedom, and the fatherland, or else that die of starvation and hardship. The other is a vagabond between the glass houses whence hypocrisy and hesitation cast stones, and where self-complacency grimaces in contempt.

It is nothing but invention when a woman, panting, throws her arms around the neck of her lover after he whispers a marriage proposal, and replies: "I am yours forever!" Such things never happen except in rotten poetry and fifty-aurar fairy tales written for maid-servants and the bourgeoisie.

When a man makes his marriage proposal the woman always gives the same answer: "What are you offering me? What will you pay me? Will I be given dining-room furniture, living-room furniture, and a piano? Will you feed me roasted chicken? Will you dress me up in ostrich feathers? Will you buy me a car?" Although I might only have the means to buy her an ordinary Ford, she would rather take the man who can give her a five-seater Fiat – and no woman can withstand a Rolls-Royce. If I don't feel like attending to her needs, she runs back home to her father's house. If I don't bring her a brace of codlings tied by the tail for lunch and plucked fowl for dinner, she takes me to court. She loves me if I give her money, baubles, houses, musical instruments, expensive clothing, plenty to eat. And if I succeed in lying my way to the highest ranks in society, I become her best ornament. But if I offer her nothing but my love, nothing to eat, no perks, then it is hopeless to count on her fidelity. If I go abroad and stay away from home for five years, she stops loving me altogether. If I ask, "Why, though I love you, should I be obliged to support you?" then I am a scurvy rogue. But beyond everything else, she hates me and scorns me if my sexual organs are out of line. Although she might have promised me all her love with the most fervent words in the language, burning kisses, and glittering tears the day before the wedding, I can rely on the fact that she will let the first Don Juan that we meet on our honeymoon take her as his mistress. There are daredevils in the south who spend their lives in expensive hotels and have made it their sport and life's work to seduce newly wedded women on honeymoons. It is said that few men are more successful in their work than they are.

42.

The older a man becomes, the more vain become the questions that he ponders, the more paltry the decisions that he makes. It is a rare exception to meet a man older than thirty who thinks. To grow older signifies a man's surrender to facts. He no longer changes water into wine, no longer gives orders, is no longer a creative philosopher. His cleverness from this point on is confined to taking a position toward things as they are, settling himself down in such a way that the flaws he fought against most often in his youth cause him the least amount of trouble as possible. To grow older is to lose the nerve to try to untie the Gordian knot, to settle with whatever one wasn't able to conquer. The soul of a middle-aged man is solidified lava.

The time will come when I no longer contemplate pressing questions. I will be sucked into pittances and day-to-day quarrels, seated with professors, members of parliament, and other wretches, honorable-looking men with well-trimmed hair, probably mustaches, discussing in solemn tones "the way out of the straits," considering myself important, and paying heed to no counsel but simmering.

The enigmas of life are stilled in my mind like water in a peat pit; they evaporate like standing water in the heat of summer. Those that never left me alone from morning till night and prevented me from sleeping at night – what are they now? The adventurous chapters in the first part of my autobiography and scarcely that, forgotten reveries. Instead my mind is filled with answers to questions that I never asked. In my youth I asked, What is God? In my old age I will write scholarly books on the details of court life in France during the reign of Louis XVI. I am quite satisfied to have forgotten the things that I wanted to know, and to know all sorts of things about which I never asked. My nervous system has reached a calmer ambit, the secretions of various of my glands have changed their function, my impulses have been stilled, the wavelengths of my thoughts curtailed.

Most pitiful is that this condition came over me bit by bit without my being aware of it. The spiritual hardening doesn't announce itself soon enough to give me any opportunity to shoot a bullet through my head in time; my adult years inebriate me like Jesuitical wine. "Dear ladies and gentlemen!" say I, sweetly and idiotically. "I pray for understanding for the convulsions of my youth!"

The adult years that lock their necrotic claws onto a man's heart muscle appear to my eyes as the most fateful disgrace. It would be more fortunate to die than to be forced to take a seat on a bench with men who stitch up the rotten holes in society and urge the paupers to simmer their potatoes slowly.

"Good gentlemen!" I write, after I have become an adult. "We must all be thrifty and economize! The remedy for mankind's troubles is to simmer, simmer, simmer!"

And if I am diligent enough in preaching simmering, I may finally receive a medal of honor from the king for my "achievements in the service of the fatherland." I will be granted the Order of the Falcon and the Dannebrog, the Order of Saint Olav, the Iron Cross and the Order of the Garter, until I clatter all over like a sea monster.

43.

London, New Year, 1925. Dear sir. I have not yet reached the conclusion of the letter that I started last summer. Allow me to add a few words.

You think that I am a communist, a stubborn pursuer of political dreams. No, dear sir, I have given up. I couldn't damn well care less about mankind. I am at my wit's end. I beg you to help me. I must be quartered – there is no other way.

Tell me, dear sir, what business does man have appearing in the light of day?

All winter long I have been struggling to nourish within me three inclinations that can overcome man: namely, homosexuality, drug addiction, and the desire to commit suicide. In these three passions I descry the highest ideals of mankind. Mankind cannot aspire to a higher ideal than to die out; life is the worst enemy of the living and "death is the victory over life," as one of the sages of our time says.

It is a madman's rage to wish to struggle for the future or for the welfare of mankind.

And I would like to know, what comfort is it to me whether people live well? People matter nothing to me. People are completely different from me. It is nothing other than Christian blather, founded on faith in God the Father, that we ought to love our brothers and do them good. But I do not believe in God, and therefore it is entirely all the same to me whether mankind feels better or worse. The only thing that makes me feel content is to live for myself, not because I love myself, but rather because I despise myself and long to destroy myself. I despise people as I despise myself. I amuse myself with the idea of sticking my bayonet through children and breaking the teeth out of ravished Negresses with the heel of my shoe, like the European soldiers in Kattinou. I have the right to do all that I will. For to whom in Hell am I obligated if God does not exist? For what do I exist besides myself? If God does not exist, then it is a sin to live for anyone besides oneself.

A living being emerges into the light of day only to die. Why should a man struggle to perpetuate his race when his only end is to die? A man is born into vanity and delusion; he suffers, endures, and fears for a few years, but each time the clock strikes, death has come nearer by one hour. My life is like a spark beneath a hoof. In one transient blink of the eye I appear on the surface of the Earth, and I am not even allowed to choose the color of the hair on my head. My heartbeats are measured, my breaths counted – just a few more times, and then it is all over. I am the husk where helplessness took up its abode, the quaking ghost in the faint glimmer between two endless darknesses, two sleeps. Why is man not commanded to cease from renewing his kin? Why this eternal work of Sisyphus, up and down the slope? A man sows but is never allowed to behold what he reaps, weaves and is clothed with derision!

> He weaves and is clothed with derision,
> Sows, and he shall not reap.
> His life is a watch or a vision
> Between a sleep and a sleep.[38]

Animals are of a dissimilar, higher nature than man; they are spiritless creatures, without investigative self-consciousness. What exists on our Earth that is higher, more perfect, and more holy than a snow-white sheep on a midsummer day? It is man's reward that he received as a cradle gift a tiny measure of passions that seek gratification. What should his goal be other than to gratify his passions and die? *"Il piacere é la sola virtù,"* "Self-gratification is the only virtue."

When I was seventeen years old I took part in Spanish and French nighttime debauchery in which naked women, painted from the crowns of their heads to the soles of their feet, performed fancy lesbian dances in between running to giant Negroes tied down to couches, while the audience lay in each other's arms on the floor. The gratification of sexual demands is man's highest pleasure, and justifiable only when it is gratified in such a way that no new individuals are born. Homosexuality is the highest level of sexual satisfaction. Of all the paths of gratification, that one is lowest and most brutish, most blind and imperfect, which leads to such a fatal consequence as the birth of new people. The goal of man is to destroy man. The goal of culture is to destroy man. The goal of wisdom is to destroy man. *"Der Mensch ist Etwas das überwunden werden muß." "Satan conduit le bal!"* [39] Homosexuality, drug addiction, and suicide are the joyful extirpation of the final and highest beings on Earth. The deepest desire of lovers is to be reminded of death in their embraces. Only death gratifies love.

Behold! These ideals point to end times.

44.

I do not think; have never thought. I know. It is my fate and misfortune to have always known without having thought or learned. He who needs to think and learn is endowed with the talent of never knowing anything. And that is a great grace. The noblest creature on Earth is the ass, because Christ rode one into Jerusalem.

A man's aptitude is a product of time and patience, says Balzac.

But my power is revealed in impatient coruscations. The deepest perceptions charge through my soul like crashes of thunder. The history of the Earth, the history of the solar system, the experience of mankind – all of it streams through my being in galvanic revelations. I am the mirror image of the development of mankind, of its grandeur and its pettiness, its distress, its wisdom, and its error. I am creation itself in the terrifying night gleam of sleepless self-consciousness. I cannot sleep; I cannot dream; I cannot forget. I stay awake, see, see through everything; I am clairvoyant; nothing can be concealed from me; I am everything, the universe my prison; the ends of the world slumber in my breast; I am alone; nothing exists but me, a feeble ephemera; I am suffering itself, dread, panic itself; death, it is I.

People suffer; all around me are people suffering. They suffer from freedom and oppression, from penury and opulence, from ignorance and knowledge, from love and hate, from God and Satan, from what they are and also what they are not. I met a little girl on the street this morning with a milk jug in one hand and bread in the other; she was walking slowly and carefully, so as not to slip on the ice, and the bread was almost as big as she was – she too was on the road to Golgotha. I felt so much pity for her, this poor little thing who walked so carefully for fear of breaking her jug, that I started sobbing when I came home.

What power do great men have? All that they accomplish is to rob the people of their ability to bear their fate. They drive the people out into the most desolate wilderness in the hope of the Promised Land, and in the wilderness the people collapse and die. At its best the Promised Land, the dreamland, proved to be seven times more accursed than the old one. It requires a great deal of childishness to fight for an ideal or solve a puzzle, because in the morning the ideal becomes soiled underwear that has gone from harlot to harlot, and the puzzle a Masonic symbol. Mankind has struggled and fought under the banners of its great men for a million years only to confirm the fact that nowhere is there a land of bliss, only various forms of suffering. There is a lichen called manna growing on rocks, and a rainbow in the sky, faith, the covenant with the Lord, but no one has ever reached its end, because it is only a mirage in man's eye – and those who eat manna get sick to their stomachs. Primitive man makes holes in the ground, and the holes gape like wounds over his suffering while he lives, and fall together over his remains when he dies, like a scab over a wound. We cannot go any further. No one has ever reached a fairer dreamland than a three-ell-long grave. After a few years the worms promenade over my rotted head.

I find myself compelled to consider the three greatest giants of the last generation: Tolstoy, Strindberg, and Nietzsche.

Tolstoy wanted to help the world with wisdom and philanthropy, and died a martyr of despair. I know of few pilgrimages more dismal than the flight of the old man from Yasnaya Polyana a few days before he died. He almost runs, as if trying to convince himself that he is young and immortal, and then disappears and dies. No one became wiser or better; in Paris a few fanatics founded a club, that is all.

Nietzsche wanted to overcome man with the superman, and when he saw that all things came to naught he wrote to Rome and requested an audience with the pope. What a lamentable recourse to descry finally his last refuge under the protective wing of the Christian delusion! And he went insane in Torino two days after he wrote the letter, then lived for eleven years like a beast, imagining that he was Christ on the cross!

Strindberg wanted to save mankind from its misery using all of the medicines that have been tried on it since the start of the history of mankind. And yet this titanic, universal homeopath lived his whole life as a wretched target for the persecutions of Jesus Christ, until he himself surrendered to this cross-madness on his deathbed, and now one may read the inscription on the wooden cross over his grave in Stockholm, worded according to his own instructions: "*O crux, ave, spes unica!*"[40]

Even the most perfect man is nothing but a plaything of derision. Man is nothing but vanity.

45.

Chi siete voi che uscite dall' eterno silenzio?

Fausto Martini[41]

What will is it that conjures up spirits from the mysterious depths of unconsciousness and makes them dance a whole lifetime by its hypnotic power, curse their provenance, and fear the way to dust? "*Gieb, ja ergieb, grausamster Feind, mir—dich!*"[42] shouts Nietzsche.

Once I was up north in Kaldidalur, in the Icelandic wilderness, where the path leads over dapple gray boulders destitute and dead, and in the distance tower the glaciers like unsculpted images of saints, those holy and soulless gods of the wastelands. But in the middle of Kaldidalur there grows a little plant. I don't know its name, but I saw it after I'd been traveling for half a day. It was growing alone there in the endless boulder-strewn tracts of land. And it bowed down when it saw me, because that was the first time since it was born that it had seen a living thing. I tore it out of the ground because it was exactly long enough and soft enough for me to use to clean my pipe.

I ask, why does the wave of life try to break forth from the mysterious depths? What is the goal of this blind struggle against triumphant death? Life is on the wrong path! It has no home in the material world; it dies! Poor being, you arise from eternal silence in order to die.

Everything that lives perishes, families as well as individuals; the sun burns out and the solar system dies of cold and starvation like little children. Ancient prophecies proclaim that the God of Judgment will come in fire. But this is false prophecy: the God of Judgment will come in ice. The sun has changed noticeably in the last ten months, says Soupault:

> And soon the sun shall darken
> The earthly clay disperse.
> And all things turn to nothing
> And no more universe.[43]

I stand at my window, look out at the fog, and ask, where will I be when the sun burns out – I, this perceiving speck of the universe, this questioning lump of earth, this trembling grain of dust, this husk of helplessness – where will I be then?

Heaven and Earth, have pity on my paltriness, for I am so weak and small, so ridiculous in my desire for the Almighty, such an atrocious symbol of death in my hope for immortality! The jackal howls in the wilderness until it drops down dead. And vultures pick the flesh from its bones, and the sand polishes them white. Far out in the desert there rises up from the sand a five-thousand-year-old monument to an ancient king. Written upon it are these words: "Tremble, pitiful man, for I am the King of Kings; all the nations of the Earth quake in fear!" All that is left of this powerful king's realm is this monument. His bones have long been lost in the sand that now covers his ancient kingdom.

Tremble, pitiful man!

46.

Where am I able to satisfy my soul? I search in the innermost recesses of my heart; I search up and down and every which way, overturn everything, like a man who has lost his collar button beneath some furniture. And I find nothing at all that could possibly satisfy my soul.

Excelsior – higher? No, it's just a name on hotels and laundry soap.

Eternal development, higher and higher, without beginning or end, eternity after eternity, where there is no boundary – what would that be? A vicious circle!

The other idea, development over the course of several eternities, until I am sucked into divinity, into a nirvana of motionless, complete perfection – what would that be? Nothing but utter lack and death.

Do I desire the Heavenly Kingdom and eternal bliss? No, dear God, I cannot even bear to hear these things named. It is as if someone were offering me eternal drunkenness. I would take a jazz band over angels' harps. I would rather go to the Tivoli or Luna Park than to Paradise. I get squeamish when I think about the elect: pure simpletons, *bonhommes,* peasants who have not even read Anatole France, Gabriele d'Annunzio, or Marcel Proust, not to mention knowing nothing about the most recent movements in literature and philosophy, such as surrealism or relativity theory! The last thing I want to do is spend all eternity in the company of patriarchs from the Old Testament, captious scholastic philosophers from the centuries before printing, fanatical martyrs, hysterical maidens who turned their backs on their sexuality, entered convents and "beheld visions," or wealthy bourgeois from Jerusalem or Reykjavík. What dainty company that would be! No – on to Valhalla, then, to fight with the fallen warriors!

Perhaps there is no paradise on either this side or the other more desirable than the Icelandic dales.

One spring day I will pack my belongings and set out for the dales. I will build myself a shack, even up the cobbles with a hammer and cut pieces of turf with a scythe, stack them in layers and put rafters on top. Though a man might have only two goats and a withy-roofed cottage, it's better than a prayer. In the summer I will rise with the birds of the moor and start to cut the grass; blessed aroma of the earth, say I, blessed mountains! And when winter arrives the lambs will eat out of the palms of my hands and the cow will stare at me with huge, blunt, tender eyes, and low when I pass by. And the dog will close its brown, faithful eyes and sleep at the footboard of its master.

There my heart is directed, there and no further.

> There where holy mountains tower
> Toward northern winds so sparkling pure
> Where Iceland thrives in winter's power
> Where you, my soul, in bliss endure;
> On peaks and passes desert fowl
> Flit through frost without complaint
> And glaciers in their vastness growl
> Awful as unsculpted saints
> Where Urðhæð, Einbúi[44] watch by night
> And white volcanoes scrape the air
> And ancient clefts proclaim their might
> At last, my nymph, I spy you there!
> Upon your lips felicity naps
> And from your eyesight vigilance glows,
> While soft about you maidenhood wraps
> Its linen frosts of tender snows.

Here is all that I love; here is my church; here will I wake and sleep, live and die. The natural beauty of the Icelandic mountains is my lover and my wife – let me die in her arms; let my soul be joined to her in death!

In Skerpla[45] the mountain hall is polished and beautified, everything hums with the purl of the brooks and birdsong on the eternal days of spring. And in Sólmánuður[46] my mountains are woven with dignity and tranquility, cloaked in mirage and dream, the nights grow darker, the songs of swans resound from moorland lakes, and from my hot springs ascend lazy bright fogs that slink back and forth throughout my dale. What mythic nobility!

It is my innermost desire to be able to walk here again, to be able to roam like a peculiar bird over the Icelandic mountains on quiet midsummer nights after I am dead.

Book Four

47.

On a cold, clear day in Þorri, 1924, the *Gullfoss* churns into the harbor. A small group of people waits at the quayside, folk who are expecting friends on the ship. The north wind is cold and bitter at the harbor: men thrust their fur hats farther down onto their heads; women hide their powdered red faces in the turned-up collars of their fur coats.

Toward the front of the group stand two women clad in fur, one elderly, the other young, and a short distance away waits their car, which the driver keeps running so that the engine will not cool down: this is the Ylfingamóðir herself, along with her twenty-something foster daughter, Diljá Þorsteinsdóttir. At a suitable distance away stands one of the Ylfingur Company's executive managers.

"The Ylfingur Company has purchased three new trawlers," writes *Morgunblaðið*. "Today Director Örnólfur is expected home from a six-week stay abroad. His itinerary included stops in Antwerp, Hamburg, and London."

The ocean liner draws slowly nearer and nearer, coated with ice from top to bottom as if returning from a trip to the pole. There was little happening on deck, few passengers; at this time of year only those who have urgent business set out on long voyages over the Atlantic.

In a short time the mother and her foster daughter catch sight of the Director. He is standing in the center of the upper deck, large-looking and strapping in his long dark overcoat, with its otter-fur collar turned upward over his ears so that it reaches the brim of his stiff black hat, wearing thick-soled steak brown boots, light-colored spats. As soon as he sets eyes on the women waiting for him on shore, he pulls a white-gloved hand from his coat pocket, waves two or three times, doffs his hat courteously, and smiles.

The ocean liner docks and stands out imposing and majestic among motorboats, small dirty fishing vessels, and trawlers; workers tie the moorings with several secure twists, and a bridge is set up connecting ship and shore. After several moments Örnólfur is standing in front of mother and foster daughter; he puts down his briefcase, doffs his hat again, and greets them. He has come home the same as when they said farewell to him here at the quay six weeks ago, his hands warm, his heart cold, his teeth pure white or banded in gold when he smiles, his hair just as carefully parted at the center of his forehead, his eyes as keen and distant as before. Only Ylfingur has added three trawlers to its fleet.

Every other hat in the group is lifted to the Director of Ylfingur; various people shake his hand; snow-white Reykjavík maidens wish him a pleasant homecoming with furtive coquetry in their glances, and the diplomat smiles to both sides in his well-known way.

He speaks privately to the company's executive manager for a moment, listens to this man's report, smiles, takes several telegrams from his pocket. They leaf through them despite the cold; he points to particular words, gives explanations, then shoves the telegrams carelessly back into his pocket. They lift their hats to each other; Örnólfur gets into the car, sits down next to his mother, and the car drives off.

When they arrive at home, Madam Valgerður sits down at the tea table across from her son and asks the news, because she is like every other mother, expecting her sons to have news to tell every time they return from abroad. But reporting the news suits no one less than the Director. For him nothing of interest ever occurs. He is like an unwilling child learning its catechism: every answer has to be specially tugged out of him. He leans back in the easy chair and raps on the armrests a few times, obviously pondering something entirely different than the news.

"Did you meet Grímúlfur?" asks the mother.

"Yes."

"Where?"

"Le Havre."

"How was he?"

"Well."

"Were you together long?"

"We went to Germany."

"Where are mother and son?"

"I don't know–" but he stopped and corrected himself: "Yes, Steinn is in England."

"But Jófríður?"

"I forgot to ask."

"You never change, my boy," answered his mother, and she offered him a piece of cake, as if to call his attention to the fact that she was speaking to him. "I don't suppose you saw Steinn in England?"

He takes a quick sip of his tea, stands up swiftly, goes to the telephone and makes a call, speaks, hangs up, and sits back down at the table. After this three-minute delay he finally answers his mother:

"Huh? Steinn? Yes, I saw Steinn."

The phone call seemed to have brought him to his senses. He looks over at Diljá, sips at his tea again, lights a cigarette, and repeats with a smile:

"I saw Steinn."

"How is the boy?" asked the madam somewhat more forcefully than before.

"Well."

"What's he up to?"

"I think he's busy writing poems," answered the Director, and he shrugged his shoulders slightly, although in such a way that the movement more likely expressed doubt as to whether he had given the correct answer concerning his nephew's occupation rather than disdain for him, because in the next breath he smiled again.

"Heaven help us!" said Madam Valgerður. "Is it out of the question that the boy will ever think an earnest thought in his life?"

"I don't know," said the Director, and he glanced over again at Diljá, who sat hunched forward in her seat, staring at several tea leaves floating in her cup.

After a moment she looked up. She looked straight at Örnólfur, candidly, and asked:

"Then he didn't say anything about coming home?"

"He wasn't planning on it."

She swirled her cup once more, making the tea leaves that had settled on the bottom float up again. Örnólfur continued to look at her.

"What do you think will become of the child?" the old madam asked her son.

"I said to him, 'You forgot to comb your hair this morning, Nephew!'" answered the Director, as if he thought this an unforgettably amusing remark.

"Comb your hair! Good Heavens! Steinn, that dandy who was always paying visits to salons to have his hair styled?"

"His shirt-sleeves were dirty," said the Director.

The madam then gasped for breath and said:

"Steinn Elliði in a dirty shirt! No, now this is not to my liking at all! Where is the child staying?"

"He lives in an old villa in one of the suburbs of London. Villa Warren Hastings in Hounslow if I remember correctly."

Diljá looked up again and asked:

"He didn't send his greetings?"

"No, now that you mention it!" said the Director, and he laughed coldly.

"Is he there alone?"

"The only one I saw there besides him was an old butler. I recall that the place had 'Carrington' on the door."

"Do you think that the boy is still in his right mind?" asked the madam.

The Director didn't answer this, but cut a wedge of the cake, ate it quickly, drained his cup, lit a new cigarette and left the other one burning in the ashtray, then stood up.

"Didn't he have anything interesting to say?" asked Diljá after he had stood up, and she hunched down again over her cup.

"I don't remember clearly what he said," answered the Director. He positioned himself behind his chair, placed one hand on its back, looked over the table, then at his cigarette. "I don't have much practice at figuring out what poets are saying; it's not all that easy to catch their meaning. But as far as I could understand, he's up to his ears in Marxism."

"What's that now?" asked the madam.

"It's that thing in Russia."

"God help me, the child's become a Bolshevik!"

"He said something about the Director of Ylfingur having nothing other to look forward to than to be executed. 'Alright then!' I said. 'Then someone better at it can take over! Maybe you'll take over, Nephew!' He said that the gospel of modern times demanded not only that disciples forsake their fathers and mothers, lovers and friends, but also that they be ready to lead them to the chopping block. 'Umm-hmm,' said I, 'we certainly are great men, my dear Hrólfur.'[47] Of course I saw that it was useless for us to try to have a conversation."

"The child is crazy!" said the old madam.

"Idealist," answered the Director, smiling.

Foster mother and foster daughter gave each other terrified glances, but the Director disappeared into the next room.

48.

Örnólfur appears like a phantom in the dining room twice a day; he is a visitor in his own house. No one knows this man; no one knows who he is; it is always as if he has arrived recently from a foreign country.

All morning he is at the company's offices, but at twelve-thirty footsteps are heard on the steps, steady and secure. He brushes the snow off his cloak in the foyer, goes into his bathroom, and sits down at the table at one o'clock. And although he speaks little it is quite wrong to think that his silence is caustic; his presence is comforting, like a protective wall.

If he has no business in town he works in his private office at home during the afternoons, most often alone, sometimes with an assistant, a young lawyer. An incredible number of people had business with him. People came and went all day: ship captains, sailors, lawyers, merchants, bank directors, members of parliament, common workers, smiths, machinists, reporters, foreigners; he must have spoken to a hundred people a day. He sat in meetings long into the nights; he was involved in lawsuits, put together court documents, had long discussions with litigators, made court appearances. This is how it went day after day.

Although Diljá was for the most part proud of Örnólfur's merits, she often regretted how their acquaintanceship had changed since she was little. He was certainly still courteous and gentle, even more courteous and gentle than he had been during his years as a student, but the cordiality in his deportment seemed to have been for the most part erased.

When Diljá was a girl she didn't know anyone more sincere or humane than him. He was even more beloved to her than her father; he was like a big brother. He alone always had enough time for her; gave her answers to everything that she asked; came to her when others had forgotten her; paid attention to her childish interests. And she never had a wish so absurd that she could not be sure Örnólfur would grant. She always went to Örnólfur. If she wanted to go to the movies, in complete opposition to her foster mother's ban, she secretly went to Örnólfur, and they both went together like little sister and big brother. And if she wanted to buy some silly thing that no one else would ever dream of buying, she could always count on Örnólfur agreeing that it was completely natural and correct; then they would both go on a shopping spree and buy and buy: she chose, he paid. If she wanted to invite her friends on a trip during the summer, she went to Örnólfur, and he would fetch the car immediately, sit down at the wheel like a dutiful servant, and ask: "Where to?" And he would be answered: "Up to Mosfellssveit or down to Álftanes," and they would drive away, and the little girls would sing and laugh in the sunshine.

During his last year in lyceum she was six years old. That winter he had taught her to read. As incredible as it might otherwise seem that the Director of Ylfingur had taught a little girl to read, it had indeed been done; she sat on his knees for several evenings and before she knew it she had gotten the trick. They looked into each other's faces, she little and bright, he grown-up and black-browed; they looked into each other's eyes and laughed from sheer delight. The spring that he graduated she had become so learned that she could read the *Book of Youth* all by herself, and *Nonni's Journey to*

Copenhagen, and she knew the stories of Snow White and Little Red Riding Hood. It was not until the next year, when she had to start learning about Abraham, Isaac, Jacob, and other boring men, that she noticed her regret at having learned to read.

Örnólfur studied economics, and spent a year and a half in America after leaving lyceum. Then he studied various subjects in Germany or Denmark and graduated from the University in Copenhagen in the spring of 1915. During the summer months he normally stayed in Reykjavík.

And although he would disappear in the fall, lost in the bottomless whirlpools of huge foreign cities, and nothing would be heard from him unless he happened to publish an excessively dry and boring essay about international banking in some journal or other, he never forgot the little girl whom he had taught to read; always when he came home during the summers he brought her newfangled things and continued to be her good old Örnólfur; she always looked forward to his annual homecoming.

Of course the difference between their ages, their knowledge, and their maturity was too great now for them to be able to associate any longer as playmates. They both developed in their own way: she grew toward her dreams, he toward a life of activity. And the more that her mind matured, the more she realized that he was too canny, too attached to the palpable gravity of reality, to be able to become a true resident in the whirling "city of beautiful nonsense,"[48] her young girl's dreams. His earnest concerns were a closed book to her, too distant to be able to touch any thread in her soul. But although the frankness of youth had surely diminished in the grown-up girl, the sympathy between them remained nonetheless, and she was more at ease in the presence of this strapping foreignish man than in that of most others. The years passed by. It was not their fault that they were two different worlds, but rather the fault of creation: friendship is like a crossroads. When they saw each other they still smiled, as if their memories of youth stirred involuntarily in their minds, and although their own particular matters of interest were incomprehensible to each other, an unwavering kindness on both of their parts bore witness to their mutual understanding. Although his face might be laden with concerns, he never forgot to treat her considerately. He always opened the door for her as he did when she was little. He would always make sure that she wasn't cold, just as before. If they went for a drive in the countryside, it was she who decided where they went, and when she didn't want to go any farther they would turn back.

All of her behavior toward him was characterized in a certain way by an impulse that is stronger in young women than in any other beings, the love of service: her concern for his welfare was ever-watchful. When he went abroad it was she who supervised the packing of his trunks, picked out his clothing, made sure that he didn't forget anything. If he had to go to a banquet or to some other formal function, she would trust no one but herself to brush his suit. During the winters she would sometimes go into his room to make sure that the heater was turned on, so that it would be warm when he arrived. If he happened to take a nap at midday, she took genuine delight in answering the phone and saying that he was not at home. Sometimes she would secretly switch the phone connection before he came to the dining room, so that it would ring in the empty office out front while he was eating, and not in the adjoining sitting room.

49.

Perhaps it had not been made clear to her that in philosophical terms the same power was required for practical accomplishments as spiritual ones, but all the same, she knew that Örnólfur was a great man. She never mentioned it, never once let it be seen in her glance, but she felt it: the air around him was charged, his will was a silent primordial element. She felt it whenever she heard his soft, strong voice in the foyer.

She knew that the productivity of the Ylfingur Company had first begun to reach its peak only after Örnólfur decided to put his powers, his knowledge and financial genius, into the company's service. While Ylfingur was in the hands of the foster brothers, Grímúlfur and her father, Þorsteinn, other fishing companies were more successful. Five years after Örnólfur entered the picture Ylfingur lorded it over every other fishing company in the country.

It was scarcely a secret that Örnólfur Elliðason was one of the chief pillars of Icelandic society: "Parliament and the government are nothing but scarecrows in the egg-laying grounds of Ylfingur," as the Socialist newspaper put it in its imagistic way. When the "Ylfingur Company" was spoken of, everybody knew that what was meant beyond anything else was Örnólfur Elliðason. When people said that the fishing industry had subsumed all of the country's other industries, people meant this one man, because fishing was Ylfingur and Ylfingur was Örnólfur Elliðason. When the loudest voices proclaimed that the country and the people were in the grip of the merciless claws of capitalism, they meant the merciless claws of

Örnólfur Elliðason. When the farmers formed a political party to protect their interests inside and outside of Parliament from the devouring practices of the fishing industry, and handed out abusive tracts vituperating the Grimsby rabble and "the trumpery," their missiles were aimed at this svelte, amicable businessman who had never said a disrespectful thing about a cat, let alone a man. And when the Socialists held their May Day parade, raised banners covered with some sort of grandiose red-lettered nonsense and delivered speeches on Austurvöllur concerning the fraudulency of capitalism, their demonstration symbolized nothing other than the groans of the people under the yoke of Örnólfur Elliðason.

There was never any rebuke too strong for him: he was the one whom untold thousands of oppressed cried out most passionately to see dragged down. It was he "who bribed members of Parliament with loans, expensive gifts, and banquets, and dictated terms to the ministers," and, "when voting takes place on important matters in Parliament the same poltergeist can always be found roaming about the antechambers. It is Örnólfur Elliðason, peering in through the doorways, keeping an eye on his subordinates. It is said that they don't betray the conservative flag so easily if they are shown 'the smile.'" "At the end of a bad year one can always be certain that an ingratiating lanky fellow with a golden tongue slinks in through the back doors of the banks: this is Örnólfur Elliðason. He makes suggestions, using carefully chosen blandishments, concerning whether it might not be more prudent for the banks to empty their vaults into his company's hands than for the state to go bankrupt. He asks, with deepest respect for the public, whether he might not be allowed to reach into the pocketbook of every man, woman, and child in the country, and filch a third of the value of every króna so that Ylfingur could continue to speculate. Although he is dapper and smiles warmly when he meets with the representatives of the workers concerning wage negotiations, various people know for a fact that he has been seen these days in Parliament, frowning and banging his fist on the table." "It is Örnólfur Elliðason who hands out hundreds of thousands in secret to newspaper reporters, to have them publicly propagate shameless political lies, scandalous stories, and insults among all of the honorable people in the country, cleverly fabricated falsehoods about the situation in Soviet Russia, praise for the noble-mindedness of the millionaires in the West, essays and poems by national poets who live by begging from the capitalists and then allow themselves to be used as dupes of advertising in order to panegyrize conservatism," and so on.

Every day Diljá read new criticisms of Örnólfur, direct and indirect. Those bigmouthed cads and hacks never grew tired of letting their printing machines spew out curses and slander over the public. How often had she gotten a lump in her throat from chagrin and disgust or struck her fists together in anger when she let herself be tempted to read those rags that were brought to the house every morning?

But at twelve-thirty his voice would be heard in the hallway, or just his footsteps, resolute and calm. And when he sits at the table, and she beholds the quietude, the security, the shine in his face, she forgets everything that had perturbed her in the morning; she feels only that this man overshadows his opponents. How wonderful to be superior to one's opponents, she thinks, because a woman admires a man's power and not his cause. And she is filled with silent pride to share her meals with a man who has willed and achieved more than any of the other 99,999 – and who walks every day like a foreigner into his own dining room.

50.

If it happened that she woke at night to the cries of the loose women who let drunken men take them home from the dances, a long time would pass before she would be able to sleep again, because those deranged voices that tore through the quiet of the night spoke the language of life. Life was not reading a novel in a soft chair. And she realized a long time ago that nothing was further from life than a peaceful sleep between white bedcovers. Life in all of its intensity and brutality was crystallized in one shout that emerged from the still of the night. In her insomnia her heart beat more briskly than during the day. Her heart remained silent in the daytime; at night she could hear it beating.

And she asked, "Why am I being kept here?" She had become too mature a woman to be able to sit at the window any longer during the spring and let herself dream something blue, eternal, and untouchable. She no longer thirsted for things that no one understands, she longed for the fulfillment of life.

Maybe people thought that she was made to be a happy spinster who would pose as a Francophile at club meetings; or just how long did folk think that she could bear to watch time stand still? Oh, how much time did she plan to waste listening to cajoling aunts, well-bred madams, and the other riffraff talk about composure, wisdom, and wariness, and spend the rest of the time complimenting themselves? Why didn't she throw herself headlong into blessed and careless mirth like other women of her age? Why didn't she misuse her handclasp and her glance like other women? Why didn't she play with fire?

Her heart in her breast accused her in her wakefulness and repeated, "Cow-ard, cow-ard" – until she promised that she would leave this place and enter into vagrancy and foolishness, lose herself and be happy like other women, and then become a nurse when she had grown too weary of being an actress. "Away, away, out into life!" she said. "Out into reality! Anything is better than novels and dreams, anything better than a sound sleep between unstained sheets! Away, away!"

But when the sun came up she opened her eyes and discovered that she hadn't moved. She hadn't gone away; instead she had slept. The walls were the same as yesterday and the day before yesterday. In the house where fate had condemned her to grow up nothing was ever said, even less done, both by night and by day, about which it would have been possible for the walls to spread rumors if they had had eyes and ears and been able to speak. And she felt that if something were done within these walls that no one ought to know, they would tumble down and bury them all alive.

And the day today came like the day yesterday and the day before yesterday; the clock kept on with its dull, silly strokes, but time stood still. Every step that Diljá Þorsteinsdóttir took was measured, every word that she spoke carefully considered. She walked about here like a phantom from another world while thousand-colored reality glittered outside, a beggar woman in her inner life while other women cried out on the squares in a blessed ecstasy of life and let men take them home.

51.

One Sunday visitors came to Örnólfur. It was late in the day: Madam Valgerður was at a meeting of the Women's Club, the servants had the day off, Diljá had to wait on the guests. They were ship captains, ponderous men, fat and red and loud like bad weather; they laughed like berserkers who had just arrived from sea and were ready to set out immediately on another sea voyage. It was like a raging storm suddenly subsiding into silence when they left.

Against his habit Örnólfur remained at home after their departure, and the girl felt an instinctive anxiety when he came into the sitting room, after all the others had left, for many years had passed since they had been alone in the house. This is something new, she thought. He walked in carrying some foreign notebooks, tables or registers, nothing but numbers, dressed in a long robe. He added several pieces of wood to the hearth fire, and then sat down opposite the girl in another easy chair in front of the fireplace.

She looked up from the seventh or eighth volume of *Jean-Christophe* and realized that it was the first time since she was a child that she returned his smile without anyone else being present. She quickly looked down again at *Jean-Christophe* to hide the blush on her cheeks.

"Where's Mother?" he asked.

But she pretended to be sunk in the book and answered without looking up:

"At some old women's meeting."

"You're not going out at all?" he asked.

"No." Her girlfriend, whom she named, had rung and asked her to come to the cinema at nine, but she had said no. "I want to go to bed early tonight," she added.

"Are you sick?"

"No." But she had slept badly last night.

"Slept badly? What was wrong? Were you sick?"

"No, no, I often sleep badly. I wake up and can't get back to sleep. But it doesn't matter."

"You've got to get more exercise during the day," he said.

"No," she said, "it's not because of sluggishness at all. It's because when I hear something out in the street I jump up."

"Hear something–? What kind of noise? Here on the street? We'd better do something about that."

"No," she said. "It doesn't matter; it's just the usual noise; jabbering; sometimes singing; sometimes laughter; sometimes–"

"Does this happen often?"

"Sometimes."

"I'll let the police know," he said. "No one has the right to disturb another's peace and quiet."

"No, no," she said, "by all means don't tell the police! That would be a shame! Because this is just ordinary noise; it–it's life. I love noise."

"Life?" he echoed in surprise. "What do you mean?"

"Oh, I don't know what I mean!" she said, and she threw her book suddenly up onto the mantelpiece and leaned back again in her chair, rested both of her arms on the chair's own, and closed her eyes. He gazed for a moment at her bosom, at her arms, bare and white. The smile on his lips faded, and, raising his eyebrows slightly as a sign that he was thinking about other topics, started to leaf through his tables; the self-control that this man had was like an overwhelming force.

And when she lost all hope that he would say more, she jumped to her feet and went to the mirror to arrange her hair. She could see his image in the mirror, and she thought: Is there really nothing between Heaven and Earth worthwhile in his eyes but the trawlers in Hali and the loads of fish going to Grimsby and Genoa? He placed a finger on one after another column in the volumes, made comparisons, memorized figures, seemed to find it interesting. My dear Lord, what abominable reading material for a Sunday!

Finally he looked up. He did not set the notebooks aside, no, but held them up as if he were ready to begin again at any moment. Perhaps he snuck a furtive peek at her because she turned her back on him, because he thought that she could not see him directly?

There was no longer a smile on his face. It was nearer the truth that his face showed signs of a hidden suffering. It was almost alarming to see how deeply the lines in his face were marked, and how dark it was around his eyes. Did he by chance always look that way when he was alone, immersed in his work? She thought, This man is carved from stone; but under his fingertips beats the pulse of an entire nation. She was frightened.

She walked from the mirror over to the little table at the window, where the ninth or tenth volume of *Jean-Christophe* was lying. Such a long time has passed since I was little, she thought. She felt like a naughty child, and was seized with an overwhelming longing to do something good for him, to affirm for him that the trawlers north at Hali and the fish loads bound for Grimsby and Genoa were not everything; that there were also human feelings in the world; that the friendship of a little girl changed into womanly concerns with the years. All the same she couldn't even bring herself to fetch his cigarettes from the next room and offer them to him. All she did was clear her throat. He also cleared his throat. And she forgot everything except that they were alone in the house. Or did it press upon her consciousness like a nightmare hidden in the air? Nothing is more menacing than the unspoken between a man and a woman.

Why had she thrown the book onto the mantel and stood up – instead of sitting across from him and sinking herself into her reading? She was a terrible actress! At the end of her pilgrimage around the room she finally sat down again, took her book from off the shelf, and started to read.

For a while neither of them looked up. From outside came the creaking of hard snow under people's feet; in here the firewood burned, the flames scrambled about the dry wood, filling the room with an Italian summertime heat. But just when she fixed her thought on her reading he slipped his notebooks down to the side, onto the seat, sat with clasped hands, and looked at her. And it wasn't until he started to speak that she noticed he'd stopped reading. He might have been looking at her for two or three minutes before she realized it.

"Sorry for interrupting you, Diljá," he said, and both his smile and his voice were less secure than usual. It was as if he intended to explain his opinions on something that he really did not understand.

"What?" she asked, as she looked up from her book, because this time she had determined not to stop reading no matter what might happen.

"It's almost a month since I returned from abroad," he said, "and in all that time I've been mulling over one particular thing."

"What's that?"

"You know that I spoke to Steinn Elliði. Why is it that you've never asked me anything more about him?"

"Me?" she said, and now she looked straight into Örnólfur's eyes. "Why should I have asked about him?"

"Have no fear," he said, "that it would ever cross my mind to ask you a personal question. On the other hand I hope that you won't be offended if I see no reason to try to conceal the fact that this has caused me some concern."

"I don't understand you," she said, and she looked back down at her book.

"You can't understand that it seems strange to me to see that you two, who used to be like – siblings, seem to have forgotten each other?"

She neither looked up nor replied.

"I'd convinced myself that you two, who seemed made to understand each other, would hold on to your friendship in spite of distance. But instead you seem to have blotted each other out: he avoids mentioning you, you avoid mentioning him."

Then she looked up and answered in a calm, measured voice,

as was usual for her when she remembered to give herself time to think:

"It's a complete misunderstanding that Steinn and I have ended our friendship – if such a thing was even part of the picture. We parted like friends three years ago, or, to put it better, like children. And we must always think the warmest thoughts about each other like good children, if we think about each other at all."

He stared at her again for a moment, but to no avail; perhaps it was useless for anyone other than a psychoanalyst or some other expert in human nature to try to understand her. And after he had lost all hope of being able to read something more in her expression than he was able to glean from her words, this indiscreet conjecture flew as if involuntarily from his lips:

"And I even thought that your friendship had been sealed with vows!"

"Our friendship sealed with vows!" she repeated, feigning indignation. "Absolutely ridiculous! Vows! Did I hear you correctly?! And I think that you are quite mistaken when you say that we were made to understand each other; he was much more of an idealist than that! I can hardly think of two children less alike than Steinn and I."

"Then how would you respond to Steinn if he were to come home one day?" asked Örnólfur.

"Is he coming, then?" she asked sharply, this time completely spontaneously, and added: "I seem to remember you saying quite clearly the other day that he would never come home."

"Certainly. He didn't mention coming home, and avoided mentioning his plans in plain language. On the other hand it wouldn't surprise me if he were to appear here when we least expect it. Who can figure out a boy of his sort? What's more, it wouldn't surprise me even if I were to hear that one day he had become the editor-in-chief of the Socialists' newspaper here, or something along those lines. How would that strike you?"

"That would be disgraceful," she said, and added, "but that won't happen; Steinn would never join a group of cads."

"He has joined a group of cads, Diljá. Their opinions are his. He hails the same solutions to social questions as they do, and would certainly be no more discreet about the means used to bring them about. And what really counts is that he is much more talented than they are. He could be a more dangerous opponent than all of them put together."

"I would hate him," she said. "But I wouldn't believe that Steinn had joined a party until I saw it with my own eyes. He's much too fickle to embrace any view for longer than a few days at a time. His views were never anything other than poetic prattle."

"Poets are the most dangerous," answered Örnólfur. "It's useless to try to meet them on the same grounds as other members of society; they stand outside society and never have anything to lose. No weapons can bite them. They have only one goal, and that's to confuse the people – if not in this way, then in another. And they have the remarkable ability beyond other men of never listening to reason. That's why I have never tired of exhorting my party brothers concerning how necessary it is for us not to lose these buffoons to the Communists. But Steinn has a private fortune and can do what he pleases without saying like the others: *'Wes' Brot ich eß, des' Lied ich sing.'*"[49]

It was clear that the danger presented by Steinn Elliði had occupied Örnólfur's mind for a long time. And although this was the first time that he found himself compelled to explain a serious matter to Diljá, it did not affect Diljá so deeply that it prevented her from turning back to her reading.

She hunched over her book, and he looked at the soft curls in her hair and seemed, despite his manifold experience, not to have any clue as to how women want to be treated. She read on, completely unscrupulously; yes, verily fluttered through the pages. Finally he grabbed his notebooks again and started paging through them. Once again crunching footsteps could be heard out in the snow, and immediately afterward the ludicrous thing on the wall struck six times without having the faintest idea that in this house time stood still.

Finally it was the girl who could no longer stand it. *Jean-Christophe* flew up onto the mantel once more. She leaned back again in her chair, clasped her hands under her knees, and broke the silence by saying:

"I want to go abroad."

He put the notebooks down slowly and carefully in the same place as before, clasped his hands in his lap, looked at her, and smiled.

"Well then," he said.

"I'll die here!" she said.

"What do you mean?"

"Oh, I don't know."

Now there was a long silence; she stared out into space, full of feminine pertinacity and whimsicality, but he tried to remain cheerful in the face of adversity and continued to smile.

"I feel like a nobody here!" she said.

"What do you mean?" he asked.

"I don't know."

All the same she added after a short silence: "I'm not living. This isn't life! I'd rather land in misfortune a thousand times! I'd rather be lost a thousand times. I hate the instrument in there; it's out of tune. I hate these tattered old books that I'm reading; they're lies. I can't stand this any longer. I lie awake all night. I'll go crazy in this deadly lifelessness. I'm going."

"Where do you want to go then, Diljá?" he asked cheerfully.

"I don't know!" she answered, and she turned around in her seat, leaned over the back of the chair, and hid her face in her naked arms. She had said it all, torn down all the walls; her desires had found their voices, all at once, and she was so ashamed that she didn't dare let the man see her face any longer. He thought that she'd started crying, and was clueless about what to do next. He wasn't used to a weapon so destructive as a woman's weakness – he stood up and touched her arm in some bewilderment, but burned himself.

"Diljá, my child!" he stammered. "I'm sorry!"

It was impossible for him to put his thoughts into words. He touched her again, involuntarily; this time placed his hand on her bright, bobbed hair. But she jolted her head out from under his hand and did not look up. Suddenly she sprang to her feet without taking her hands from her face, ran out of the room in silent horror, and left the door open behind her.

52.

For the next two days she was ill and did not emerge from her room.

On the third day she sat down at the table without looking up, smiled at no one, ran her slender fingers through her hair. She looked glorious after her two-day stay in her room, a jewel newly unwrapped from its linen cloth, and yet more precious than all other treasures: a woman in the flower of maidenhood, a materialization of grace. Bewitchments dripped from her fingers; she magnetized everything she touched; her femininity surged through her body with every breath, glittered in the algal gloss of her eyes, quivered about her mouth; her body and soul were one. It was as if she knew all of this herself, because she did not dare to look up any more than a Persian noblewoman who has lost her veil. Her mouth was shaped like Cupid's bow.

Örnólfur looked at her three or four times, but she did not return his glance. He asked about her health, and she said that she was quite well. He poured wine into her glass and passed her the strawberry jam, but she was as appreciative as a discourteous child. Lunch was hardly finished before he was gone.

She did not come to dinner, nor did Madam Valgerður.

"Where's the madam?" he asked.

She was at a club meeting.

"Where's the missus?" he then asked in a hugely carefree tone, as if it didn't matter to him at all, and sat down.

"The missus has been out with her girlfriend since noon and won't be home until late; they're going to the theater." He sat alone at the table and regarded the steam from the dishes, emptied his bowl of preserves, smoked a cigarette, and drank a glass of wine.

"Perhaps the Director doesn't like the steak?" said the maid.

"The steak is heavenly," said the Director, and he stood up and left.

He did not sit down at his desk as usual. Instead he paced the floor in his office, back and forth, lit one cigarette after another and threw them all aside half-smoked, looked at the watch on his wrist, forgot just as quickly as he looked what time it was and looked at the watch again. The bell rang in the foyer and he had a servant say that he wasn't at home. The phone rang and he didn't answer.

Finally he put on his overcoat and went out. The street was slippery as glass, with a blustery wind from the north. He headed downtown and stuck to a course along the least traveled streets so as to draw as little attention as possible to the director of the Ylfingur Company. The clock in the theater foyer struck nine thirty; the last act had begun. He goes up to the balcony without taking off his overcoat, sits down in a half-empty box, and looks around. But he does not see Diljá or her girlfriends anywhere. He stands up and peers about even more carefully in the half-darkness, examines box after box. No one noticed him; everyone was waiting eagerly for the climax onstage. Diljá was not to be seen anywhere. He sat down for the conclusion of the play and listened distractedly to the gab on stage, then slunk out of the balcony before the curtain fell and waited in the foyer until the audience exited. But she was not among those who exited the hall. He waited again for a little while by the outer doors, in case he had overlooked her, looked carefully at everyone, but she wasn't in the theater. He couldn't understand what was going on, drank a cup of coffee in the next café, and headed home.

It wasn't until half an hour after midnight that the rustling of her clothing was heard on the stairs, and then her footsteps in the hall. She walked carefree, contentedly, opened the door of her room briskly, and stood there in her unbuttoned coat, hot, winded, her eyes dusky from the nighttime and the luxury, perhaps still intoxicated by the flattery of the boy who had walked her home. But in the doorway she stopped in surprise, because she did not expect a light to be on in her room, and was even less prepared for a man to be sitting there with his hand on his cheek.

Her eyes widened and she gasped for breath. "Örnólfur!" she said. "You here!"

"I'm sorry," he said as he stood up. "Forgive me for waiting up for you; for sitting here in ambush like a highwayman–"

"I'd been planning to be home a lot earlier," she said, as if she felt some need to apologize. "But I was at the theater," she added. "And afterward we went to a café. Time flew by."

"How is it that I didn't see you at the theater? Where were you sitting?"

"Were you at the theater?" she asked, and she blushed to the roots of her hair.

"I dropped in."

"Yes, that is to say, we decided not to go at the last minute," she hastened to correct herself, pale and disconcerted. "But we were going to go. We even booked seats. If I had known that you were going too, then–"

"I went down there just to find you," he said. "It's so slippery and windy. I wanted to walk you home. And besides that – I can't put it off any longer–"

"Put what off?"

"I've got to talk to you, Diljá."

He stood in the center of the room and stared at her with dilated pupils, rigid breaths, as if something perilous were about to happen, his arms hanging down at his sides.

"Almighty!" she said in alarm. "Are you mad at me? I'll tell you exactly how it was: I was at home with Sigga P. all evening. There were guests. We danced a little, actually only a tiny bit. Don't be angry with me."

"What reason should I have to be angry with you? Nonsense, Diljá!"

"Sit down," she said calmly. And when he had sat back down: "I'm sorry I lied, Örnólfur. But we did book seats; that's absolutely true. But it was so icy and windy."

She went into her bedroom, put her coat in the closet, took off her hat, fixed her hair, powdered her face, and then came back into the sitting room. She pushed over the silver box of cigarettes that stood on the little table next to him, sat down opposite him, and continued to run her fingers through her hair.

After a little silence he said:

"I've been very distracted since last Sunday evening, Diljá. It's no exaggeration to say that I haven't had any sleep or anything to eat for the last twenty-four hours. The time has come; in fact it came a long time ago – I haven't kept my mouth shut for any other reason than cowardice. There's nothing that I fear as much as my own feelings. I've been gnawing the backs of my hands because I lacked the words for it when we spoke together last time, or, to put it better, lacked the courage to tell you what's been in my heart, what's been in my heart for many years–"

She was at that stage of understanding instinctively the female art of changing oneself into all different forms of living creatures, and now she put on the best face she could manage of a complete moron who couldn't discern one thing from another:

"I beg you, Örnólfur," she said, "it's hopefully nothing terrible!"

"I haven't been able to forget what you told me on Sunday, that you want to go away."

"No, Örnólfur," she interrupted, "I don't want much of anything. I just want a little – sometimes."

Now there was a short silence, punctuated by a feeling of dread that ran through the girl when she beheld his face so heavy with passion: she'd never seen him like this before; his voice, his glance, the lines in his face, his entire being had transformed. But no matter how much he had pressing on his mind, he did not break out of the basic mode of the businessman at this moment any more than usual, and he told her, straight out, the entire story of his heart in this simple declaration:

"Diljá, I have loved you for many years."

"Örnólfur!" she said reproachfully, as if he'd been swearing. "I think that you're not quite in your right mind! What dreadful foolishness has gotten into you, man?" – at the same moment she grabbed the powder box from the table and started to powder herself from old habit, but he placed a finger on her wrist so that she would stop this foolishness.

"Diljá! Listen to me!" he said, and his eyes were burning. "Listen, when I finally open my heart! I've been sitting here waiting for you because I can't put off telling you my deepest secret; I know precisely what I want to say. Listen!

"I've been sitting here waiting for you to tell you that I love you, Diljá, I love you and have always loved you. In fact I've never loved anything but you. My life is founded upon nothing but love for you. I've loved you from the time that you were a little child. It might be ugly and sinful for an adolescent to love a little girl, but I didn't care about that. The truth is that I've loved you since you sat on my knee when you were a six-year-old girl. Deep inside your child's eyes I saw the woman dozing.

"I lived abroad for many long years," he continued, fixing every word precisely, with soporific calmness, although his eyes were moist. "I won't bore you by describing the nature of the training that I undertook. You would never understand it, and I would never require you to understand it. But I have lived many sad, empty days and racked my brain between dawn and dusk over problems that are thoroughly counter to personal life. I lived like an ascetic, and this has certainly made me strong; I struggled mercilessly against everything human in my nature, and that struggle has given me the strength to raise myself over the populace. What do you suppose has been my only pleasure all these years? It was to think about a little fair-haired girl who had sat on my knee when I was a youth far in the north of the world. There was only one picture for my guests to look at in my apartment; it stood on my desk: a photograph of a seven-year-old child, a smiling girl with two golden braids, in a white dress and white shoes. At night I dreamt childish dreams: I dreamt that we walked side by side, hand in hand in the sunshine through green valleys, that we picked flowers on the banks of streams and listened to the songs of the birds."

After a short silence he continued:

"I have never before spoken of my feelings, Diljá, and I know that I have difficulties expressing myself clearly. I don't know how to speak, but I know how to feel. I trust that you will not only listen to my words, but also to their spirit. You understand things that are not possible to say with words. I would have felt that I was committing blasphemy if I had ever dared to speak about the things that I kept hidden inside, so sensitive were my feelings to me.

"All of my life I have despised those peddlers, those naked whores who shout about human feelings out in the streets. This repulsion gripped me first one summertime here at home when I heard Steinn Elliði read one of his poems, when he was fourteen years old.

"Diljá! I have been disgusted by Steinn Elliði since the time when he wasn't such a bigwig that I couldn't spank him with one hand. From his earliest days his entire personality has been tinged with treachery, every one of his movements, every look of his eyes, every word of his fit for the mouth of a sorcerer. His mother is a harlot, and it's from her that he inherits this poetic caprice; in our family we've never been given to any sort of libertinism. Steinn Elliði is a degenerate and malefactor who has no ability to live for anything other than his own hallucinations.

"When I saw the gleam of sympathy in your eyes it became clear to me that in my nephew dwelled the archenemy of my life. I knew that he had all the requirements to be your beloved; he was almost the same age as you, he was your companion, and last but not least – a poet! A woman is a more innocent, more simple being than a man, always ready to let herself be deceived by the illusions of a clown. One quick flash of an illusion enchants her more than the mighty lifelong work of an honorable man.

"Diljá, I would have looked upon it with equanimity if you had fallen in love with a wholesome and true man, a man who desired only to be able to be everything for you. I would have wished you congratulations for having such a man and kept silent until my dying day about my own feelings toward you. But it was clear to me from the beginning that Steinn was a man who would do nothing other than ruin your life, unless you were to part ways. Love is only of any worth to poets when they can sing about it on the streets and corners, like the Salvation Army about God. A woman is only of any worth to them if they can deceive her. Lost souls and shamed women are to these members of the Salvation Army of love their most beloved topics for song. The poet is a talking mannequin, a conscienceless imp; his soul is nothing but a perfidious monster. Because men only become poets if they are prepared to defend lies: everywhere, in everything and always. I hate Steinn Elliði.

"And I told myself: 'Be quiet and strong. Don't speak with words, but with deeds. Prove to Diljá that greatness is not found in high-flown gurgling and marvelous babbling, but rather beyond anything else in the productive might of the iron will of a quiet man, who surpasses thousands and hundreds of thousands of others. Perhaps someday she will understand that no matter how glorious she thought the gab, the clownish antics, and the castles in the clouds, it on the other hand takes manliness to dare to place unwieldy reality beneath one's chisel, to choose a working-place in the center of the battlefield of life and there raise a monument around which the children will play, securely and fearlessly, long after the chatter-boxes with their castles in the clouds have fallen silent and been forgotten.'"

She sat there hunched and motionless, reluctant to look at his face so as not to distract him; her ears were thirsty. But here he fell silent, and she felt that he was waiting for her to say something.

"I've always known that you are a great man, Örnólfur," she said, and looked calmly into his eyes, because she had somehow managed to steady herself, "a much greater man than all the others. And I have, what's more, often thought, especially the last two years, that Steinn Elliði cannot compare to you in any way."

Then she looked down at her lap and continued: "I've sometimes feared that you were too selfish to be able to let yourself admire anyone in any noticeable way. Actually you are merciless, Örnólfur; you can't deny it. It's almost as if there are spells on you, as perhaps there are on all great men, to wish to put everything under you and to stop at nothing to do so. Have you at any time considered whether your desire for dominance is actually not the strongest of all your feelings? Domineering men frighten me."

"My dear Diljá!" he answered with a pained smile. "I see that you haven't understood me, that you haven't realized the main point, the thing that I named the foundation of my life. If I didn't love you, Diljá, it never would have crossed my mind to reach down to pick up the glove lying on the stage before the jaws of the lion. I would have ended up out in colorless banality somewhere, among other mediocre men, without having spent any time on great works, set course into the storm, or played a risky game. A man's love is a man's omnipotence. It was to be elevated in the eyes of the woman I loved that I made a vow to become the most powerful man in the country or else be destroyed. It was for her that I longed to be able to dive into the deepest depths and fight against all the monsters of the deep, like the man who sought the cup, because I thought myself unsuited to stand in her presence until the tribulations had consecrated my might. Because of her I reared my work with affectionate care, as if it were my foster child, working days and nights. Because of her my work became not only my art and my science, but also my world.

"It's true, Diljá, my work was never contained in whatever it is that's called doing good; it is, in general, impossible to express earnest work with a vain phrase. And it is also true that my love for mankind, of which these so-called men of the soul boast, is greatly lacking. But neither do I hate mankind: I am artless enough to admit that people are all the same to me. I discovered early on that all goals outside of my work were pointless and nonsensical. A serious man sets no goals for himself beyond his work. It is only through the perfection of his work that a man becomes powerful; to make one's work one's whole life is to realize this. A lawyer does not defend a case because he desires to advocate the cause of a client who claims to have suffered injustice, but rather because he loves the art of advocacy. A doctor does not heal because he loves the patient; he is quite indifferent to the patient. He heals because he loves his art, his science. I have nothing against the fact that you call whatever it is I have that surpasses other men selfishness, mercilessness, and a desire to dominate. If someone proves to be stronger than others in his lifelong battles, then he ordinarily possesses such qualities. Christian virtue always upholds and praises the weak; but we will not speak about that. I just wanted to remind you that if I had not been selfish, merciless, and domineering, Ylfingur would never have become anything other than an ordinary small retail company; wealth would not have been exploited; the lives of a thousand people would have been much sadder than they are now; their children would still be crying from hunger at the close of winter; a whole nation would have been timid, helpless, less educated, less independent. Because of the fact that my selfishness and my domineering nature have cost me many sleepless nights full of worries and headaches, yet another risky chess move played after the one before it was thwarted, I have still managed in the end to give my business enterprises a solid foundation. And although I am not the man to write a psychological essay about my feelings or to consider in any philosophically long-winded way how this so-called domineering desire of mine relates to my other feelings in certain situations, I would dare well stand in comparison with those in this country who have shouted most beautifully about brotherhood and the universe, the solar system and the cell, for in my hands I have felt the wealth well up from the wastes of the sea, seen children satiated and gladdened, the backbones of the cotters straightened, the condition of the entire nation blossom, its honor increase, its culture become fragrant with newfangledness. I am not seeking praise, either from you or from others; those who compose the poems have earned the right to be carried on golden chairs – they belong there. But face-to-face with the woman I love I find myself no less worthy than any other suitor, no matter how glorious his name might be."

Book Five

53.

The home that Steinn had lived in as a youth had neither center nor periphery. It was scattered here and there throughout the world. Reykjavík and Bilbao, Genoa and Baden-Baden, Brighton and Paris – newly refurbished mansions where the furniture smelled of polish – hotels, trains, and ocean liners – these had been his youthful homes. Each of his parents had had a different fatherland.

The life and work of Grímúlfur Elliðason was founded on the aphorism *"Ubi bene, ibi patria,"* or, better put, *"Ubi pecunia, ibi patria."*[50] He was like a machine that God had created to calculate where and how a soulless company might make its greatest profit. He did everything in the right way and was lucky in everything as if by natural assignation, because he never gave himself time to think about the reasons why man was born into the world. He did not complain about making ten trips over the Alps in five weeks, provided that his trips might possibly profit a company whose only aspiration was greed. His zeal was as single-minded as that of a child building castles out of sand. He was actually a childish artist who lacked the ability to find his way through such an adventure as to think a thought from top to bottom, an imbecile who sat out and counted the stars not because he longed to know how many there were, but rather because he enjoyed counting, a sleepwalker in the hands of providence. After Steinn Elliði matured to manhood he never considered his father as anything but a fool.

Existence meant something completely different to his mother. She lived in another world, was subject to a different type of providence. These two human beings had jumbled their fates together in a kind of blunder, without their souls possessing any sort of preconditions for meeting – if in fact they weren't both soulless. His mother had her own fatherland, her heathen god: namely, her tuberculosis. She lived for this fatherland. And there was no doubt that one fine day she would die for it like a French soldier on the field of honor. Her disease was everything to her. Whoever met her was immediately led into a chapel with pale blue curtains and pale red flowers on the walls, and there stood the idol on a pedestal: pulmonary tuberculosis. Everyone was expected to bow down and kneel before this god. Around this daemon everyone had to tiptoe and lie prostrate. It was forbidden to speak loudly. No noise! Perhaps some vermin of a doctor had originally come up with the idea of telling her this lie in the hope that he could keep himself employed afterward by plying her with prescriptions and all kinds of old wives' tales. After being diagnosed she took her greatest pleasure in maintaining the company of old and half-dead aunts and feebleminded boys who would lose heart over her wretchedness. Her son, on the other hand, was sincerely averse to fearing God because of tuberculosis. He never felt sorry for his mother. He became angry whenever he heard her talk about her sickness. But when he grew up he made it his habit to treat her with more consideration than in his youth, not out of love, but rather because he felt that nothing else suited good manners. It was a crime against common courtesy to jostle his mother. When he drove with her through Reykjavík on calm, bright days or sat at her side one hour a week and read a chapter from the fabrications of Blavatsky, Trine, Besant, Leadbeater, or the other false philosophers whom she most loved, it was cant; it was clear to him that the day was coming when he would be forced to cut all ties to his mother. Now that day had long since passed. His mother was no longer anything but a base fairy tale from his childhood. When she wrote to him he threw her letters unread into the wastebasket.

And when he was handed a telegram informing him that his mother was dead, he thought to himself: My precious Lord, why are they sending me telegrams though a woman died down south! What does it matter to me whether she's living or dead? The only thing I care about is whether I myself am living or dead, and not even that! He did not, however, immediately throw the message away; instead he read it over and over, in a trance: "Your mother deceased last night. Bradford."

He started to rummage through the wastebasket, which was full to the brim with crumpled paper and other trash, until he finally found several of his mother's last letters. He straightened them out, opened them, and ran his eyes over the dates. And then it came to light that the last one was dated to Taormina, Hotel Regina, one month ago, 15 April 1925. Taormina was a tourist town in eastern Sicily, halfway between Messina and Catania.[51]

Her letters were, from beginning to end, nothing but the tormented sighs of a belabored soul, which hopes for what it fears, and fears that for which it hopes. She was reluctant to dredge up palpable pictures, but constantly bade her son to come to her and protect her, without clearly stating from what she needed protection; it was as if all of her thoughts were shrouded in hot steam, and he felt sick at reading the letters. He ran his eyes over page after page until he stopped at a little passage in the last letter, the only place where he thought a fish might be hiding under a rock:

"It has perhaps been my most grievous affliction, my dear Steinn, this last half year, while I have been sinking bit by bit deeper and deeper into a laughing despair, to think about the spite that I deserve from you. And I often feel that if I had always had the good fortune of having you with me, my beloved boy, many things would have turned out differently. Once you were my little guardian angel who protected me from taking a terrible step, and so it might have been again these last months if I had only gotten to look into the clear blue eyes of my boy one or two more times; it is as if I understand it for the first time now, when all the bridges have been burned behind me, that the child alone is the savior of woman. Steinn, forgive your mother at least after she is dead, because the dust does not deserve to be hated."

Nothing was clearer than that these lines had been written with the last drops of blood of a human being for whom fate had passed final judgment; behind every line revolved a whole universe of the sheer despair of a lost soul. It is absolutely ridiculous how one little human being is able to suffer. A man falls over a cliff, is torn to pieces by the rocks on the shore, and there he howls until the next day when the sea flows over him; a woman's child falls into a little pot and she boils it by mistake; a lover climbs up the Eiffel Tower to jump and break his neck; all of these are greater events than the eruption of Hekla or an earthquake in California, and yet people forget such events in exactly five seconds after they read about them in the papers. Why do people forget these great events so easily? It is because nothing is as common as human suffering. In London fifty people a day have their limbs torn off or suffer other such accidents from motorized vehicles. Steinn Elliði felt that if he were to take any notice of the distresses of these victims of bad luck, he could not get away from buying a car and doing nothing from morning to night but driving from accident to accident in order to pour carbolic acid into the wounds of people nearly dead. When he considered that mankind had from the beginning of roads been run over by buses and locomotive engines, chocolate wagons and other wheeled contraptions, he realized that in order to love mankind, no less love would suffice than that shown by God, who came down from Heaven and let himself be crucified out of pure compassion. He crumpled up the telegram from Taormina as well as all of the letters and threw them back into the trash, muttering one of Nietzsche's aphorisms: *"An seinem Mitleiden mit den Menschen ist Gott gestorben."*[52]

54.

The voice of the heart is more powerful than philosophy. Night after night Steinn's mother came into his room in her burial shroud, bloody and filthy. She never opened the door; it never seemed to perturb her to walk through solid objects. At first Steinn felt sorry for her, such a fine woman, to have to go about in such a filthy shroud; but he couldn't bring himself to address her decently for any length of time, because the face of the ghost was sad and distressed. Sometimes she thrust her clasped hands up toward her breast. Was her breast still sore? he thought. Couldn't even death cure her breast? "Oh, Death," she said. "He is the lover par excellence! No woman was born so haughty that Death would not be able to satisfy her affections. I fought against his obtrusiveness for many years, but he always snuck up to my bed at night after I had turned out the light, and touched my naked bosom with cold, slender fingers, and breathed the stench of the grave into my nostrils. And finally he possessed me completely. Life! – God bless life; I certainly do not reproach it! But Death took me before life had offered me any sort of sweet wine or kissed me with a cozy kiss on the cheek in the sunshine out in the woods. But if I had been able to have you with me, my beloved boy, many things would have turned out differently."

Of what use is philosophical reasoning when one is speaking to a ghost? For when Steinn thought that he had convinced her that he bore no responsibility for her death, and that she might thank her lucky stars to have gone down belowground while other souls were exhausting themselves aboveground, she started dancing like the great dancer Anna Pavlova, who was at that moment rehearsing for a trip to South America. He asked her to go away, but she would not. He recited the Lord's Prayer, but she did nothing except nod, as if she thought the Lord's Prayer were worthless. He heaped abuse on her and told her to go to Hell, but she bored her idiotic and soulless ghost's eyes into his consciousness and stood still. He frowned and shouted, but she paid no attention and stayed. And although he was completely innocent from a philosophical point of view, his soul suffered the mental anguish of a murderer, like Raskolnikov,[53] who killed the old lady and then spun around in a hundred thousand circles: he felt that he would never find peace until he had seen the place where he had committed the crime.

When, after a nonstop trip of five days, Steinn Elliði stepped out of the train in Giardino, the station-village nearest Taormina, his whole body was in pain, like that of a martyr who's been left on the rack for several days. After untold countless zigzagging turns up along a cactus-grown hillside, the car dropped him off at the entrance to the Regina Guesthouse in Taormina. It was at the time of day when the heat was at its worst, shades drawn before all the windows in people's homes, and no one out on the streets but German tourists and dogs. No sooner has he been shown to his room than he throws himself down onto the couch – without having the energy to wipe the dust and sweat from his face, change his shirt, or brush the train soot from the pleats of his Wembley trousers – and falls asleep.

It wasn't until suppertime that he went to find the landlord, a dark-skinned Sicilian with a well-formed potbelly, clad in white flannel trousers and a sport shirt, cut and colored according to the latest fashion. Steinn gave his name and asked about his mother.

The landlord put on a face of sincere sympathy when he finally figured out whom he meant. With two-thousand-year-old pliancy he explained that it would be his true pleasure to share all of the information at his disposal concerning the last moments *di Signora Ellidaso*,[54] with emphasis on the "a," the wonderful Scandinavian woman whom it had pleased *il buono Dio*[55] to call to himself so far away from her kin and fatherland. No one who knew the madam had any doubts that she was of a great lineage, and furthermore, that she was surpassingly well educated: she spoke fluently in English, Spanish, and French. Yet he gathered that there was perhaps another man who might know more of the small details in this case: namely, the madam's friend, Signor Bambara Salvatore, a scientist and shopkeeper who had been her guide when she and her English maid came to Taormina at the beginning of April. It was fortunate, he said, that Signor Bambara Salvatore had not yet set out on his planned scientific expedition to Russia, and he added:

"It will be your true pleasure to meet Signor Bambara; he is a millionaire from a family in Milano, a dealer in antiquities and an archaeologist, and he has traveled throughout the whole world; he has a special interest in iconography. He has spent time in all the corners of the world and his knowledge is limitless. And neither does he look down on *le bellezze della vita,*[56] as so many scientists do, and thus he never says no to a dance with a lucky woman. Therefore I make bold to inform you of the trial undergone by Signor Bambara Salvatore, to have to witness such a fortunate woman give up the ghost in his arms in an innocent Charleston one evening at the end of the season, when we had arranged a tiny *soirée internationale*[57] in the social hall downstairs. No one suspected that the madam your mother suffered from tuberculosis, and therefore you can imagine the terror that gripped us all when the madam suddenly started to spit up blood during the dance. After supper the signora your mother and Signor Bambara went out for a refreshing walk, north toward Hotel Castello a Mare to view Isola Bella[58] in the moonlight, and nothing out of the ordinary happened. Two hours later she was a corpse. We suddenly saw that Signor Salvatore's shirt and vest were red with living blood, and that the madam had fainted in his arms. In the same breath he lifted her in his arms and carried her into a side room, and there she gave up the ghost in just a few minutes. A young British doctor, one of the guests, said that it would have been beyond any human power to do anything for her. A half-healed sore in her lungs had reopened, and she bled out in a number of minutes. The madam's death was at the same hour reported by telegram to the signor your father in Genoa, and two days later he came here, along with a Danish consul from Palermo and an English Protestant priest from Rome. We had all witnessed an unforgettable tragedy, and I can assure you that we are inconsolable, sir!"

When Steinn Elliði came down into the hall accompanied by the landlord a few minutes before dinner, he saw a man sitting in one corner in a deep armchair, hidden behind an *Il Mondo*,[59] small and slim, with chestnut hair carefully curled, a cadaverous face and black bags under his eyes, a monocle over his left eye, wearing a fascist shirt of raven black silk. This was Bambara Salvatore. He put the paper aside, took the monocle deftly between small slender fingers, and bowed in deep deference:

"My dear sir," he said to Steinn Elliði. "I am smitten with deeper delight than words can express to have been finally granted the fortune to be allowed to do what I have desired for so long: to greet you."

He not only spoke flawlessly in English, but his accent and diction were characterized by a particularly grand Bostonian quality.

"I feel as if I have known you for a long time," he continued. "I can assure you that I have heard more good things spoken about you than any other man. And it is scarcely a week since I ran across an English literary journal that had printed your picture and the most praiseworthy reviews of your newly published poems: in them you were openly compared to the greatest spirits of genius."

After they had taken seats at a table, Bambara Salvatore switched to French, since most of their table companions were Americans and other English speakers who were busy conversing with each other.

"It truly pains me," said Bambara Salvatore, and it quickly became clear that his French was no less fluent than his English, "that I shall not be able to have the pleasure of enjoying your company during the time that you perhaps intend to stay in Taormina. The fact is, I am forced to set out on a journey tomorrow evening, and tomorrow morning I have been asked to go to Giarre, a town located some twenty-five kilometers from Taormina, to give my opinion in court concerning some newly sold antiquities that are under suspicion of being forgeries. These blessed Americans let themselves be so heartily duped like dunces, as one might expect, because they have no knowledge of anything but stocks and bonds, and dash off to a judge just as soon as someone tells them that their Adonis with the unbroken nose is a forgery. But I have an exceptionally special desire to be able to speak with you before I go, and although it might be late I hope that you do not take offense at my request that you grant me the honor of paying me a visit this evening. I am staying on the second floor, numbers five to eight."

A half an hour later they sat beneath the leaves of palm trees in the garden and drank coffee. Two northern Europeans of the twentieth century, two masked souls, two actors. If Fra Angelico had lived seven years after the European war, thought Steinn, he would have used Bambara Salvatore as his model for saints.

Steinn was a child in comparison to Salvatore. Without a doubt, Salvatore had lived a thousand more adventures than Steinn. Without a doubt, he had dived for the cup. He must have run the race of ultramodernism backward and forward and ring after ring while Steinn was still a greenhorn and his fatherland the *terra nullius*[60] between the trenches. Salvatore had found his own little sanctuary and paid homage to the Babel of vanity, dressed like a Fascist, with a monocle. He studied iconography. No one does such a thing unless he knows the whole world by heart. Bambara Salvatore had dwelled in Rome among prelates, in Monte Cassino among canons, in Britain among lords, in Paris among artists, in Berlin among homosexuals, in New York among rich capitalists, in California among movie actors, in India among yogis, in Moscow among chess players. While Europeans squeezed their hands around each other's necks for freedom and the fatherland, Bambara Salvatore lived alternately in the Orient and America and scoffed at those baboons. He nimbly picked up the thread where the conversation had broken off when they had left the dining table, and spoke entertainingly about his trips through Rajputana[61] in 1917, about his stay in Jaipur,[62] the Paris of India, about the heathen and godlike grandeur that rests over the architecture of the sun-white palaces and magnificent temples of Jaipur.

55.

I see, dear sir, that your eyes widen when you behold the images of saints around me, as if you were asking in your heart: Is it possible then that he has not overpowered God?

Indeed he has, dear sir. You are mistaken; I know precisely as well as you that the image of God, or, to put it better, the feebleness of imagination, is the foundational flaw in the soul of man, the chief cause of human suffering. But I collect antiquities and have a proclivity for finding pleasure in things that are older than I am and that can outlast me. Before the gaudy Christs and Buddhas I reverentially burn my candles, because I rejoice to think that some things are able to endure. And when you consider that the Catholic Church is the ancient relic of all ancient relics you will come closer to understanding what religion I actually profess. I love it, to wit, as he alone is able to, who has seen through its ideology, that most peculiar crossword puzzle under the sun; I love it as one who has gazed into all of the phosphorescent phantasmagoria of worthlessness that descended from Heaven and took up its abode in Peter's bones. Catholicism is as old as God, as me, as the world, dear sir. It is the first and the last illusion of all illusions, the one true lie poured from the breasts of creation, the harp song of the deep, over everything and in everything like Fujiyama in a hundred prints by Hokusai. A thousand years ago I leaned up against the pillars in its forecourt and left. But it stands there and calls out after you as you leave: *"Vous vous en allez; moi, je reste."*[63] A thousand years later I take my rest under the pillars in its forecourt, and it asks, "Where have you been?" I love it in a sinful way, like an ignorant man who perceives the harp song of the deep in the smile of his lover, love it because it stands unmoving while the world perishes, because it will remain like Fujiyama in the paintings by Hokusai, will remain when I disappear. And I will disappear and it will remain.

Perhaps now you fear, dear sir, that I am preparing to lecture to you on the ascetic life, just as if I saw nothing in the Catholic Church but a divine institution against whoredom, homosexuality, or *crimine bestiali,*[64] but it is not so: I have, since my childhood, investigated its tenets, and although you see saints and the crucified Christ here, I can assure you, after having looked deeply into the ascetic culture of the Church and found nothing there but a very primitive and deficient type of sadism, that the highest wisdom and the sweetest bliss can only be drunk from the breast of jocundity. This is how Signor d'Annunzio put it, our peerless d'Annunzio: *"La vita . . . c'insegna che il piacere è il più certo mezzo di conoscimento offertoci dalla Natura, et che colui il quale molto ha sofferto è men sapiente di colui il quale molto ha gioito,"* "Life teaches that bliss is the most secure medium of knowledge that nature offers, and that the one who suffers much is less wise than the one who lives in pleasure."

A purebred criminal nature is the highest degree of all human perfection. If you understand German I would rather choose to word this wisdom in this way: *"Der reine Verbrecher ist der einzige wahre Erkennende."*[65] Dostoevsky, entirely Dostoevsky. The perfect criminal is holy as a dove. His crimes are not kneaded out of the imperfection of a slavish nature, which breaks the laws of God and man only from blindness, but rather they are the calculated wisdom of the superman, who must attempt to break free from the conspiracy against genius which the world signifies. The world is a conspiracy of impotence against the soul of genius. Of what use is the bourgeoisie in the eyes of the superman? It is suited only for snapping at the flies that have gotten into its mouth, and for raising wives and daughters who prostitute their honor in secret while swearing oaths of fidelity and who turn out to be pregnant long before they are due for insemination according to the almanac.

The superman enters the world to make the world suffer. He comes to ruin girls' virginity and the honor of madams, if I may speak metaphorically. It is in the nature of a powerless man to sacrifice himself to a powerful man, but the powerful man is easily distinguished by the fact that the smoke from the sacrifices is a foul stench in his nostrils, and he never rewards weakness with mercy. A man who makes a woman happy makes a fool of himself. The harlot, the image of self-abnegation, is the revelation of the highest and most noble female nature. She is holy, because she has chosen unhappiness as the reward for her sacrifices, and no one has granted her a title for not throwing her integrity into the bargain. The wise do not touch her, because she has found the highest bliss in the lowest form of misfortune and cannot be tormented. But the criminal, who loves the game of tormenting and believes in the sanctity of pleasure, knows that the fate of modern woman can be read in the depths of her eyes and cries out: "Pereat!"[66] Her path leads to perdition, because she seeks in her loves the ultimate bliss. Over the flames of lust hover imps who ceaselessly sing "Pereat!" while her soul and body are destroyed. Nothing can quench the primordial elements of blind lust that cry out in the breast of the modern woman, nothing but the embrace of death. Laughing and anxious, expectatant and lamenting, she worships her own destruction. She ladles out her heartache in grotesque profanities, cries, bites, genuflections, sluttishness, tearful convulsive laughter, and blind acceptance of your most repugnant caresses.

You work, dear sir, because you are a Scandinavian man, slow to develop; you have hardly run half the race. But when you have finally been convinced that work is the most wretched and vulgar form of opium that human society is capable of giving its slaves, then you find yourself obligated to fight against holiness, and have it either better or worse for years on end until you have attained the highest state of all mortality, the state of the complete criminal, which finds its final rest, if not in suicide, then in the lowest form of pleasure: addiction to the greatest type of poppy that is produced on our Earth, opium. When sexual vigor slackens, this pivot-point of life and center of gravity, the thrill of the game disappears, and then it is just as pleasant for the wise man to lose his consciousness in narcotics as it is for a Buddha to find peace in nirvana after a thousand-year migration from man to beast, beast to man. As for me, I have already run such a huge part of the race that I can now devote myself peacefully to iconography. As an example of how far I have come along the road of the perfect criminal, let me say that when an American friend of mine, one of the greatest bacteriologists in the world, asked if I would like to let loose a pestilence that could wipe out mankind in half a month, I shrugged my shoulders, like this, and answered, no, it is much more entertaining to watch them die out gradually from cocaine, syphilis, and psychoanalysis.

56.

Steinn Elliði walks along Corso Umberto in the midday heat, out through Porta di Messina, asks his way along until he sees tall cypresses looming to the west of the town. He feels as if he is carrying a column of fire on the crown of his head. It is good to dwell in this country if one is going to Hell and wants to get used to the heat. White dust spins up from the road at every step. The Mediterranean Sea is a beautifully green weft in the golden blue haze out near the rim of the horizon. The ripples on the calm sea disappear from view out in the radiant mist, like truth transformed in poetry, or reality that ends in an abstract dream. In these countries men condemned to death, like Saint Anthony, suffered lustful visions.

He walks along the wall and stops in front of the gate of a graveyard where the cypresses tower over with a Böcklinish,[67] solemn air in the glowing midday sky. He had never found himself in a more astonishing neighborhood. Finally he placed his hand on his forehead as if to defend himself against attack, and his palm became drenched with sweat. Two farm girls with black eyebrows and eyelashes came down the road from the west, bearing huge baskets on their heads; they stopped near the graveyard gate, lowered their baskets, and sat down quickly on the crumbling wall to catch their breath. Their backsides were burly and they began to read the inscription over the gate with difficulty.

"Questa soglia divide due mondi. La pietà li congiunge."[68]

The other girl looked at the first, solemnly and contemplatively: *"È vero!"*[69] she said, and nodded her head. Inside the gate stood two lissome banana trees; then a broad pathway lined with cypress trees crosses the yard, and from the conical crowns of the trees came a constant chirping of cicadas. On both sides of the main pathway were first-class graves, for the yard was divided into three sections according to rank. Here each gravestone was showier than the last, for under them lay men of rank, while most of those who were buried in the third section on the outskirts of the yard lay under bare stones. Steinn searched and searched without finding; he examined the inscriptions on the memorials and had no scruples about treading on the graves, elated that, despite the intensity of the parching drought, he was able to promenade aboveground, while these wretches had to remain still, down in the dirt, thoroughly rotten.

Finally he came to a gray brick wall, covered completely with compartments. It is quite common in the southern lands to dispose of corpses in a Saracen way: the coffins are shoved into compartments in the walls, and then a plate is screwed over the compartment and the name of the occupant is inscribed on the plate. Gaudy green lizards crawled back and forth along the wall, nimble and quick, and disappeared into the most unbelievably narrow holes like the souls of the departed. Their eyes were like living pinheads. Steinn read the minute inscriptions on the plates, to see if his mother might have been thrust into one of the compartments. But he found nothing.

He finally realized that it was childishness to try to find one foreign woman in such a large town. Nothing was more likely than that she rested under some bare marker in the third section, so he saw no other way than to visit the sexton. On the left side of the gate, within the yard itself, was a little house with a doghouse out front, wherein lay an old, sagely guard dog with its head on its front paws. The dog looked at Steinn as he walked by, saw immediately that this man was secretly grief stricken, did not think once about barking, and instead regarded him with a look of sincere compassion, as if wanting to say, *"Nihil humani a me alienum puto."*[70]

The house stood open and two bulky women worked in the kitchen; one was the housewife. She came to the door and stood there opposite the traveler, clad in black, tall and shriveled, like the women who are paid to weep at the cheapest funerals. Steinn lifted his hat and asked about a foreign woman who had been buried here.

The housewife answered that her husband had gone to take a midday nap; otherwise he knew everything about those who had found their rest here in the graveyard.

"But maybe I could help in some way," she said, and added: "I wonder if this foreign woman was one of the faithful or if she was a heretic?"

"She was certainly one of the faithful," said Steinn, in the hope of avoiding any fuss.

"Catholic?" reiterated the woman.

"No, she wasn't strictly Catholic, but all the same very faithful," answered Steinn, and he laughed in his heart, since this was the first time in his life that he had given credit to his mother for anything.

"Then other rules apply here," said the woman. "Since she is not Catholic, then she is lying in the other graveyard."

"What other graveyard?"

"Yes – there is actually another tiny yard a short distance from here, for Turks, Jews, and heretics. They don't receive any church service, you know, but instead are buried like dogs."

"Yes, very pitiful," said Steinn Elliði.

"But all the same I think that the good God who rules the universe has mercy on them," said the woman. "By the way, I can hear by your accent that you're from northern Italy, sir," she added.

"Yes, I'm from northern Italy."

"Well that's good luck," said the woman. "Because my husband actually comes from northern Italian stock. If you give him a few soldi[71] for tobacco, I almost think he'd be willing to get himself up and dressed and take you over to the heretics' yard. Wait just a moment, sir; after five or ten minutes my husband will be ready."

When the woman had gone back into the house Steinn clenched his face with both hands. In front of the doghouse lay a donkey-load of firewood. For a moment he felt as if he would lose his balance and faint. He let himself sink down onto one of the bundles of firewood, supported himself with his elbow on his knee, and covered his face with the hollows of his hands, sat in that way motionless for a while. But his body was suddenly seized with uncontrollable shaking. It was as if his chest were going to burst, and the sobs were forced like unstoppable laughter up out of his throat, sore and dry. The guard dog looked at Steinn Elliði like a wise man, but Steinn Elliði howled like a guard dog.

He himself didn't know whether he was laughing or crying. But he certainly laughed and cried all at once. His heart was ungovernable. Neither Heaven with all of its might nor Earth with all of its wisdom could break the back of this power. The tears burst forth like water that suddenly sprays from cliffs; they fell down below his hands and were lost in the white dust on his feet, the dust that thirsts ceaselessly for human tears, the dust that swallows all human tears. And the worm writhes back and forth in the dust.

57.

Ego autem sum vermis et non homo:
opprobrium hominum et abjectio plebis.[72]

On the steps on the Via dei Vespri, the steep street leading up to Villa Valverde, where Steinn had rented a room, sits a one-legged beggar playing a flute. Every time that Steinn walks along the Via dei Vespri the beggar grabs his flute and blows one measure in a show of respect. And on the days when Steinn sits out on his balcony and watches the smoke from his cigarette creep out and in among the fronds of the palm trees in the calm, he hears the whistling from down on the Via dei Vespri, and the cicadas in the crowns of the trees provide accompaniment. The beggar knows three short melodies and mixes them all together into one, and usually ends up playing off-key like a young cock that hasn't yet gotten the hang of crowing. But the flute always resounds with redemptive jubilation and heavenly delirium. The spirit is greatly uplifted in listening to such music.

This virtuoso is named Leonardo Peppino, in Icelandic, Ljónharður Pípín. He has a yellow dog, emaciated and abject, tied with a rope to his remaining leg. But Ljónharður Pípín is not merely a virtuoso; he is also an instrument maker. Wind instruments are his specialty. And more than an instrument maker, he is an instrument decorator: he decorates wind instruments. He makes them from hollow stumps of wood, and decorates them with carvings. His etchings are matchless; his grasp of style unfailing. He whittles all sorts of supernatural species of cabbage, and peering out from between the cabbages are faces like smirking corpses or half-awakened ghosts; an icy and fatal dead man's bliss shines from their eyes. Twice a day a dark-eyed and filthy little girl comes from a nearby house, gives him a loaf of bread, an onion, and water in a clay jug with two handles. She says nothing and leaves.

Pípín is a small man, shabby and grizzled, with gray strands of beard here and there upon his wrinkled face. He has cinnabar eyelids, and is usually dirty about the mouth because he kisses the ground whenever an American passes by on the street. But he is a happy man and smiles the whole day, celebrates the glory on the visage of things from morning till night. He smiles at the countenances of the apparitions that are revealed beneath the point of his knife, smiles at his dog as he checks it for lice, smiles at the Americans who buy his flutes, *ricordo di Taormina*,[73] smiles at the bald-headed gentlemen and gracious ladies who hand him two soldi as they pass by, just because such a man should exist, and when night falls he lies down and smiles at good God in Heaven before he goes to sleep. And he sleeps in the Via dei Vespri, on the open street in the five-finger-thick dust, and sleeps deeply and sweetly. Fortune lives in Taormina in Sicily, and Taormina is called the pearl of Europe. Fortune sleeps in the open on the Via dei Vespri.

Steinn had difficulty withstanding Ljónharður Pípín's charm. He often stopped on the stairs where the beggar sat, and listened to his Sicilian when he talked about his flutes and praised the magnanimity of the Americans, those God-fearing people whom God sends to care for the poor. Otherwise Steinn did not have the bad habit of giving alms, for such a thing offends God, who has given into people's hands an entire planet, full of bounty. Pípín's blissfulness and his arts were, on the other hand, of such quality that twenty soldi was not too much to pay for the pleasure of his company. It was not in Steinn's power to grant this foundling any fortune other than admiration. And he laughed in his heart to be considered *gran' signore*[74] in the Via dei Vespri, because he felt himself unworthy to untie the shoelaces of a man who has conquered himself so thoroughly as to be able to kiss the dust before every American.

And one day when Steinn sat at his meal in the Villa Valverde, and the flute-song was borne in through the open window, the waiter said:

"Signore must excuse this everlasting noise from that beggar's shrieking tool. But he once received permission from the police to sit here on the street, and although we've complained about him many times to the authorities we still haven't succeeded in driving him away."

"Do you think that you can play the flute better than Leonardo Peppino?" answered Steinn.

But since the waiter had to admit that that was not the case, it consoled him to mention the fact that this wretched ragamuffin had spent fourteen years in a workhouse.

"Workhouse?" asked Steinn Elliði.

"Yes, he was sentenced to prison, signore!" said the man.

"For what?"

"*A fatto malo a una piccola ragazza,*"[75] answered the waiter, without going into any more detail. And so the day passed by. In the evening a brass band played at the Piazza Sant Agostino, and a pink moon burned in the green haze over the horizon of the Mediterranean Sea, and with this magical world as a background stood the cinnabar red balustrades at the edges of the square, octagonal pillars at every twentieth baluster and a flowerpot on the top of every pillar, with acacias in the pots. And in the crowd of people meandering back and forth over the square stood Steinn Elliði, leaning back against a tree trunk, smoking a cigarette and looking out at the sea. The brass band played a whole act from *The Barber of Seville,*[76] and Steinn knew each and every note by heart and felt the breath of mastery in every wave, but *"durch alle Töne tönte ein zarter Liebeston,"*[77] and it was the flute of the beggar, singing of slavery and prison, quivering with joy and thankfulness, like birdsong in the spring.

"Saluti, saluti, Eccellenza!"[78] exclaimed the beggar, as Steinn walked by in the evening. He rose from the dust to wipe his flute and play to Steinn Elliði's glory. Steinn stopped, leaned up against the wall opposite the virtuoso, watched him and waited for his meandering rigmarole to wind down. Then he asked:

"Is it true, Leonardo Peppino, that you committed a crime against a little girl?"

The beggar bent his head from side to side several times and gave a sidelong glance, then played a long, wailing note on his flute and answered:

"Dear sir, I am a horribly wicked man. Why am I such a bad man while other men are so good? The notary's daughter was twelve years old, sir, and was standing in the doorway. And in the evenings when I came home from work she was standing in the doorway. She had two pigeons. And in the evenings when I came home from work I saw how she stood on the threshold, leaned up against the doorframe and held her pigeons by their legs and kissed them on the breast. She was careful not to look at me as I walked by. But when

I'd passed by she would follow me with her eyes. But God and men have justly punished me. I feel as if I always understand better and better how God and men are just. Fourteen years in the workhouse, sir, fourteen years in prison with consumption in my leg, fourteen years. But what's that? I am just as happy having those behind me as I would have been having reigned as a king for fourteen years, because who counts the hours once they've passed? It is said that God hears the tears of the wretched fall, and if God hears my tears fall, would I really be better off as a king living in a palace in Rome? And since God and men are good, do I deserve anything else but to be a dead wretch before God and men? Don't I have reason to thank God and our Lady for being allowed to sit here and play my flutes for the blessed Americans who are so good? When I came from prison worse than dead, with a crutch under each arm and only one leg, then there was no one to help me, absolutely no one, sir, except for good God who rules the entire world. And then I thought to myself: But oh how sweet it is to be allowed to draw breath under your sky, my Lord, free and wide. And you let yourself be crucified under your sky, my Lord, for love of me. But a murderer from Calabria,[79] who was a tremendous musical genius and had been a coal burner up in the mountains all his life – he taught me to play the flute in prison while I lay sick with consumption. And the day before I was set free we were allowed to say good-bye out in the prison yard and he gave me his flute as a parting gift, the only flute that he owned. And ever since then he's been fluteless."

58.

It was Steinn's resolute intention to put an end to all vanity, to everything that tied his being to the laws of existence, and he had, not without lustful feelings, tried to envision how he could bring about his death in the most ridiculous manner possible. He longed to die with storylike disgrace, and asked himself again and again: "What would amuse Bambara Salvatore best?"

He was born in Kashmir, the valley of roses, with a harp in his hand like the gods. One day he awoke from his harp playing and saw himself: the roses had paled and died beneath the soles of his feet. But human society can only do two things for all of its sages: turn them into either criminals or suicides. Before the door of the sexton he had sobbed away his last human feelings. And this entire ridiculous tragedy had its roots in an event no greater than this: his mother had forgotten to use contraceptive precautions. But now he was reborn. His suicide did not signify his fear of becoming a criminal, as did Dr. Otto Weininger's suicide, but rather his escape from a dungeon.

He was truly reborn. His feelings were far from dancing a deranged dance in his breast as before, when he had been a normal person. Tonight he did not despair. He muttered to himself almost involuntarily this foolish aphorism of Maupassant, the conclusion of *Une vie: "La vie, ça n'est jamais si bon ni si mauvais qu'on croit."*[80] Suicide was actually not a more horrid act than, say, eating a slice of bread with sausages. There is, generally speaking, not a more trivial or insignificant act. But from a dead man the power of destiny is wiped away; a dead man has cut himself free from the yoke of his existence. A dead man is freer than God. What prompted Steinn was the desire to defeat this God of the deeps and dawnlight, who can never be eluded, to defeat this power which itself was forced to live and let live. How indigent and worthless is all the glory of existence compared to the strange, victorious smile on the face of a dead man! Even the poems of the divine Omar Khayyám pale before it! He sits in the armchair on the balcony, malevolent like a troll in a grave mound, his mind ice-cold. Down on the Via dei Vespri a lantern shines, and the electricity and the moon join hands in illuminating the garden beyond, while bats, *bêtes à bon dieu,*[81] and locusts play in the crowns of the palms and poisonous mosquitoes hum like fiddles. He lit a new cigarette, tore a page from his pocketbook, and wrote:

"*Til det dansk-islandke konsulat, Palermo. Sicilien.*[82]

"*Jeg undertegnede*, etc. request that you excuse the fact that I am forced to trouble you to come here to Taormina to oversee my burial and other things concerning my departure. As I take it for granted that the embassy in Rome shall demand more detailed information concerning my death, it is my true pleasure to inform you that I intend to ingest cyanide tonight at two o'clock. There is no reason for the suicide. With deep respect, etc."

He read the letter over, and felt that he had never actually been in better touch with himself than tonight. He had a dismally clear head. On the other hand he regretted most painfully that he was to die without ever having raped a girl or torn out a man's throat with his teeth. But when he considered it more carefully he concluded that his intention was in fact not to scandalize human society.

He had only one letter left to write before he died, to Bambara

Salvatore, only a very few lines, some clever rhetoric that would be enough to convince Bambara of the fact that the son of Signora Ellidaso had not lacked the courage of a visionary soul. His mind searched everywhere for brilliant words. But the moon over Etna sneered straight into his face, making it more difficult for him to think seriously the more roguish it became; it was as if the moon sucked out from his narrow pupils the mere pittance of genius that remained in his soul; it derided this pitiable soul of his like an insolent prostitute who puckers her lips in the face of a saint. Finally Steinn could bear it no longer and hurled himself off the balcony like an acrobatic clown, turning twelve somersaults in the air before hitting the ground.

59.

A little girl sat among the geese by a blue pond in a green meadow. And the geese dabble and drabble or preen their feathers with their beaks. Sometimes they stick their heads into the water and look toward the bottom, with their rear ends up in the air, because these are very discourteous birds. And the girl sits cross-legged in the grass and knits a red sock for her dowry, because she plans to get married when she grows up.

"I'll steal her away!" says Steinn Elliði, and he walks straight over to where she is sitting. But when the girl realizes what he has in mind she slips out of his grasp and takes to her feet.

Damned fox! he thinks, and he runs after her shouting and

cursing. "I'll kill you if you don't stay still!" The geese start craning their necks and screeching piteously. The sun is squarely in Orion and will soon enter Aries, then Libra. The girl rushes around the pond as fast as her feet can pull her. Steinn follows, singing the newest operetta by Verdi:

A dunderhead mobile
By Snowpachy Jón
From seamobby Frón
A lioncub profile!

The gander's lights went on when he heard this, and he and all of his wives started to chase Steinn. The chase lasted for three days. Then Steinn suddenly remembered that he was one-legged and had forgotten his crutches down on the Via dei Vespri, and thus could not actually run. He sat down on the bank of the pond sadly and picked up his flute to comfort himself, while on the opposite side of the pond sat the girl with her half-knitted sock, singing:

The sun in the west shines just to be mean
just to be mean to be mean
ach du lieber Augustin Augustin Augustin
ach du lieber Augustin Augustin Augustin
the sun in the west shines just to be mean
just to be mean to be mean.

Steinn noticed that the flute was not a flute at all, but rather a paltry water gun made of an angelica stalk with a hole at the end. Now he started to shoot it with all of his might, until he watched the girl fall lifeless to the ground. Steinn was seized with painful remorse, but he resolved, all the same, to go to the girl's father and ask what he should pay – then again, this was only fantasy.

60.

The Situation in Cairo

In Cairo a great banquet is being held. He was told that the sultan's wives had risen up against the sultan and castrated him. This was criticized in the papers, and men blamed the collusion of the Bolsheviks. But to make amends the women invited all of the most prominent men in the country to a feast. Steinn dismounted his horse, tied it to the columns in front of the palace gate, and went in to examine the caricatures on the Gobelin. All of the carpets on the floor came from countries famous for textile weaving. Velvet flowed in sumptuous folds from the couches onto the carpets. The windows were near the roof, and sleeping birds cuddled in every window, with the twilight blue sky in the background and a star here and there. Eunuchs carried in wine, and the maidens stepped forth from their bowers and appeared in the banquet hall, clad in long trailing silk veils that could be torn off from top to bottom with one quick hand movement, embroidered with long-legged pelicans and other noxious birds, while their hips and breasts swelled beneath the silk like heavy sea-waves in sunshine mist. Their eyes glittered like black diamonds. And the dandies entered, with white teeth and long mustaches and fezzes on their heads, otherwise dressed like gentlemen from London and Paris, and appearing to be jacks-of-all-trades, alchemists, and diviners.

After a drawn-out ceremonial greeting two women and two men sat down at each table; the cups are filled to the brim, and a conversation about politics begins:

"Mosul," said one man.

"Angora," replied a girl, and she laughed.

"Moscow," said another man.

"Afghanistan," said another girl, and she laughed.

"All things must once begin," said a third man, as if to inject a philosophical profoundness into the conversation.

"All things have been once before," said a third girl, and she laughed.

"Bena Kipa!" said a fourth man, as if in agreement.

"Bena Kipa, Bena Kipa!" they all said, and they laughed raucously. "What, might we ask, didn't the Chinese know two thousand years before us? Cheers!"

Steinn Elliði had never witnessed a more soulless or idiotic gathering.

The clinking of glasses was heard throughout the hall, and the wine splashed into the air in long arcs, then fell down like rain. Everything was one great Babel of burning eyes, sparkling diamonds, swelling bosoms, sweating hands, and gleaming lips.

"I dream golden dreams," says one man.

"Behind cinnabar palace walls," answers a girl, as if attempting to distort his meaning.

"I dream of poison mistresses!"

"Who never existed!" the girl distorts.
"Never existed!"
"Never existed!" echoes the crowd.

And songs
arise,
claps
resound
in hundredthousandmillionfold myriads of primitive forests
where gigantic steeds of stormcloud rear,
and drunken hippos lie upside-down on cliffs
like *Rhodymenia palmata,*[83]
stand on their hind legs and fume,
neigh,
rear,
hiss,
snort,
pish

like the fate of the millions. *"Il piacere, il piacere!"* my lords.[84] The goal of life is joy. Or better put, the joy of life is the death that swallows the consciousness of the living in the bottomless oblivion of the lunatic. From every direction, "Hurrah! Hurrah! Hurrah! Hurrah!" "Up with the wine, Ave Dionysus!" In howling laughter and weeping song slumber the mysteries of the lotus blossom. "OM! My lords and ladies, OM!" And the men pour cup after cup into the faces of their wives and drink the wine madly as if from living springs and groan the Tibetan prayer like fiddles with slackened strings:

"Om mani padme hum!"[85] And they lean over their concubines like lotus blossoms over turbid ponds. Oh, the joy in the lotus blossom! Until everything starts to fall into silence; the revelry is at its climax; here and there silk is heard torn, frenzied creatures pant, and the eunuchs sprinkle wine and perfume over the gathered guests, who entangle themselves like kelp on the floor and up on the couches; they strew roses over the corpses and howl like devils in this glorious graveyard. And it is twelve midnight, and from the nearest minaret comes the cry:

Allah is Allah,
And Mohammed is the prophet of Allah!

And the birds in the windows respond with a sleepy chattering:

Allah is Allah,
And Mohammed is the prophet of Allah!

The pelicans lie in the torn and soaked tatters scattered here and there or hang like signal flags from the legs of overturned tables. And from the minaret comes the chant, for the third and last time:

Allah is Allah,
And Mohammed is the prophet of Allah!

The jacks-of-all-trades, the alchemists, and the diviners stand up dreamily and sleepily and wrap their heads in the drenched silk rags woven with the images of pelicans. It is three minutes past midnight. "Gentlemen, we are almost late for the nighttime prayers; let's hurry to the mosque, or, if nothing better, out into the fresh air, where we might be fortunate enough to locate the east. Let us honor the memory of the prophet!" The outer doors are opened and the blue night steps in; a fresh breeze from the stars blows throughout the hall; and the men hurry off to prayer. But behind them lie the maidens like saplings, strewn across the floor and over the couches, dead drunk and naked.

61.

Salvation is much closer than most people suspect. On the doorsteps Steinn met a Benedictine monk whom he recalled having had as his traveling companion on the Rome-Paris express. And this Benedictine monk addressed him with redemptive words.

"Leicester Square! Leicester Square!" said the monk as he laid a hand on his head, and Steinn grabbed the monk's cowl and followed him. And the monk repeated the redemptive words at every third step:

"Leicester Square!" one two three. "Leicester Square!" one two three, "Leicester Square!"

In a short time they arrived at Leicester Square, where a great celebration was clearly in full swing. The crowd was so enormous, both on the square itself and on the streets leading to it, that the streetcar and automobile traffic had been stopped, while old women and children were trodden under by the thousands, without anyone noticing or taking the trouble to gather these poor wretches together and bring them safely away.

What was happening?

Steinn pressed his way through the crowd and didn't stop until he could see the cause of the celebration. In the center of Leicester Square, Jesus Christ was being crucified. It was the crucifixion that everyone had come to see; around him circled the throng. Christ hung there upon an enormously tall tree and had obviously been nailed up in a hurry, probably without having been judged or subject to due process of law, because they hadn't given a thought to tearing off his clothes. He was dressed according to the latest fashion, like a young intellectual, poverty having long since ceased to be a virtue; his shirt was of fine-woven silk with a pattern of tiny stripes and golden buttons on the sleeves, diamonds on his tie, his hair carefully curled, his socks of bright-colored silk, a crease in his trousers, shoes with a gentlemanly cut. The bright, close-shaven face had radiated visibly with talents and virtues up until today, but now it was sweaty and deformed, the eyes bloodshot. Steinn could not understand at all why the man did not frown at the mob clustering around him.

What a mob! Because no matter how far he looked out over the crowd his eyes never came to rest on anything but whores! Mere whores! All of mankind, nothing but simple, accursed whores! Whores who demand bridal gifts and bridal gifts and bridal gifts! Whores who want to clothe themselves in silk and diamonds, feathers and furs, and demand music, roses, and happiness! – either emaciated whores or fat whores, dirty whores or spruced-up whores, dainty to the depths of their souls, beautiful whores or ugly whores, foolish or gifted, their voices dusky or fair. They stand here in one mass like sardines, and shout at Jesus Christ the crucified: "I, I! Me! Me!"

And then Steinn noticed that he was no exception: he himself was a whore just like all the rest, and when he glanced down he noticed a huge stain on his jacket, just below his chest. There he had spilled his champagne glass during his last orgy. And he was even about to ask the Crucified One for a new jacket when lightning started to flash and thunder to boom, and Heaven and Earth to quake. The day of wrath was at hand. The sun darkened and the cliffs were cloven, and from them ran dead men in underwear, at their wits' end. And it seemed to Steinn as if the curtain of the temple was torn asunder from top to bottom.

Book Six

62.

"Brussels – Berlin – Moscow!" calls out the train attendant in the first-class waiting room at the station in Basel, as if these were three villages situated next to each other, and the clock strikes. It is morning, and within two minutes the express train is on its way. And all day such a heavy rain patters on the compartment windows that one could imagine that the train was running along the bottom of a rushing river. Through the rain one can dimly see forests, fields, and human dwellings like moving pictures behind mica, and the rain claps robustly on the station pavements like applause in a huge hall. Evening comes and the light dwindles.

In a Belgian village the train ejects cramped souls into the darkness and the rain. Among them is a foreign traveler, his collar dirty and the ends of his sleeves dark with locomotive soot. The travelers who step out pull their cloaks tighter, turn their hat brims down and their collars up, hurry through the station building, and disappear into cars and horse-drawn carriages. But the foreigner stands alone, unmoving, on the platform after the train has gone, looking about like a man who has fallen into a crater, with no protection against the flood of water but for a tattered English hat on his head, sweaty and sooty. When he had started out his only luggage had been a dirty handkerchief, which he had lost two days ago between Rome and Florence. Here he stands destitute, and the rain trickles down his neck; only after all of the others have turned in their tickets does he dare to make his way through the station gate. He asks the station manager in a whisper, his heart pounding like that of a newly confirmed youngster who asks for the first time of the man in the street where the prostitutes can be found:

"Is there an abbey here?"

"Unfortunately not here at the train station, sir!" replies the Fleming, and he looks around to see whether anyone was near enough to hear how clever his answer was and to admire his wit.

"I mean whether there is an abbey here in the vicinity," corrected the traveler.

"That's another matter," said the man. "I'm afraid that it would be more advisable for you to spend the night here in the village, because it's both dark and raining."

"Would you please be so kind as to point me in the direction of the abbey?" asked the other.

"It's up the mountainside. You cannot walk there in less than half an hour in daylight. And in this darkness and foul weather it seems to me fairly impossible for a complete stranger to venture up there."

All the same the man condescended to accompany the foreigner out of the station, and then he pointed straight up in the air.

"There's the abbey," he said.

Some workman or other showed him where the path to the abbey turned off from the village road up a slope; at first there were steps leading up so that one could walk fairly easily for a time. A dim light from a lantern down on the road cast a gleam up along the foot of the mountain, but as one ascended into the trees the gleam disappeared. The traveler found himself in a palpably black night on a narrow path between tall pine trees; the rain poured down. Now it took a great deal of work not to lose the path, and he used his hands and feet to probe his way forward.

After skulking along in this way for some time he discovered that it was all for nothing: he was no longer on the path, but instead on a slanting ledge on the hillside. He searched around for several moments to see if he could find the path again, but it was no good; he ended up in tighter and tighter spots the longer he searched. The slope was spongy with wet earth and rotting leaves; he lost his footing, and it was only by luck that he was able to grab a tree trunk to stop himself from falling. The soil wet his ankles; his shoes filled with mud.

Should he turn back?

But before he gave himself time to decide what he ought to do he turned automatically upward, facing the slope. He advanced both on his knees and on all fours over the drenched earth, searched for handholds in the branches above him, scratched himself on nettles that stung like fire, muddied his hands. Now and then he thrust his feet against stumps or grabbed on to a tree trunk. He scrambled his way higher and higher, drenched, sweaty, dirty, and exhausted, and the ascent seemed to him to take an eternity. Finally he thought he caught a glimpse of the ridge of the hill against the sky.

Awaiting him here was the most difficult stretch: a dense thornbrake more than waist-high. He felt his way along a clear, narrow hollow, but the brake grew as thickly everywhere along the ridge, leaving him no other choice but to break through. And so he broke through. The thorns stung his bare hands; they hooked on to his clothing and tore it, pierced through his clothing and into his bare body, wounding him. But he no longer cared about anything, no longer winced at any pain; instead he grabbed handfuls of the thornbushes, pushed the resilient branches to the sides and stood in the next instant upon the ridge.

The darkness was too deep for him to be able to distinguish one thing from another; he glanced about to try to discover a light in a window, but to no avail. He roamed around for a short time, until he decided that his best course would be to try to find himself a place to sleep. But then powerful bells started to clang a short distance away; the air quivered at this mighty sound. They can't be more than fifty steps away, he thought, and he walked overjoyed toward the sound. Presently he was stopped by a high wall; he found a gate and in a moment stood in the courtyard between tall gables. The metal of the bells rang and rang, and the heart of the stranger hammered with fear and trembling as he stood there in the courtyard of the abbey. At each gable was an entryway; on one side the abbey, on the other the church. After some hesitation he ventured up the abbey steps, felt about, found the string of a bell, and rang the doorbell. And after he had rung the bell it finally dawned on him where he was; he awoke like a sleepwalker. What business did he have here? He knew no one here and no one knew him! This house wasn't built for men of his sort; here dwelled holy men. Here dwelled men who believed in God and Jesus Christ, but he was the most heretical of men and believed neither in God nor Jesus. What was he searching for here? His homes were waywardness, the wilderness. No, he thought, I'll hide and lie down to sleep in the churchyard until dawn.

But it was too late; inside, someone was fiddling with the door, then a little hatch on the upper part of the door was opened and a nose poked out. In the next moment the door was opened, and a lay brother in a brown cloak, with a hood drawn forward over his head, let a lantern cast its gleam out through the doorway. And the gleam fell upon a wretched wreck of a man who appeared to have fallen into the hands of robbers on the road from Jerusalem to Jericho. He stood there at the threshold of the monastery with large horn-rimmed glasses shielding his dilated and fear-stricken eyes, dirty and ragged as if he'd emerged from a peat pit, his hands bloody like those of a criminal, soaked to the skin like a keelhauled castaway. The rain took the color from his cap, and the drops trickled down his face like streaks of tobacco juice: the Great Weaver from Kashmir.

The doorkeeper glanced at him sharply and appeared to conclude that the man had recently escaped from a madhouse. He gave no greeting, and asked, with no introduction:

"What do you want?"

"Is there a man here called Alban?" asked Steinn Elliði.

"If it is the prior whom you mean, Father Alban de Landry," answered the brother, "he is not available before seven o'clock tomorrow morning. The fathers have just finished the *completorium,* and now it is *magnum silentium*."

"Magnum silentium?"

"Yes, *magnum silentium.*"

The dryness of the doorkeeper's answers was enough to call forth the dominant in Steinn Elliði's heart, and without digging any further into what this *"magnum silentium"* meant, he ordered:

"Go to Father de Landry, and tell him that there is a man here who absolutely needs to speak to him right away."

"Since so much is at stake, sir," said the servant, after discovering by the foreigner's voice that he was an educated man, "might I then invite you to step into the foyer" – he showed him into a comely waiting room situated next to the entrance hall, turned on the light, and left.

A substantial amount of time passed, and Steinn waited. Everything was silent, as at the bottom of the sea. On the wall hung a graceful portrait of our Lady from Luxembourg, *Consolatrix afflictorum:* the Mother of God with the child, her countenance like a spruced-up mermaid, her dark purple, golden-stitched gown lined with crinoline, a crown on her tiny head. It was almost comical that this woman should be the consolation of the afflicted. Over the door hung a replica of the Spanish Crucifix of Holy Christ from Limpias, one of the most poignant representations of the crucifixion in the world, because the sweat, tears, and blood that ooze down Christ's breast are not like painted-on sweat, tears, and blood, but rather like sweat, tears, and blood. And the eyes waver back and forth in the death struggle; they look sometimes at me and sometimes at you, admonitory as if they wish to say, *"Memento mori,"* and sometimes to God in Heaven crying, *"Eli, Eli!"*[86] Hanging there upon his cross is a living man who will likely give up the ghost this very night.

63.

Father Alban opens the door quickly and stops in the doorway. He is clad in a raven black full-length cloak, his hands hidden in the arms of the cloak, his palms clasped. The strongly built, magnificent head of the canon is uncovered except for a black skullcap on its crown. He is pale-cheeked, but the look of his eyes is therefore even more powerful, his mouth closed; from him radiates strength and cold austerity. But when he sees his visitor an incredibly gentle smile comes over his face, and in one instant the austerity has changed to clemency. He recognizes Steinn Elliði again at first glance, bids him good evening in a bright Gregorian voice, extends both his hands, and greets him joyfully. It was by no means clear to Steinn Elliði as to what controlled his actions, because he threw himself down onto his knees before the cloaked man and kissed his hand. Perhaps it was due to the monk's personality that he greeted him with such affection and feeling, or rather, and more than anything, due to the hope of his own salvation.

"Forgive me for coming here at night and disturbing you," he stammered. "But I have come a long way to ask you to help me. I have come to ask you to tell me what I should do. If God exists, then everything is vanity except for him. My sufferings have overstepped all limits. Tell me, do you think that God exists? And what does this God demand?"

"Stand up, dear sir, and let's be bold!" answered the ascetic. "It's God himself who has led you here, and a great celebration awaits you. If you had remembered to put your address on your letter to me, for which I thank you sincerely, I would have written to you a long time ago. But now you have come, and I am given not only a chance to praise God for leading one and all where he pleases, even without me writing a letter, but also to glorify once again the most precious message in the Gospel, that is, that neither death nor life nor angels nor principalities nor the realized nor the untold nor powers nor heights nor depths nor any other creature is able to part us from the love of God, who revealed himself in Jesus Christ our Lord. What does God demand, you ask? He never demands anything but this: that you come to him as a little child. When Christ challenges modern man to follow him he does not demand that a man leave his father and mother, sisters and brothers, wife, children, and home, because modern man turned his back on all of these things long ago, and they are of little worth to him. Modern man has opinions, interests, ideals, convictions, and knowledge. These things are most precious to him, in the same way that men of old loved their fathers and mothers, wives and children. For this reason Christ says to modern man: Forsake your opinions, interests, ideals, convictions, and knowledge; lift your crosses to your backs and follow me. Unless you turn around and become like children you will never be able to enter the Heavenly Kingdom–"

He helped Steinn to his feet and smiled into his eyes with deep clemency. And all of this touched Steinn's heart.

"This house stands open to you," the monk continued. "Imagine that you have come home. In this place peace reigns. We monks of the Benedictine order have two mottoes: one is *'Pax,'* the other *'Ut in omnibus glorificetur Deus.'*[87] Let us make them our truths! Now please follow me into the monastery, friend, and the brother will fry some eggs for you, because you must surely be hungry. And what a great wonder it is to see how you look, my good man – and bloody all over! You surely haven't been in a fight? And where is your luggage? Oh, fine; since you have no luggage I shall provide you at least with dry undergarments, since you are thoroughly wet. *Eh bien,* now we'll go to the refectory."

A heavy, black oaken door was opened, upon which the word "*Clausura*" was painted near the top in red letters; then came a corridor that extended a very long way, silent as a crypt, but the footsteps of the men echoed in all directions. The lay brother walked ahead of them with a lantern. Finally came a wide hall, cold and empty: the refectory, with a great crucifix at the far end, bare tables and benches along the walls. In the center of the hall was a little table laid with a cloth, chairs around it; Steinn was offered a seat there. Speaking was permitted in hushed tones only. Both the lay brother and the father left, and Steinn sat in the dark hall like a spellbound character in a folktale. All was quiet.

A short time later the lay brother reappeared and was now the reverse of what he had been before, completely cordial; he served the guest thick porridge in a bowl and fried eggs on a platter, strawberries, salad and bread, and poured sour wine into a glass. Then Steinn discovered that he was as hungry as a horse left outside in the winter, remembered that he hadn't eaten since this morning when he had coffee with wheat bread at the train station in Basel. But he was so befuddled that he started with the salad and ended with the eggs, and did not have the sense to cut them into pieces and transfer an appropriate portion over to his plate according to good manners, but rather pulled the platter over, strewed salt and pepper over the eggs, and emptied the platter in an instant. When this was finished he was full, and he stood up. The lay brother waited a bit for him to give thanks to God at the close of the meal, but when this did not happen he picked up the lantern once more and asked the guest to follow him. The hallways seemed endless again; they were like a labyrinth; finally came a stairway; Steinn followed the brother; the echo of their footsteps once again became a discordant concert that disturbed the nighttime silence of the house; more hallways and stairs followed, and finally the door of the room intended for Steinn.

The weather was cold and raw although it was only slightly past midsummer, and Steinn was drenched. When he stepped over the threshold and saw Father Alban on his knees before the fireplace, he was seized with a feeling of gratitude so deep that it struck him speechless. The burning sticks crackled. The room had been prepared in haste; a broom stood by the door, a witness to the fact that Father Alban had just finished sweeping, the bedcovers white on the bed. Against one wall stood a padded prie-dieu, and over it hung Christ made of white plaster on a cross of ebony, with a green garland stuck behind it. On another wall was a portrait of "*S. Benoist, Abbé, Fondateur et Patriarche de L'ordre des Bénédictins.*" He was wearing the same kind of cloak as Father Alban, and offered his hands to Heaven and prayed to God; around the head of the saint beamed rays of light.

The glimmer from the hearth fluttered through the half-dark room, and everything had an air of antiquity. Life did not change here with the years and centuries; the mottoes were still the same as in Subiaco: "*Pax*" and "*Ut in omnibus glorificetur Deus.*" Outside the rain poured down. Father Alban stood up, turned to Steinn, and smiled.

"Eh bien!" he said. "You see that we have laid dry underclothes there on your bed. You should hang your outer garments on the back of the chair and let them dry by the fire. We hope that you won't be too cold. Now sleep deeply and well. *Tout ira mieux!* May God send his angels to keep watch over you, my good lad! I look forward to seeing you in the morning. God give you holy dreams!"

And the monk took both of his hands and pressed them, then left and shut the door quietly. This house was like the heart of a good man. Such quiet, such peace! Steinn Elliði wept like a little girl.

64.

He woke to the ringing of bells early in the morning, dressed quickly, emerged from his room, and lost his way for a long time in the labyrinth of twisting passageways and spiral staircases. Black-clad beings in long robes, whom he dared not address since their hoods were drawn over their faces, appeared before him now and then; they hurried silently past and disappeared. But through the windows, which were set so high in the wall that he could barely reach them with his outstretched arm, he could see the clear blue summer sky, innocent and deep like a child's eyes.

Finally he came to a door at the end of the lowest hallway, large, broad, and sturdy, with this inscription written above it: *"Hæc est domus Domini"* – "This is the house of the Lord." Finally, was his first thought as he stood before the door of this house, and his heart began beating hard. Should he turn away or dare to open it? Either choice could be dangerous. He was like a rheumatic old geezer who racks his brain over whether he should pick up his staff or let it lie. And finally, what would the Lord say if such a man, the son of waywardness, dared to step over the threshold of his house? Wouldn't such a man profane the company of the blessed and God's saints?

He had never set foot in a more astonishing house than the Lord's. Down from the dome peered long-faced beings, beardless and alien, with closed eyes and palms pressed together; it was difficult to guess whether they were dead or living; perhaps both at once, or rather, neither; but they gazed beyond life and death into the depths of themselves and the Almighty. Around their faces grew the most astonishing plants, like those on the flutes of Ljónharður Pípín. On the columns to the right stood tall bearded men in Roman togas; one held a key, another a sword, a third a book, a fourth a crosier, a fifth a house, and so on: these were various saints of God. One thing was astonishing: the key in the hands of the first was much larger than the house in the hands of the fifth; it seemed supernatural that such a little house could be opened with such a huge key. To the left stood noblewomen in long gowns that covered everything except for their toes. Veils covered their hair, and their necks and breasts were enwrapped in bright cloths, but their bright and blessed faces were thrust forward from their head coverings and their long, slender fingers from their sleeves. Here was Scholastica, holding a dove as if she believed in the virtues of birds. Hildegard also held a feather ("It takes only one feather to make me die of laughter," says Joseph Delteil), Gertrude, Valborg, and Mechtilde, all brides of Christ, and long since gone to Heaven. At the far end stood a great altar on a marble platform, and over it a white canopy set with golden rhombuses and other adornments, standing on four pillars, with a green velvet cloth stretched between the rear pillars; on the altar stood a variety of shining objects whose meaning no one understands, with a crucifix above. High, high up in the vault over the altar was a golden triangle, a symbol of the Holy Trinity, and within the triangle a white lamb with a pennant under its feet, lying on a large, old-fashioned clasped book. How in Heaven was the blessed lamb supposed to flip through the pages of the book if it wanted to read? Because with two cloven hooves it is impossible to turn the pages of a book; and what would happen to the pennant if the lamb were to stand up? Because a lamb walks on four legs and is absolutely unable to hold on to a pennant. Along the side walls were numerous small vaults, and beneath each of them one altar, and over each altar events depicted from the life of God and his saints here on Earth, some carved from wood and painted with glistening colors, others painted on limestone, still others sculpted in stone, with the altars made of polished marble the color of chocolate pudding. The most distinctive things in the house of the Lord were the mysterious men standing before each altar, with their backs turned, their faces toward the wall. They were wearing ornate chasubles, and under these, snow-white gowns. Some of the chasubles were red as blood newly dripped from a wound, others bright gold like the noonday sun, still others green like a field glittering with sun between showers of rain, others purple like Mount Etna at five o'clock on a July morning, and finally one could see chasubles black as tarred coffins; and on the altars burned three-stemmed king's candles. And all of these supernatural beings spoke in half tones, each before his own altar: they said *"Gloria," "Misericordia,"* and *"Secula seculorum,"*[88] and their chatter was blended into a continuous purl that sounded throughout the vaults like a westerly breeze in the leaves. Sometimes little bells were rung, with weak voices like newborn lambs, and the vaults echoed like forests, and at the foot of each altar behind the magicians knelt a little brown-cloaked being that beat its breast and repeated *"Mea culpa, mea culpa, mea maxima culpa."*[77] And Steinn felt as if he were standing at the bottom of the sea among divine mermen who could neither sin nor die, and who had stood there since the creation of the world and read from the Psalter to the glory of God while mankind sinned and died. Everything was magnificent in the house of the Lord, and he threw himself onto his knees before one of the altars and gazed with tearful eyes at the cross.

65.

I.

Si me vis esse in tenebris, sis benedictus, et si me vis esse in luce, sis iterum benedictus. Si me dignaris consolari, sis benedictus: et si me vis tribulari, sis æque et semper benedictus.

If it is your will that I remain in darkness, may you be blessed. And if it is your will that I come into the light, may you again be blessed. If it pleases you to comfort me, may you be blessed. And if it is your will that I be afflicted, may you again and always be blessed.

God, I approach your altar and kneel; I throw myself down prostrate. I cast myself down onto my face before your altar and cry out. I cry out to you and implore you. *In manu tua sum; gyra et reversa me per circuitum!* I am in your hands; turn me this way and push me back that way, just as it pleases you. If it is your will that I remain in darkness, may you be blessed. And if it pleases you to lead my soul into great light, may you lead my soul into great light. Praised be the name of the Lord now and forever.

II.

It is my soul that cries out. It cries out loudly like a little child, when other voices have become weak and hoarse. For so long, so long have I stifled this child's voice, but now it cries out. It cries out in the darkness, asking, "Are you there? Answer me only this one thing, whether you are there!" And all will be answered. Then I will know that it was you who poured the darkness over my soul and held the cup of despair to my lips. And I bless your will. Because if you are there, then you are my God, and if you are my God, then your will is holy, and it is my salvation, and my afflictions gifts of grace. And whether you turn me this way or push me back that way, I am in your hands. My soul cries out in the darkness and longs to know this one thing: are you there?

Listen! The voice that speaks is prodigious, deep and steady, and answers with these old words of wisdom: If you had not known that I was there, you would never have thought to call on me.

Yes, my God, I have always known that you were there. I had a suspicion of you always in the unknown. And I mocked you precisely because I believed that you existed. And although I mocked you, my conscious life never actually had any other pillar of support than the suspicion that you existed. Perhaps it was never more clear to me who you were than precisely when I exalted the merits of men over your omnipotence; I was never more near to falling at your feet than when I mocked your name most bitterly, never more terrified in the consciousness of my shame than when I had silenced your voice with the most pandemoniac acts of my intellect. My revolt against you was the lowest level of my cowardice.

III.

Now I have come before your altar. Do you see me? Do you see this ludicrous worm in the dust; do you see this dust of the dust? And I, who am nothing but dust, dare to speak! I dare to speak to you!

I have come before your face so that your eyes can see my heart. Look into my heart! This is who I am, exactly as you see me. *Respice in me, Deus, et miserere mei, quia unicus et pauper sum ego;*[90] I am precisely this: indigent and alone. I am the husk where impotence took up its abode. I beg you to crush me. I beg that it might be your will, and not mine. I pray that your will be done on Earth as in Heaven. I pray that I might be nothing from now on, and everything nothing but you. Blessed be your will! I beg to be lost in you.

IV.

I peer into the darkness that envelops me. Yes, I know that you are there! I believe nothing except that you are there. There can be nothing there but you! What indeed should be there but you? And still I bless you; I know that your holy decrees have not led me for nothing into the darkness. I believe that you have prepared for me a brighter light than ever my darkness was dark.

Look! My breast waits for you to lay your healing hand upon it. Yes, it is true: sometimes I have suffered. Sometimes I have even started to bleed again from a wound healed long ago, and I have often felt as if seven arrows of steel had been shot through my heart. Why should I not confess to you that I have wept? As soon as night fell I was alone. I felt so ill; I was destitute and alone. My God, I wept all those long winter nights because I was destitute and alone. I felt that nothing existed except for me. I was too selfish to have friends, too arrogant to call to you.

I have never told anyone that I wept. And I shall tell no one else, only you. I am telling you everything because I believe in you. Tell me whether you are listening to me, so that I conceal nothing from you. Will you permit me to forget that my heart is completely covered with scars from old wounds? Help me to rejoice in the one thing that I learned from this, that it was you who created my heart.

V.

I thank you for inviting me home. What fortune to be allowed to speak with you! What unspeakable abundance of joy to know that I am with you! All despair is diminished to know that you see me and hear me. My God, my God, I have found you and have come to you!

The world lies behind me full of deluding enchantments and enchanting delusions. Help me to forget these horrific visions! Allow me to love you and to forget all else. Allow me to be near you always; let me never again lose the certain knowledge that you are near me. Will you watch over me? Will you be everything to me? Take your little senseless child in your arms and comfort it.

See, my God, I come to you like a little senseless child. I know nothing, want nothing, am nothing. You, Creator of the worlds, Heaven of the heavens, God of the gods, are my father. My father, I have come to you.

VI.

If it is your will to lead my soul into great light, then lead my soul into great light, for I am a little child, and all that I desire is the great light. And now I have thrown myself down before your altar, where your servants worship the truth. And I beg you with the humility of a little child: will you tell me whether it is your truth, the only truth, that your servants worship, or is there some other truth? I know you wish me to know nothing but the truth. And I know that you have created me to live in the truth, because I will never be free and will never come to you unless I know the truth, because you are the truth. You are the only truth and all is untrue but you. Will you whisper to me whether what they teach is the truth? Did you found a Church among men as your apostles say? And why did you found this Church? Is it true that you have founded it to preach to them the truth, and to free them? Whisper, whisper! My ears thirst! For if it is true then I will enter your Church and devote my life to the truth from this moment on.

And if it is not the truth that your apostles preach and your servants worship, and if it is untrue that you founded the Church or gave it the task of preaching the truth, and if the Church is fallible and no more knowledgeable of the way than any other human establishment, then I beg you to lead me away from this altar. I beg you to lead me to the other altar, where the only truth, your truth, can be found. If you tell me that your truth can be found on the far side of the world, then I am ready to set out today.

Father, are you there? Hear your child!

VII.

Is it true that in the beginning you created the world and made man in your image? And is it true that afterward man directed his will toward things that are of less worth than you? Is it true that man's will is inclined toward things that are at variance with your will? Is it true that sin exists, and that sin is a revolt against your will? Is it true? If the opposite is true, that man's will is in complete unity with your holy will, then tell me so, my God, because I cannot endure this uncertainty.

Only this, and I will start a new life. Is it true that you are displeased when a man turns his longing toward the created, but that you find it most pleasing when he bends all the energies of his being toward his Creator, the eternal reality behind the created world? Is it true that the man who pushes God away and dedicates his life to delusions is eternally lost; and that he who dedicates his spirit to his Creator and fetters his physical desires with asceticism celebrates eternal life? Is it true that he who lives according to nature is on the road to perdition, but that he who lives according to the demands of the spirit shall see your glory? Is it true? If it is true then I shall, from this moment on, live according to the demands of the spirit, for I long only to behold your glory.

VIII.

Take uncertainty from me. Does this Church tell the truth? Is it true that there once lived a man named Jesus Christ? Is it true that he was the envoy of perfection, the Adam of the highest humanity, as your wise men say? Is it true that Jesus Christ is raised over all creation?

I have never asked such huge questions before; now I ask in childish earnestness; I know that you hear the expectation of a child in my voice when I ask. Is it true, my God: was it you? Was Jesus Christ, this son of sorrow, this homeless child among men, this outcast from everything, whom they spat on and scourged – was he you? Is it true that you have taken upon yourself man's tatters in order to conquer man; that you have clothed yourself in man's weakness in order to teach man to conquer the world? Or is the opposite true, that you have always hidden yourself in your Heaven and that it is not possible for man to know you, not even whether you exist? What is true, what is false?

Who was this Jesus Christ if he was something other than you? I do not understand Jesus Christ if he was something other than you. And if he was not you, then I beg you to teach me to understand Jesus Christ.

IX.

I have read the Gospels in one sitting; read them time and again without intermission; read them backward and forward and yet have not dared to trust, in any way, the one conclusion that I felt could be drawn from them: that Jesus Christ was you. For the longest time I have shunned placing any faith in such a glorious message. Imagine what disappointment I would have felt if I had later realized that I had been mistaken.

I have tried to convince myself that Jesus Christ was a liar. I have read all of the Gospels under the presupposition that he was a false prophet. But how unfortunate is the liar who lets himself be crucified for his lies! When has that ever been done before? In spite of all of my prudent attempts to convince myself that it must be a lie that he and you were one, no sooner had I finished my reading of the Gospels when this conclusion cleared all the rest out of the way: yes, he and the Father are one. It is not possible to read the Gospels otherwise; one must come to this conclusion. The beginning of the New Testament and the end are precisely this: he and the Father are one. What a joyous message if it is true.

I have read all of the Gospels with the presupposition that he was insane; that he was a megalomaniac; that he was psychotic; that the idea of his own divinity was a schizophrenic obsession; that he was not The Way at all; that he was neither the Truth nor the Life. But I always found myself forced to ask, during times of trouble, how can an insane man have done all this? And on the other hand: how can it be justified that the New Testament, the book in which the wise men of the world descry the pinnacle of perfection, is all about a lunatic? In order to do this, all ideals built on sound reasoning would have to be turned inside out. In order to do this, new criteria would have to be formulated, and that deemed lowest which everyone believes to be highest, that most imperfect which everyone believes to be most perfect. Then the most perfect thing known to the soul of man could be considered madness and delusion, and the beast a paragon. Sound reasoning could never justify considering Jesus

Christ a lunatic. Quite the contrary: sound reasoning can comprehend the perfection of Jesus Christ only when it realizes that he and the Father are one, can worship his teachings only when it sees the perfection of God in Christ himself. Human wisdom cannot separate God and Christ.

And yet if I persuade myself that all of the humility and equanimity that he displayed to his revilers and tormenters was a type of arrogant madness, I would certainly be forced to halt at this final question: how could any man be resurrected from death, even if he did have delusions of grandeur? Because no matter how I consider the New Testament, it is not at all possible for me to ignore that astonishing event, which turns all of the science of the world into vain prattle.

I have read all of the Gospels under the presumption that they are works of fiction; that Jesus Christ never existed. But then I always arrive at this question: who wrote this work of fiction? My God, will you lead me to the person who has made up this story about Jesus Christ? And if many others have helped in doing so, will you lead me to them? I am sufficiently experienced to know that it is impossible to fictionalize about anything except for oneself. It is impossible to make poetry more beautiful than a man is himself. It is impossible to describe a man better than oneself, or, in fact, a man worse than oneself. Only someone who was as great as Jesus Christ himself could have written the story of Jesus Christ. If you tell me that I may not believe in Jesus Christ, then I will believe in whomever wrote the story of Jesus Christ. The one who wrote the story of Jesus Christ has revealed to mankind your perfection. And I believe in your perfection. After I had rattled off to myself all the *videtur ut non*[91] about the divinity of Jesus Christ and finally thought that I could celebrate my victory over this man from Galilee, I discovered that this song of praise echoed stronger in my soul than at any other time:

Unus Altissimus Jesus Christus.[92]

My skepticism could not defeat the man from Galilee.

My God, help me. He persecutes me. I cannot negotiate with this man from Galilee. I am like a cotton-grass wick in his hands.

X.

I believe in Jesus Christ. I cannot help but believe in Jesus Christ. Everything is worthless to me except for Jesus Christ. I will die if I am not allowed to believe in Jesus Christ.

And I think that I can hear you calling to me to believe in him. Stop me if I am on the wrong path! Are you not telling me that it was for Jesus Christ that your saints were blessed? Are you not telling me that in his name mankind is forgiven its sins? Are you not telling me that no one comes to you except through Jesus Christ? And are you not commanding me to lift my cross to my shoulders and follow him?

XI.

"*Si quidem aliquid melius et utilius saluti hominum, quam pati, fuisset, Christus utique verbo et exemplo ostendisset*," says the Master.[93] "If there were anything better or more useful for man than suffering, Christ would have taught it to us by his words and examples."

Finally I have come before your eyes to ask you to open to me the way that leads to unity with you, the way that Christ has marked out, the way that all the saints and holy men have trodden since time immemorial, *regia via sanctæ crucis*.[94] And I have come to ask you to place the cross on my shoulders. I pray to you and nothing but you and grant myself no refreshment except in you. You alone are my hope, my health, and my freedom. And the way to you is the way of the cross. I know that wherever I go and wherever I search I will find no road higher or more secure than the *regia via sanctæ crucis*. There is no other road to life, to life in you, than the king's road of the holy cross. The cross – the scandal and the foolishness – it has now become my only hope, because without it I would never be able to shun myself, and now I ask you for the grace to be able to bear it.

I pray for the grace to be able to die to myself so that I might be allowed to begin to live in you. You have led me out into the darkness, and have filled my soul with forebodings of my perdition, to reveal to me that there is nothing within the limits of existence that could possibly comfort me while I have not yet denied myself. You have led my soul into great darkness in order to make me lose all faith in my own power and to find you. You have allowed my pride to sink into the waywardness of waywardness so that I might find the footprints of Jesus Christ, *hanc regiam viam quæ est via crucis*,[95] the bloody trail of the cross on the hard frozen ground. And now I know that you will lead my soul into great light. A man finds no solution to the riddles of his soul before he has thrown himself down to the ground and fallen onto his face before the cross. In the cross is good fortune, says the Master; in the cross life, in the cross protection against enemies. In the cross is the infusion of heavenly blessings; in the cross the most sublime bliss; the cross is the condensing lens of all true virtue;

our souls derive their strength from the cross; in the cross and nowhere else is perfection.[96]

O crux, ave, spes unica!

XII.

"*Factus sum omnibus humillimus et infimus, ut tuam superbiam mea humilitate vinceris*," says the voice of the man from Galilee. He shouldered his cross for me and allowed himself to be crucified for me so that I might learn to shoulder my cross and die to myself upon the cross. If I die with him, I will live with him. And if I share in his suffering, I will also be granted a share of his glory.

Over the gate of the royal road stand the words that reveal the key to the forecourt:

Nothing to you is worthy of pursuit or admiration, and nothing to you of value but for God alone and that which belongs to God.

The comforts granted to the created are to you worthless chaff.

The soul that loves God despises all that is inferior to God.

God alone is eternal and unchangeable, fills all, is the comfort of the soul and the true joy of the heart.

66.

The flowers here in the monastery garden smell best on days after rain. There stands the rosebush with three hundred and fifty roses. Behold the beds with the huge multicolored blossoms! Those in the middle are called Georgias, because they come from Georgia, a land that lies on the other side of the Earth. Aren't they delightful, the paths between the young trees? The leaves tickle your cheeks. At the western end stands the fountain in a glade, with beautifully green, mown grass all around. At the eastern end is a little grove. And in the grove stands the Virgin Mary, who nurtured the Lord for us. The Virgin Mary is blessed among women, as it says in the angel's greeting: *"Ad Christum per Mariam."* We love this image of Mary in the grove; it is well made; supple ivy covers the pedestal upon which it stands. Notice how the linen falls about her head and shoulders. The same comeliness shines also from the boy's mantle: the swathes are almost transparent; behold the Lamb of God! There is something wondrously human in this image of the child; his face just like any other infant at the breast; you see here not a trace of the elated air of divinity which so many portrait artists have taken to putting on his face. The child of Mary is like every other child, and so is Jesus Christ in his mature years: we think of him as we do every other man. *"Homo factus est,"* says the profession of faith, short and sweet. He himself was so conscious of his humanity that when he was called good he answered, "No one is good but God alone." The merits of our Lord Jesus Christ are to us most richly comforting because he came to us as a man, lived as a man, died as a man. In his veins streamed blood, just as in your veins and mine. This is how God chose to teach mankind to overcome the world: he himself came to us as a man and overcame the world as a man. For the only way that we are able to shoulder our crosses bravely is because the man Jesus Christ carried his before us. Think not upon your sorrows, but entrust everything to the Lord, past and future; the Lord calms the wind and the sea. You have been led to a holy place, but the Lord directed the journey; allow his mercy to trickle over your soul. Remember that man is nothing without the mercy of God, and look around you: around you reigns *Pax Benedictina,* the Benedictine peace. Yesterday it was windy and rainy. Last night it cleared up, and this morning is full of promises. God's world spreads itself out before your eyes beautifully, as in the first light of the sun. Imagine that you are a new man, that you were created last night and saw the sun for the first time when it appeared over the edge of the forest this morning. Greet this world in which we stand not as a child of Adam, but rather as a son of God, limbs on the body of Christ, the re-created man, who does not live according to nature, but rather is above nature. Reason no longer according to your own understanding, but rather be certain according to the revelations of God. Drink no longer from the salty well of philosophy, but rather strive for purity of heart. A pure heart sees through Heaven and Hell.

I told you last evening that God loves you. I tell you the same thing today. I will tell you the same thing tomorrow: God loves you. I will not stop saying this to you until you have come to the understanding that it is the most precious of all the things that have been said in the world, the kernel of all joyous tidings. God himself, the Almighty, the Creator: he loves you. He loves you so much that he cannot think of losing sight of you for a single moment. His eyes follow you wherever you go. His ears have heard the falling of every tear from your eyes. He has loved you ever since you were an infant. Yes, he loved you before you came into being, has loved you since the creation of the world, and created you to allow you to revel in his glory. And he has descended from his Heaven in order to make your path to his glory more passable, has become the lowest and smallest of all. He let himself be nailed to the cross for you, precisely as if no other person existed on Earth except for you, so that you would not have to suffer the consequences of your apathy toward his love and your revolts against his will. It is he who protected your steps while you roamed throughout the world, friendless, wayward, and disturbed, watched over you like a mother at the foot of her suffering child's bed. And now he has led you here to us, his wretched, unworthy servants, so that we might serve you.

In your countenance one glimpses the understanding of a mature soul; I perceive clearly that you are a much wiser man than I. And I am humbled to walk here by your side, daring to speak to you, as if I were so conceited as to think to teach you. I myself am the least learned of the disciples. The only thing that I have the power to do is thank God that he has displayed to me, so unworthy, the grace to show a soul whom he loves the way to our house. All that I am able to do is to receive you, just as a poor servant is required to receive the nobleman whom the king summons to council.

Do not look up to me, dear sir; I beg you this as fluently as I can, because I am not in any way more worthy in the eyes of God because I wear a monk's cowl, or because the holy office of priest has been placed upon my shoulders. Neither of these things does anything but increase my obligations. I am the weakest of men and the most frail, and I perpetually forget the presence of God; keep this in mind every time that you speak to me. No one has further to go than I. If you want to see a miserable wretch of God, then look at me. I have not fallen seven times like the righteous, but rather four hundred and ninety times, like those who are most pitiable. But every time I fall I stand up again with these words of Saint Augustine on my lips: "*Potuerunt isti et illi, quare non ego!*" – "These and those were able to, why not I?"; and then I fall once more. You are justified in finding me ridiculous.

It is the hallmark of a Christian man to know the key to true perfection. Never let God's presence slip from your mind. The key to your perfection is to remember at every moment of your life that you stand before the face of God. Therefore let your life be an uninterrupted prayer, all of your work in the service of God, every movement of your mind *ad majorem Dei gloriam* – to the further glorification of God. In the same way that the love of God enwraps you, so are you obligated to direct your thoughts to him, forever and always. In the morning when you wake let the first movement of your consciousness be a song of praise to him. And when you close your eyes to sleep in the evening let this be your final thought: *In manu tua sum.*[97] Every step that you take, every word that you speak, every glance: let all of your thoughts be directed toward this one thing. It is the hallmark of the saints that they forget themselves in the sight of God. Pray and busy yourself with nothing but prayer. Pray to God. Pray always to God. Pray everywhere to God. For everything.

67.

Several days later, at the close of supper, the investiture of two novices took place in the abbey's chapter hall. Steinn Elliði was invited to attend, and the Guest Master showed him to a special seat. Two young men were being accepted as novitiates: they had during the preceding months learned the abbey's traditions and participated in the life of the novices, in layman's dress and with full freedom of action. One was from The Hague, the other from Paris. Steinn had noticed them immediately in the choir, two men of the world surrounded by eighty canons, looking perpetually confused by everything that was happening. The Dutchman looked as if he had been a bank clerk or an office worker for an important company: he had gold-rimmed eyeglasses and his hair was gleaming with hair cream, his clothing and shoes were styled according to last year's fashion. His shirt and tie were handsome without awakening any special notice, just like those worn by employees of upright commercial institutions. He had a fountain pen and a pencil in the breast pocket of his jacket. The man from Paris was still quite young, obviously from a bourgeois or perhaps aristocratic family, admirably raised, with dark eyes and eyebrows, his skin bright and pink like a young girl's. His mouth, like his hands, displayed sensitivity, and his clothing was as tasteful as it was unostentatious, the mark of a good upbringing. These two youths had said farewell to the world in order to be consecrated to the cross from this day on.

All of the windowpanes in the hall were stained and let in only meager light, but above the abbot's seat burned a small candle that cast a dull gleam over the hall's Baroque style and the facial portraits of abbots many hundreds of years old, maintaining watch along all the walls. Everything is silent. Finally a bell rings dimly from a distant tower somewhere; the hall doors are opened and the monks step in two by two. They are clad in black choir robes, with their hoods pulled forward over their faces; each walks to his own seat in the hall. Last to enter is the abbot, with a white miter on his head; he sits in the high seat. Finally everyone is seated; eighty black-clad beings stare straight ahead, their faces expressionless like stone statues; everything is as quiet as before a beheading.

68.

Father Alban, this fool of the Lord, *"le fou de bon Dieu,"* as he called himself, who emphatically denied that he was a man able to teach himself, much less others, became in fact the one whom Steinn looked upon as his master ever afterward. Father Alban had found the way that the son of waywardness had sought all of his life. Although Father Alban was extremely busy with his work, which consisted of attending five hours of divine offices every day like a regular monk, as well as serving the brotherhood as prior and Novice Master, two positions laden with responsibility, he still never seemed to lack the time to speak with the foreign guest. Steinn sat for long periods of time conversing with him in his room, as the sun shone in through the window and the summer breeze, blowing in from the garden, brought the perfume of roses. Or they walked side by side through the young trees, where the crowns were low enough to brush a man's cheeks, and the days passed by so quickly that the sun seemed to set before noon. And our Lady stands in the grove.

It did not take long before the monk knew all the details of Steinn's life and spiritual journey, the hopes and disappointments of his youth, his dreams and reality, his plans and shipwrecks, his struggles, victories, and defeats. And he knew what was sick in Steinn's soul and what healthy. Steinn studied Christian ascetic theory, either by listening to the monk's living words, or by reading the books that he recommended. *De Imitatione Jesu Christi* became by and by his fondest reading, then *Introduction à la vie dévote* by Saint François de Sales, the *Exercitia Spiritualia* of Saint Ignatius, Master Eckehart, Pascal, and finally the Doctor Angelicus himself.

Little by little Steinn became part of the household of the abbey. Its astonishing aspect disappeared: he discovered that daily life here was just like anywhere else among mortals. He learned to find his way through the halls, got to know the monks. He attended services, dipped his finger in the holy water at the church door and signed himself, kneeled whenever he walked before the cross, received a Psalter and participated in the Gregorian chant, came to understand the Mass better and better, and would not be satisfied until he had come to understand the meaning of every last little detail of the liturgy.

The monks were the most educated of all men, gentle in their conduct, cheerful, modest. When they were at Mass their faces reflected strong determination, and during the chanting, deep adoration that no outside influence could perturb. They would not have been vexed even if the house had collapsed. But in the refectory, where guests were invited to come, they were extraordinarily cheerful, and in the free time at the conclusion of meals they told antic stories from east and west, or wonderful tales about everything under the sun, and laughed in such a way that no one without a good conscience could possibly imitate. Over time Steinn came to know what each of them was named; behind each name was a man with distinct characteristics, although all of them seemed cast in the same mold at first sight. Father Alexandre had a huge nose; he was exceptionally learned and just as absentminded, knocked on everything that came into his hands as if he wanted to find out whether it might be hollow inside, peered into his glass as if gazing into a crystal ball, held his knife to his ear like a tuning fork while he was eating. He seemed to be the type of man who held many interesting discussions with himself, and who saw most things in a philosophical light. Father Benjamin looked like a portrait of a saint from the Beuron school, both solemn and personable. His eyes shone with a childish purity and deep understanding; out in the world others take it upon themselves to trample down such persons. Father Boots' usual expression consisted of pursed lips, flared nostrils, and a furrowed brow, making one believe that he had recently committed some misdeed or other and was preparing to commit yet another. In conversation, however, he proved to be meek and harmless; he pressed his palms together as if begging for mercy and smiled out to his ears, causing one to forgive him of all his misdeeds at once. Father Benoit was handsome and dignified, portly like a medieval canon, around sixty, with an abrupt manner of speaking, gentle laughter, and frolic in his eyes. Dorval, the Guest Master, was lighthearted and animated, companionable and inquisitive; he thought it great entertainment to be told the news if there was any news to tell, told the news himself if no one else knew any, and read the newspapers. Word went around that he sometimes smoked a pipe out in the garden, but everyone adored him and found no fault with him for this. He was *un homme du Midi* and went to the Riviera for three-week stretches each winter to undergo treatment for asthma. "The climate in Belgium," he said, "now that's a miserable climate!" He had played as a child beneath palm trees. The Venerable Father, the abbot himself, was an aristocratic and honorable man, his smile and glance warm and paternal; they had all wept with joy when he returned to them after a half-year mission to the Congo last year. His bearing was determined and stately, his voice slightly cracked when he began the Benedicite at meals. He was sparing with words, but unsparing with his genial smile, and he would warm everything around him wherever he went. He was the incarnation of Benedictine dignity and gentility. And in the midst of these men went Father Alban, strong and gentle, kingly and meek, wise and childish, inspired and taciturn, smitten with the guilty conscience of a saint, because he was a holy man. Other men faded from Steinn's mind when he thought about Father Alban. *Voilà un homme!* Such a countenance! Such hawk's eyes! Such a bearing! His profile was pure of form, like a portrait on a Roman coin. Whenever Steinn thought of Benedict of Nursia, the nobleman who became the father of Christian monasticism, it proved impossible for him to call to mind any other image than the likeness of Father Alban.

69.

It was one of Father Alban's particular characteristics that he never spoke about himself except during those few times when he could not refrain from saying what a contemptible and imperfect person he was, frail and helpless, unworthy in the eyes of God. He never made any mention of his former life. Had he put all of his memories to sleep or had he been born with a scapular on his shoulders? The information that Steinn received about the upbringing and former lifestyle of his master came from others, in particular the talkative Guest Master, Père Dorval.

Father Alban's story was in certain respects parallel to the life of Charles de Foucauld, his compatriot, an ascetic who lived in the Sahara desert and was killed by the natives there in 1916. Landry was an aristocrat like Foucauld, a member of an old and renowned family, born in Paris, brought up either there or at his family's estates in the Pyrenees and on the shores of the Mediterranean Sea. Early on the astonishing artistic ability of the young aristocrat came to light: his violin playing earned him the admiration of virtuosos by the age of seven. His father, however, did not believe in prodigies, and thus the boy was made to follow the normal course of schooling. But along with his schooling the boy continued to practice the violin with extraordinary gusto; his energy for work seemed inexhaustible. And after he had *fait son droit*[98] he entered a conservatory at the age of twenty, and it did not escape the notice of any musicians qualified to judge that here was a manifest gift of grace, and that he surely had a shining future as a virtuoso ahead of him. After studying for almost two years at the conservatory his teachers sent him away with the testimonial that he had surpassed them. In the winter of 1910 he held his first public concert in Paris, when he was twenty-five. His performance became legend. At that time Alban de Landry was worshipped in the concert halls of Paris, the stately man with a genius' youth behind him and a prospective future as a superman. But he was cool and reticent; in his eyes dwelled the perception of another plane; the ways of men were not his ways. He did not let the adoration of women or the veneration of masters seduce him into a more comfortable way of life; instead he drove to his old estate in the Pyrenees and hid himself from the world for two years, following the example of Paganini. There he cultivated his art, playing the violin days and nights, roaming about in the countryside in between and hearkening to the echoes of the Aeolian harp. No other environment is better suited to raising a true troubadour than the land of the Gascons, and when he felt that the time was right he reappeared in the world of men and embarked on a concert tour throughout the various capital cities of the Northern Hemisphere, leaving a trail of fame from Stockholm to Rome, from Saint Petersburg to Madrid. In 1913 he was heard from in America; he continued his victorious journey from one great city of North America to another, and then on to Brazil and Argentina. It was there that snow started to cover his tracks, until finally it was no longer possible to follow his trail. Months pass and people cannot agree on what has happened to him. Some believe that he has returned to Europe to prepare new concerts. One newspaper claims that he is living on the island of Capri in the company of another virtuoso, a Spaniard, and that they spend their time together composing music. Another newspaper suggests that he has returned to his estate in the Pyrenees to refresh his health.

But none of this turned out to be correct. At the end of 1914 his family hears the first true reports of his fate. He had certainly returned to Europe, but not to prepare new concerts or compose music; even less to refresh his health in the Pyrenees. He is no longer in the same class as Kreisler and Elman – he has shattered his violin, cut his bowstrings. He has become a novice at the Benedictine seminary of Saint Anselm's in Rome.

The attempts made by his family to remove him proved futile: even their last resort, a report from his family doctor claiming that he had always been mentally ill, failed. At the end of 1917 he earned a doctorate in philosophy. Two years later he was consecrated a priest and sent to the French Benedictine monastery of Solesmes. In 1921 he was sent to the abbey of Sept Fontaines, where he accepted the office of Novice Master and was later appointed prior.

"There is no one else like him," said one of the older monks to Steinn once, when the conversation turned to Father Alban: "He governs us with an iron fist wrapped in silk. We don't know whether we love him more as a father or a brother. He is humble like the man Jesus Christ, stern like the judge Jesus Christ. He is the one man who never loses sight of what is deepest and highest in all ideals. Everything but the utmost is worthless to him. As a teacher he is an authority on every subject. He teaches canon law with the same expertise as he expounds Greek and Hebrew texts. Biology, mathematics, history, literature, art, languages, he is well versed in all of them. Every day he spends five hours in choir for the mandatory divine offices; he conducts practices with us and the novices for three hours daily, attends to his duties as prior and receives visitors. On his shelves one can see ell-long rows of manuscripts: the history of the monastery, commentaries on the Psalms and other texts, philosophical and theological essays, and lectures on asceticism, all in Latin. When he has had time to write all these things, no one knows. It is no secret in the abbey that he prays long into the night, and yet is the first one to arrive at choir in the morning."

70.

After the conviction that Jesus Christ was the incarnation of the highest power had become entrenched in Steinn's mind, there were no other obstacles on his path; after this he considered himself a Christian. Man's will was free to choose between the Creator and the created, the eternal and the perishable. There was no lingering doubt that the will of man inclined more toward those things that strengthened his perdition rather than his salvation, toward the visible and inconstant rather than the eternal truth behind creation, toward his yokes rather than his freedom, toward his vanity rather than God. This inclination led to what Christian moral philosophy designated with the name sin. To sin is to turn one's desires from the Creator to the created. Jesus Christ is the way to the highest reality; no one comes to the Father except through him. As long as God exists, as long as his love has appeared to mankind in the person of Jesus Christ, then Christianity is nothing but the plain truth, the one certain healthy wisdom. Now finally Steinn appreciated the statement made by Robert Hugh Benson, which he had previously thought to be far too bold, that if God exists, then the doctrine of the Catholic Church is also one logical integrity all the way down to the font of holy water at the church door.

If Jesus Christ established a Church, as was made clear in the apostles' statements written in the New Testament, then no doubts crossed his mind as to what this Church was. It would never cross his mind to imagine that the churches of Luther, Calvin, the Methodists, Baptists, or any of the others among the six hundred Christian inventions of recent times could be the Church of Christ. It required neither contemplation nor cleverness to choose between churches on the day when he finally considered himself a Christian. Jesus Christ had vowed to support his Church all of its days until the end of the world, fifteen hundred years before the churches of Luther and Calvin were founded. And it was absolutely clear to Steinn that if Jesus Christ himself had founded a Church to lead mankind to the truth, it was a scandal and an outrage to imagine that that Church could teach a lie, and that other churches that were founded by men and were under the custodianship of men could teach the truth. Various offshoots of the Church did not exist: there is only one flock and one shepherd. Either all of men's ideas concerning the Christian Church were blather and nonsense, or the Church of Christ is the unfailing envoy of the truth – *ancilla veritatis*.[99] Other churches are rootless branches, Bedouin tents at the foot of a pyramid, raised for one night; when the tents are gone and the Bedouins are lost out in the desert somewhere the pyramid still stands. A church that hazards teaching one thing today and another tomorrow cannot be the Church of Christ, because God is unchangeable and his truth eternal. The divinity of Jesus Christ and the infallibility of the Church stand and fall together. No matter how improbable Christianity might appear, its full validity is guaranteed by the fact that the Church is founded on the magisterium granted by Christ to his apostles in these words: "Whoever hears you, hears me." If God founded the Church, then its teachings are true. If men founded the Church, as they did, for instance, the Lutheran and Calvinist churches, then one has sufficient grounds for considering its teachings lies. They were false churches, the harlots of falsehood, which gathered together and held a conference in Stockholm during that jubilee year. They feasted for twelve days and debated bourgeois politics, but no one dared to mention Jesus Christ except in vague terms, because each delegate to the conference was firmly entrenched in his own lie about Jesus Christ. And if this flock of ravens had actually tried to discuss Jesus Christ, then their lies would have drowned each other out and the conference would have turned into a riot.

And then there was the Church of Christ, the maidservant of the truth: the Catholic Church, the ancient Church, which gathered to Rome, its capital, its children from all the continents, all the lands of the east and west, all the corners of the world, in the same year, the jubilee year, 1925. The crowds entered through the colonnades of Saint Peter's Square: men, women, and children, with the Apostles' Creed in their hearts, the sign of the cross on their breasts, and their pilgrims' scrips upon their backs, streaming into the chief cathedral of Christendom to sing the *Te Deum*. Here knelt poor and rich, high and low, learned and laymen, confederates united in their faith in the same Jesus, Lord and Redeemer, the true God, whom the apostles taught on the first Pentecost, born of the Virgin Mary, crucified, died, and buried, resurrected on the third day, ascended into Heaven. They prayed here. Here offerings were made. Here they wept and gave thanks. Here the living history of the living Church was being made. Around the representative of Peter, to whom Christ entrusted the keys of the Heavenly Kingdom, was unbreakable concord; certainty; undefeatable power, the power of the congregation, the power of Christ over the hearts of the people, the power of the Holy Spirit. And a poor old woman who did not have enough money to travel to Rome set off on foot from up north in Rhineland, over an entire kingdom, over mountains and wildernesses, through villages and towns, alone, hungry, and tired. She lay out under the sky at night, slept beneath the walls of churchyards. And by the time she reached Italy she had worn away her shoes and was walking barefoot. And onward continued this foreigner, in the roasting heat of summer, along the dusty highways of Italy week after week. She continued on, barefoot. She had with her one ten-aurar postcard from her parish church at home, the building that she had known to be the most glorious on Earth. And she had planned to show this postcard to the pope. The prayers of this woman beneath the eternal lamp of Saint Peter's Basilica were more powerful and more holy and a thousand times more pleasing to God than the entire "church council" in Stockholm.

Jesus Christ knew that written words were erasable. For this reason he never wrote any visible letters, except for once: these he wrote with his finger in the sand. He knew that palaces and temples crumble; thus he never built a house for himself, but took his lodging under the roofs of his friends or slept outside under his father's sky. And the houses that his friends build for him, even the cathedrals themselves, are never so robust that they cannot be tumbled down in the next assault. The papal residence itself can tumble down when least expected. But he scratched his mark of ownership with invisible letters in the hearts of mankind and built a living temple in the hearts of men: ". . . and the gates of Hell will never overwhelm you," he said. The Church that God has built for himself in the hearts of men will never fall while one man's heart still beats. *"Anima naturaliter christiana,"* says the Church Father.

The soul of man is Christian by nature.[100] God's Church will be slandered, disgraced, refuted, and attacked by the armies of its enemies until the last day, just as it has been until now. But it will stand. The Christian sects, which even out east in China wage war over Christ, chase after the latest fashions and teach one thing today and another tomorrow – they perish in the desert today, like the Bedouins who pitched their tents beneath the pyramids last night; they die out silently and soundlessly, the Lutherans and the Arians, Calvinists and Nestorians. And history chisels the words of Voltaire onto their bald-headed watchmen: *"Rien n'est plus désagréable que d'être pendu obscurément."*[101] The first Church shall be the last. The kingdom shall be overthrown; the king shall tumble from his throne, new forms of society established. Black savages shall conquer the Northern Hemisphere, build up a new civilization in those places where white savages evolved into maturity a thousand years ago, but the words of the British master of history will be proven true: around the time that the natives of New Zealand dance on the ruins of London, yet another renaissance for the Catholic Church will be nigh.

"Behold," says the Lord, "I am with you through all days, even unto Doomsday."

71.

Of course Christ's Church has for ages been subject to danger, as history tells us, but has never been defeated. *Ecclesia militans,* the shield-maiden of God, has been beset by swords and spears. Sometimes its worst enemies filled its highest offices; more often, however, its most bitter detractors were those who had fled from beneath its banner and wished its destruction because they knew that they lacked the strength to live according to its teachings. But at the conclusion of each trial it arose more powerful than before. It is always new, a different Church at the turn of each century, yet it is always the same. Christ not only keeps watch over it, but also in it, and that is what determines the outcome. Its core is the holiest sacrament of all, Christ's body and blood, the supernatural nourishment of souls, found on every Christian altar.

"I beg you, my God, to allow me to forget that my heart bears the scars of old wounds," says Steinn Elliði. "Now I beg you to still the tongues that cry out malevolently about the wounds of your Church and deride it because it has been stabbed by swords and spears, for these are precisely the same tongues that mocked the scourged Christ. My enemies are sucklings of heresy, who hope to be vindicated at Doomsday by the fact that the treasures of the Catholic Church should have sometimes fallen into the hands of the unworthy. But they err grossly, for on Doomsday they will discover that they still have things left unswept before their own and their women's doors."

The fate of man slumbers in his will. Man goes where he wishes, as high as he wills, as low as he wills, neither higher nor lower. The one who loves God goes to God. The one who loves the Devil goes to the Devil. It is simple. Whoever directs the powers of his body and soul away from the illusions of the visible world and defeats the desires of the flesh and the arrogance of the intellect, practices asceticism, humility, amity, peace, willingness to make sacrifices, and prayer, defeats the created, himself and his own demands, and lives as a pure spirit before God, he will surely achieve the condition that is called the Kingdom of Heaven. The Kingdom of Heaven signifies union with divinity. When his life in the pinch of mortal fetters ends, his soul is free.

He who sacrifices his life to illusion, lives to eat and drink, reckons whoredom and harlotry as the highest good in life, pursues riches, reputation, power, fame, and praise, considers more important how he appears in the eyes of men than in the eyes of God, mocks holy things, suppresses all the aspirations of his soul toward a higher state of being and knows nothing higher than himself, he will go to Hell, or, better put, from one hell to a worse one. He might just as well abandon all hope. The one who holds himself higher than the Lord has already chosen the Devil; he has pushed away the love of God. He has no hope of resurrection to eternity, without repentance. Hell is eternal; that is to say, the condition of the soul in the next world is fixed. Time no longer passes by. The condition of the soul of man at the hour of his death is its eternal condition. It is too late to repent after death.

No one has placed man on a higher pedestal than the Church. In truth man is holy, because he exists by the will of God and has an imperishable soul, created to enjoy the highest glory throughout eternity. Man has been created to be saved, and nothing else. Therefore all of man's goals other than his salvation are contrary to the will of God. And God so loved the world that he gave his only begotten son so that whoever believes in him, that is, walks in his footsteps, will not perish, but instead will have eternal life. Man and woman are consecrated by God in the sacrament of marriage because their offspring are created for heavenly predestination; the sacrament of marriage is holy because man and woman are not creatures void of responsibility: their child is the living temple given into their hands by God, and they will be held accountable on Doomsday for how they have maintained this temple. A child that has not learned from its parents to love God will curse its mother when it grows up, and call damnation down upon her on Doomsday because she failed to teach it the Lord's Prayer.

The Church provides everything to all of its children and to each his own. It feeds its wise men, its simpletons. It feeds its ascetics and its laymen. It sanctifies the life of the layman with its sacraments and gives a higher dignity to his work. Each one of you should do your work in the name of God and for God's sake, says the Church to the layman, through the mouth of the saint from Sales, the gentleman saint. It commands the apostles to seek the kingdom of God above all else. It grants to its ascetics the strength to endure. To all who heed its message and believe in its truth it guarantees happiness in this life, salvation in the next. It has made marriage a divine service, the home a chapel. It has called the common layman to the same glory as the one whom God elects to a holy way of life, has given mankind the saints as measures of perfection, and although the virtues of the layman are slight compared to those of the saint it promises the same wage to each. The Lord gives one man a hundred talents, another man two. One is granted the grace to take upon himself the yoke of the ascetic, another to polish the boots of the bourgeoisie. But both are promised the same wage.

72.

Father Alban was Steinn's guide in Christian studies, and he decided that Steinn was prepared to join the Church in the fall. Steinn was baptized *sub conditione* and accepted the faith.

During the week leading up to this he was required to pray before the most holy sacrament and was not allowed to speak to anyone other than his teacher. The ceremony took place on a clear and fair Sunday morning, before High Mass. All of the monks were present, along with a crowd of visitors, because it had been announced in the newspapers that an "English poet" would swear off heresy in the abbey church that day and would accept the true faith. It was standing room only in the church that day.

Before the high altar he renounced the Lutheran heresy in which he was raised. The bishop then released him from the church ban that lies over the Lutherans, and chanted over him grand incantations that drive the spirit of Satan from the heretic. When this was finished Steinn placed his hand on the Holy Bible and recited before the apostolic servants the creed of the Church in Latin. Next he was sprinkled with water and anointed with holy oil back and front, and then the *sal sapientiae,* the salt of wisdom, was placed on his tongue; this, however, he spat out, because of its disagreeable taste. At the end of the baptism he changed into a white woven garment and was led to the sacristy, where he was to make his confession before he could receive communion. The sacristy was a great hall draped with tapestries; it had high windows, and outside, the sky was replete with morning rays. On one of the walls hung a simple rood, and beneath it, in a low seat, sat Father Alban, who stood on his feet and turned toward the penitent as he approached; his smile had never before been so gentle.

Then the canon sat back down, asked Steinn to kneel on the prie-dieu at his side and at the same time stroked his head with the palm of his hand as if he were a little child. Here had Steinn come, to receive, for the first time, absolution for his sins from the apostolic servant, according to the power that Christ gave to his Church with these words: "Whosesoever sins ye remit, they are remitted unto them; and whosesoever sins ye retain, they are retained." "Whatsoever ye shall bind on Earth shall be bound in Heaven: and whatsoever ye shall loose on Earth shall be loosed in Heaven."

Steinn trembled from the crown of his head to the soles of his feet when he kneeled on the prie-dieu by the side of his Father Confessor and began the Confiteor for the first time. He had prepared himself for his confession the day before and accounted for most of what his conscience deemed his most outrageous crimes against the will of God. And when he began his confession it was in a voice that he did not recognize, although it came from his own throat; it was as if his speech organs had been borrowed from another being. He spoke the language of a distressed child who has been shaking for a long, long time from suppressed weeping, and the Great Weaver from Kashmir was no longer anything but an empty shell.

In his youth he had despised his father and mother, never heeded their biddings or prohibitions, lied to his mother on a daily basis, scarcely spoke to her without lying, generally had constantly lied in his youth, lied about every conceivable thing to anyone and everyone. He had had a special fondness for torturing animals. He had sought out wicked company, trained himself in abominable language, held obscene conversations with his companions and thought with the greatest pleasure about everything that leads to the consternation of the spotlessness of the pure soul, surrounded himself with pornographic pictures on foreign postcards. He had taunted and offended his companions and bribed them into keeping quiet about it. At home and in the company of adults he had always pretended to be the guileless, well-mannered boy. When he was eleven he had gotten drunk for the first time, when he was fourteen committed an actual sin against the life of chastity.

The Father Confessor said that whereas actual sins against the holy life of chastity were mortal sins, they required more detailed confession. He asked how many times Steinn had fallen, but the penitent could not answer this with certainty; he could only make a rough guess.

And the confession continued. With the exception of the hysterical fantasy about creating a "masterpiece for mankind," he had never thought a congenial thought for anyone, had never been appreciative of anyone. He had of course admired certain individuals for their virtuosity, their intelligence, and their knowledge, but had usually become disappointed in these people after getting to know them better, and looked down on them afterward. Then he had made a sport of uncovering people's defects. In general he had never looked upon mankind as anything other than *Staffage zu gewissen Ideen*.[102] Concerning others' opinions he had never considered them of any worth – the only thing he thought excellent was what he thought of himself; these were crimes against sacred humility.

He had never done anyone any good *secundum intentionem puram*,[103] for the love of God.

He did recall, however, three good works that he had done at one time, although they weighed little against his sins. Once he had come out of a chocolatier on Oxford Street with a package of Nestlé's chocolate, and as he was about to shove the first piece into his mouth he came across an urchin looking for cigarette butts on the ground. He gave him the package of chocolate as if in capitulation and continued on his way. Another time he was walking along Hverfisgata in Reykjavík on a summer day. In front of the National Museum he noticed an emaciated wagon jade standing on the pavement. But in the yard in front of the museum there were patches of beautiful grass. Steinn had made little of it, had taken hold of the jade's goatee, led it across the street, opened the gate of the yard, and let it in. Then he had closed the gate and continued on his way. Once he had been at a trattoria in Rome, not far from Saint Peter's Basilica. At the next table sat a German pilgrim, drinking beer, an old peasant who had neither Italian money nor any understanding of Italian. *"Wie viel?"* he asked, when the pitcher was empty. The waiter held up five fingers, meaning five lira. Then the farmer took out a five-gold-piece note, intending to pay with this without any grumbling. Steinn saw that the man was poor and humble, butted in, and paid for the pilgrim's beer, letting him keep his gold. These were all of his good works. Were not all the good works of the world something like this? It is no trouble to perform good works. It is a far heavier burden to keep oneself from doing bad deeds; there the best and most respectful men wreck their ships. No one becomes more famous for good deeds than the worst crooks and wretches, like American millionaires.

On the other hand he had never missed the opportunity to deride God and repudiate Christianity, did everything he could to silence the voice of God in his heart, defended with the utmost pleasure the teachings that were most inimical to men, listened spellbound to the Devil in human form unravel his own scriptures on the destruction of man and mankind, and from this became extremely eager to commit an abominable crime. Finally he had decided to lay hands on himself, but providence had taken hold of him and sent him into a deep sleep.

It was as if putrid pus had been squeezed from a pustule; his soul felt lighter like the sky after hail. He no longer composed clever philosophical systems to justify his sins, but instead walked humbly before God and prayed for forgiveness. He begged for mercy, redemption from the righteous punishment that his sins called down upon him. Some of his sins were so difficult for him to admit that he had to use all of his strength. But he knew that nothing could heal his soul until the wounds were completely cleansed, and that he could never start a new life as a new man without receiving absolution, even for the most hidden sin. He knew that nothing but God's forgiveness could cleanse his sins, because even though he might come to possess from that moment on a faith so powerful that it could move mountains, or if he were to give his wealth to assuage the poor, or sacrifice his body on the fire for the cause of the kingdom of God, none of this could compensate for his crimes. None of these things were, in the eyes of God, anything but plain duty. Even if he were to live a holy life from that moment on, his sins were nevertheless inexcusable without forgiveness, and his holy life could never become anything other than his obvious obligation in the eyes of God; there would never be compensation or propitiation for his sins. No matter how much good a man does, he can perform no good deed over and above his most simple obligations to God. God's mercy sanctifies a sinful man if he repents his misdeeds and mends his ways. Steinn was to a certain degree aghast at the thought of the horror and repulsion that his lifestyle must surely awaken in the soul of this man, who just a short time ago had greeted him with love and tenderness, but on the other hand he was elated to know that he could kneel in the sight of God and receive absolution for his sins from the servant of the Apostolic Church, one of those to whom Christ had given the authority to release and to bind.

When Steinn finished his confession there was a momentary silence; all that could be heard was the organ sounding from within the church, as if from a great distance. He will surely be shocked, thought Steinn, and he sank still deeper into the prie-dieu. Finally he felt that when Father Alban opened his mouth it would be to proclaim to him that a righteous God would never be able to forgive such sins. And Steinn would not have found such a proclamation remarkable in the least. The Great Weaver from Kashmir squatted here on his knees, suppressing sobs, his face in his hands, fearful that even Almighty God would not be able to wipe away such crimes.

But then Father Alban began to speak.

No, it was far from being the merciless voice of the prosecutor. The voice that spoke was gentle, bright, and pure, heavy with love, woven with radiance. Not even half a word of rebuke, no astonishment at the volume of his misdeeds, not once a sigh over his wickedness.

"We thank God for having granted us the mercy to accept us into the lap of his Holy Church. At the moment that I grant you absolution for your sins you will stand as a pure spirit before God, as a newborn child, as the angels themselves. Today your prayers are as powerful as the prayers of the angels, as the prayers of the saints. Human understanding can have naught but the tiniest fleeting suspicion of the abundance of grace overshadowing you at this moment. Protect your baptismal grace! Pray for your father and mother. Pray for all of those whom you wished to have done well. Pray for mankind. Pray for us, the unworthy servants of the Lord, that we might acquire the strength to stand faithful in holy servitude. Pray for God's Church on Earth, for the representative of Jesus Christ, the Holy Father in Rome. And pray for the spirits of those in prison. Glorify God from this moment on with your entire being, in the humility of a pure soul, and with all the strength of your being, all of your life and each footstep of your life, with no exceptions. Now I grant to you the apostolic absolution."

When the words of absolution had been spoken in Latin, the Father Confessor stood up, raised Steinn from his prie-dieu, took both of his hands, kissed them, and said:

"Pray for me, a wretched and unworthy servant of the Lord!"

73.

The venerable Père Abbé had invited Steinn to remain with the monks as long as he pleased, and Steinn accepted the invitation with thanks, because he knew that he would never find a better opportunity to unite himself with the Catholic spirit. In his life with the monks he found himself in the first group of friends he had ever had in his life; the thought that the day would surely come when he would be forced to say good-bye to Father Alban only served to awaken in him a sorrowful apprehension.

The desire to work was rekindled in him; he sunk himself zealously into the study of Catholic doctrine, the history of the Church, the lives of the saints, philosophy, theology. Beyond all else, however, he loved the study of asceticism: everything that touched on prayer and one's inner relationship with God. All of his affections were directed toward the cultivation of his prayer life; he attended the divine offices, including Tenebrae, which started before dawn. At first he had made it a rule to pray for one hour a day; a bit later he found himself compelled to double his prayer time. Finally he found that the entire day and the night along with it were insufficient, so much did his soul have left to say to its Creator. He prayed at times following the systematic contemplative methods of the Jesuits, at others the simple rules of the Rosary. He tried to bring his piety into accord with the ritualistic life of the Benedictine monks, but knew that it was best to approach God as a little child approaches his father, according to the practices of the Carthusians. The most sincere prayer is not prayed in words, but rather in the tears of a child. He took on the task of translating into his mother tongue the *Imitatio Jesu Christi*, which he considered the most precious pearl of all that had been written in the world, studied Hebrew with one of the fathers, and tried to translate the psalms of David into rhythmic verse.

With each day that passed, his mind became more balanced; few things are better suited to soothing a troubled disposition than Benedictine gentility. He slept undisturbed at night; his groundless fears disappeared; his thoughts became ever more calm, stronger, more firmly coherent. He recalled that long season devoid of joy, full of stress and insomnia, when he had stayed at the Villa Warren Hastings in Hounslow near London; it made him shudder like someone who has experienced being buried alive. He recalled the rooms where everything had been in chaos, as in the graveyard at Doomsday, books and papers all over the floor or up on the furniture, and in among all that mess floated innumerable notebooks containing English lessons marked over in red by Mr. Carrington, as well as endless drafts of poems that their author had deemed dead and banal after having struggled so much to try to knead them together; where everything had been covered in dust and filth, because it had been strictly forbidden to tidy up; where every single thing had been thoroughly soured by tobacco smoke. His room in the abbey was a dwelling place of another sort, clean and simple, only a few books on the shelf over the desk, everything in order, no decorations, nothing for comfort, and Steinn adapted himself to the monks' habit of having nothing at hand that was unnecessary. Two large windows looked out at the abbey garden and remained open most of the time, allowing fresh air to stream in, blended with the smell of decaying vegetation and rainy soil. At the start of winter the leaves dropped from the trees, and the bare branches appeared against the evening sky like an image of man's brain drawn on a gray tablet, while the moon sat at the edge of the forest like a bronze kettle on a shelf.

But in the same way that his condition had become more natural, the life of his soul more healthy, the stronger became the voices of his needs, which *la fureur intellectuelle* had fettered during the last few years. Who knew but that the storms of the intellectual life had only been an outflow of the unquenched demands of sex? If a man did not suffer like a beast, he suffered like God. He was reluctant to disturb his new condition by probing into his former life, tearing open old wounds. But the days of temptation were facts that he had to look in the eye. On days when such images crept into his consciousness he worked at overcoming them by dipping his fingers into the bowl of holy water at his door, making the sign of the cross over his breast, or reciting a short prayer to Mary. But on Sundays when a crowd gathered for High Mass, feverish fires flamed around him if he heard the sigh of a young woman break through the silence of the Offertorium. He could smell the odor of women throughout the whole church. His sensitivity for even the weakest of waves in the streaming current of the female body became for him an intolerable plague. But he fought valiantly and faithfully. While Mass was being sung he never yielded to his longing to glance behind him at the women seated at the front of the church, so that he would not turn into a pillar of salt, and when he walked along the highway for exercise and met a girl by chance, he was careful not to look in her direction. He used the same approach if he was passing through the village, and the women stared giddily at him from their doors or windows, but it cost him incredible effort to conquer himself in this way. In one house by the road sat a beautiful girl at her window, sewing. Every time she spied him from a distance on the road she stopped sewing and did all she could to get his attention; he felt the lust from her eyes burning like fire around him, but he never once looked into her eyes. Yet he dreamt of her at night.

Unclean dreams became one of his most serious afflictions. Naked lustful women encircled him. He would start up in the same way that he had previously started up in the middle of the night with thoughts of death. He got out of bed, turned on a light, knelt on his prie-dieu and prayed for a long time beneath the cross.

He trusted his Father Confessor with all of this and learned that what plagued him was nothing unique. The saints had all found themselves in the same battle, *propter regnum coelorum.*[104] Saint Benedict's temptations cannot soon be forgotten; the same went for the temptations of Saint Francis. And how had the saints triumphed? All in the same way: humility, dear sir; solitude, prayer, ceaseless prayer, endless prayer all their lives. God has sent his heaviest temptations to his most holy; Christ himself was tempted with every conceivable trick, even after a fast of forty days. He was led up onto a high mountain and given a choice. Let your vigor never be broken, friend, least of all when you find that you are capable of nothing. "Strength is perfected in infirmity," says the apostle. Never trust ourselves, but trust God always and in everything. He defeats our weaknesses; he is in charge of our lot. Let him be everything! We must let our prayers ascend to him, and he will let his grace descend to us.

74.

Steinn Elliði had now decided what to do. After thinking the matter through the entire winter he had become convinced that his monastic ideal was not a simple dream: everything but the ascetic life was vanity, was chasing after the wind. All the same his Father

Confessor advised him to consider his decision carefully, and not to give an answer until he thought it sure that it was the voice of God calling him.

Otherwise they discussed his plan as if it were already decided, and talked about the most opportune way for Steinn to seek admission to the monastic life. Steinn desired most of all to begin his training under the guidance of Father Alban, but the father particularly recommended Solesmes and said that it was uncertain whether he would continue on in his work as Novice Master. When spring came, however, Steinn began to think of Iceland. He thought of the blue bays of Reykjavík, and the mountains that watch over the bays. He saw these things in his mind's eye in the same glory as they had appeared to him in his youth, and he dreamt of the wilderness like a young man who dreams of the bosom of his lover; he could not sleep for their songs. He thought of the peaks, the tranquility of the peaks, the glaciers, the light of the glaciers, because he loved the godlike purity of the natural wilderness at home, the depth and expansiveness of the sky vaulting over that royal world. God in Heaven is somehow completely different there than here – the God of our land.

The enchantments of the land of memory are powerful. He longed to feel once more beneath his feet the earth from which he had grown, the country that had nourished his family for a thousand years. In July the nights begin again to grow dim; the songs of the swans resound from moorland lakes, and from the hot springs ascend bright, sluggish clouds. And he felt as if he were in a swoon in the melodious calm of midsummer nights, and the Mother of God stood in the grove.

Thy visage, O mother, shine over my head
In teardrops of dew, and free from cumber.
'Neath midsummer sky be my rest and my bed,
O Iceland, rock thy little child to slumber![105]

He became sad with homesickness, like an ancient Icelander. And even if he had been a saint, he could not have avoided recalling the young girl to whom he had bid farewell near a mountain almost five years ago. She must be happy now, even if she'd complained about it then. No, he would not even touch her hand; he would only look at her from a distance. I'll ask God to protect you, he thought, and then I'll leave and never return. He begged God to forgive him if all of this was sinful.

"Father Alban," he said. "Is it wrong of me to wish to see my country once more for the last time? If it is your opinion that this is harmful egoism, I will not go. But you would not believe how passionately I desire to spend this last summer of mine at home. I have never prayed to God at home in Iceland."

Father Alban was far from thinking this wrong.

"There is, might I say, nothing more likely than that your journey to Iceland will turn out to be exactly like a pilgrimage to the Holy Land," he said, and he immediately began to give Steinn various healthy pieces of advice for his journey, counseling him to guard his faith and remain attentive to his prayers, and warning him against three things: "Never attack the faith of another man, never engage in disputation over your own faith, and never discuss your plans with anyone."

Several days before his departure Steinn participated in a minor ceremony of investiture and became a Benedictine *oblatus secularis*.[106] Father Alban presided over the investiture, which took place at the altar of Benedict in one of the side chapels. Only three monks served at the ceremony. Steinn was neither required to swear oaths to the rules of the order nor to make any other promises relevant to the monastic life, but he did accept the obligation to live according to the spirit of the Catholic faith. At the conclusion of the ceremony Father Alban slipped a tiny scapular over his head; this he was to wear beneath his clothing night and day. When this was finished Steinn knelt before the altar and prayed. The monks did the same, and now all was silent for a long time. Steinn covered his face with his hands and repeated over and over: "God, I offer you my body and my soul; God, I offer you my body and my soul!"

To Steinn this minor investiture meant that he was now connected to the supernatural with unbreakable bonds: he felt that he was married to the foundational ideals of the Church. And if he placed anything before this it would mean a breaking of a vow, harlotry. *Credo in unam sanctam catholicam et apostolicam ecclesiam*.[107] He called on all of the saints to intercede for him.

When he finally looked up Father Alban was still kneeling next to him, but the other monks had gone.

Book Seven

75.

"A ship came out to Leiruvogur" [108]

The ocean liner glides into Faxaflói on a bright night during the dog days and is opposite Grótta by midmorning. Few passengers are up and about to greet the glory of the summer morning, even though the ship will dock within half an hour. Last night a great drinking party had been held, and folk went to sleep drunk around the time that the sun of the Northern Hemisphere began to redden the mountains around the bay. Now they enjoy their dreams most deeply and sweetly, until the stewards are ordered to wake the assembly with the news that the ship has reached harbor. Then folk are startled awake and start the day by trying to comprehend exactly where in the world they are now. Compare:

> Mörður Fiddle is his name,
> His heart for greatness yearns,
> To Australia he turned his ship
> And landed midst a flock of terns.[109]

A foreign couple, dressed sportishly, lean up against the ship's rail on the lee side and look out spellbound at Kjalarnes. It may be that they have dreamt of making this trip for years, to the arctic island where the ancient saga has its holy sanctuary and the language of the gods was written in books. They hold hands, rapt and pious like oriental pilgrims who have espied the towers of Benares from afar.

Before a gable in the smoking parlor sit two businessmen on a bench, smoking their morning pipes and enjoying the bliss that is granted two elderly bourgeois who pretend to take an interest in each other's family affairs. One is from Copenhagen, the other from Oslo. One speaks deeply, the other feebly. Neither of them took part in the drinking the night before. The bourgeois virtue of frugality, which no unspoiled Icelander has understood to this day, was the fundamental ideal of both. Neither was touched by the beauty of the land, because they had sped a hundred times over the Atlantic Ocean on company business, and Sagaöen[110] was in their eyes nothing other than a run-of-the-mill herring-salting station.

But at that moment another early-rising traveler joined the crowd: a big, strapping young man, confident in his step. He walks leisurely along the rail, with his hands in his coat pockets, gazing shoreward, finally leans up against the gunwale on the starboard side, looks first over Reykjavík, which resembles a poorly made Cubist painting, then lets his eyes wander over the mountains from peak to peak. Wind gusts against him, cold and fresh, the mountains open their valley laps, green and blue. The beauty of the summer morning rests upon the land, from the town to the countryside, where the heart of the nation has beaten for a thousand years, where the noble mountains keep watch over the straits, the same mountains that kept watch here of old; they bid the Icelander welcome after long periods away from home, now as in ages past. And he greets the land that preserves the footsteps of his childhood, silent and emotional, like the heathen Viking who brought his ship into Leiruvogur a thousand years ago, after many a dangerous journey to foreign harbors, pirate raids in far-off lands. Many times he had suffered shipwreck; he had fought against the overwhelming force of armies, been thrown into dungeons, delivered poems to kings to ransom his head. Now he is carried once again to the shores of the land of his childhood.

76.

Shortly before nine in the morning the bell in the foyer of Director Örnólfur's house is rung. Who could possibly think of ringing on the foyer side so early? The cook hurries bewilderedly upstairs to call on the chambermaid; the chambermaid looks quickly into the mirror, then runs down and opens the door, but not until the doorbell has again sounded several times.

"Good day!" – a foreign accent can clearly be heard in the visitor's speech. "Is Madam Valgerður home?"

"Madam Valgerður is unfortunately unavailable. The madam hasn't risen yet."

The visitor looks at his watch in half surprise, as if he has no idea that in this town it is not the custom to get up before noon.

"Is Örnólfur home?" he asks next.

"Örn – the Director? No, the Director is unfortunately not at home. The Director is in Spain. The Director left last week. The Director will not come home until the end of August."

Some director! thinks the visitor, and he looks again at his watch.

"Is mademoiselle home?"

"What?"

"Isn't there a girl here named Diljá?"

Now Stína lost all faith that the visitor was in his right mind, but still she replied:

"You don't perhaps mean the Director's wife?"

"The Director's wife? Who is that?" he asked. "Is Diljá Þorsteinsdóttir here or not?"

"If you mean the Director's wife, she hasn't gotten up yet. That is to say, the Director's wife is still asleep. Who might you be, if I may?"

But he did not introduce himself, and instead gave the girl a penetrating stare, completely dumbfounded.

"Go inside," he finally ordered, "and announce that I am waiting for them here in the foyer."

"From whom am I to say this message comes?" asked the girl again.

"That's not your concern!" he said, and he walked into the foyer past the girl, took off his coat, removed his hat and threw both to the side, then sat down in the nearest chair. The girl paused for a moment before leaving. A brindled tomcat came in from the next room, courteous and coy like a valet de chambre, greeted the guest by rubbing itself against his foot, and then continued on, out through the front room, over onto the stairs, to look at the birds. Afterward there was no other sign of life in the house for a quarter of an hour.

Finally the Ylfingamóðir herself appeared on the stairs in a simple morning dress, her hair set loosely up, distinguished and strong, entirely unchanged, stout and heavy-stepped. But when the visitor stands up to walk over to her, she stops in her tracks, unable to believe her eyes any longer.

"Steinn Elliði! If it isn't you, child!"

"Hello, Grandmother," he says, and kisses the old woman in greeting. "Yes, I have come."

She looks him over from tip to toe, and tears come involuntarily to her eyes. She kisses him again on the cheek, because he is, after all, her grandson, whom she lulled to sleep when he was just a babe in swaddling clothes.

"Welcome, my dear," she says. "And how you have become so different-looking, so doleful. I've often pitied you, poor thing, for the misfortune of never having anything resembling a family home. You certainly must never have felt very well."

But the Ylfingamóðir was, generally speaking, not a sensitive soul, and she quickly switched to a more lighthearted tone.

"But what were you thinking, child, not to send us a telegram so that we could come meet you at the ship? How could it cross your mind to surprise us all like this?"

"It's not my habit to send telegrams," he said. "And now I'm here, anyway. What's new?"

"Oh, everything's been fairly decent lately, thank you very much. But what can you tell me of your affairs? Sometimes we've been worried about your fate, but now you've certainly become famous, isn't that so? They've written about you in the papers here; and at one time those poems of yours were being circulated here; they've been praised as paragons! But I didn't understand them, my boy, though that certainly doesn't make any difference whatsoever. How is your father?"

"That I don't know. I haven't seen him for several years."

"Didn't you write to each other?"

"I never write to anybody."

"Then you didn't have any contact with your blessed mother during her final years?"

"Nothing that could be called contact."

"Well now, my boy. We won't talk about that. She's at peace now."

"Everything is in God's hands."

"It pleases me to hear you say that, my boy," answered the old woman. She showed him to a seat and sat down opposite him.

"But listen, my dear, have you had anything to eat or drink this morning?"

"I had some coffee at the hotel."

"Hotel? What did you say, child? You haven't taken a room in a hotel? For goodness' sake, why didn't you come straight here from the ship? We would have had a room prepared for you immediately."

"I don't doubt that. But I'm staying at Hotel Iceland. Don't trouble yourselves on my behalf. I'm going up to the mountains."

"There you go again. You don't think much, do you, about what folk might say."

"Folk? What folk?"

"Then aren't you here to stay?"

"No."

"I can't think of letting you stay in town, Steinn. Do you hear me?"

"The girl told me that Örnólfur is married."

"What is this, child? You didn't know that?"

"How was I to know that? People get married without asking me."

"They've been married since April before last."

"Are they happy?"

"Why do you ask, child?"

"Are they satisfied?"

"Thanks, they feel fine enough under the circumstances, God be praised."

"Circumstances – what circumstances? Are they poor?"

"Poverty is a blessing – not a curse, dear Steinn. But poor Diljá has met with deep misfortune."

"Have things gone poorly for Diljá? I'm sorry to hear that. And I hear that Örnólfur has gone to Spain."

"Their boy died in February."

"Their boy? What bad news!"

"Such a gloriously fair boy, and he was getting on so well. He was named Úlfur. He suddenly fell sick and died, ten months old. Yes, those were sorrowful days for Diljá, the poor dear."

Prior to this Steinn had listened to his grandmother as if he were reading an ordinary newspaper article. But the news that Diljá had not only become a mother, but had also had to see her child buried, shocked him thoroughly, and he asked:

"How did she handle it?"

"Well, what can I say? As you must surely understand, it is a more painful loss than one can put into words for a young mother to have to see her child buried."

But it was a family trait to put little stock in human feelings, and he asked:

"Couldn't she always have another one?"

His grandmother gave him the calmest of looks.

"It is little comfort for a young mother to tell her that she can have another one," she answered. "Of course the mother knows that she can have another one; yes, maybe even five or six more, but she can never have the same child again."

He kept quiet for a short time and harbored doubts as to whether what his grandmother was saying was rubbish, or whether it might contain dearly bought life experience.

"Did she cry?" he finally asked.

"I would have thought that you wouldn't have had to ask me that," said the old woman, and she added, unprompted: "She had the little body kept in the room there, behind that door to the left," and she pointed to the door whence the cat had come. "For a whole month afterward I slept with Diljá in her room, the poor dear, and tried to do what I could for her. It was strange at first: she seemed not to be able to understand that little Úlfur was dead. It was as if she were angry with us for having thought of telling her the truth. Time and time again I had to go and bring her down here in the middle of the night. When she thought that I was sleeping, she'd sneak to her feet. And there I would find her, as she sat with the stiffened corpse on her knees, rocking back and forth. It was as if she always believed that he was still alive. It was horrible, my dear Steinn. But that's in the past; wounds of grief heal like other wounds."

The old woman's entire bearing appeared to become more gentle in relating this tale, and her grandson asked nothing further.

"Rest here a little while, my dear. I'm going to wake Diljá and tell her that a visitor has come. I hope that you'll have morning coffee with us and tell us your news."

77.

They greeted each other like two cousins who are raised in separate countries and meet for the first time today. At the last minute they realized that their relationship was only a misunderstanding resulting from a genealogical error. They were simply two strangers. The smiles on their faces were stillborn. To her his return was no more unexpected than if he'd gone off to Stokkseyri the day before yesterday. All the same she welcomed him back to Iceland. She was wearing a sleeveless pink dress, which hugged her bosom and hips; her hair was cut *à la garçonne*. Her eyes shone with a fatal gleam; in her bearing there was not a trace of the exultant joy of a happy wife; her face was marked with lines of age, long before she had aged at all.

She listened to her mother-in-law go on and on about Steinn's return, and about the unseemliness of his having gone to stay at a hotel; it was out of the question that he should stay at Hotel Iceland – he must have his luggage sent here immediately. What's more, he wanted to go up to the mountains, which was certainly opportune, since they would be going for their annual summer holiday to the

Ylfingabúð, starting next weekend; he would of course have to come with them. Diljá looked at her mother-in-law, then quick as a flash at him.

"We must have a little party here tonight or tomorrow night, Diljá," continued the old woman, "and invite some of those blessed artists and writers and others whom Steinn would be pleased to see."

"No, Grandmother," he interrupted. "By all means spare me from such a thing. I can't stand parties. I've long since stopped enjoying mingling with people. I've got nothing left to say to anybody."

"Nothing to say! Once upon a time you didn't think yourself too great to grant people the pleasure of your conversation! Don't you know that you're renowned here at home as a poet and a celebrity for those poems you published in England? Word would get around, to the family's shame, if we pretended not to know about this."

"Celebrity! Me? Damn it! Great poet! Me? *Vanitas vanitatum!* They might just as well have written that I'd gotten gastritis. Nor have I published any poems. That's untrue. They were stolen. I don't care to see anyone. I'm going up to the mountains."

"What is this, child? I thought that you would have been in seventh heaven for publishing a book of poetry in the most widely read language of culture in the world!"

"Stop it, Grandmother; I'm tired of this. Language of culture! Rubbish! What is a language of culture? Perhaps Aramaic, the mother tongue of Jesus Christ.

"English is the language of pirates. Where were the English when the Gospels were written? Where were they when Lao-tzu composed the *Tao Te Ching* or the Indians the wisdom of the Vedas? No, dear Grandmother, don't invite anyone here."

"You're the same as you were when it comes to exaggeration, dear Steinn," said Madam Valgerður. And the Director's wife glanced at him without lifting her head. Her eyes looked outward and inward at the same time; she looked at him as she would a phantom in an insomniac dream, all the while comparing his voice to that of her childhood memories.

Madam Valgerður poured coffee into their cups and offered them cakes. They sat in the sun-drenched foyer before open doors, surrounded by Keilir and the mountains of Langahlíð. Steinn felt it almost unbelievable that he should have returned home to his fatherland, so cold were the mountains before which he had knelt in his dreams.

"Where have you come from, Steinn Elliði?" asked the Director's wife courteously.

"I've come from Belgium."

"I see. How did you get on there?"

"Well."

"They speak French there?"

"Yes, they speak French there. Also Flemish, and actually all sorts of other languages and dialects."

"This Flemish is similar to Dutch?"

"With slight differences."

"It often happened that those so-called Flemings stranded their ships out east, not far from where we were living when my husband was a bailiff," said the old woman. "Sometimes we put up whole crews of them. They were courteous and gracious."

There was nothing more that anyone could think of to say about Flemish or the Flemings, and so there was silence.

"You didn't spend much time in Italy," began the Director's wife again, just as courteously as before.

"I went there last year, shortly after my mother died."

"I'm sure that she couldn't bear the climate there, down south by Africa, or wasn't it in Sicily where she died?" asked the old woman warily.

"Yes."

"Was the grave properly looked after?" she asked next in a low voice, full of delicacy.

"I know nothing about graves," he answered coarsely, silencing the speakers again momentarily.

"It must be terribly hot down there in Sicily," said the Director's wife; she could not get past geographical locations.

"Winter there is similar to summer here."

"Aren't people half-savage down south?"

"The people there are like they are everywhere else."

"Do you mean to say that people are the same everywhere?"

He looked quickly up, in precisely the same way as he always had, and answered as sharp as lightning:

"You remind me of my mother."

Both women felt the tactlessness in this remark, and were reluctant to respond. He had again snapped the thread of conversation with an unwieldy answer, and again they all fell silent. Finally Madam Valgerður said, in a half-cheerful, half-insulted tone:

"I scarcely recognize you as the same man, dear Steinn, you've changed so much."

But suddenly the Director's wife lost control for a moment, and she said without any forethought:

"Yes, he has changed completely – terribly!"

As she spoke these words a cold shiver gripped her. She paled.

"Once I heard that you'd become a Bolshevik," said Madam Valgerður. "I hope, God willing, that that was a misunderstanding."

"I'm a Catholic," he said.

"Catholic?! Catholic?!" repeated mother- and daughter-in-law flabbergastedly.

"I've been baptized *sub conditione*."

Madam Valgerður could not keep from laughing to herself at this nonsense.

"Well, it's not worse than being a Bolshevik," she concluded. "After all, Catholicism is just an innocent sect. Catholic! I do declare!"

"You don't believe in saints, do you?" asked the Director's wife.

"Why not?"

"Surely you must know that they're just men."

He glowered at her again and asked:

"You don't believe in Örnólfur?"

The blood rushed to her cheeks, and her mouth quivered slightly. In spite of all appearances she must have been extremely sensitive. But when her mother-in-law saw her biting her lip she butted in and answered:

"It's quite a different thing to adore one's husband than to pray to dead men, as I hear they do in Catholicism."

"Or the sale of indulgences!" began the Director's wife again. "I hope you don't believe that it's possible to buy forgiveness for sins from the pope!"

"No," he said, still glowering at the pale young woman as if she were his enemy. "I don't believe it because that is nothing but ordinary

Lutheran slander. Only God forgives all sins. On the other hand, it is no mystery that the road to Hell is an easy one."

"Do you think that I'll go to Hell?" she said, and tried to laugh lightly.

"That depends on whether you wish to see the essential difference between right and wrong," he answered coldly.

Madam Valgerður still chuckled to herself and shook her head.

The Director's wife, however, was frightened, and could not bring herself to look at the guest. He was no longer a civilized man; he was a shape-shifter. The brilliancy of his youthful years had disappeared from his manner, replaced by something repulsive and dangerous.

"God Almighty, how you have changed, Steinn!"

Then she looked at her mother-in-law, tried to smile, and asked:

"What do you think Örnólfur would say?"

78.

Steinn was not able to accept his grandmother's invitation and instead stayed at the hotel. He gave in, however, to her plea that he come daily to supper.

In truth he had changed a great deal; it became more and more apparent as the days passed. Before, he had spouted his heart out whenever he had the chance, with an unsteady glance; now he hardly ever said anything and brooded on unspeakable things, his pupils fixed in a stiff gaze; before, he was vigorous and flexible, held his head high, stuck out his chest; now he was slow and looked constantly down at the ground, his movements slight and resolute. He no longer spoke with his hands, no longer fingered a cigarette case nervously; now he listened to others speak without showing any signs of impatience, whereas previously this had been impossible for him to do. Before, his lips had always been open, revealing his two front teeth; now his mouth was usually closed, and this change gave his face an expression of sternness. His face was marked with clear, strong lines, bearing witness to austerity and self-denial. His eyes were even more fleeting than in years past, and were shielded by heavy glasses with light-colored horn-rims. If he looked at a book, he took off his glasses quickly and read with bare eyes. His voice was clearer and fuller than before, but his pronunciation was tinged with a foreign accent. Sometimes he found himself lacking the right word, forcing him to change his sentences around in order to be able to say what he was thinking. Before, he had been a pretentious dresser; now his clothes were not only simple, but also coarse: his trousers were baggy, his boots of thick brown waterproof leather, his shirts and collars of nappy flannel-like material. His hair no longer reminded one of a lion's mane nor hung down the back of his head in comely waves, as it had in years past. Carelessness had spoiled its color; despite the reddish tinge it was almost ashen, cut badly, combed even worse. His locks hung in disorder upon his forehead. The backs of his hands were hairy up to the knuckles.

He no longer let himself be enticed into discussing thought-provoking topics, preferring most to add something to the conversation only when it turned to a completely worthless topic, seemed no longer to voice his own opinion about anything except when he insulted the things that most others enjoyed, and then used logic that kept everyone thoroughly confused. When least expected he would come up with questions or comments that were either far-fetched or unbecoming. In his presence any kind of weather could be expected: people could not help but feel apprehensive about what he was going to say next. No one was safe when he was around. Although he listened calmly to those who spoke to him and never objected, one got the impression that people suspected him of considering everything that was said to him vanity and idiocy. He hardly ever smiled.

And how completely different was the woman sitting here than the child to whom Steinn Elliði had said good-bye at Þingvellir one summer night five years ago. What had happened to the light-hearted, thoughtless laughter of the young girl? It no longer sang out; eternity had locked it away. Her countenance no longer shone with naïve expectations and unfulfilled dreams. Her eyes were like silvery velvet or splintered lead. She was a woman, tall and lissome, the shape of her body roundish and soft, causing her smallest movement to become a stylized performance. Her vaulted bosom and thickset, strong hips revealed incessantly in their charming comeliness the copiousness of female fecundity, her bearing was locked in the fetters of habitual kindheartedness, puritan precaution, and anesthetized passions.

79.

Once at dinner he was seated opposite the chair of the master of the house. There were no other guests but the Director's wife's best girlfriend, whom Steinn had known in his childhood, always called Sigga P., now called Madam Sigríður Geirdal, the daughter of an official in town. Steinn spoke to her informally.

He was asked how he had spent his first day at home. Thanks very much, he had walked over to Kleppur,[111] then had gone to his father's house and met with old Guðmundur. Finally he had sat in the hotel for three hours and read Icelandic. He hadn't seen an Icelandic book for five years.

What had he read?

"*Morgunblaðið*." He had borrowed several of last year's issues from old Guðmundur.

"Is that what you call literature!?" said the young women.

"Ellingsen is advertising patten overshoes and sailcloth," he said.

Silence.

"The firecrackers from Cremona come in countless colors and styles," he said.

Madam Sigríður picked up her handkerchief.

"I the undersigned need a wife immediately," he said.

First Madam Sigríður laughed out loud, then Diljá.

"Didn't you read anything other than the advertisements?" asked his grandmother.

No, he hadn't read anything other than the advertisements. They were the most interesting part of the newspaper. The other stuff was blather.

"But sometimes there are articles in *Morgunblaðið* by Sigurður Þórólfsson and Halldór Kiljan Laxness," said his grandmother.

When Madam Sigríður had stopped laughing he looked at her and asked:

"How long ago were you married?"

"About two years ago. Diljá and I were married at about the same time," answered the young madam, frankly and innocently.

"Do you have children?"

"No, not yet," and she laughed shyly.

"Why not?" he asked.

Both young women reddened and looked ashamed, but Madam Valgerður reminded her grandson that in this country it was not customary to ask women such things in such a way. Then there was a short silence, and Madam Sigríður took a bite of food in a dignified and noble way, as if she were offended.

"I hope we're not eating rotten dog," said Steinn Elliði. His lack of respect for the sensitivity of his table companions seemed to be entirely limitless.

"You certainly can be terribly rude to the young ladies," said Madam Valgerður.

"Is there a Latin dictionary here?" he asked.

"A Latin dictionary, yes, there's some sort of dictionary rubbish out on Örnólfur's shelves. Hopefully you're not planning to delve into Latin at high summer, child!"

"Is it forbidden?"

"You've read far too much during your days, Steinn Elliði," said the Director's wife.

"Yes, he has certainly read too much for his own good," said Madam Sigríður perkily. But the Director's wife wanted to turn the conversation toward a more harmless topic, and asked:

"What poet do you regard most highly these days, Steinn Elliði?"

"David," he answered.

"David from Fagraskógur! No, now that's a new one!" said Madam Sigríður.

"King David who taught," he corrected.

"Hopefully you don't mean the one in the Bible?" asked the madam.

"Yes, I do."

"I can scarcely believe you've become attached to the Bible," she said.

"The Bible doesn't really go down very well in my case," testified Madam Valgerður. "We aren't what you'd call champions of the faith in this house."

"Otherwise I find it hard to believe what I've heard, that you've become a Catholic," said Madam Sigríður.

"Curious people, those witless folk at Kleppur. They were supposed to be mowing the grass. One sat with his legs stretched out in the grass and sang. Another was trying to stand on his head. They don't believe in bourgeois decorum. It was as if I saw standing before me the incarnation of what Jacques Maritain calls *l'avènement du moi,* which he considers to be the hallmark of Lutheranism."

"But you don't mean that all Lutherans are crazy?"

"As soon as you, my dear ladies, stop believing in bourgeois decorum, you will be admitted to Kleppur."

"What do you mean by bourgeois decorum?"

"Oh, it's something left over from old Catholic ethics, which have long since been worn out."

"I've wandered into Catholic churches several times," said the Director's wife, "and they are the most wretched buildings that I've ever seen given the name 'houses of worship.'"

"That's sad," he said.

"Their robes, however, are showy enough," said Madam Valgerður.

"Or, one might add, how those Catholics kneel there in front of each other and pray out loud!" said Madam Sigríður. "I'll be damned if that's better than in the Salvation Army. It's absolutely disgusting to see such fawning before God. It's downright perverse."

"We'll let them say their prayers," said the Director's wife. "What scandalizes me most are those Catholic preachers. Such damned nonsensical harping I have never heard in my life. The last time I was in a Catholic church the priest talked about the redemptive work of Jesus Christ. And what wisdom, good gracious! The way he told it Jesus Christ didn't resemble a person at all, but instead some sort of theological gorgon; he had one foot sunk in dog-boring references to the Old Testament, the other in preposterous stories about the apostles and the church fathers. ("There now, Diljá, you've said enough," interrupted Madam Valgerður.) It was like the romance about the bishop from Aberdeen by Sigurjón in the bank."

80.

He did not show up the next day. Perhaps he couldn't bear the atmosphere of bourgeois society. They kept food warm for him that evening and finally telephoned the hotel, but he hadn't been seen there since early in the morning. No one knew where he was.

"You insulted the boy yesterday with what you said about the priests, Diljá dear," said Madam Valgerður gravely. "It doesn't do to be so blunt with folk even if they are of another faith. I would never do that. One can hint at one's opinions if necessary, but such words as you used – no, Diljá dear, we've got to be pleasant to the poor boy. There is no doubt that he hasn't had as many as seven happy days since he left this country, the poor dear."

"Didn't he start by saying that we were all crazy?" said the young woman sharply. "Every last word that he said at the table last night was an insult."

"Absolutely true. Steinn's comments are a little insensitive, but I can understand him much better like this than the way he was before, when he never said anything that wasn't poetic prattle; now he's more like one of the family. His grandfather was never gentle. And what do we women know about religions, Diljá dear, which is right and which wrong? We shouldn't trouble ourselves with such questions. And if someone believes in something different than we do, that's his business. It could very well be that their popes are just as good as the bishop here. How would we know? And concerning Jesus Christ, no one knows anything for sure, so it should be all the same to us whether he's preached in a different way in the other religions than we're used to hearing from the Reverend Haraldur."

"If Steinn keeps on in the same way as yesterday, I'm not eating at this table any longer."

"Such caprice, Diljá dear! We should be pleasant."

Then the Director's wife became a little girl: "Yes, Grandma, I really wanted to be; but I always feel like I'm about to lose control of myself, Grandma. And what did he mean last night when he was talking about bourgeois decorum? It almost seems like he hates me. Oh, I wish Örnólfur were home."

Next morning Steinn's grandmother phoned the hotel again, but he hadn't returned during the night; no one had heard anything from him. "God grant that the child hasn't put himself in peril," said Madam Valgerður. She rang again and again throughout the day, but there was no news of Steinn, and she became much more restless, more taciturn, than Diljá had seen her for years. God grant that the child is safe! The Director's wife tried to appear unmoved, but she avoided looking into her grandmother's face all day. She wandered restlessly about the house and accomplished little, until the atmosphere at home became unbearable; then she put on a coat and hat and fled to Madam Geirdal.

"Almighty God!" she said, after they'd kissed each other in greeting. "I didn't sleep a wink last night!"

"Goodness help you, dear Diljá!"

And after a bit of prattle back and forth about insomnia and medications for it, there came this question:

"Listen, Sigga; did you think that I was terribly rude to Steinn the other night?"

"Good Lord, Diljá! Hopefully you aren't kicking yourself over what you said to Steinn! What you said didn't do anything but serve him right, that insolent cad who thinks he's so famous that he can do or say whatever he pleases!"

"But, dear Sigga, he hasn't come home for two days."

"What does that matter?"

"No one knows where he is."

"Thank your lucky stars, you and your grandmother. What a boor!"

"Sigga, you don't understand how much it's bothering me. Imagine if–"

"If what?"

"I've been thinking about him the whole time since he arrived. Don't you think he must feel terribly bad? Oh! I thought that someone had to feel absolutely terribly bad to decide to become a Catholic. That's a frightful step! Didn't you notice the lines around his mouth? I'm certain that Steinn has suffered much more than we can imagine. Imagine how lonely he must have been–"

"The other day when I sat down at the table with Steinn I felt that for the first time in my life I beheld a wicked man."

"Dear Sigga, how can you say such a thing?" rebuked Diljá.

"I'm just saying what I feel. There's something disgusting about him."

"No, Sigga, not disgusting, but something that makes one afraid. It's his suffering that makes one afraid, not Steinn himself. You must have noticed how beautiful his eyes are. They're as clear as when he was a child. Sigga, do you remember Úlfur's eyes?"

"My dear Diljá, how could it possibly cross your mind to compare him to your baby?"

"They were cousins. I remember Steinn when he was a little boy with a straw hat and a red walking stick."

"He was much better when he was a boy, even if he was abominable."

"But Steinn and I were friends once. We gazed at the sea when we were children and held hands."

Her girlfriend gave her a look of surprise.

"Think about it, Sigga! Steinn has come home! How often did I long for Steinn to come home!"

Her girlfriend said nothing.

"He has returned to his homeland because he feels horrible. He has come alone, helpless as a pilgrim out of the unknown – the solitude, where no human comfort can be found, where no heart communicates any warm feelings to another; no friend takes part in the woes of the abandoned. He never heard a friendly word all those long years, and when he comes home everyone has forgotten him. And imagine if–" she whispered, "if he had committed suicide! And all I did was ridicule his faith, which he reached out to when he had no other hope of human help. What excuse would I have had then? No, Sigga, I have no excuse at all; none."

She leaned forward across the table, hid her face in her arms, and shook; her girlfriend came over to her, sat at her side, and placed an arm around her shoulders.

"Diljá," she whispered, moved. "You love him."

At these words she lifted her head from her arms and looked at her girlfriend. Her face was puffy, her pupils dilated behind her tears; her jaw quivered.

"I forbid you!" she hissed more than whispered. "I forbid you–"; the young women looked at each other for several moments.

"Forgive me, Diljá dear, if I've offended you with insensitivity."

Then she thrust a kiss onto her girlfriend's hand. Women understand each other.

"We'll hope that nothing has happened to him, Diljá dear," she said.

81.

It was cold, and raining heavily outside.

When Diljá came home, Madam Valgerður was sitting in front of the fireplace with Steinn Elliði opposite her, ragged and unshaven; his face was streaked all over with mud. He was wiping the mist from his glasses with his gloves.

She stopped in the doorway and could scarcely believe her eyes, so strongly had the mad fear that he was no longer to be counted among the living seized her. She relieved her own tension with a quick sigh of joy:

"Steinn," she said. "We thought we would never see you again!"

"Good evening," he said.

She wanted to go straight over to him and give him her hand, but he continued polishing his glasses without paying her any further notice.

"Where have you been all this time?"

He'd been up in Kjós.

"I don't understand this child at all!" marveled Madam Valgerður. "To undertake such a thing! He left at six o'clock yesterday morning, on foot! And climbed up Esja!"

Then she addressed him directly:

"You must have forgotten that our car is available to you whenever you want, boy! What do you think people are saying? It won't do at all, Steinn, for you to be seen walking around the countryside like a beggar; do you hear me?"

"You haven't asked me the news, Grandmother," he said, holding his glasses to the light to check if they were clean. "You didn't ask how the view was from Móskarðahnúkur; didn't ask how I'd been received at the farms; didn't ask once about the well-being of the farmers in Kjós."

"Oh, they can go to Hell in Kjós!" she said, and gave her grandson a look that showed how delighted she was to have gotten him back from death, then stroked the hair back from his forehead and patted him on the cheek. The Director's wife stood at some distance and watched.

"I'm hungry, Grandma," he said.

Supper was ready; a maid was called to wipe off his shoes, and the girl knelt down and performed this task. The Director's wife stood at some distance and watched. Finally she came to her senses and hurried out.

He was famished and ate thick slices of pork chops as if they were Danish pastry, and Italian salad with a fork like porridge. He devoured the cheese in huge chunks. He talked about skyr,[112] flatbread, dulse, Iceland moss, codheads, and the Icelandic nation. He had walked forty kilometers in six hours and answered everything that was said to him distractedly.

"When I got up to Kjós I came to my senses," he said. "I've been sleepwalking all my life. Reality is in Kjós. The rats were holding a political rally between the planking and the wall in the place where I slept last night."

It seemed at that moment as if the old Steinn Elliði had been resurrected from the dead. His grandmother offered him a cigarette after the meal, but he had long since stopped smoking.

After supper he found the Latin dictionary, sat down in front of the fire, looked up the definitions of several words he needed, and wrote them down on a slip of paper. His grandmother addressed him several times, but he answered haphazardly, as a true member of his family. Finally he stopped answering. He turned his back to mother- and daughter-in-law, let his head fall to his chest, and didn't move. It was quiet in the room, the slightest movement perceptible. First they heard a little thump, as the dictionary fell from his hands onto the floor. But it didn't look likely that he would pick it up; he sat as dead still as before; a little later his deep and regular breathing sounded throughout the room; he was sleeping. Daughter- and mother-in-law looked at each other and smiled without saying anything. He slept peacefully before his family's hearth after five years of exile, after having undergone countless trials in distant lands where reality most resembles the coral world at the bottom of the sea.

The embers in the fireplace were starting to cool down – they needed to be careful to retain the room's warmth. He could catch cold, thought the Director's wife, he's so sweaty from the hike – and she bade the servant fetch a quilt. She didn't cover him herself, but instead handed the quilt to Madam Valgerður. The old woman laid it as carefully as possible over his chest and tucked the corners under his shoulders, but at this he woke with a start.

"Let Grandmother tuck you in," said the old lady cheerfully, but he had no liking for such sensitivity, muttered something, stood up with a shudder, and wiped his eyes.

"Sleep here at home tonight, Steinn dear," said his grandmother, "and don't go out in the rain; you'll catch cold from it!"

But he asked for his hat and left, without even saying goodnight. His grandmother followed him out onto the doorsteps. When he was gone Diljá stood up and picked up the book from the floor.

82.

On the next day the hotel phoned and said that Steinn Elliði was ill. Had a doctor been sent for? Did he have a fever? Pneumonia? He had scarcely escaped from one difficulty before he found himself in another! Madam Valgerður immediately put on a coat and went to see him.

When the Director's wife came to bring flowers to the patient that evening, he was lying there without his glasses on, disheveled, in dirty, blue-striped pajamas, with all the newspapers of the town on top of him, reading the advertisements. His greeting was not unfriendly, and he rose up halfway and stretched. He smelled the flowers and laid them on top of a copy of *Tíminn*.[113]

"I've rented two horses," he said.

"Horses? How do you feel?"

"I'm heading east."

"East? Aren't you ill? Steinn, you can't imagine how startled we were this morning when they called to say you were ill."

"It's just stiff muscles," he said, and yawned again. "I felt as if I'd been thrashed by cudgels when I woke up this morning after that damned trip to Kjós, and I had a cough into the bargain."

"Would you like some bonbons?" she asked, and unwrapped a decorative box of sweets.

He was overjoyed at this kindness, rolled over in bed and tumbled all of the flowers to the floor, thrust a hand toward the box, and said: "Give me!"

He obviously took no liking to the package's artistic decoration, because he ripped off the lid and threw it aside. The pieces in the box were wrapped in fancy paper of various colors. "Thank you very much!" he said, and started to eat. He pulled the box of chocolate into bed with him, leaned on one elbow over it, tore the paper off one after another of the pieces, and munched on them like meat. His hair was so disheveled that it was tempting to offer to comb it for him. His arms stretched far out of his sleeves and his nightgown was unbuttoned at the neck, revealing his chest when he moved. His chest was covered with hair. "Do you want some?" he said after eating for a while, and he handed her one of the pieces, wrapped in beautiful green paper. But after finishing half the box he was full, and he handed her the rest and said: "I don't want this! This is awful! Give me a glass of water!"

She poured a glass of water and gave it to him, and when he'd drunk his fill he said:

"I don't feel so well. All day I've been training myself to think like *Tíminn* out of fear of coming under the influence of *Morgunblaðið*."

But the concerns that pressed upon her mind made her unable to reply to this; she was earnestly concerned about everything but *Tíminn* and *Morgunblaðið,* and Steinn hadn't spoken a word in earnest since he had come home. It was as if he were speaking with an idiot. In his presence it was as if everything were vanity, killing every attempt she made at earnest expression. She longed to be able to give voice to all of the serious things in her life, since what is serious to one soul is serious to all existence. She longed to ask; she thirsted for an answer; she longed to sigh; she thirsted for comfort. But she knew that he wouldn't answer in any other way than to say that reality was in Kjós and that he was afraid of being influenced by *Morgunblaðið*. She stared straight ahead and kept quiet; if he had been ill, she thought, then I could have done something for him. Now she couldn't do anything. His table was strewn with written papers and books bound in black leather.

"It's better to go east," he said.

"So you're not planning to humor us at all, Steinn, during the time that you're here. If you knew how much your grandmother cherishes you."

"Ufff! Women!" he said. "She sat here for two hours today."

"I won't sit here too long, Steinn," she said.

He lay back and said nothing. Was he beginning to suspect that a human being had come to visit him? Finally he raised himself up again onto his elbow and looked at her for the first time, with deep, clairvoyant eyes that gazed from one world into another. She blushed.

Finally he said, as if he'd been examining his conscience the whole time:

"The only thing that I do not need to be ashamed of for saying to dear God is this: I am an uncontrollably wicked man!"

"Steinn, why do you say this!?" she answered sharply, since she did not understand how much depravity it takes to analyze other souls.

Then he said:

"Dear Diljá, I wish I had good reason to be grateful to you for something."

"Once we were friends, Steinn."

"You hated me, Diljá."

She looked up, met his clear eyes again, and said, distressed:

"Will you forgive me, Steinn?"

He looked at her as he did before, without moving, without answering, and she longed to veil her face or to flee or to put her hands over his eyes so that he couldn't see her. Finally she said:

"You never wrote to me, Steinn."

He continued staring at her.

"If you had written to me, Steinn–"

It was almost as if his eyes absorbed her life; if she had had a will of her own, they would have robbed her of that as well.

"I haven't understood anything, Steinn. What has been happening all these years? Who controls the world? Why didn't you ever let me know where you were? I was alone. Forgive me!"

He still stared, and she spoke his name with a sob in her throat, like someone begging for mercy:

"Steinn!"

In a kind of nervous confusion she touched the hair on the back of his hand without touching his skin. But he did not move.

"For just one thing, Steinn," she said. "You can deny me your forgiveness for everything else. The other day when I saw you again I was seized with guilt for this one thing, because I saw that you had never stopped turning your face from God–"

Finally he shook his head and answered coldly:

"Man and woman hate each other. It is better that we do not forgive each other."

"Steinn," she wailed again, as if he had hit her with an iron rod. "Try to understand that I am a human being."

"God has mercy on people and understands them, not I," said he.

She leaned forward in her chair, hid her face with one hand, and with the other grabbed his arm resting on the blanket.

"When I lost Úlfur, I thought the vow that you had taken from me when I was a girl had called down God's punishment upon me. I hated you because you'd hidden yourself from me. When I was little I believed in you, Steinn. Don't be angry with me, even though I'm just a woman. But you are a great man, and there is no God so holy or terrible that your will would not lead you to his footstool."

He shook off the chain that she had placed over his arm: her bright, warm, female hand.

"Stop this!" he said impatiently, and added: "God alone forgives women!"

She did not extend her hand to him in farewell. But at the door she turned around and looked at him. Her smile was a grimace of pain. Her flowers lay on the floor. The candy that she had brought him stood on the nightstand. The air in the room was still heavy with her perfume.

"It's really a shame that I've stopped smoking," he said to himself as he climbed out of bed to open the window. It was certainly her car that he saw disappear around the next street corner.

Mein Herz pocht wild beweglich,
es pocht beweglich wild:
Ich liebe dich so unsäglich,
du schönes Menschenbild.[114]

Oh, this is quite possibly the most beautiful avowal that has ever been made on Earth. But it is still a sin to love a human being for any other reason than its predestination for eternal life. Yes, all love of human beings is sinful except for the love that shines forth in the beneficent act of plying humanity with the blessed formula for the composition of divinity, the profession of faith.

Ich liebe dich so unsäglich,
du schönes Menschenbild.

He sits at the window and looks down at the street, where human children are running races at the street corner. Nothing is at once so painful and so delightful as to love life and the image of man. Such a love is truly lyrical. But the truth makes a man neither blessed nor free. The truth makes a man a pilgrim, a foreign prisoner. The pope is a prisoner in the Vatican. It was almost unbelievable that man should have been created for the truth. God, be not too hard on these souls! Have mercy on men, because they are nothing but wretches! Men cannot help it if they do not care for the truth.

Mein Herz pocht wild beweglich,
es pocht beweglich wild–

And he sits here motionless until the sun sets in the fishing grounds to the west, and the history of mankind once again goes through his mind, everything like a bizarre dream, and he sees everything and knows everything in his imperfection. The perfect were like this from time immemorial. No one but the imperfect saw and knew. The way of perfection is the way of imperfection. "God help me," he said, "God help me!" because he found himself lacking strength like all perfect men. Thus spoke Yajnavalkya long before the days of the Buddha: "Those who bind themselves to error find themselves in darkness; those who bind themselves to the truth find themselves in even deeper darkness."

As happened many times before when he encountered trouble, *The Imitation of Christ* became his refuge. He turned to Book Three, Chapter Twenty:

"It is often merely a trifle that leads me into great temptation. Yes, sometimes when I think myself secure I am caught off guard and blown down by the slightest gust of wind," says the master.

He still saw in his mind's eye the young woman who had filled his room with sorrow and perfume, this questioning soul, this weeping human being. And she had held him by the arm as she made her confession, as if she hoped that she would find a redeeming power there. Why is woman made this way?

He hastened again to the wisdom of the master:

"Look down, O Lord, upon my weakness and paltriness, which you know through and through. Have mercy on me and lift me up from the mire, so that I do not sink entirely and perish.

"It often vexes me and shames me in your sight, how frail I am and weak in my struggle against my passions.

"Although I do not give in to them entirely, their perpetual pursuit of me is troublesome and grievous, and it wearies me greatly to endure this daily strife.

"My weakness lies in the fact that foul imaginings are quicker to attack than to retreat."

Ich liebe dich so unsäglich,
du schönes Menschenbild–

No woman was possessed of a more desirable femininity in the wax of her loins. Her movements were inexpressible. In her breast breathed vitality itself. Deep in her skirts slept the born and unborn, generations that waited to be awakened to eternal life. Her bosom was entirely perfect. Was there a power stronger than the one that feeds the white suckling infant? He looked at his arm, which she had so quickly fettered, and knew that without her there was no work of creation. Woman is not only the mother of men, but also of the saints, even of Jesus Christ himself. *Ave Maria, gratia plena, Dominus tecum.*

But when he became aware that the air around him eddied with lustful visions he tried again to sink himself into the book of the master:

"O mighty Lord of Israel, the goad of faithful souls, behold the sufferings and trials of your servant, and be near to him in everything that he undertakes. Strengthen me with heavenly power so that the old Adam does not prevail, the wretched flesh that I must fight against all my miserable life, until my last breath . . ."[115]

No, thought Steinn Elliði, woman has never been satisfied with the power granted by God to the arm of man. When Adam walked in the garden to rejoice in the Lord's creation, Eve sat in council with the devil under the tree. Does anyone doubt what happened at this meeting? Bontempelli has the last Eve say this to the fiend Bululu:

"Qui, qui, in mezzo, sotto questi alberi cosi spessi, tu potresti–"[116]

Everything around him was replete with hideous images: naked women with serpents coiled about their hips, Leda with the swan, pelicans feeding their young with their blood –

"De profundis clamavi ad te, Domine," he prayed. "From the depths I cry out to you, Lord: Lord, hear my voice! Incline your ears to my pleas!

"When you behold our misdeeds, Lord, Lord, who could withstand your judgment?

"But your judgments are words of reconciliation, and thus I yearn for your coming, Lord.

"In his words my soul yearned for its end; my soul awaits the Lord.

"From dawn until dusk Israel fixed his hope on the Lord.

"For the Lord is merciful and from him comes a plenitude of redemption.

"And he will redeem Israel from all of his sins."[117]

"I love him, because the Lord heard the chirrup of my prayers, because he bent his ear to my pleas. And I will call on his name all of my days.

"The dread of death encompassed me, and the terrors of Hell overwhelmed me.

"I suffered grief and hardships, and I called on the name of the Lord;

"O Lord, free my spirit, you who are merciful and righteous! And the Lord has remembered us.

"The Lord is the defender of the poor; I humbled myself, and he redeemed me.

"Direct my spirit to your peace, because the Lord is my bliss.

"Because he freed my spirit from death, my eyes from tears, my feet from stumbling.

"And I will rejoice, Lord, in the land of the living."[118]

83.

The next day, when Madam Valgerður came back to check on her patient, he was gone. He had gone east along with some English tourists and a guide. They had taken a large number of horses and planned on being gone for a long time. Hadn't he left a message for anyone? No, he hadn't said good-bye at all.

The summer passed by.

Mother- and daughter-in-law stayed at Þingvellir at midsummer, as was their custom. The Ylfingabúð was set up as a comfortable residence wherein people sat in deep chairs, read from *Tidens Kvinder* and the *Times Weekly*, played instruments, received visitors. On fair days the visitors and residents roamed the paths through the lava and smoked cigarettes in the birchwood copse, discussing their plans for the work of the charitable society during the winter. Polished cars on the highway sparkle in the sunlight. Sometimes the area is shaken by shouts of hurrah and singing from Hotel Valhöll, where banquets are held for foreign and native snobs, but in between everything is quiet, since the temporary residents are for the most part artistic old spinsters, bookish teachers who have lost their femininity, painters with bow ties, and middle-aged ladies who have lost their husbands to the wearisome toil of life. The painters are trying to create moods and stand bent over on the heath, observing the landscape through their legs in order to better collect their thoughts. These people yearn for the theosophical peace of the soul in the groves of the Summerland, and read in *Morgunblaðið* about the miracles of Conan Doyle and the elf Friðrik, as well as the romances written by Sigurjón in the bank and the holy man Krishnamurti.

One evening shortly before mid-August several guests had gathered at the Ylfingabúð, acquaintances who were spending their summer holidays at Hotel Valhöll, several elderly ladies and young women, as well as a spiritualist businessman from the north. They talked back and forth about the new movements, as they are called in Iceland, even if they had become passé in England twenty years earlier. Everyone agreed that Ford's autobiography had many exceptional qualities, but were reluctant to take sides with Dr. Helgi Pjeturss concerning bioinduction.[119] But if the solution to the mystery of existence was not that the Earth stands on an elephant and the elephant on a tortoise, as is taught in Indian mythology, then it was certainly very likely that Dr. Helgi Pjeturss was right, that men go to other stars and propagate there. Unfortunately, however, it was a waste of time to invent a new religion that was not based on paranormal Americans or lamas in Tibet. The demand for homegrown truth was constantly waning. From the next room came the sounds of the *Serenata* by Toselli.

Madam Valgerður generally never contributed to the conversation when it focused on religious matters, because it is best not to concern oneself with things that are both insignificant and sacred at the same time.

"By the way, Madam Valgerður," said one of the women, "I've heard it said that your grandson, the poet, has become a Catholic."

"So he says," replied Madam Valgerður, as if she still had some doubts as to whether that was anything but pretense.

"How does he like being a Catholic?" asked another woman.

"Do you think that there are actually great differences between all of these religions?" answered Madam Valgerður. "I imagine that their God is neither better nor worse than other gods."

"It takes an incredible amount of courage to take such a big step," said the spiritualist businessman from the north. "Now that's what I call conviction!"

"Have they stopped excommunicating people in Catholicism?" said a divorced minister's wife softly.

"No," shouted the businessman, "of that you may rest assured, madam; they haven't stopped excommunications. They would excommunicate you in a living flash. They excommunicate, excommunicate vigorously. Now those are what I call men!"

"But the granting of indulgences was surely done away with a long time ago," ventured another woman.

"Indulg–, no dear young lady, you can name a dog after me if they've stopped granting indulgences!"

"And I wonder, do they still charge for them?"

"Charge for them!? Yes, of that you may rest assured! They accept all types of payment, either on account, or up front in butter or livestock, exactly as they have for ages. They would pick your bones clean, my dear! – Those indulgences are no laughing matter, any more than they ever were!"

"It is truly sad that the Catholic Church is so narrow-minded," said one of the women. "It recognizes absolutely none of the new movements."

"New movements! No! That's something else entirely! They're not going to get caught making a fuss about those new movements there, no, ma'am! They believe in God and Saint Columba just as they did in the old days. They're not about to eat their words!"

"But their ceremonies are incredibly beautiful," said one of the women, and the others chimed in: "The ceremonies, yes, the ceremonies, ceremon, cere . . ."

"I'll never forget one Sunday last year," said the first woman, "when I and another woman went together to the church at Landakot. It was around midafternoon, and the sun shone on Jesus Christ. The nuns sang in Latin, and the altar boys swung the censers, and at the front of the church a few Catholic individuals were kneeling in prayer. Don't you find it wonderful to see folk kneeling? And the sun shone on Jesus Christ. I felt that God was much nearer to those people than to us."

"Conviction is nowhere but there!" howled the businessman. "But there's nothing enviable about getting caught in their claws."

In the next room Dvořák's *Humoresque* was being played as if it were the accompaniment to a prankish kiss of gloom.

"I've really been wanting to see your grandson, Steinn, Madam Valgerður," said one woman. "I haven't actually read his poems, because my understanding of English is limited, but I've heard him often spoken of as an entirely incomparable young man."

"I've read his poems," admitted another. "And it's not everyone who can understand them, because they're both deep and dark, and besides that written in such difficult English that you have to look up every third word. And it always seems that a poet's brain isn't put together like regular people's brains. His harp isn't tuned to either flats or sharps. You ask yourself involuntarily at every other line: 'Are these sounds, or what is that I hear?' I realized only this one thing: the man's got to be quite exceptional."

"I remember when he was a schoolboy here at home," said a third woman. "He was really a lovely boy. All the young girls had crushes on him, especially since he was raised for some of the time down south in Europe. Isn't he going to hold a lecture in Reykjavík before he leaves Iceland again, or give a public poetry reading?"

Madam Valgerður thought this unlikely. "He's not much of a socialite these days. I've always said that the traits he inherited from his family would show up sooner or later. And he takes after his kin more and more with age. His grandfather went on long trips without telling anyone beforehand. Three weeks ago Steinn left town, and I didn't hear any news of him until he'd reached Skaftafell out east."

"Couldn't we get him to speak at a dinner party for the Twenty-Five-Aurar Society?" said a respectable old madam, the president of a charitable society that funded itself by charging innocent people on the street twenty-five aurar for useless paper stamps. "I've actually been given the duty of finding a good speaker for our meeting a week from next Saturday."

In the middle of this hubbub Steinn Elliði showed up. Speak of the devil! Outside, bridle bits clinked and horses snorted; in the next moment he was standing in the doorway, wearing a gray sporting outfit covered with loose horsehair and dirty travel boots laced up to the knees, with long gloves, a bare head, a dusty, tanned face, and disheveled hair; 180 centimeters tall. "Good day," he said, at ten o'clock in the evening. And when he smelled a familiar odor, he asked:

"Tea?"

"Steinn! Welcome, child!" said Madam Valgerður as she got up from the table to go and greet the visitor. "Where have you come from?"

He had come from Gullfoss, had spent the night at Kjóastaðir, wanted tea.

Whispers went around the table and greedy, inquisitive eyes fixed themselves on the doorway. The Director's wife informed everyone that this was Steinn Elliði. Madam Valgerður led him to the table and introduced him to her guests: "My grandson, Steinn Elliði Grímúlfsson–"

"Was there a wedding here?" he asked.

He had come all the way from out east in Öræfi, had set out from Reykjavík with three Englishmen but had lost them on the way, no more about that. Beautiful countryside, wonderful weather, excellent haymaking, good milk. Icelanders are akin to the saintly ancient peoples of Asia. "Is there more tea in the pot?"

Several years ago a French trawler was stranded in Björg. The farmer in Björg is a poor man, but a good fisherman, and he was able to save every last man on the ship. He saved the lives of fifteen men single-handedly. It was written up in French newspapers. He brought them home to his cottage, and the family gave them their beds and slept out in the stackyard. He slaughtered his fattest cow, like a rich man holding a wedding feast. On the next day he set out walking in bad weather to procure tobacco for his guests. But no one in that district smoked, so he had to go to another district, returning home after a twelve-hour journey; and they held a great feast and smoked tobacco.

Six months later, on a summer day, a French warship dropped

anchor out by Björg. They sent for the farmer, and on the ship's deck a great feast was held for him and his family. And before they left the table, the commander said: "Dear sir, you have saved the lives of fifteen men for a powerful state far to the south. It is called France. And I have been entrusted the duty of offering you anything you might wish, up to fifteen thousand gold-crowns' worth, or in ready cash if you prefer."

But the farmer in Björg tried to excuse himself for a long time and said: "God be praised that the men were able to make it home. They were innocent men."

But when he saw that there was no way that he could refuse the reward, he had this interpreted to the commander:

"Esteemed sir commander! God bless France and the king of France. Tell him that I live by the sea and the soil here is scanty. My salvation is the sea. But my yawl has started to leak, because it's so old, and sometimes I've thought about how I might get myself a new yawl. And I've seen nothing in my life that has awakened in me such an unchristian desire as the ship's boats here on deck. Those are fine boats, my Lord, I said to myself, and if Torfi in Björg could have one of those he wouldn't need to fear for his children's future."

"Now that's an Icelander!" bawled the businessman, and he hammered his fist on the table so hard that tears of fear came to the women's eyes.

"More tea, more tea!" said Steinn Elliði. "The cheese is like rubber, Grandmother. And how come there aren't more of those fine cakes on the table? I hope that the guests don't have stomachaches?"

The mandarins in China are said to take three hours to greet each other, for the rules of courtesy demand that they hop, kneel, cast themselves down and stand on their heads, sing, shout, whistle, warble, crack their knuckles, and stand on one foot in front of each other untold times before they dare to ask the news or mention politics. When Saint Francis of Assisi addressed the birds in the forest he did so halfheartedly, because he found himself unworthy to speak to God's handiwork, and he began this way: "Forgive me, dear brothers and sisters, that I should be so bold as to disturb you! When you have finished your conversation might I be permitted to say a little something that lies in my heart?" And who has ever compared to Beinteinn from Fagurhóll for courtesy? A well-mannered man, when he bids his guests farewell, accompanies them at least out over the threshold. An even more well-mannered man accompanies his guests out through the outer doors, even to the gate of the yard. Beinteinn from Fagurhóll accompanied his guests back to their own homefields. The parish there lies far from the main routes, and therefore every visitor to Fagurhóll is received as a divine revelation. Three times Beinteinn has accompanied his guests from Reykjavík all the way from the paving stones at Fagurhóll south to the Elliða River. And that is a journey of eleven days, as from Paris to Peking on the Trans-Siberian Railroad. The road crosses twenty parishes, sandy wastes, and extremely dangerous rivers. Beinteinn won't hear of allowing his guests to ride their own horses the whole way back. Several years ago an agronomist from Reykjavík, with degrees from Askov, Hvanneyri, and Voss, stayed at Fagurhóll. He was researching agricultural conditions in the eastern part of the country and came riding on a clumsy, haggard nag that he'd probably stolen somewhere out east in the Múli district. He went and fetched two small rocks up in a ravine, hammered them together until they broke, scrutinized the fractures, and then measured the waterfall. He was received like a king at Fagurhóll, and when he left, Farmer Beinteinn accompanied him out of the yard and then rode with him for eleven days. When they came to the slope above Ártún, five kilometers east of Reykjavík, Farmer Beinteinn dismounted, and they put the visitor's saddle on his jade and bade each other farewell with a kiss, as was customary.

"Listen, Beinteinn," said the agronomist when they had said their farewells. "You don't suppose you could possibly loan me ten krónur? I'll send it back to you by post."

Nothing was more self-evident. Beinteinn removed the safety pin from the opening on his breast pocket and took out his wallet, wrapped within three white handkerchiefs, and from the wallet took ten krónur and gave them to the agronomist. After this they parted.

Twelve months passed and the post came twelve times, but nothing was heard from the agronomist. Beinteinn had never known a debt to go unpaid, and such a thing chafed against his conscience, so he thought the agronomist might be dead. But two years later he took a steamship to Reykjavík and learned that the agronomist wasn't dead, but had actually set up an experimental farm employing the latest methods in Kjalarnes. Poor man, to have forgotten to pay his debt, thought Beinteinn, and he took this so sorely that he set off on foot up to Kjalarnes in stormy fall weather. The experimental farm was comprised of one tomcat, a woman, and three chairs of American design. "Those few krónur were somehow forgotten over the past few years," said Beinteinn, "it doesn't really make much difference, but still . . ."

"That's good luck, because just this morning I happened to buy five hundred lambs," said the agronomist, and he rounded them up, drove them in, and gave Beinteinn a small, late-born lamb in payment for the debt. Beinteinn begged forgiveness for having had to remind him of this trifle, thanked him, said good-bye and set off again for Reykjavík with the lamb upon his shoulders. But it had started to grow dark, the weather was rough and the fall night dim, so Beinteinn decided to stop for the night at the first big farm he reached. In the morning when he woke he suddenly remembered that he'd left the lamb at the foot of the homefield the night before. But he wasn't going to work himself into a lather about it, and instead paid for his lodging graciously, bade farewell to the householder with a kiss, and left.

"What an unparalleled delight it is to listen to the man!" sighed the madam from the Twenty-Five-Aurar Society devoutly.

But Steinn Elliði had his grandmother pour more tea into his cup and kept on eating.

"At Hvolur I spent a night with Aðalbjörn from Hrísar. He'd been a respected farmer and parish administrator in Lón. But due to his good deeds for both the worthy and the unworthy, the parish coffer was emptied, and Aðalbjörn was taken to court; he was ordered to relinquish all of his possessions, but this still wasn't enough to cover the loss. He had six sons, strong, promising men. Two were lost at sea, another in a river, a fourth from tuberculosis, and a fifth went to America. The sixth became a scholar and drunkard down south. Because of their bankruptcy the parish administrator and his wife were forced to go begging, and the wife died of exposure. Then Aðalbjörn was alone. He is eighty-two years old. He is like a cardinal, infirm and august, uglier than anyone but to children the kindest of all men. He invents machines, slaps his thigh and says: 'Oh my dear children, I have so many machines to invent!' He has far too serious work to attend to give himself time to die. We spoke together for five hours about machines. He told me about seven machines that he had invented during the last few years, and claimed that they had become so much in vogue that I would find them on every farm in the Eastern District and every other farm in the Western District. Then he asked me whether I'd invented any machines. And since the answer to that was no, he entrusted me with a secret. He was, to wit, on his way toward inventing a new machine, more remarkable than any previous one, an eiderdown-cleaning machine that would surely make all of the other methods of cleaning eiderdown obsolete, and would use about seventy-five percent less labor. He had come on foot over mountains and wastelands and was heading west to Vík to have a talk with the bailiff there about this grand innovation. He wanted to try to get a patent on his invention and later bequeath his parish the patent, so that it could build a children's school there after a time. He set off early in the morning and worried about the cough that he would get along the way, because his route put him headlong against a breeze. The path curled like smoke up a steep slope. He wanted to make it to the western side that same day. He walked on with bent back south of the lane and staggered in his steps, supporting himself with a large staff. The breeze blew through his silver white locks. A spotted dog followed him, but otherwise he was alone."

84.

Steinn came to the breakfast table after a long morning hike and sat down at it alone. But shortly after he has begun eating, the Director's wife walks in. She is pale as usual in the morning; her body is still a mirage, but her soul is everything; even her hands are nothing but soul.

"Good day!" he says with his mouth full. "I thought that everyone had eaten already. I walked east to Vatnsvík through the entire copse. Such a fragrance!"

She sat down wearily and poured herself some tea.

"I always get up late," she said, without looking up.

"That's unhealthy," he said, and kept chewing.

"I usually don't sleep until around dawn."

"Why is that?"

She shrugged her shoulders and made no reply. Twice he had seen her appear in the hallway in the last few days, but both times she had disappeared through the nearest doorway and acted as if she hadn't noticed him. Yesterday she'd been walking with one of her girlfriends along a path from the east; he had come from the west. But the two women quickened their pace so that they could turn up the road to Hotel Valhöll before they met him, and they disappeared into the hotel.

He acted as if he had no idea that she was afraid of him, ate easily, and kept on talking.

"Who knows, maybe I can give you some advice about insomnia, my good lady," he said. "I've spent time studying homeopathic remedies and was for a time a specialist in painful mental conditions."

She leaned her elbow on the edge of the table and ate half a biscuit out of a sense of duty to breakfast.

"You should determine never to sleep until you have reviewed all of the happy moments in your life. I guarantee you that you won't have finished reviewing the sixth before you relive the seventh in your dreams."

"I've never lived any happy moments" – her answer came like an echo out of a frigid vacuum.

"Except for your honeymoon," said the doctor, and he gulped down an egg in one bite.

"No."

"What the hell?" said he. "That's a sad story indeed. Have you ever tried taking the multiplication table to bed with you? Or read *Manhood* by C. Wagner? That's such a hateful book that it could put a five-year-old bull to sleep."

"Oh, Steinn, stop it!"

But he was not about to stop; he was eager to give his wholesome advice, like an elderly bourgeois.

"The best way to deal with a disturbed mental condition at night is to accustom oneself to going to bed in alignment with the compass. All the perturbed movements of a person's heart are caused by its not being aligned properly with the magnetic axis. As soon as one lines oneself up with the magnetic axis, the heart is calmed and the thoughts become as fair as lilies of the valley. If I were a Protestant, I would invent a religion that would aim at aligning the heart of man with this particular axis."

"Steinn, you are mocking me! Why can't you speak seriously anymore?"

He looked at her with wide eyes as if he were completely surprised, but there was some devil in his heart that giggled unrestrainedly. How was it possible to imagine that he could speak a word in earnest in this pestilent atmosphere?

"Am I so despicable in your eyes, Steinn?"

Finally he stopped eating and looked straight at her:

"But you certainly couldn't think that I look upon human feelings as sacred?" he asked. "Such ludicrous vanity!"

"Then are people even more ridiculous in your eyes the worse they feel?"

"Yes," he replied unequivocally. "I am grateful to you for wording this question so well. People are even more ridiculous in my eyes the worse they feel."

"Is that Catholic?" she asked.

"No, it's Buddhist."

"Steinn, I feel that I still haven't begun to speak to you, to your essential self. Why aren't we allowed to see you as you are?"

He couldn't hold back his laughter.

"I have lived my life among giants and ogres," he said.

"Do you know what I really long for, Steinn?"

No, he had no idea.

"I really wish that we could be friends, Steinn, all three of us."

"Three?"

"True friends, Steinn; like brothers and sisters. Örnólfur, you, and I."

"I'll remember you in my prayers after I've gone."

"Why do you have to go? Your friends are here."

"Friends!" he said contemptuously.

"Imagine what a great man you could be here at home!"

"Stop this shameful nonsense!" he said, and stood up.

"Steinn, you're hiding something!" she said hotly, and her eyes started to glisten. He looked at her dumbfoundedly, unable to make heads or tails of her vehemence.

"Yes, I'm hiding something," he said, and he left.

85.

"Det var en vas med roser."[120]

Skjaldbreiður is enwrapped in coarse clouds. It has started to rain; Almannagjá is like a dark, dirty streak traversing all existence, from the mountain above down to the lake, broken in only one place by a waterfall. Otherwise the mountains are not nearly as holy as Steinn had fancied in Belgium. Of what worth are mountains? He roams to and fro along the paths through the lava, and the raindrops fall from the sky. The drops come from Heaven and land in different types of soil, like good tidings. He shuddered most to think of how he enjoyed being a wicked man, entirely contrary to his conscience. He could care less about being better. He loved the Devil by leaps and bounds more than God. He started thinking about a certain medieval prioress who had made a contract with the Devil in her cell. It was a lengthy, detailed contract. She gave herself head and foot to the Devil. To him she dedicated her body and soul, her deeds and all of her thoughts. Because it is so delightful to give oneself to the Devil – it requires neither contemplation nor concern; nothing is easier. The contract is written on calfskin. It is stored in a certain archive, and is signed by both parties.

He thought to himself: is a man the same today as yesterday? If this is so, then there exists no more merciless truth, and the hopes of the Kingdom of Heaven dwindle. "The bird flew featherless and alighted on the wall boneless. Then came a man handless and shot the bird bowless." Meaningless.

Now for the first time in a long while he recalled Hounslow, the suburb of London where he had studied Strindberg, and said: "I'm no better off here than there!" There he had suffered from angina; there he was stuck on a spit and roasted over a slow fire like Savonarola. One night he had bitten his own tongue, causing blood to flow from the corners of his mouth. All night he had cried out for the comfort of the downtrodden, for the God whom he neither believed in nor trusted. On one side death screamed: on the other insanity howled. He prayed the Lord's Prayer nonstop, over and over again, incessantly, without rest, like a sailor who curses when his life is in extreme danger. He prayed for twelve hours at a time, from dusk until dawn, without believing in God.

On the days when he tried to read, the letters started dancing around and turned red; they were playing; the pages burned with corposant. And dismay lurked behind the entire dance. The little that he understood were hints and insinuations predicting his damnation. Finally he had ordered James to hide every last book that he found in the house. Where? Down in the basement. The shelves were emptied, the table and the floor cleared; the furniture was poked under to see if any volumes might have crept into hiding, until finally the rooms were emptied, but for a few bugs in the corners. When it was least expected, however, a very thick old book fell down from one of the shelves that had recently been emptied. It was a train timetable; an omen, he thought; some left at 10:15 and others at 12:45. He did not doubt that the book had come like a *sending*,[121] in a fiendish way, and terror welled up in his heart the more he thought about its contents: a conspectus of trains that transported lost souls to Yorkshire and Devonshire, Budapest and Prague. He threw it out the window.

And as Steinn drank his afternoon coffee at Hotel Valhöll, he pulled *The Imitation of Christ* from his pocket to see whether the saint might not have something up his sleeve. Wherein could he find lasting peace of the heart and true advancement?

"If you have finally become so sturdy and perseverant in hope," says the master, "that you are able to submit your heart to even more hardships when it feels as if all of your inner comfort has been taken from you – when you no longer try to make excuses as if you felt you were too guiltless to suffer hardship, but rather admit Christ to be righteous in all of his dispositions and worship him as holy, then you will find yourself on the true path of peace." One cup of coffee with cakes, two krónur fifty. He killed two flies with one swat of the book and stood up.

When he came home late that afternoon he wondered why the door to his room was ajar. He hung up his wet coat and went in. The Director's wife was standing near the table in his room, arranging flowers in a vase. He saw her profile. There were violets from the slopes, forget-me-nots from the priest's yard, and various other flowers, all Icelandic, beautiful, and small. They grew at the heart of the country.

"Good day."

Unsteady fingers upset the bunch the moment he walked in; her pupils were dark, but she did not blush. She looked at him and started to rearrange the flowers.

"I'd planned to have been gone," she said.

"Are these flowers?" he asked.

"I don't know," she said.

"What are flowers for?" he asked.

"Flowers? I don't know," she said, and continued to arrange them. She tried to keep the violets on the outside, the forget-me-nots on the inside, because they were the smallest. "We always have flowers here in this room. I picked them for fun, because they grow–"

It was almost bizarre how her hands had gotten smaller since she was a girl; at that time they had appeared large; now small; then, her arms had been slender; now, her wrists were cylindrical, her skin more delicate, softer, whiter. She had had braids before; now her hair was bobbed. Her neck was strong, yet had soft lines, her femininity woven with a distinctive velvet blueness, her calves stout, adamantine, and beautifully shaped. And there she stood, arranging flowers.

Finally she walked over to him and said:

"Tell me, Steinn, what we can do for you. Now you've been outside the whole day. We've been worried about how lonely you must be."

"I'm thinking of taking up smoking again," he said. "Do you think you might have any decent cigarettes at hand?"

"Yes, there's plenty to smoke here," she said. "Listen, do you want some wine?"

"Wine? Have you lost your mind?"

"No, Steinn," she said in a pleading voice, and touched his arm. "Can we drink a bottle of wine together? Yes, let's do that, alright? Please don't be angry that I've come with these flowers; they're just ordinary flowers; I found them, forgive me for that, alright?"

"It's criminal," he said, pointing at the flowers.

She closed her eyes quickly and sighed; grimaced as if she were going to start crying, and turned away. Finally she looked again toward him and asked with wide eyes:

"Am I really so corrupt?"

He took her in his arms. He was very strong. She gave herself completely to his embrace. But this only lasted a moment; then he shoved her away, turned, went to the table and started looking at the flowers. Finally he asked impetuously, looking sharply toward her at the same time:

"What am I supposed to do with these damned flowers? Get these damned flowers out of here!"

He grabbed the vase and threw it full force at the wall, causing shards to fly throughout the room and water to stream to the floor. But he was not satisfied with just breaking the vase; he also trampled the flowers under his heel, yelling, "Down with flowers!"

But she had never been more calm nor determined than at that moment; this meant she was a woman; she looked at him without moving an inch and said coldly:

"How you hate me!"

He continued to trample, she to strengthen her resolve:

"You make a game of trampling me to pieces!"

He went straight over to her and struck her on the cheek with the palm of his hand, causing her to sink at the knees.

"I love you!" he said.

But she did not start crying, and instead sat calmly down, felt her cheek, and said:

"I know that you're hiding something. And I know what it is you're hiding. I might as well say it. You're married."

"I am a man of God," he said.

"A man of God!" she repeated, and she laughed contemptuously.

"I'm going away to become a monk."

"But you're not married otherwise?"

"I'm going to become a monk."

"Where?"

"In France."

"Where in France?"

"Solesmes."

"Can I come visit you after you've become a monk?"

86.

He walked quickly westward along the road, as if he had pressing business. But when he reached Þingvellir he realized that he had no business there after all. Some Germans rescued him: several scientists with close-cut hair, newly arrived, thirsty for knowledge, asked him, *"Sprechen Sie Deutsch?"* Steinn was delighted to meet educated men, and was eager to guide them and explain things to them. They went first to the Byrgisbúð, then west along the river-bank and examined the outlines of the booths, finally sat down on the eastern rim of the ravine and talked about the place. Twilight fell over the mountains and the valley; the rain abated; the winds died down along the paths; the lake was placid and white; loons cried out. Next they went to Valhöll, ordered drinks, and discussed European cultural affairs and British and Russian politics in Asia; Steinn sounded like a telegram from Agence Havas. He came home half an hour before midnight.

The Ylfingabúð did not have electric lights, because it was not used during the darker part of the year. He lit a candle and looked about; both the shards and the flowers were gone. She had gathered them herself, cleaned the floor with her prim wife's hands without anyone else knowing. He sits down and reflects in the quiet of the night on how wonderful it would be to break more. But after sitting like this for some time he catches sight of something new upon his table: a bottle of champagne and two glasses. A bottle of champagne and two glasses, he thinks, and his heart stands still for a long time. Sticking out from beneath the bottle is a folded piece of paper, upon which are several typed lines and an address: a telegram. He picks up the note. It has already been opened; the address is Madam Diljá Þorsteinsdóttir, *pro tempore* Þingvellir, and its contents as follows: "London this morning, 9 a.m. On my way home to you. Örnólfur."

He pretended to have no idea as to how these things had mistakenly found their way into his room, did not even suppose there might be someone insane in the house, thought to himself, "There was a man named Joseph," understood nothing. Steinn Elliði was determined to admit the righteousness of Christ in all of his dispositions and worship his holiness. In the tranquility of midnight, when the world sleeps, the Lord is near to everyone who calls upon him. The Lord is awake all nights. *Sicut tenebrae ejus sicut et lumen ejus.*[122] As his light, so also is his darkness. Lord, teach me to love you as your saints do, in such a way that nothing will be of any worth to me within the boundaries of existence except for you alone, the ultimate reality! Teach me to submit my heart to even more trials, even if all spiritual comfort might be taken from me! Make me a pilgrim in this world, which gives only stones for bread and worms for fish, and let me find no refuge until this sorrowful existence is at an end and my bones find their rest in you. He reached into his pocket for his rosary and started to contemplate the five sufferings of Jesus, who died for the sins of men: he sweat blood in Gethsemane, was scourged, was crowned with thorns, bore a heavy cross, was crucified. Amen.

His fingers feel their way from bead to bead, and at every tenth bead he makes a large sign of the cross, brings the Rosary's crucifix to his lips and recites the Lord's Prayer, then begins the next set of ten.

But even the smallest movement outside disturbs him; the night is so quiet, so still; somewhere in the house a door is opened carefully, and then quiet footsteps can be heard. His concentration is broken for several moments, a short time passes, and all is as quiet as before; his fingers feel their way along another five beads.

Then a rustling noise is heard again, and no longer in a distant wing of the house – instead he hears the unmistakable sound of someone walking outside his door: movements, footsteps, a brushing against the wall. He sticks the rosary quickly into his pocket and blows out the candle. For a moment he hears nothing but his own heartbeat, heavy like the boom of a cannon, but then the door handle is turned from the outside, thrust downward until the latch is free of the jamb. There is a slight hesitation again, until the door is opened very slowly, and in through the thumb-sized crack between the jamb and the door falls a stripe of dim light.

The door is opened halfway. It is Diljá who stands there in a wide-sleeved pink negligé, with naked feet in high-heeled silk slippers; in her hand she carries a little red night-light. The gleam from this faint red light falls on the lines in her pale face, rigid as a wax mask, and her wide-open eyes, pupils dilated, stare into the room. She stops in the doorway, her hand still on the handle, and continues to stare; it is almost as if she has lost the ability to move her eyes; she stares and stares. The fetters of reason are broken, blind natural power appears in these nocturnal eyes, liberated on the ruins of God and man, gleaming red. Her personality has disappeared into the void, where all form vanishes; she appears here as the embodiment of nameless powers, the image of the first and last living being, blind, devoid of thought, and gruesome.

After staring at him for a time she sighs quickly, and convulsive shivers of either bliss or woe run through her body. She steps over the threshold and closes the door behind her. He walked over to her with almost perverse calmness, took the lamp from her hand and put it on the table, took her by the arm and led her to a seat in a deep chair. But when he was going to release her arm she took him by the hands, held them tightly, stared agonizingly into his face, and sighed:

"Oh-h-h, wine!"

He sat down opposite her and said:

"God has blessed both of our lives. We may not reject his mercy, because our health in the next world is far better than our sin now. Love Örnólfur, Diljá; he is worthy of your love; he is your husband. God desires that you live a stainless life as a faithful wife, not for your sake or his, but rather for the sake of the children that God gives you. For before the judgment seat of eternal life it will not be asked how passionate your loves have been, but whether you taught your children to love God. And I have been called to die to myself for the name of Jesus Christ."

"Take off your mask, Steinn," she pleaded.

"You are not free tonight, Diljá."

"You said you love me."

"Forgive me for what I have said. I am not in control of myself. Everything that I say is a lie. I am nothing but an illusion. This is why I have turned my back on myself. God alone is real."

Then she squeezed his hands, tilted her head back, and closed her eyes. Her voice welled with passion as she started to speak:

"All of my most sublime feelings would enclose this little holy innocent. How blissfully I would have thanked God when I held him to my breast to feed him. For his sake I would without a grumble take every single burden of fate upon my shoulders. Steinn, I am prepared to sacrifice everything, everything! That cannot be a sin!"

"What are you talking about, woman?"

"The memory of you, Steinn, the incarnate memory of the god in you, the truth in you, your clear blue eyes, your bright curls, your mouth, Steinn, your mouth; the memory that you are going to give me, that I want to bear in my womb. I can no longer evade you, Steinn; it would be ridiculous if I tried to hide myself."

"This is sinful, Diljá."

"If I have sinned, then God sinned before me when he created the world."

"Diljá! Beware, child! God is holy!"

"He is heathen," said the woman, "and neither Catholic nor Lutheran; heathen! I hate all of this disgusting religious prattle!"

She sat up in her chair and looked him straight in the face, her eyes wild. He feared that the savage beast would burst out uncontrollably if he did not try to calm her down, so he stroked the back of her hand with his palm and said:

"Calm down, Diljá dear. We shall be friends as you suggested yesterday morning, pure and simple friends, like sister and brother."

"Fie," she said. "I never said that, never wanted that! Sister and brother! It's disgusting! Oh, Steinn, Steinn!"

He tried again to calm her mood and continued to speak in a friendly, relaxed tone of voice:

"Diljá. I will never forget you. You will continue to be my most cherished memory from youth. I shall pray for you every day, every night pray to God to let his angels watch over you. But God has called me; he demands me; all of me. I have made an unbreakable vow to worship God, entirely. I begged him to preserve my chastity long before I humbled my arrogance before his omnipotence. And he desired that I live chastely long before it pleased him to let me hear his voice. If I were to sin tonight, I would stain my baptismal vow. I cannot bear to think of taking a willing step contrary to the will of God."

"Fool!" she shouted, shaking her fist in his face, her face disfigured from the anger of humiliation. "You disgrace me! This is what it means to disgrace a woman! Get out of here! You do not belong in this house! I own this house! Away!"

Then he acted humble and wretched, cast himself on his knees before her, begged for forgiveness and kissed her hands, but she grabbed handfuls of his hair; they remained in this posture for a short time. Then he stood up. She turned away, went to his bed, threw herself onto it in a heap, and started to weep. She lay there for a long time and wept, in painful, heavy sobs. He waited. Then he showed her to the door.

87.

Peace between a man and a woman is the worst, except that one thing might be even worse: their friendship. On the next day they sat together for three hours and spoke harmoniously. He told her everything that had happened from the time that he abandoned his mother in Naples in the fall of 1921 until he set foot in Iceland again six weeks ago. He described to her Hounslow near London, the abominable city; told of his pilgrimage to Sicily, where his mother's gravestone, inscribed in Danish, stands in the heathens' graveyard, and where green lizards run around and squint in two directions at once in the midday heat. Then he told her about his stay in the abbey in the Ardennes mountains, where he was converted to the true faith. He spoke about his growth in the faith, using exemplary tales like a public school teacher. He explained to her that God himself established the Catholic Church, and that the other churches were heretical. He proclaimed to her that the soul of man is predestined for eternal life. The way to freedom requires the sacrifice of one's own will. Afterward he was annoyed with himself for all of his prattle. He felt as if he'd been making excuses.

She listened, but he couldn't tell whether she was distracted or attentive. Perhaps she was thinking of only one thing the entire time. Of course women never think about anything else. Women don't understand spoken words. One can only speak to them as to children and dogs. Where can one find enduring peace of the heart and true advancement? What woman understands this question? If she had had a lucky night, she would spend the entire next day thinking about it. If something had disappointed her in the night, she would start contemplating her revenge.

Then they went out for a ride.

The evening was cloudy, but the clouds and the peaks were tinged with sunshine and the air was calm. They had gotten a late start, because the boy had taken a long time rounding up the horses. By the time they came down from Meyjarsæti after sunset and rode back toward home, rain clouds covered the sky and showers fell in the mountains. Soon the first drops fell on them, and in just a short time it was pouring. They would rather have let the horses run the rest of the way home, since they weren't dressed for the rain, but as it turned out, one of the horse's hind hooves was shoeless and it limped, forcing them to walk. The light grew dim.

When they had crossed the lava halfway they stopped for a rest in a hollow. They sought shelter from the rain and found an overhang, but the space beneath was so narrow that they had to sit squeezed closely together. He took their gloves and wrung them out. They cursed the stable boy for not having inspected the horses better before they set out, said that sloth was to blame for his tardiness in rounding them up. They agreed that he should be fired. Finally she said:

"I hope I don't have a cold tomorrow, because I'm going to Reykjavík early in the morning."

"To Reykjavík?"

"Yes. The *Bothnia* arrives tomorrow evening. I'm going to meet Örnólfur."

He said nothing. It rained on the lava and the birch; the twilight deepened. She was sitting nearly in his lap. All he needed to do was lean a little to the left and she could have rested her head against his chest. But neither of them moved. They even took care not to let each other hear their breathing. Both of them seemed to have forgotten that they were wet and needed to get home quickly so that Grandmother would not be alarmed.

Finally it was she who flared up, as if she were startled; she turned her face quickly toward him and whispered:

"Steinn, what must you be thinking of me?! You must think the very worst of me! Oh my God, if you should have misunderstood me; if you should think that I am loose!"

And now she tugged at his shirt and whispered imploringly into his face:

"Promise me that you will never think that I came to you out of wantonness. I could never bear that. God Almighty knows that I hate wantonness, Steinn, I hate it!" – and at this point the sobs once again broke through her sighs, and at the same moment she wrapped her arms around his neck, cuddled up to him, trembled and wept:

"Steinn, you cannot imagine how I hate wantonness!" she professed. "I could die!"

He walked out of the lava hollow and looked for the horses, but they were gone. "Wait!" he called, and then ascended the nearest hill, but the rain and darkness clouded his sight so much that he caught no glimpse of anything resembling their horses. He crept about in the hollows around him, climbed from hill to hill; she waited for him. She had no inclination to crawl into a shelter again, but stood there where she had emerged, staring trancelike into the night and allowing the rain to trickle down into her bosom as it did into the earth. Finally it crossed her mind that Steinn Elliði might be in mortal danger due to the deep clefts in the lava, and she started to yell: "Steinn, Steinn!"

He answered from a distance.

"Come here," she yelled. "Come here!"

She waited again for a little while. Finally she heard his spurs clinking on the lava rocks, and the drenched birch brushing against his clothing.

"The nags have bolted," he said. "I can't see anything in this darkness. We'll have to walk home."

88.

The path was not easily trodden, and was worst where it lay across bare lava; it was very difficult to make out the road, but where it crossed soft ground pools of water gleamed in old hoofprints.

"You must be soaked to the skin," he said. They walked for a whole hour without saying anything, splashing, slipping. She lost her whip, he one of his gloves; the mud piled up on the outsides of their boots; she fell behind. Finally he recalled that she was a woman and offered to take her arm.

"We must be almost there," she said.

He answered, annoyed: "I don't understand this at all."

This night walk continued for quite some time without them finding themselves anywhere near the Ylfingabúð, until dogs started barking loudly a short distance away – and now three or four dogs came at them, making an angry racket and a fuss. And when these unpleasant night watchmen were assured that these were not ghosts, their vehemence subsided, until they lost all interest and slunk away.

"We've come to a farm," said Steinn. "This is clearly a fence, and it looks to me like the outline of a farmhouse, just over there."

They felt their way along the fenced path to the farmhouse and after a few moments arrived at the paving stones before its door.

"Where in the hell did this farm come from?" she said. "There's no such farm near Þingvellir."

But his only reply was a curse, and he pounded the door with the toe of his boot, causing the farmhouse to creak and groan and the dogs to bark and howl once more.

"Dogs and devils!" he muttered angrily, as he continued to pound on the door. "Damn it all, I'm sure we've gone in the opposite direction–" and he continued his hammering.

In a few moments a rustling was heard at the door, and a human nose stuck out through the gap. A sleepy voice, which it was impossible to guess came from the throat of a man or a woman, but which was obviously surprised by the noise of the dogs, asked who was outside.

"Folk from Reykjavík," answered Steinn. "We've lost our horses and our way. Could you possibly put us up for what's left of the night and give us something to drink?"

"Well, damn, I really don't know what you'd settle for; there's nothing you could call high-class housing here, as you can see, but naturally you can try to fit yourselves into what we have resembling a guest room, instead of hanging around out there in the squall."

It was an old woman. She invited them to follow her down a pitch-black hallway that smelled of rotten turf and other earthly materials, cautioned them not to break their necks on the stairs, and then led them into a little room with a four-paned window.

"I don't dare to wake anyone else, because everyone's exhausted; it wasn't even possible to gather what we'd spread out to dry yesterday morning before the rain started; and I'd only just gone to sleep when the whelp started barking; and there's still nothing to feed the lamps here on the farm; still there ought to be a bed made up there if you'd care to go to sleep, and somewhere there ought to be a chest if you want to have a seat while I try to get something for you to drink. Are there more than two of you?"

Steinn Elliði said no.

After several moments the woman returned with a large pitcher full of fresh milk and two large cups. She placed these on the table beneath the window and invited the guests to help themselves.

"You don't have to worry about the bed at all," she said, "because we've often housed people from Reykjavík here in the past, and we're clean folk here."

"When does it get light?" asked Steinn.

"Oh, it'll start glimmering pretty soon, considering it's already three," answered the old woman, "but don't you worry about that, because when I get up I'll tell the housemother that there are guests here, so she'll wake you up with a cup of coffee."

The old maid seemed satisfied that everything was in order, because she bade good night without any further ado and left the guests and their muses alone in the darkness.

The milk proved to be a most outstanding thirst-quencher, and they gulped it down as the rain hammered on the corrugated roof of the house.

"What do you think Grandmother will say when we don't come home?" he asked.

"She'll think we're dead," said the daughter-in-law remorselessly. "She'll think we've fallen into a ravine and broken our necks. It won't do her any harm to be upset for one night."

The Director's wife took off her hat and fixed her hair in the darkness, just as if she were absolutely delighted with this change of plans.

"You must be soaked to the skin," he said.

"That doesn't matter. I'm not wetter than you."

"When it gets light I'm going to look for the horses."

"And I'd already told our boy at home to have the car ready by nine tomorrow morning. I've got to be in Reykjavík in ten hours. At this particular moment I feel like I'm somewhere in Alaska. Steinn, imagine! We're in Alaska! Alaska!"

"You've hopefully noticed that there's only one bed for the both of us in this damned den," he said.

"What does that matter? I'm used to sitting up all night when I can't sleep. Take it easy and go to bed; I'll sit here on the chest."

"Are you crazy? You're wet and tired and a woman besides, and you could catch a cold! You go to bed; let me sit on the chest. I'm going anyway to search for the horses as soon as it starts to brighten up."

"I'm going too when it's light enough to find my way," she said. "You mustn't imagine that I would let anyone find me sleeping here tomorrow."

"No, let me sit on the chest."

"No, I'm not moving an inch off this chest."

"Yes, but you can see, woman, that there's no sense in letting the bed remain empty."

"Then lie down!"

"Are you nuts, woman? It's only fair if I stay awake for a while."

"I'm not going to sleep before you."

"Before me? I'm not going to sleep at all."

"Well, fine then. But you can be absolutely certain that I won't go to sleep."

"Diljá dear, what is this waywardness supposed to mean?"

"The bed will remain empty as far as I'm concerned; I'm telling you that once and for all."

They sat there for a while, stubborn and silent, and listened to the rain. He drank a cup of milk. Then he stood up, stricken by a fit of shivering from the cold.

"I don't understand this idiocy at all! Will you use the bed or not?" he asked.

"Haven't I said that this blessed bed can stand empty until Doomsday as far as I'm concerned?"

But it was a long time to wait until Doomsday, and still several hours until dawn. He walked around in the darkness for a few moments, stopped at the window, reached out and found her. He took hold of one of her arms and whispered:

"I'm going to bed."

She said nothing.

He started taking off his clothes and threw them carelessly onto the floor, slipped himself finally beneath the soft bedcovers and pulled them up to his chin. She didn't stir for a long time. Rock-a-bye baby, he thought, and tried to make it sound as if he were sleeping. A long time passed, and the rain continued to patter on the roof. He perceived no movements in the room until he felt someone standing at his bedside and the top blanket being touched. In the next instant the blanket was quickly lifted, and in a split-second she had climbed into the bed and slipped beneath the covers by his side. His searching hand brushed her naked breast and bare hips, and soft arms slipped beneath his head and entwined about his neck.

"You won't throw me out of bed naked?" was whispered in his ear.

"No. I thank you, my love, for how you have allowed me to torment you. Lovers torment; and are tormented."

"The time has come," she sighed. "Then you can kill me."

"No, my love, I won't kill you; I'll torment you, torment you, torment you. I left Iceland last time with the intention of tormenting you; and when I leave again I leave in order to torment you. Because you are all that I love. The love between a man and a woman is the only truth in life. Everything in my life is a lie, Diljá: God and the Devil, Heaven and Hell, everything a lie but you."

89.

When he woke it was late in the morning; the sun shone ceremoniously through the room's single four-paned window, gilding the destitution within: under the window stood a table of unpolished wood and upon this a pitcher and two cups. Of his female companion there was nothing to be seen. He got out of bed, drank what was left of the milk in the pitcher, and lay back down. His clothes lay scattered about the floor, in the places where he had cast them in the night.

He pounded on the wainscoting several times and called out: "Hello!" Finally a young woman, the housekeeper, came in, bade good day in a friendly way and displayed obvious surprise at seeing only one guest, because she'd been told that two had come there during the night.

"My companion left early this morning to search for the horses," he said. "We were a bit tipsy yesterday and the horses escaped us when we stopped for a rest. Might I ask you to dry my socks?"

The woman was most hospitable, collected his clothes and left with them, but returned in a short time with steaming coffee, hot pancakes, and waffles. Around noon Steinn sauntered away in his dry clothes, feeling very contented. The air was clean and clear after the rain, the view of the mountains was bewitching, the scent of the copse intoxicating; all around him the birds of the heath tuned their voices; the butterflies slipped through his fingers before he was able to catch them. He walked leisurely westward through the lava and recited a stanza from the *Völuspá:*[123]

She sees rising
a second time
earth from sea
eddying green:
waterfalls stream;
the eagle overhead
wings to fells
to hunt for fish.

He was far from feeling anything akin to remorse; on the contrary, he was elated, full of the confidence of a healthy man, masculine pride. He had learned to perceive the guiles of the Devil in a woman and to value love of chastity as the most precious of all the passions of mortal man. Today he adored man for having been granted the ability to take part in the glory of creation of the living universe. Two human beings encounter the immortality of their own deathliness in the ultimate offering of their bodies and souls – could a more beautiful gospel exist? That night he had had the courage to forsake himself and speak the most truthful lie of human imperfection.

And he allowed his ideals to evaporate like a web of dew in a brake beneath the rising sun. His monastic ideals? Vain threads, the woof in the warp of a sick soul, the same kind of fanaticism as composing fifty poems about God in English. God cannot be served any better with monasticism than with poetry. Man does not triumph over his imperfection any better with monasticism than with poetry. To live in affluence in a stately monastery all of one's life, to go to bed at nine o'clock and get up at four to sing some sort of rigmarole from the Old Testament, to sing masses in multicolored silk chasubles and to ring bells was not a bit more Christlike than to live in Hounslow in London, to go to bed at one and get up at eight to quarrel with Mr. Carrington over oatmeal about the value of ancient writers. He was determined now to start reading Freud as thoroughly as possible. Self-denial! People would be better off following the example of Lao-tzu and trying to overcome sanctity! The greater part of mankind lives under more stringent forms of self-denial than the most austere monks. In Great Britain there are five hundred thousand people unemployed at this moment; and they don't even have the means to buy the milk for their porridge, let alone to own a one-shilling edition of the works of Bernard Shaw! In the evenings they get drunk and steal. The life of the fifth estate, the unemployed, drunkards, prisoners, and harlots – their life is the true asceticism. Monasticism does not mean asceticism to anyone but lustful gourmands, and not even to them. Don Quixote-ism! All this time I've been fighting against windmills for Dulcinea del Toboso!

Fais le testament de ta pensée et de ton cœur, c'est ce que tu peux faire de plus utile.[124] Make a pact between your flesh and your spirit, those savage combatants, calm yourself and make peace between your heart and your mind, impulse and reason, and pay to each its own! Nothing in the world is more prudent! No one achieves a goal more glorious than to be a human being as God has created him. I will shed the skin of the supernatural monster and start a new life, as a human being, a servant in the kingdom of reality, a simple son of my nation:

> And that which I choose for myself is the love of a woman
> And the kingdom of the common man.

And when he looked out at the ring of mountains surrounding Þingvellir, a sight that appeared before the eyes of the fathers of the country for a thousand years, he thought to himself that it was indeed of consequence to have a fatherland, that it befitted the dignity of the inexpressible, and he concluded that no one could wish for a better lot than to be fitted out with all of the preliminaries necessary for becoming a good Icelander. Nothing could be more worthwhile than to be a good Icelander.

Book Eight

90.

Ostende. Hotel Windsor Castle, 10 Sept. 1926. R.F. Dom Alban O.S.B. Dearly beloved friend and Father. I returned to the continent two days ago, and now write to you a few lines while I rest after the voyage, respectful and beloved Father, to make you aware of my expected arrival at Sept Fontaines in several days.

My stay at home in my native country became for me a true wellspring of satisfaction and self-recognition. Whereas I had previously thought that the first step was to have realized that all is vanity, I am now much more inclined after my trip home toward the view of the ancient Greek philosopher who proclaims that the beginning of happiness is for a man to know himself. I wish therefore that you would view me in a somewhat different light than you did last time, as I view myself.

I am the living incarnation of the type of man who has seen the light of day the last ten, twelve years, but never existed before: an Icelandic Western European man of the spirit of those times that have pilloried the history of mankind, my mind free like that of a man who rained down from the stars in August 1914 and afterward lived his life in world news bureaus and editorial offices. A poet grown from the cohesive hereditary culture starting from ancient Greece has nothing more conterminous with me than a fossilized fern from earth's prehistory. My thoughts play on the stage of the most gruesome expressionism and most nonsensical surrealism, and will never be compatible with the calm, faultless, and simplistic in the life-view of noblemen in wigs and ladies in crinoline, not to mention lapdogs and commodes in the Rococo style. I could never imagine citing a book composed before 1914; although I have read all of the most important ones, to me it's all the same old porridge in the same old pot. I forbid any man to try to understand me or to form an opinion of me on the basis of the classical criteria that have been in vogue up to the days of the French psychological novel.

There is no history of mankind except for myself. I have mankind on my conscience like my old knavery, know it by heart and have already forgotten it like the multiplication table. The future shall be grounded on living thought instead of old facts, on life as it is lived instead of historical "truth," on the dreams of God instead of excerpts from old documents. The world of thought is the true world, taking precedence over laws, facts, and deeds; the world of history is in the graveyards. History speaks of labor and achievement, but the chief characteristic of man as opposed to nature is that he has been given clarity of vision, is raised above labor and achievement. There is no such thing as history when all is said and done. The history of mankind is a political essay, and most unedifying when it is composed by bookworms who either do not know what politics are, or who take pains not to know. If a man surmounts the boundaries of abstract thinking, he becomes a political creature. Thus the history of mankind is narrated by conservatives or liberals, aristocrats or republicans, capitalists or communists, Catholics or Protestants, Romans or Germans. A true man is raised above the history of mankind and everything that takes place outside of himself. If he works, he is so far removed from his work that by the time he reaches his goal he has forgotten where he started. He takes things as they come. Victory and defeat are to him two alien notions, and the experiment that works is to him precisely as worthless as the one that goes awry. He stands before the revolutionary tribunal and gives the orders as to who should be taken to the guillotine, just as impartial as when he tips his hat to a beggar on the street.

91.

I do not doubt that men crucified the Son of God. And that the Son of God died for the sins of men. In the same way I am certain that the one who denies the existence of the Devil is in the Devil's grasp. The monastic way of life is, on the other hand, not the least bit more remarkable than ordinary housekeeping. Several bachelors build themselves a mansion. They are eager to be able to add several acres to their land and devise a clever scheme to inflate the price of pork. You must not think that I have lost my respect for man's endeavors; I have as much respect for a bad monk as for a bad poet, because both do the best that they can. On the other hand I cannot deny that I have more respect for a good poet than for a monk who has not matured beyond his prayer book. All aspiration is good as long as a man is independent of it, all prayers good as long as a man has forgotten them, like the three holy elders in Tolstoy's folktales.[125] But the greater part of monks and priests are like chests of drawers. In one drawer is philosophy, in another theology, in the third ethics, in a fourth mysticism – all according to what has been placed in them; in some one finds nothing but weird tales in kitchen Latin. The greatest part of the scholars in the religious orders are anachronistic phenomena who pore over age-old texts of fairy tales written during the time when superstition was called mysticism, and experimental science was grounds for imprisonment. Most of them are slaves of wisdom. Jesus Christ is the Redeemer of mankind because it is unwise to believe that mankind can redeem itself. It seems that it is wisest to label everything that is irreconcilable with this blessed wisdom a miracle, either from God or the Devil. Men worship as a miracle Jesus Christ's having changed water into wine and other such paltry contrivances, but no one would think to give the name of miracle to the paintings in the Sistine Chapel, Dante's *Divine Comedy*, the Oratories by Palestrina and Bach, or the Ninth Symphony, which Beethoven composed deaf. They believe that it is a more glorious miracle to resurrect people from death than it is to create works of art. I admit that I find nothing more believable than that Christ should have resurrected people from death, but I find this so base and disgusting that I feel nauseous even mentioning it. I would never once think to tip my hat to a dead man who has been resurrected. Jesus Christ is the highest that the human intellect can imagine; in other words, he is our God. And I am too thoroughly convinced of the divinity of Jesus to have any need of such an equally piggish proof as resurrection. The thing that first made it most difficult for me to believe in the divinity of Jesus Christ was precisely this: that he should have resorted to tricks. And it pleased me to no end when I learned that it was not part of the doctrine of the Catholic Church that Christ performed miracles, but that this was instead only a pious presumption gleaned from the stories of the New Testament. There is nothing in the kingdom of nature as far from being supernatural as miracles. Nothing is supernatural but nature itself. For example, I do not believe in the *conceptio immaculata* for any other reason than that the Church has made it part of its official dogma that Christ came into the world in that way, just as Christians have believed since the time of the primitive Church. If men had been sufficiently acquainted with science to worship the most supernatural of all, nature itself, then they would have believed in something else: that Christ came into the world the ordinary way. All the endless rubbish about the virgin birth chafes me as both pornography and blasphemy at the same time. Yet that is not to say that I think it likely that the Virgin Mary had between ten and twenty children, as the Protestant church teaches in order to warrant its glorification of the family. On the other hand it is simply unintelligible to me as to how any thinking man could believe the *conceptio immaculata* to be more remarkable than the *conceptio maculata*. Is there anything but a supernatural explanation for the fact that a man is born into this world with a soul that has been granted the ability to worship the Lord? I was absolutely overjoyed when I discovered that Thomas Aquinas did not believe in the bitter truth of this so-called Immaculate Conception.

When the fakirs make plants spring from seeds in an instant, and when yogis promenade on water, or when clairvoyant men spirit themselves off like Óðinn to distant lands on their own and others' errands, people say: "Beware, good children, it is the Devil!" As if the Devil would not be welcome to make seeds sprout, men promenade on water, clairvoyant men carry out their errands, and mediums experience ectoplasmic vomiting and diarrhea? If the Devil were as harmless as that, it would be great fun to live. I admit that I hate the Devil and know best of all men that he possesses a completely astonishing power, even the power to heal the sick and comfort the sorrowful. But it is no explanation whatsoever to say about any phenomenon: "That's from the Devil!" I ask: "How is it from the Devil?" Just as it is nothing but a distortion of fact when someone who asks about the existence of this world is given the answer that it was created by God. I ask: "How did he do this?" In the same way I say to the Devil, if he comes into my room at night: *"Bonjour, monsieur le Diable! Je suis bien charmé de vous voir. Comment allez vous? Voudriez vous bien vous donner la peine de vous asseoir?"*[126] And I do not let him leave until I have examined him carefully, peered down his throat, looked under his tail, and listened to his heart.

When all is said and done I hope that you understand, dearly beloved Father, that I am as firmly Catholic now as I was before. Allow me to repeat it: I believe in God the Father, Jesus Christ, and the Holy Spirit. And I believe in the one Holy Catholic and Apostolic Church. The Church with its precious teachings has lifted me beyond the boundary of the temporal world, and I have the Church to thank that I find myself a free spirit. It has interpreted my dreams of God for me. Its creeds stand in my imagination as holy places of refuge, redeeming monuments. I perceive the brighter Heaven of truth behind every one of its most ordinary expressions better than the clerics themselves: I cannot compare my perceptions to anything other than the inexpressible in the visions of mystics, saints, and other free men. On the other hand I eagerly admit that I have not become what is called a "better man" by becoming Catholic; no, God is just as far above me as he has always been. The Church has only granted me security; it is my life's anchor. Without it I could no longer bear to exist. There and nowhere else can I bear to live and to die. There I say my prayers unafraid. If I did not believe in Jesus Christ, I would die.

In the hope, beloved Father, of being able to greet you face-to-face within the fewest number of days, I am your obedient and compliant son in Jesus Christ.

92.

After a three-month absence Steinn Elliði stood again at the gate of the abbey in Sept Fontaines. Grapevines droop down off the edge of the wall. He peeked shyly into the abbey garden, where he had left innumerable footprints among the flowers. It was in fact this garden that preserved the footsteps of his childhood feet; here he had become a child of God; he had been lost and the Kingdom of Heaven had awaited him in this garden. For a whole year he had wandered about this garden, where every twig had been planted by consecrated hands and God let his holy designs drip down into his soul. There were the tree-lined paths to the grove, and the young trees; and God created Heaven and Earth. Grace serves the inner being of the man who has forsaken everything for the Kingdom of Heaven. He had left this place as a member of its household three months ago; now he stood again as a visitor at its gate. He was so heavyhearted that he longed to slink away and disappear with the first train into perfect oblivion and utter darkness. Nothing is as alluring as oblivion. And the greatest thing to look forward to is death: nothing is nearly as exciting as to die. Death is like the raisin in the whale's ass.[127] What might be on the other side? No, he thought, I will speak with Father Alban and take his advice. It would be cowardice not to dare to stand face-to-face with Father Alban.

Evensong sounded throughout the church. God bless these men who believe that God is served with worship, music, and hymns of praise. It would be cruel not to allow them to sing. The music of the familiar old Gregorian chants was carried to his ears. The blessed Church has sung through the mouths of its monks in the same way for many years, for many hundreds of years, for many thousands of years – because the verse and the song originate from the eastern part of the world, from the temple of Jerusalem.

Lætatus sum in his quae dicta sunt mihi:
in domum Domini ibimus.[128]

The most remarkable invention on Earth is the Lord. Electricity is a trifle compared to him.

Stantes erant pedes nostri
in atriis tuis Jerusalem.[129]

He prayed in the shadows before the door, and his ears drank in every syllable of the ancient psalm. In the choir sat the men of God with their hoods drawn over their heads like Santa Clauses, looking into their souls as they sang. The souls of monks are like beautiful countries. He recognized all of the faces again, every line of every face. These were his faithful friends, and he was unworthy of tying their shoestrings, although of course they already tied their own. But no matter how much he searched he did not see Father Alban anywhere. There was a new monk sitting in the prior's seat. What happened to Father Alban? Was he ill, or on a trip somewhere? Finally Steinn came to the conclusion that he must have died, since a new man had taken his seat. What reason could the Lord have had to let Father Alban die? Steinn waited impatiently for the monks to finish singing the divine office. If Father Alban were truly dead, he thought, all joy would be swept from existence. It isn't so bad to live if a man has had the fortune to become acquainted with holy men. If a man has not become acquainted with holy men, then there is no advantage to living, and it would be just as well if one had never been born. How often had he regarded Father Alban and said, like Maxim Gorky when he saw the elder from Yasnaya Polyana[130] sitting alone at the seaside one sunny day: "I am not so badly off while this man inhabits the Earth!" A silent payer follows the last *Deo gratias,* which ends with a hammer stroke. The monks rise to their feet and walk two by two from the choir, with their hands on their chests, covered over by the billowing arms of the choir robes, without looking to the right or left, a silent host.

Several minutes later Steinn sits in conversation with the Guest Master, the loquacious Père Dorval, in the refectory. Father Dorval lets the questions rain down as before; he takes completely limitless pleasure in hearing news. Perhaps he in fact thinks that there is nothing so terribly boring as the news, but he asks and asks because he has been chosen by God to speak with guests. How did you feel about visiting your homeland? Is there any likelihood that your people will be converted from Lutheranism in this century? No. Arianism lingered for four hundred years, Nestorianism has lingered since the fourth century and still lingers. And in the seventeenth century a group of Nestorians was reunited with the Church. Protestantism would have been finished a long time ago if it hadn't been kept afloat by kings. Isn't Copenhagen a brilliantly beautiful city? Isn't seasickness amazingly unpleasant? How many departments are there in the university in Reykjavík? Are the Freemasons well established in Iceland? Finally Steinn was given space to interject the question that had been burning on his lips the whole time:

"I didn't see Father Alban in the choir. Is he away?"

At the mention of Father Alban the smile disappeared from the monk's face, and he became pious and solemn:

"Yes, you have every right to ask about your friend and Father Confessor, our good Father Alban! But you have seen that he is no longer with us. God has called Father Alban away from us."

"Are you telling me that Father Alban is dead?" asked Steinn.

"No, monsieur, that's not what I meant. Father Alban is not what is ordinarily called dead, but rather he has gone away. He has entered a stricter order. He was so eager for the ascetic life that his life with us did not fully satisfy his demands. It will be nearly six weeks now since he left us and went to Switzerland. He has started as a novice with the Carthusians in Valle Sainte. It is high up in the mountains."

"Him, the Novice Master, starting as a novice! That's unbelievable! What does he think he will find with the Carthusians that he did not find here?"

"His humility and piety were great, monsieur. He was that man who never lost sight of the highest goal. He had felt the calling to the Carthusian life before he became a Benedictine monk, but his state of health prevented him from beginning his clerical life in a lifestyle that demands such limitless self-denial. He was originally nothing but a weak violin virtuoso who had been coddled all his life. But during the last few years his health started to improve daily. Now he starts again at the beginning, the humblest of all the Lord's poor. He will start by scrubbing the floors and feeding the pigs. The Carthusians have no freedoms resembling ours. They may not speak together except for one half-hour a week and must fast for eight months of the year, and never eat meat. Each monk lives in his own cell, and his daily bread is thrust in through a hole in the wall. They spend their lives in constant prayer. They get up at midnight and attend choir for three hours. No one is allowed to see them or to speak with them. The world does not know that they exist. Whoever becomes a Carthusian dies to the world and is buried. Dear friend, allow me now to accompany you to the refectory, and to give you coffee, milk, bread and butter and honey. *Maintenant c'est exactement l'heure pour goûter.*"[131]

Steinn Elliði rambled away from the abbey and disappeared into the forest. Autumn's change of colors had come to the forest. Steinn thought about what an uncomfortable feeling it was to be startled. Perfect men never allow themselves to be startled.

Father Alban sets out from Sept Fontaines and buys himself

a ticket in third class. He takes his seat among spitting workers, screaming children, and unclean mothers with naked breasts nursing swaddling infants. No one suspects that this poor monk with his cowled head and his hands beneath his scapular had at one time been the golden idol of the concert halls in Paris and shared toasts with potentates and geniuses in Saint Petersburg and New York. He does not even have a knapsack on his shoulders or a staff in his hand. He is free. There is nothing between Heaven and Earth that binds him anymore, not even a flute. He chimes in with the poet and sings:

Ich hab' meine Sach' auf nichts gestellt,
und mein gehört die ganze Welt.[132]

He has abdicated all positions of rank, the names of nobleman, virtuoso, and scientist, forsaken his gold and green forests, mansions and thrones, horses and cars, dogs and cats, lovers and loves, family and nation, country and arts. Finally he has said farewell to the sunshine of the Benedictine life, its beauty and peace, his rank within the monastic order: his positions as prior and Novice Master, the conversations and his friends – everything. Only one thing remains – God the Father Almighty, the Creator of Heaven and Earth, his only begotten son Jesus Christ, and the Holy Spirit. Now he dwells in a cold district in a coniferous belt of the Alps, among the prisoners of the Lord, scrubbing the floor and carrying draff to the pigs, he whose cheeks are like those of a Roman emperor! What was it to walk the steep slope to Golgotha with one's gibbet on one's shoulders, if not this?

Soon Steinn Elliði emerged from the other side of the forest and stood on the highway. On the side of the road stands a little chapel with a coarse crucifix above the door. Steinn stops and looks at it. The body is straight-trunked, like a stuffed-up sack, blue gold in color, with a hideous, huge wound on the chest from which blood oozes, dark red sealing wax. The legs are far too short and far too stout; they are chunky! The face is broad and unshapely, resembling a grotesque caricature of a ragamuffin clipped from *Punch* or *Strix*.[133] He who wishes to follow me must forsake everything. Steinn Elliði took off his hat and prayed. Christ, Christ, if only you could suspect all that you have on your conscience.

93.

The monastery gate in Valle Sainte has been opened for Steinn Elliði. He is shown in to a bright and high-ceilinged waiting room in the guesthouse. He asks to see Father Alban, and the lay brother leaves silently. Steinn waits a long time without any further sign of life appearing in the house. He gazes at the copper etchings of Saint Bruno and the first Carthusians adorning the room, and then leans out the window and runs his eyes over the countryside. Over the mountains, the pine forest, and the river hovers a cold and gray autumn sky, but no human dwellings are to be seen. Valle Sainte is as far out in the countryside as a mountain monastery in Tibet; a man could sooner imagine standing face-to-face here with statues of the laughing Buddha and lamas than with Jesus Christ and his sons.

Finally the rustling of robes, the rattling of a rosary, and brisk footsteps are heard out in the hallway. The door is pushed open, and in walks a monk of indeterminate age, clad in a thick, white robe, with his hood pulled forward over his head. His face is marked with deep, sharp lines and is extremely pale, his lips pursed; his eyes burn with power; he gives the visitor a piercing glance; in the crest of his nose are two deep creases. He pushes his hood back from his tonsured head, bows deeply, and extends his hand, blue and cold, to Steinn.

"God bless you, sir! You are speaking to Brother Pascal, whose duty it is to greet the visitors whom he sends to us. What is your business?"

"Venerable Father! I longed to be allowed to speak with Father Alban, whom it was my honor to come to know among the Benedictine monks in Belgium. He was my confidant and Father Confessor."

"You wish to speak to Brother Elias," said the monk.

"Forgive me, Venerable Father, if I have not explained myself clearly. But it is with Father Alban that I wish to speak."

The monk smiled broadly and replied:

"I know whom it is you mean, sir. The one you seek is here called Brother Elias, and he is one of our novices. I shall ask for permission from the master. Would you like to have a light meal now or later?"

Steinn had eaten on the train and chose to speak to Brother Elias first.

The monk asked Steinn to follow him and walked quickly ahead of him down silent and endless hallways; these corridors connected the solitary cells of the monks. They walked past numerous small doors and one broad oak door, and there the monk cast himself facedown, kissed the floor, and lay motionless for several moments.

Steinn knelt down; this was the chapel where the most holy sacrament was kept. Finally the monk knocked upon a door, and they waited for a moment until there appeared in the doorway an old monk, with a huge domed forehead and glasses with rust-colored frames in front of bright and shining eyes; he muttered something like *"Deo gratias."*

"Forgive me, Père Maître," whispered Steinn's guide. "But we have here a foreigner who wishes to speak with Brother Elias. He is one of Brother Elias' old confessants, from Sept Fontaines."

"Outstanding!" said the master, as if he had always been expecting this, and he shook Steinn's hand with a smile and bowed several times, then looked into his face with his sapient, elderly eyes, which still bore witness to his unbroken joy of life. He examined Steinn's soul but asked nothing, not even his nationality. The master gave Brother Pascal brief instructions, said farewell to Steinn with a handshake as if he were an old friend, and then returned to his immortal life; but Steinn and his guide undertook a new journey through the labyrinth. Finally the Guest Master showed Steinn into Brother Elias' cell and left after conveying the instructions from the Novice Master.

They greeted each other in monastic style by pressing each other's cheeks, and Father Alban led Steinn to a seat and closed the door. He was clad in a coarse gray cowl, far too close-fitting at the shoulders; his scapular reached only to his knees, as a sign that he was a brother of the lowest rank. His shoes were rustic, coarse, ugly winter shoes, his hands tanned and scraped from toil. His countenance still displayed the peculiar mixture of eagle and lamb, but the beauty of bereavement had replaced the severity of the superior; his voice was still mild and clear, woven with musical effulgence. His home was this single room with a window in the front wall overlooking a small garden. Against one wall was a bench with a gray woolen coverlet, while the rest of the furniture consisted of two chairs and a prie-dieu, a little workbench upon which lay pliers and wires and half-finished rosaries, a wooden image of the mother of our Lord on a shelf, and a crucifix hanging on the wainscoting above the prie-dieu. On the door was a hatch through which a monk put his food at mealtimes.

"I have been granted permission to speak to you for half an hour, friend," said Father Alban, and he laid his watch on the table and sat down opposite his guest. "I know that you have news to tell me of your soul. Your letter from the Netherlands has been sent here, but Carthusian monks are prohibited from receiving letters, so I have not read it. It is in the hands of the master. I am prepared to do for you what God wills, and now I ask you to speak."

But all of Steinn's thoughts spun chaotically through his head, like cold suns in dead solar systems. He was situated opposite eternal life itself and there was no world in existence any longer where he could gain either a handhold or a foothold. He had hoped to have had the chance to speak with Father Alban about everything, over the course of several days, to let the monk observe the condition of his soul as it was now rather than for him to have to speak of it plainly. Business! He had no business here at all. He had come here as a simple traveler, wishing to speak to an old friend. He didn't have the slightest idea where to begin! All the same he felt that there was no excuse for hesitation on his part, so he let his tongue run free and took his chances on what might come out.

"It's a pity that you should not have been permitted to read my letter, because it is overflowing with observations. To be frank, I have a tiny bit of experience at being a man, and have spent time studying the things that the Catholic Church has for the most part neglected, and which therefore the Church is rather apt to overlook. I have investigated modern man to a nicety and understand him much better than the Catholic Church does. Telling these hounds to come to Jesus is an abuse of the name of God. They stick their tails between their hind legs and run howling away. It is useless to think that one can drive the Devil out of them with kindness. Evil shall be driven out with evil. The missionary sphere of the Catholic Church is neither in Africa nor Asia, as some believe, but rather in our own culturally straitened hemisphere, where the white race is on its last legs. And in the midst of those straits lies my homeland. And I have decided to use my life to reconcile the views of modern white men with the truths of the Catholic Church. It is good that there are monks, because the monasteries are the banks of the Catholic Church, the roots of the oak tree. But *oportet et hæreses esse*,[134] and the history of the Church shows that nothing apart from the virtues of the saints has proven better for sweeping away the refuse from the Church's doctrines, for strengthening and consolidating its powers, revitalizing its ideals, and elevating its honor than precisely this: heretical teachings and lies. Of course I do not have the fortune to be a heretic, but I do know that the only way to fish for souls in our time is to clothe the truth in the costume of a lie and have one's writings blacklisted by the pope. Just as the Devil can be clothed in the garb of Christ, or establishes puritanical societies and home missions to beguile simple souls, in the same way the apostle of our time must clothe himself in the guise of Satan, if he wishes to save modern men from eternal damnation. Because those apes are so misguided that they pay no regard to those who come in the name of the Lord."

Father Alban looked with steady, calm eyes at his protégé and waited until he finished speaking. He gave no sign that he would discuss how necessary it was for the apostles of Christ to make their appearance disguised as Satan in order to preach the good news. On the contrary, he quickly saw that his protégé must have somehow betrayed himself, because every word that he spoke bore witness to his having fallen away from what should have been most pure in his conscious life, his soul stained by the fingerprints of the Tempter. It was obvious from what he said that he still wished eagerly to be a Christian, but not without making some sort of a deal with Satan; he must still be hiding something. And when Steinn looked into the monk's eyes he was startled, and found himself speechless and confused. Father Alban had not only listened to what he said, but also tuned his ear to the deepest movements of his soul as he spoke. Steinn sat here before the doctor, having concluded blurting out his description of his sickness, and he realized that the doctor would know the precise Latin name for his sickness, as well as the composition and doses of the medicines that he required.

The monk stood up slowly. He moved his chair over to the wall beneath the crucifix, took out a threadbare stole, put it over his shoulders, and sat down. Next he gave Steinn a sign that he should come over, pointed with his other hand to the prie-dieu at his side, and said simply:

"Confess!"

Something in Steinn Elliði's facial expression made him resemble a terrified idiot when he looked in the monk's face; or perhaps more than anything else an animal in a slaughterhouse awaiting its death-blow. His plea for mercy found no words; this order, at once unexpected and humiliating, robbed him of speech; the canon's hypnotic power enchained his personality, and he found that he had no other choice than to fall to his feet, completely exposed. His pride was given no space to secure a hold on his heart so that he might rise arduously against the lack of respect that this cowled tyrant was impudent enough to display to him; Father Alban's eyes rested on him, insurmountable and omnipotent, as he waited for his protégé to stand up falteringly and kneel beneath the cross. Finally Steinn stood up. He fell to his knees upon the prie-dieu and automatically recited the penitent's opening words:

"*Benedic, pater, quia peccavi.*"[135]

And the Father Confessor made the sign of the cross over him and answered:

"*Benedicat te omnipotens Deus: In nomine Patris, et Filii, et Spiritus Sancti.*"

There was silence in the cell.

For several moments Steinn buried his face in his hands without finding an outlet for his thoughts in words, and when he finally started to speak his voice was stern and brittle.

Before he confessed particular sins he spent a long time chastising himself for the crime of the complete corruption of his soul, his strong, intractable passion for concealing his personality, his limitless joy in kindling marsh-fire over his own vanity, his lack of courage to come forth with the sincerity and humility of a clean soul;

in everything he had shrunk from assimilating himself to the will of God. He loved every single most unrighteous movement in the depths of his soul and had created for himself as quickly as he could a philosophical system as an excuse, found himself guilty of crimes against the will of God. He believed in God and God's Church, but had chosen his own lies and delusions over the redeeming truth. He knew precisely what was true and what a lie, what vanity and what reality, what was right and what wrong, and he loved a lie knowing full well it was a lie, chose vanity over the eternal truth, and wrong over right. When he rejected God and joined hands with the Devil, it was neither from blindness nor weakness, but rather, quite bluntly, because he was enchanted by the Devil and loved him. He longed, quite bluntly, to revolt against eternal life and Almighty God and sell his soul to the Devil. He had, time and again, considered whether he ought not call upon the Devil sometime during the night and make a contract with him for his soul. He frequently and sincerely longed to be able to go to Hell so that he might take part in the revolt against the eternal and Almighty God of judgment for all eternity. He would not yield a hair's breadth to this almighty tyrant of being. He knew well that the Devil and his imps were condemned to eternal suffering; but he chose eternal suffering rather than the alternatives, to lose himself or submit to God.

Such were his thoughts, such his will. He considered himself lost, felt that there was nothing left in him that could save him; when he looked in the mirror he thought he could see *poenam damni*[136] in his own face. Nothing could help him but the hand of God himself. He did not wish to mend his ways, could not do this voluntarily; nothing could correct him but God, the author of his soul. If he were not to be lost, God would have to take him by force and renew his soul from its bottom up, think for him, will for him, make him put one foot in front of the other as if he were a lifeless doll, because if he controlled his own footsteps, he would walk straight into perdition. He was so deeply sunken that he had lost all hope of being able to lift himself out of the depths.

Next he counted up specific sins in thoughts, words, and deeds, one after another, the last being that he did not repent of anything that he had done, but rather presumed himself entirely lost, and concluded by saying that he considered himself completely unworthy of being granted absolution. A long silence followed his confession, and the penitent again hid his face in his hands.

Finally the silence was broken by the voice of the Father Confessor, gentle, lyrical, and bright: no despair, no surprise, no disquietude, no sign of any desire to blame or to rebuke.

"*Domine, si me vis esse in tenebris, sis benedictus,*"[137] he began. "We must never forget to thank God when he has led our souls into the darkness whence we see no way out. For Jesus Christ is our Redeemer, not we ourselves. It is he who seeks out the soul of man in the darkness and leads it forward into the light. In truth, we are nothing unassisted. My friend, we both know that the way toward blessedness is narrow and steep. But on that road Christ himself and all of his saints are our guides, and the angels of God our defenders. We stumble. There is nothing more certain than that we will stumble. We fall and lie there where we have fallen. Again and again we are convinced that we can do nothing unaided; that even our best will is worthless without God's grace. Then all we have left is to allow our lament to ascend to God. But God has never refused his mercy to those who consciously lament their weaknesses. Remember that the holiest men have fallen before you ever did. They have lain powerless and despairing in the dust like you. And they decided to lie there where they had fallen. Nowhere do we behold God more powerful than in our weakness. God reveals his power in our weakness. The more powerless that we find ourselves, the more securely we may trust the guidance of God. And the saints recalled how Christ himself fell three times to the earth beneath his cross on the road to Golgotha. He even prayed in Gethsemane that the bitter cup might be taken from him. And his sweat was like drops of blood that fell to the earth. And when the saints recalled this they got back up, like Christ who had to get back up three times before he carried his cross to the end of its trail. My friend, remember that Christ himself fell beneath his cross before you did. The cross of Jesus Christ is the one joy of a sinful man. Christ, Christ, it is you who carries your cross before me, scourged and crowned with thorns, and who calls me to follow you to the heavenly wedding feast! I love only you, my Creator and Redeemer, my Lord and God, who have descended from your Heaven for my sake."

94.

Copenhagen. Hotel Phoenix. 2 February 1927.

My most dearly beloved friend.

Have all of my letters been lost?

Or am I to believe that you have forsaken me, after I have forsaken everything for you?

Time and again I wrote to you at the abbey in Belgium without receiving any answer, and now I am told that you are somewhere in Rome; therefore I send these lines to the Danish embassy with tearful pleas that you answer me if they reach you.

Steinn, do you still not know what has happened? Fate has made everything happen as it must happen. Steinn, you disappeared without saying good-bye, and yet you must have known that the vow you took from me would surely cut two threads that were wound together. Do you not know, Steinn, that I have become a murderer for the vow I was made to swear to you that last night? Where are you, Steinn, so that I can make more vows to you? Will you never answer me again?

Yet Örnólfur was perhaps the best man in the world, the only noble man whom I have known, the only good man. He gladly did everything he could for me when I was little.

He lived for me and believed in me ever since I was little.

Steinn, can't you believe in anything but God? Steinn, God doesn't love you as much as I do.

When I told Örnólfur that I was no longer true to him, all things became worthless in his eyes. I know that they will hound me to death, those terrible words that I let fall from my lips in sheer panic the first night he came home. I said that I hated him, that he terrified me, begged him to kill me rather than to touch me any longer as his wife. I have written you all of it in long letters, but you haven't answered. Do you then have no word of comfort to lend to your lover who has sacrificed everything for you and sold the peace of her soul for her freedom? Yes, she has sacrificed the health of her soul to you for as long as any eternity exists, has become a murderer for your sake. Now she awaits your order. There is no crime so unspeakable that she would not commit if it were your will.

Don't you also know that I carried your child for two months in my womb, and didn't know until after a long illness that I had miscarried? Steinn, I have carried your own progeny in my womb. And when I came to my senses after the delirium I met your grandmother's glance. And I understood everything at once. For two months, while I was recuperating, I had to live and breathe in the piercing, contemptful cold that is reserved for whores and murderers in the eyes of that soulless witch.

One morning in the fall I found myself alone; someone came to me and said that Örnólfur had been found dead with a bullet in his head. I was all by myself, alone, and no one farther away from me than you.

But what is it that I have endured, Steinn, if you have faith in me? Nothing! A game! A game! One can endure anything for the person one loves, yes, even reject God and all goodness and commit outrage after outrage; I shall be exactly as you wish, do with me everything that you will, because you own me entirely in body and soul, every hair on my head, every cell in my body; it is all yours; but I ask you only one thing: do not drive me away from you! Only one thing can repair what I have broken, and that is if you allow me to love you and live for you, endure for you. God will forgive me if you allow me to love you. And if God exists, I have no reason to believe anything but that you love me. You cannot push me away from you so long as you believe that God has created us, reigns over us, and will judge us! Because if you do not love me then no atonement exists for our sin within the boundaries of existence!

Oh, Steinn, let it no longer be proven that everything that touches me dies! No, Steinn, I know, I believe, that you love me. I want to believe it! Wrap your arms around me and allow me to become the mother of your happiness and your children! I shall forget everything and bring them to my breasts and suckle them so that I am not lost for eternity. And I shall teach them to cry out to God. And we shall pray to him to erase the past entirely. Steinn, Steinn, come and speak one word in my ear! No saint has desired God as passionately as I desire you, no saint has ever loved his Lord more profoundly than I love you.

95.

Roma. Convento Salesiani, Via Romagna.

I do not ask you to forgive me for anything, because it is not in your power to forgive. I am bound to answer to another mightier God for my sins. When you say that you love me you have no suspicion of what it is you say. You have never seen me as I am, do not know who I am, do not want to know who I am, would die if you knew who I am. You have only caught a fleeting glimpse of the part of my being that turns from God. You have been bewitched by the hallucinations of the Devil in my nature. A woman does not love a man, but rather the beast in a man. You love the part of myself that I hate and despise, my imperfection. My perfection hates you. To the side of my being that turns to God your eyes will never be opened; because the only thing that panders to a woman's nature is deception. You have no higher desire than to be allowed to join with the part of my being that the Lord commands me to defeat for the sake of the Kingdom of Heaven. I am an immortal soul, created to rest in God and eternal life. Nothing is of any worth to me but the predestination of my soul for eternal life. "My heart lacks all peace, until it rests in God." All is vanity but God. Nothing is true but God. My soul longs for the eternal reality behind creation.

96.

Rome in all of its glory has incredibly little attractive power for a young, fatigued woman who has traveled night and day for seventy-two hours in order to rescue her lover from the hands of trolls.

On a raw, cold morning early in the last month of winter, she steps out of the Munich-Rome express, exhausted after a sleepless night, alien and speechless. After getting directions from thievish porters and larcenous cabbies she sits down to breakfast with her maid in a dirty hotel, in a large hall open at both ends, where savage dogs slink in and out and scowling salesmen offer stolen rubbish at half price. The city is one street after another of filthy, dilapidated houses, black ugly hulls of churches, abominable statues. Thus does Rome greet a grieving and wretched pilgrim of love. Would she like to buy a fountain pen? *Prima qualità, signora, pure trente lire!* Or a meat grinder? *Piccola, facile, signora;* might I have the honor of taking it apart and showing the madam its insides? Or a violin? Stradivarius, built in 1728. Would the madam like to peek inside and see the stamp as proof? *Di una originalità assoluta, signora–*

She looks at herself in a mirror in her large and shadowy room, where every piece of furniture is rickety; beetles crawl across the floor, and from her bedclothes wafts a stale human stench. She is gray and jaded, her eyes bloodshot: the lines beneath her nose have never been so visible as on this morning; oh, she is a world-weary woman who has nothing left untouched in her possession; in just a few years she will have become a witch. Her youth had come and gone like a rainbow or a multicolored butterfly. She had dreamt dreams by the window; reality is never anything other than the relics of the palaces of dreamland. The young girl who once upon a time felt the dream of life give her precious chills has now brought death to all; what touches her dies. She throws herself onto her bed to let the gnawing weariness pass from her limbs.

The Tiber River tumbles on with the history of mankind in its brown waves. It is a senseless satire, without beginning or end, like a dance of death in a graveyard. And a certain man fords the river on a braying donkey and reaches the bank right where she is standing, and the donkey shakes itself and continues to bray. "Greetings!" says the man; he is dressed in a nappy black overcoat and has turned the collar up and pushed his hat down over his eyebrows to make himself look odd; he is wearing light gray spats and steak brown shoes.

"How lucky it is for us to meet, since your journey has led you here," he continues. "Because then I get to enjoy the pleasure of showing you a little of Rome. Please climb up here in front of me."

The man did not say his name, but she recognized immediately who he was, longed to flee but was unable to do so, finally saw that her most hopeful chance was to pretend that she took him for a stranger who worked as a guide, and mounted the donkey in front of him trembling in anguish. But the man was determined to talk and certainly thought he was likeable: he was well-informed in history and gave her a summary of the most important events in the Roman Empire, old and new.

"Look here!" he said when they set off. "Rome is exceptionally rich in history because it is built on seven hills; it is built on seven hills, and that's why it's called Rome. It was very wise of you to take a trip to Rome once you had decided to take a trip at all. Helen the Fair, who is famous from the Trojan War, was the daughter of the brothers Romulus and Remus, and they had two sons as an only child, named Paris. Now once after Paris the king's son paid Romulus and Remus a visit, Romulus and Remus pursued him, because he kidnapped Helen the Fair. And she was given this name because she was the most beautiful of women. A certain king named Achilles comes into the story, and he was descended from Paris and Helen on his father's side, since he had kidnapped the couple's daughter, and he put his ships to sea; history says nothing more of his journey."

97.

When the story reached this point they arrived at the gates of Saint Peter's Basilica. The man helped her dismount, tied the donkey to one of the columns and opened the church doors. The church was packed with people; on one side stood countless little aristocratic women with tall silk hats, and on the other side big railway officers from Milan, chewing tobacco. But before the altar stood the holy apostle Peter, consecrating to the true faith young boys who had abandoned their sweethearts. Then the sweethearts were used as fill where new roads were being laid. "That's better!" said the poor woman. "Yes, no one can defeat them now," said her guide, who had taken off his hat and scratched his head where the bullet had gone through.

The boys walked in a single-file line up to the altar, clad in ceremonial chasubles made of pieces of chintz, and the holy apostle Peter consecrated all of them to the true faith and gave each of them a map and compass. But one towered head and shoulders above the rest, with a mane like a lion and a glance like a flash of lightning, bright and limitless. She waited burning with impatience until he reached the front of the line, whence he walked solemnly up to the altar and knelt before the apostle Peter.

"I hereby permit myself to consecrate you to the true faith," said the apostle, "and call upon you not to behave in any foolish or ridiculous way–"

But the woman saw that it was now or never if she were to put an end to this wickedness, so she sprang up from her seat and ran in through the church, stopped in front of the altar, thrust her fists at the apostle's face, and shouted:

"You have no right to take him from me, Peter; he is mine!

"Steinn, I call Heaven and Earth as witnesses that I and no one but I own you! Neither God nor men have the right to take you from me."

"Filth!" said the aristocratic women.

"Who does she think she is?" said the men, and they jeered and spat.

Steinn Elliði saw that the crucial moment was at hand, and that no one who stands in debt to a human soul could become a saint. And he threw aside his chasuble quickly, took the woman by the arm and led her out of the church, but the entire congregation fussed and cursed, because they could all see that these were sinful folk, and the master of ceremonies had a hard time silencing their shouts. But when most of the clamor had dwindled the men came out onto the veranda and informed the people of the latest news:

"Doomsday tomorrow. Starts at eight o'clock sharp. The house will be opened at 7½. Admission one króna. Children under 16 not admitted."

98.

Nightfall in Rome.

A car stops outside the Salesian seminary on the Via Romagna and a woman steps out. She walks up broad and broken doorsteps and stops in the open entryway. There sits an old man in a cloak at a little table, clenching his sinewy hands around a rough-hewn rosary, reciting the Ave Maria. The light falls upon his wrinkled face and bare cheeks. He rocks forward and back and laughs from sheer old age.

She asked after Steinn Elliði, and for a good amount of time the doorman understood nothing. Finally it came out that this ragamuffin of a doorman was a French lay brother.

"You mightn't mean the young man from Scandinavia who has been received by the fathers here as a guest?" he finally asked.

Yes, that was exactly whom she meant. She wished to be permitted to speak to him.

"He is not available at the moment, madame. He is training with the novices, and when the training is finished they sing the *completorium* in the chapel, and will not be finished until shortly before midnight. It would be more advisable for you to come tomorrow, madame; he will be available for conversation during the free time between one and two."

She stared straight ahead for some time without knowing what to do. After contemplating for a moment she felt that it would be cowardly to return to the hotel the way things stood, and she addressed the brother again, more boldly than before.

"I am determined to wait for him," she said. "If you do not dare to disturb him until he has completed these exercises, then I must ask you to show me to his room. I am a family member and have come here to Rome to discuss a very important family matter with him; this matter must not be delayed any further. Look at my passport, please, so that you can be sure of who I am."

The old man examined her for several moments with the extraordinarily discriminating look of an experienced doorman, and laughed. Finally he admitted that "*Madame n'a pas l'air d'une intrigueuse,*"[138] and after making several attempts finally got himself to his feet, then lit a lamp and bade her follow him. She followed him through a large waiting room decorated with statues of the blessed Don Bosco and other saints, then through a broad hallway, until he opened a door and invited her to step in.

"If this young man were one of the novices," said the brother, "then I would not be allowed to show visitors in to his room, especially at this time of day. But the young Scandinavian is staying here like any other guest at an inn; a friend of the superior, who is a monk in Switzerland, sent him here to spend a winter reflecting on his vocation. But since you are his cousin, come from a distant country on an urgent errand, then–"

He lit the gas, offered her a chair and left. The room was bleak, with a high ceiling and shuttered windows. On one wall hung a simple cross, and under it stood a prie-dieu of polished wood. On another wall was a portrait of the meal in Emmaus: three men sit eating beneath a tree, Christ in the middle, radiant: he looks toward Heaven, raises his right hand in blessing, and holds a loaf of bread in his left. On the table in front of him are a chalice and paten and a cluster of grapes. At the same moment that he blesses the bread the eyes of the disciples are opened and they recognize him; one extends his hands; the other clutches his hands over his heart. Wonder and adoration shine from both of their faces. A pockmarked moon glistens in the twilight sky behind them. At the foot of the portrait stand these words of Gregory the Great:

"*Deum quem in divinae scripturæ expositione non cognoverant, in panis fractione cognoscunt.*"[139]

In one corner stood a bookshelf with thick black books, in the middle of the room a desk covered with open books and notes written in Steinn Elliði's hand, all in Latin.

She looked through the half-open door into his bedroom, and was surprised to see a framed picture of a woman on the nightstand. She was immediately seized with the thought that the picture was of her, but it was not so; it was a completely different woman. It was a pauper woman from Judea, dark brown in the face after fetching water in the heat, sad eyes dark and dreamy, her mantle sewn with gold and silver seams as a sign of grace. The boy rested in her arms. Both of them had pancakes over their heads, the lady a large one, the boy a fritter. And beneath the picture was written this passage:

"Oh, dear mother Mary! You are the refuge of sinners. You never forsake me. Have mercy on me. If I have offended your son, then I repent with all my heart, and I am ready to lose my life a thousand times sooner than his grace. Oh, mother of mercy, have pity on me! I hear you named by all the hope and refuge of the sinner. Be also my hope and refuge. Help me for the sake of your beloved son Jesus Christ. Extend your hand to help a miserable, fallen wretch. Verily, my past is greatly stained with sins, and that is because I placed no faith in your help. Now I glorify Almighty God, who by his grace has granted me faith in you. Mother of God, be my mother!"

99.

Time passes. She waits motionless in the chair before his desk, and stares either at the white-painted doors or at the unintelligible Latin in the open books. Twice or thrice the weak resounding of a bell is heard from another wing of the house. Mass is rung out and rung in. At times robed beings make a rustling in the hallway. Finally a church bell is rung, and a faint resounding of monotone song comes from either down in the cellar or out in the garden. On the street all is quiet.

Finally deep-voiced bells are rung, first slowly, then little by little more briskly. Now all the day's holiness is rung to a close. There is a swishing of clothing from various directions outside the room. In the woman's breast something trembles. The door handle is turned with a brisk, determined movement. And the door opens.

Steinn Elliði is wearing a black full-length soutane, tight-fitting, with small closely set buttons; around his waist is a broad black silken sash, tied with a knot; at his neckline stands a white gleaming collar, buttoned in back. His hair has been cut down to the roots. She had never seen his head so bare. It was peculiarly long and slender, convex at the forehead and back. She had never before noticed that his face was so big, almost gigantic. His glance was cold and clear, like that of a man who has a goal but still has a long journey to make to reach it, his lips pursed. The frames of his glasses were of iron.

He stopped in the doorway and looked at her, then shut the door.

"Well now," he said, without showing any emotion. "You here."

"Yes, Steinn, I have come!" she said, and she stood up, went over to him, and extended her hand. "Bless you, Steinn!"

But instead of greeting her he took one step backward.

"God help you, woman! What do you want here?"

"Dear Steinn, my beloved Steinn; weren't you certain that I would come when I was free, as I promised? Steinn, I've traveled night and day."

"How dare you come here by night like a thief! Try to imagine how discourteous this is toward the masters of this house! Get out of here, quickly!"

But she came to him, laid her hands on his shoulders, her face against his breast, and spoke as if she wanted to whisper to his heart:

"Steinn, I have come to you because I can do nothing else. I cannot live except with you.. Have pity on me! Do with me anything that you will; anything except reject me. God does not want you to reject me after all that I have endured for your sake ever since I was a child. And God does not want you to be here. He cannot want that. God wants you to be happy. God does not want you to waste your life in a foolish battle with your soul. Steinn, allow me to free you from the claws of these soulless, merciless men who keep you in this prison. Steinn, follow me out into life where happiness awaits us."

She slipped her naked hands beneath the sash around his waist.

"At least do not let me leave without this. God cannot wish for you to drive me away like a harlot out into eternal darkness. No God could be so vicious."

He freed himself from her arms, grabbed his face in his hands, and stumbled across the room like a drunken man, until he kneeled down on the prie-dieu beneath the cross.

"My God, my soul desires no peace until it rests in you; it was created for nothing other than you; eradicate, my God, all that I call my own; for everything that is not yours comes from the Evil One.

Humble me, Lord, humble me; let me never forget that I am the most sinful of all sinners and the weakest of the weak; let me neither hunger nor thirst for anything but your grace, and give me the humility of the saints who have drowned their sins in your wounds. Send me out into the street to beg for alms. Let me drink the water used to cleanse the sores of lepers, so that I might learn to break the blade off the spear of my arrogance. Holy Mother of God, you who bear the Creator of the universe in your arms, be also my mother and whisper to me words of wisdom as you did to your child of old. Holy maiden, protect the one who flees to you in need; pray for the one who calls upon you in despair, pray for me. My God, if you call me into your wilderness, I shall set out tonight, because I know that if you call me, you have also prepared for me a little cave in the mountains where I shall be allowed to await the final dawn facing your cross. Place upon my shoulders the heaviest cross that I can carry, my God, because I deserve it, and do not deny me your grace, because without your grace I am lost for life. Condescend to look down on me, Lord, and have mercy on me, because behold, I am destitute and alone."

He raised his hands and his face toward the Crucified One and remained in this position for a long time. Finally he stood up and looked in amazement at the woman.

"Poor child!" he said, and his face was so radiant that she had never seen anything more beautiful in her life. "Man is an illusion. Go and seek God your Creator because all is illusion except for him."

100.

The night sky is heavy with bitterly cold, raw weather.

She wanders in the darkness throughout the streets of the holy city of Rome, dead tired like a drunken harlot, sits down on a doorstep or on a bench in a public garden and lets her head sink down, drifts off in a delirious dizziness and disquietude, starts with a chill and feels a feverish weakness pass through her limbs, hastens away again. It did not cross her mind once to try to find her way back to her hotel. All roads meant nothing to her. She had come to Rome, where all roads led; now no road was right any longer, no road wrong. The world is like a night in Rome. The streets crisscross, and who knows where they lead? Some folk are sleeping; some are awake; some are being born, others are dying. And the life of man is an attempt to arm oneself for war against the eternal horror that laughs behind the day. If the illusion is swept away and a man sees himself, it goes the same for him as for the fool: he discovers that comfort is found neither in Heaven nor on Earth, and then he dies. And Rome is a particularly famous city because it is built on seven hills, and through the center of the city the Tiber River rolls along with the history of mankind in its brown waves. It is a meaningless satire, sprinkled with Spiritualism, like something written by Arthur Conan Doyle; it has no beginning and no end, like a dance of death in a graveyard.

Once again dawn breaks over the tribulations of mankind. Once again the dim blue morning sky proclaims the victory of day over night, and the ghosts thrust themselves head down into their graves.

At the time when the March sun starts to redden the tallest towers, the woman wanders among massive columns set in four rows in a semicircle around a paved square. She stands beneath the columns, which in ancient drama mark the stage of tragedy, and looks out over the square, which in ancient drama marks the stage of comedy. The square is deserted and empty, because the actors are not yet awake; they still have a long time to sleep. In the background towers a great church, Saint Peter's Basilica, the terror-laden monument to God's Christians.

How he is holy and terrible in his Church, this God! His Church is even more powerful than the laws of nature and calls to itself the souls of men from east and west, north and south, calls them from all directions to rise against the nature of the created and lift themselves from the dust to eternal life. Jesus Christ is a comical tyrant: his enemies crucified him, and he crucifies his friends in turn. The Church is the kingdom of the crucified. What power did the love of a wretched created woman have against the holy Church of Jesus Christ, which is more powerful than all of creation?

She sat down on the steps of the colonnade to the left of the main doorway, leaned her back against a column, and looked wearily at the facade of San Pietro; she was staring straight into the face of Catholicism. And there, written in huge letters, stand these words: TU ES PETRUS: ET SUPER HANC PETRAM AEDIFICABO ECCLESIAM MEAM. Which means: "You are Steinn, and upon this Steinn I will build my Church."[140] The yearning of the imperfect for perfection is the earthly foundation of the Lord's Church.

The first trams clatter in nearby streets. A car rushes madly around a corner. Farmers drive horse-drawn wagons loaded with vegetables to market. And the bells begin to ring; the Catholic world wakens. The first clapper strokes are weak and mild, and in the intervals the air is filled with gentle resounding. But the chiming gradually gains strength until it sounds like a deafening crash of surf. Presently the bells stop ringing; everything quiets down and the sounds of the bells dwindle into the distance in calm, harmonious echoes.

Two maidens of Christ who have set out early on a trip to market appear between the columns with their baskets, just as the echoes of the bells begin to dwindle away. They stop here to recite the Angelus face-to-face with San Pietro, cross themselves hurriedly, and begin now to mutter these divine mysteries of the Holy Spirit and the maiden Mary:

To Mary the Angel: "Greetings be thine,"
And by Holy Spirit the virgin gave birth:
The Lord's will be done, in all be mine,
I am the Lord's handmaid, a thing of no worth.

Hail the Lord's word, man's living breath,
And the cross of the Lord over sin and death.
Hail, Mary, full of grace, Christ's fairest flower.
Of women be blessed and blessed in Earth's bower
Christ Jesus, woman-born, heavenly king.

Blessed Mary, mother of God, hark to our plea.
Pray turn your son's anger to clemency.
Grant grace, O Queen, on our last mortal hour.
Behold! All creation bends to your power.

Their voices as one ring out their string of rhymes with the word "Amen!" which means: Yes, yes, let it be. Finally they cross themselves quickly, hitch up their skirts a bit, and then waddle out through the Porta Angelica, bearing their baskets.

Taormina, summer 1925

Pronunciation of Icelandic Letters

The modern Icelandic alphabet consists of thirty-two letters, many of which do not appear in modern English; however, the sounds that these specifically Icelandic letters make all have near-equivalents in English:

ð, known as "eth" or "crossed d," is pronounced like the (voiced) *th* in *mother*
þ, known as "thorn," is pronounced like the (unvoiced) *th* in *thin*
æ is pronounced like the *i* in *time*
á is pronounced like the *ow* in *town*
é is pronounced like the *ye* in *yes*
í is pronounced like the *ee* in *green*
ó is pronounced like the *o* in *tote*
ö is pronounced like the *u* in *but*
ú is pronounced like the *oo* in *loon*
ý is pronounced like the *ee* in *green*
au has no English equivalent; it can be approximated by an exaggerated slurring of the *oay* sound in *sway*. Perhaps closer is the *œ* sound in the French *œil*
ei and ey are pronounced like the *ay* in *fray*

Endnotes

1 The quotation is from the third book of Dante Alighieri's (1265–1321) *The Divine Comedy, Paradise*, and is spoken by Dante's ancestor Cacciaguida (giving Dante advice on how to act after he is exiled from Florence, in response to Dante's suggestion of prudence): "But none the less, put every lie aside,/and make thy vision clearly manifested,/letting them scratch who have an itching hide;/For, though thy word be grevious, barely tasted,/it will at length become a vital food/nutritious, so it be but well digested" (trans. Melville B. Anderson, *The Divine Comedy of Dante Alighieri, Vol. III, The Paradiso* (London: Oxford University Press, 1921), p. 173; this is the edition of Dante that Halldór Laxness had at his home at Gljúfrasteinn).

2 Þingvellir: The site of the Alþingi, the general assembly that was held for two weeks in June throughout most of Iceland's history (it was held for the last time at Þingvellir in 1798; after being held in Reykjavík in 1799 and 1800 it was abandoned, until it was reconvened in Reykjavík starting in 1845). At the Alþingi lawsuits were settled and laws enacted beneath the cliffs of Almannagjá, a dramatic ravine formed by the separation of tectonic plates. Súlur (or Botnssúlur) and Skjaldbreiður are the names of two mountains that can be seen from Þingvellir. Esja is the name of a mountain close to Reykjavík (to the west of Þingvellir).

3 Ylfingabúð is the name of the summer house of the "Ylfingurs," that is, the brothers Grímúlfur and Örnúlfur Elliðason. (The word "ylfingur" is a diminutive form of the word "úlfur," "wolf," the second element in both brothers' names. Ylfingabúð means, literally, "the booth of the Ylfingurs"). Many Icelanders have summer homes and cottages in the area around Þingvellir and Þingvallavatn ("Þingvellir Lake," a huge lake just south of Þingvellir).

4 *Morgunblaðið:* the name of Iceland's main daily newspaper (literally, the "Morning Paper"), founded in 1913.

5 Ylfingamóðir: the mother of the Ylfingurs.

6 Eine feurige Begabung (German): A flashing talent.

7 *Eimreiðin:* an Icelandic journal founded by Valtýr Guðmundsson, published in Copenhagen, 1895–1918, and in Reykjavík, 1918–75. The journal published stories, poems, and scholarly articles about literature, but during its final years it focused primarily on politics and government. *Skírnir:* an Icelandic journal, published yearly since 1827 by Hið íslenska bókmenntafélag (The Icelandic Literature Society) in Copenhagen, and from 1890 in Reykjavík. The journal was originally concerned with news and culture in general, but after combining with the *Journal of the Icelandic Literature Society* (*Tímarit Hins íslenzka bókmenntafélags*) in 1904, it has published articles on Icelandic literature, as well as, in recent years, philosophy and other scholarly topics.

8 Karl Finnbogason (1875–1952) was an Icelandic teacher, school principal, and member of parliament. His book *Landafræði handa börnum og unglingum* (*Geography for Children and Teenagers*) was first published in 1907 and reprinted numerous times.

9 Marriage is an ignominious capitulation . . . : This quotation, from George Bernard Shaw's (1856–1950) *Man and Superman* (1902), is given in English in the Icelandic text of *The Great Weaver.*

10 Væringjar: A scouting organization run by the Icelandic branch of the YMCA.

11 Painted veil: a reference to a sonnet by the English Romantic Poet Percy

Bysshe Shelley (1792–1822), starting with the lines, "Lift not the painted veil which those who live / call life . . ."

12 Tjörnin: "The Pond," the name of the large pond in central (downtown) Reykjavík.

13 Grettir Ásmundarson: The eponymous hero of *Grettis saga Ásmundarsonar*, one of the medieval Icelandic sagas. Grettir was a poet and an outlaw, and was finally killed by his enemies on the island of Drangey in the north of Iceland.

14 Drápa: A variety of Icelandic skaldic verse, consisting of a series of stanzas (in general, at least twenty) broken by one or more refrains at regular intervals.

15 Lazzaroni (Italian): Beggars.

16 Gotaterri (Italian): Incessant pleading, begging.

17 Vedi Napoli e poi muori (Italian): An Italian proverb: Behold Naples and then (you can) die.

18 Tendresse sans passion (French): Affection without passion.

19 La meta profetata fuori del mondo (Italian): The promised boundary beyond the world.

20 Pricked by a sleep-thorn: A metaphor for "drugged," referring to a magical technique used by sorcerers and others in Icelandic sagas and legends. Pricking one with a sleep-thorn in the ear or hair caused that person to fall into a deep sleep.

21 H/f Ylfingur: H/f is an abbreviation for "hlutafélag," or joint-stock company.

22 Einar Jónsson (1873–1954) was an Icelandic sculptor. He bequeathed the Icelandic people his works, and they are now displayed at the Einar Jónsson Museum of Art in Reykjavík.

23 Jón Sigurðsson (1811–1879), an Icelandic literary scholar and politician, was the leading advocate for Iceland in its struggle for independence from Denmark (Iceland was granted free trade in 1854, domestic autonomy in 1874, home rule in 1904, and sovereignty under the Danish Crown in 1918. On June 17, 1944 Iceland became an independent republic, and

Independence Day is celebrated annually in Iceland on this day, the anniversary of Jón Sigurðsson's birthday).

24 Jeg kaldte dig mit . . . (Norwegian): "I called you my messenger of joy / I called you my star." Lines from the poem "Stambogsrim," written by the Norwegian playwright Henrik Ibsen (1828–1906) and put into a musical setting (*Stambogsrim. Op.* 25, *no.* 3) by the Norwegian composer Edvard Grieg (1843–1907).

25 Leise flehen . . . (German): "Quietly my songs beckon through the night to you," the first line of the poem "Serenade," by the German poet Ludwig Rellstab (1799–1860), set to music by Schubert ("Ständchen," D. 957 no. 4 (1828), from *Schwanengesang*, no. 4).

26 Heinrich Heine's (1797–1856) *Doppelgänger* reads as follows in the original German:

> Still ist die Nacht, es ruhen die Gassen,
> In diesem Hause wohnte mein Schatz;
> Sie hat schon längst die Stadt verlassen,
> Doch steht noch das Haus auf demselben Platz.
>
> Da steht auch ein Mensch und starrt in die Höhe,
> Und ringt die Hände vor Schmerzensgewalt;
> Mir graust es, wenn ich sein Antlitz sehe–
> Der Mond zeigt mir meine eigne Gestalt.
>
> Du Doppelgänger, du bleicher Geselle!
> Was äffst du nach mein Liebelsleid,
> Das mich gequält auf dieser Stelle
> So manche Nacht, in alter Zeit?

27 Ô, doux printemps . . . (French): "O sweet springtimes of seasons passed, you have fled forever." These lines are from Jules Massenet's *Élégie,* published in 1869, and originally written by the French librettist Louis Gallet (1835–1898).

28 Eviva la bandiera rossa (Italian): Long live the red flag.

29 Moine bénédictin (French): Benedictine monk.

30 Johohoe . . . (German): From *Der Fliegende Holländer* (*The Flying Dutchman*), an opera by the German composer Richard Wagner (1813–1883), first performed in Dresden in 1843. ("Yohoho! Yohoho! Hoyohe! Have you seen the ship upon the ocean/blood-red the sails, black the masts?/On her bridge a pale man,/the ship's captain, watches without rest./Hui! How the wind howls! Yohohe!/Hui! How it whistles in the rigging! Yohohe!/ Hui! Like an arrow it flies on,/without aim, without end, without rest!")

31 Panem et circenses (Latin): Bread and circuses.

32 Psalm 143:4.

33 Greif hinein . . . (German): Grab all you can of human life. From Goethe's *Faust*.

34 Deadly mistletoe: An allusion to the killing of the Norse god Baldur with a missile fashioned of mistletoe, an event that heralded Ragnarök and the destruction of the gods.

35 Garçonnes (French): Tomboys; boyish girls.

36 Jóhann Sigurjónsson, *Fjalla-Eyvindur*: Jóhann Sigurjónsson (1880–1919) was an Icelandic writer who lived most of his life in Denmark and wrote mainly in Danish. His works display a great Neoromantic spirit, and he became famous for his play *Fjalla-Eyvindur*, but he is now highly regarded as both a dramatist and a poet.

37 The character is from Marcel Proust's (1877–1922) masterwork, *Á la recherche du temps perdu (Remembrance of Things Past),* published 1913–1927.

38 He weaves . . .: Cited from the chorus of "Atalanta in Calydon" by the English poet Algernon Charles Swinburne (1837–1909).

39 Der mensch . . . (German): Man is something that must be defeated. Satan conduit . . . (French): Satan conducts the ball, a reference to the title of the book *Satan conduit le bal . . . Roman pamphletaire et philosophique des mœurs de temps* (1925), written by Georges Anquetil. This book had a great influence on *The Great Weaver from Kashmir*.

40 O crux, ave, spes unica (Latin): O cross, hail, my only hope.

41 Chi siete . . . (Italian): Who are you that emerges from the eternal silence?

42 Gieb, ja ergieb . . . (German): Hand yourself over to me, you most vicious of enemies. From Nietzsche's *Also Sprach Zarathustra* (1883–1885), Part 2, I, "Der Zauberer" ("The Magician").

43 This translation of Soupault's poem is from the incomplete, unpublished translation of *The Great Weaver from Kashmir* made by Magnús Arason and Halldór Laxness in California in the 1920s, and that exists in manuscript form in the National Library of Iceland.

44 Urðhæð, Einbúi: Common generic names for mountains in Iceland ("Rocky Height" and "Hermit," respectively).

45 Skerpla: The second month of summer in the old Icelandic calendar, beginning on the Saturday of the fifth week of summer (19–25 May).

46 Sólmánuður: The third month of summer according to the old Icelandic calendar, beginning on the Monday following the 17th of June.

47 "We certainly are great men, my dear Hrólfur": This idiom is used in Iceland to silence or humble prideful or egotistical people . The idiom is associated with *Göngu-Hrólfs Saga*, one of the so-called "Legendary Sagas" (*fornaldarsögur*), mainly fantastical tales composed during the thirteenth to the fifteenth centuries; in the saga a character named Vilhjálmur claims responsibility for some of Hrólfur's great deeds.

48 Possibly a reference to the romantic novel of the same name by the Anglo-Irish author and playwright E. Temple Thurston (1879–1933), published 1909 (and subsequently made into a film).

49 Wes' Brot ich eß, des' Lied ich sing (German): Whose bread I eat; whose song I sing. A German proverb, akin to "He who pays the piper calls the tune."

50 Ubi bene. . . (Latin): Where one is well off, there is his country. Ubi pecunia… (Latin): Where there is money, there is one's country.

51 Messina is a seaside town in northeast Sicily. Catania is a seaside town in eastern Sicily, at the foot of Mount Etna.

52 An seinem . . . (German): God died of his pity for mankind, from Nietz-

sche's *Also Sprach Zarathustra*, Part 2, XXV, "Von den Mitleidigen" ("The Pitiful").

53 Raskolnikov is the protagonist of Fyodor Dostoevsky's (1821–1881) *Crime and Punishment* (published in 1866).

54 Di Signora Ellidaso (Italian): Of Signora Ellidaso (Madam Elliðason).

55 Il buono Dio (Italian): The good God.

56 Le bellezze della vita (Italian): The magnificence of life.

57 Soirée internationale (French): International evening party.

58 Isola Bella (Italian): "Beautiful Isle," the name of an island near Taormina in Sicily.

59 *Il Mondo* (Italian): The name of an Italian newspaper.

60 Terra nullius (Latin): No-man's land.

61 Rajputana (Rajputstan): A historic region of northwest India, coextensive with the modern state of Rajasthan.

62 Jaipur (Jeypore): The capital of the state of Rajasthan, India, known as the "Pink City."

63 Vous vous en allez; moi, je reste (French): You go away, me, I will stay.

64 Crimine bestiali (Latin): Bestiality.

65 Der reine Verbrecher . . . (German): The purebred criminal is the only one who truly knows.

66 Pereat (Latin): Let her die.

67 In the spirit of Arnold Böcklin (1827–1901), a Swiss Symbolist painter.

68 Questa soglia . . . (Italian): This threshold divides two worlds. Mercy binds them.

69 È vero (Italian): It's true!

70 Nihil humani . . . (Latin): I consider nothing that concerns mankind alien to me, a famous Latin phrase used by the Roman playwright Terence (190–159 BC) in his play *Heauton Timoroumenos* (*The Self-Tormentor*).

71 Soldi (Italian): Italian currency (1 lira = 20 soldi).

72 Ego autem sum vermis . . . (Latin): Psalm 22:6 (But I am a worm and no man: a reproach of men, and despised of the people).

73 Ricordo di Taormina (Italian): A souvenir of Taormina.

74 Gran' signore (Italian): A great gentleman.
75 A fatto malo . . . (Italian): He hurt a little girl.
76 *The Barber of Seville*: An opera by Gioacchino Antonio Rossini (1792–1868), first performed in February 1816.
77 Durch alle Töne . . . (German): Through all of the notes sounded a tender tone of love.
78 Saluti . . . (Italian): Greetings, greetings, Excellency.
79 Calabria: A region in southern Italy (the toe of the boot).
80 La vie, ça n'est jamais . . . (French): Life is never as good or as bad as people think.
81 Bêtes à bon dieu (French): Ladybugs.
82 Til det dansk-islandske . . . (Danish): To the Danish-Icelandic Consulate, Palermo. Sicily.
83 *Rhodymenia palmata* is the scientific name for dulse (edible seaweed).
84 Il piacere (Italian): The bliss.
85 Om mani padme hum: A Tibetan mantra, "Hail to the jewel in the lotus," intended to create and maintain a state of compassion, both in the chanter and the world.
86 Eli, Eli! (Latin): My God, my God; part of Christ's final words upon the cross (*"Eli, Eli, lama sabachtani,"* "My God, my God, why have you forsaken me?").
87 Pax (Latin): Peace; Ut in omnibus glorificetur Deus (Latin): That God might be glorified in all things.
88 Gloria, misericordia, secula seculorum (Latin): Glory, mercy, ages of ages (now and forever, throughout the ages).
89 Mea culpa, mea culpa, mea maxima culpa (Latin): Through my fault, through my fault, through my most grievous fault; a phrase used in the Confiteor, a general confession recited in the Roman Rite at the beginning of Mass, in confession, and on other occasions in preparation for the reception of grace.
90 Respice in me, Deus . . . (Latin): Look upon me, God, and have mercy on me, for I am destitute and alone (Psalm 25:16).

91 Videtur ut non (Latin): It is not seen.

92 Unus Altissimus Jesus Christus (Latin): Jesus Christ, alone and highest (a variation on a phrase of the Gloria, a prayer in the Ordinary of the Catholic Mass).

93 *De Imitatione Christi (Of the Imitation of Christ),* Book 2, 12:15. *De Imitatione Christi* is a great devotional work that is thought to have been written by the Dutch theologian and Augustinian Thomas à Kempis (1389–1471).

94 Regia via sanctæ crucis (Latin): The royal road of the holy cross. Book 2, chapter 12 of *De Imitatione Christi* bears the title "De regia via sanctæ crucis."

95 Hanc regiam viam quæ est via cruces (Latin): Here, the royal road, which is also the road of the cross.

96 In the cross is good fortune . . .: This passage, loosely translated from *The Imitation of Christ,* Book II, chapter XII.

97 In manu tua sum (Latin): Into your hands (from the seven last words of Christ upon the cross).

98 Fait son droit (French): Fulfilled his (academic) duties.

99 Ancilla veritatis (Latin): Envoy of the truth.

100 Anima naturaliter christiana (Latin): "The soul of man is Christian by nature," a famous statement made by the Roman lawyer (and Church Father) Tertullian (born ca. 160) in his *Apologeticus* (a defense of the Christian religion against the pagans).

101 Rien n'est plus désagréable que d'être pendu obscurément (French): Nothing is more disagreeable than to be hanged in obscurity.

102 Staffage zu gewissen Ideen (German): Afterthoughts; accessories to fixed ideas (figures in paintings that are secondary to the main concept are called *Staffage* in German).

103 Secundum intentionem puram (Latin): From pure intent.

104 Propter regnum coelorum (Latin): For the Kingdom of Heaven.

105 The English translation of this poem is, like the Soupault poem earlier, from the Arason/Laxness translation of *The Great Weaver* from the 1920s.

106 Oblatus secularis (Latin): Secular oblation; worldly service (an obligatory regulation, without being attached to it).

107 Credo in unam sanctam catholicam et apostolicam ecclesiam (Latin): Part of the Creed, "I believe in one holy Catholic and Apostolic Church."

108 A ship came out to Leiruvogur: This is a translation of a line from the medieval saga *Egils saga Skallagrímssonar (The Saga of Egill Skallagrímsson),* ch. 79: "Þat var eitt sumar, at skip kom út í Leiruvági . . ." ("One summer a ship put in at Leiruvogur"). The ship's captain is a man named Þormóðr, and he brings Egill a shield sent by Þorsteinn Þóruson in Norway; Egill composes a verse in thanks (Egill is living at the time in Mosfell, where Halldór Laxness grew up). Leiruvogur is in Kollafjörður, the bay bordering Reykjavík. The references to viking "activities" (battles, shipwreck, head-ransoms) at the end of this chapter are for the most part direct allusions to events in the life of Egill Skallagrímsson. (*Egils saga Skallagrímssonar,* ed. Sigurður Nordal, Íslensk Fornrit, Reykjavík, 1933, p. 275.)

109 Mörður Fiddle (Mörðr Gígja): the name of one of the main characters in *Njáls Saga*, one of the greatest of the medieval Icelandic sagas.

110 Sagaöen (Norwegian): Island of sagas; that is, Iceland.

111 Kleppur: The name of a mental hospital in Reykjavík.

112 Skyr: A traditional Icelandic food, smooth curds made from skimmed milk and cheese rennet.

113 *Tíminn:* An Icelandic newspaper, founded in Reykjavík as a weekly paper in 1917, published as a daily paper since 1947. *Tíminn* has been the mouthpiece for the Progressive Party since 1938.

114 Mein Herz pocht wild beweglich . . . (German): From the song "Die Meerfrau," written by the German poet Heinrich Heine, and set to music by the German composer and conductor Franz Paul Lachner (1803–1890) ("My heart pounds so wildly turbulent, it pounds so turbulently wild: I love you so unspeakably, you shining human child."

115 O mighty Lord of Israel . . . : From *The Imitation of Christ,* Book Three, chapter XX ("Confessing Our Weaknesses in the Miseries of Life").

116 Qui, qui . . . (Italian): "Here, here, in this very orchard, you could . . ."

117 De profundis . . .: Psalm 130:1–8.
118 I love him, because the Lord heard . . . : Psalm 116:1–9.
119 Ford: The American businessman Henry Ford's autobiographical work, *Today and Tomorrow*, originally published in 1926, was read in Iceland in Danish translation, *Idag og imorgen*. Dr. Helgi Pjeturss: Helgi Pjeturss (1872–1949), the first Icelander to earn a B.A. in geology. He later devoted himself to philosophy and psychology.
120 Det var en vas med roser: There was a vase with roses. (Apparently Swedish, but with *roser* misspelled (should be *rosor*)). Unidentified quotation.
121 In Icelandic folktales, a *sending* is a ghost conjured and sent by a sorcerer to attack an enemy.
122 Sicut tenebrae ejus sicut et lumen ejus (Latin): "And as is his darkness, so is his light" (Psalm 139:12).
123 *Völuspá*: The *Völuspá* (the "Prophecy of the Sybil") is a famous mythological poem from the *Elder Edda*, a collection of poems dealing with ancient Scandinavian mythological and legendary subjects. In the *Völuspá* a sybil relates the story of the creation and destruction of the world, predicting the creation of a new world following Ragnarök, the final battle between the ancient Scandinavian gods and giants.
124 Fais le testament . . . (French): Make a pact between your intellect and your heart; that is the most useful thing that you can do.
125 Three holy elders in Tolstoy's folktales: A reference to the story, "The Three Hermits," published in 1886.
126 Bonjour, monsieur . . . (French): Good day, Mr. Devil! I am charmed to see you. How are you? May I offer you a seat?
127 A variation on an another Icelandic idiomatic expression, "*Rúsínan í pylsuendanum*" ("The raisin at the end of the sausage") akin to English "Icing on the cake."
128 Laetatus sum . . . (Latin): I rejoiced at the things that were said to me: We shall go into the house of the Lord (Psalm 121:1).
129 Stantes erant . . . (Latin): Our feet were standing in thy courts, O Jerusalem (Psalm 121:2).
130 The elder from Yasnaya Polyana is Leo Tolstoy.

131 Maintenant c'est . . . (French): Now is the exact moment for eating.

132 Ich hab' meine . . . (German): "I placed my trust in nothing, and the whole world belongs to me," from the poem "Vanitas! Vanitatum Vanitas!" published in 1806 by Goethe.

133 *Punch:* A British magazine of humor and satire, founded in 1841 and closed in 2002. The works of some of the greatest comic writers and cartoonists were published in *Punch*. *Strix:* unidentified.

134 Oportet et hæreses esse (Latin): Even heresies must exist (1 Corinthians 11:19).

135 Benedic, pater . . . (Latin): Bless me, Father, for I have sinned.

136 Poenam damni (Latin): The punishment reserved for the damned.

137 Domine . . . (Latin): "Lord, if I am in darkness, may you be blessed." From *De Imitatione Christi*, Book III, 17:2.

138 Madame n'a pas l'air d'une intrigueuse (French): Madam does not seem to be a conspirator.

139 Deum quem . . . (Latin): God whom they did not recognize in the exposition of the Holy Scriptures, they recognize in the breaking of the bread.

140 The Latin Biblical quotation is from Matthew 16:18–19 ("And so I say to you, you are Peter, and upon this rock I will build my Church"). Laxness extends Christ's play on the meaning of Peter's name (Greek for "rock") to his protagonist (*steinn* means "rock" in Icelandic).

Acknowledgments
The translator gratefully acknowledges the encouragement and support of Pétur Már Ólafsson, the International Center for Writing and Translation at the University of California-Irvine, the Sigurður Nordal Institute (Reykjavík), the Árni Magnússon Institute for Icelandic Studies (Reykjavík), the Fund for the Promotion of Icelandic Literature (Reykjavík), Auður Laxness and Guðný Halldórsdóttir, Norbert and Judy Roughton, Regina Carlyon and L. Michael Bell, Halldór Guðmundsson, and Jill Schoolman.